KU-339-911

i.
C
B
(SL

PEO
DISA

10 A
2 4

1

He   d grabbed both of her legs, the water in his dimples
shining   onlight. With his firm tug, Manny slipped off the
bench   he hot tub, wineglass and all, her head dipping
beneath   ecause she had not expected the move. She came up
sputteri   a ruined mess. She had no chance to speak, however, fo   er's head lowered and he claimed her mouth in a
blisterir   rocked Manny to her toes.

Wh   ased her lips, Christopher looked deep into her
desire-b   tare. "Good," he said. "I was hoping you'd remember. Sta   e right back."

Ma   the dripping hair out of her eyes, her frowning gaze
glued tc   ttom as he left the tub. By the time she thought to
ask him   was going, Christopher had disappeared into the
house.

B6 SIXTH FORM COLLEGE

534611

ENCHANTED DESIRE

WANDA Y. THOMAS

LONDON BOROUGH OF
HACKNEY
LIBRARY SERVICES

BFM

LOCAT CL4

ACC. No.

CLASS

Genesis Press, Inc.

Indigo Love Stories

An imprint of Genesis Press, Inc.
Publishing Company

Genesis Press, Inc.
P.O. Box 101
Columbus, MS 39703

All rights reserved. Except for use in any review, the reproduction or utilization of this work in whole or in part in any form by any electronic, mechanical, or other means, not known or hereafter invented, including xerography, photocopying and recording, or in any information storage or retrieval system, is forbidden without written permission of the publisher, Genesis Press, Inc. For information write Genesis Press, Inc., P.O. Box 101, Columbus, MS 39703.

All characters in this book have no existence outside the imagination of the author and have no relation whatsoever to anyone bearing the same name or names. They are not even distantly inspired by any individual known or unknown to the author and all incidents are pure invention.

Copyright© 2006 by Wanda Y. Thomas

ISBN: 1-58571-176-4
Manufactured in the United States of America

First Edition

Visit us at www.genesis-press.com
or call at 1-888-Indigo-1

DEDICATION

This book is dedicated to my brother, Keith Erickson Thomas.
We miss you son.

THE SIXTH FORM CENTRE
BROOKE HOUSE
LEARNING RESOURCES:

LOCATION: LRC

COLLECTION: Loan

CLASS MARK: THO

BARCODE No: 534611

DATE: 16/04/09

ACKNOWLEDGMENTS

To my family. We've experienced the loss of our father, our mother, and our brother in the last few years, but our love for one another has only pulled us closer together.

To Alvin Barnes, one of Baltimore's finest, for his knowledge and willingness to share that information with me.

To Sidney Rickman, who edits my manuscripts and points out my writing mistakes in glaring, bright red ink! Thanks, girl.

To my sister-authors whose support is a great inspiration to me: Angie Daniels, T. T Henderson, Natalie Dunbar, and J. M. Jeffries; you ROCK!

To my best sister-friends in the whole world: Jacci Gooden, Lynn Joseph, and Carolyn Alexander. Most people can count themselves lucky if they have one good friend; I am blessed to have three.

To my fans, who have repeatedly requested and waited patiently for this story.

PROLOGUE

The young man stood statue still.

His mind told him to run, but he was unable to make his body move. He felt as though he was passing through a dream, an unreality of his own making, even though his mind was fully aware of the signs of life going on around him. The sun beamed down hot on top of his head while cars whizzed by, their back wind tousling his glossy black hair as the squeaky squawk of a female voice and intermittent beeps came from a radio in the car that was parked a few feet away. When his startling blue gaze rose and he saw the birds soaring in the sky above him, he wished with all his heart that he could grow wings and fly off with them.

He looked down at the man lying on his back in the street and squeezed his eyes shut, blocking out the pool of blood that surrounded his head. He clenched his fists as a loud scream reverberated inside his mind. *What in God's name had he done?*

"Dexter, let's go!"

He heard the voice of his friend Carlos and opened his eyes, but he still couldn't make himself move.

"Santangelo, get in the car! We can't stay here!"

Carlos grabbed his shirt from behind and began dragging him back, while Dexter struggled to get away. The man needed help; someone had to help him. "B-but w-what about—"

"Ain't nothin' you can do for him, he's dead! Come on, man!"

Dexter pulled away and looked down at his hand. It began to shake uncontrollably and tears welled in his eyes. Sunlight glinted off the shiny black metal and the heaviness in his hand suddenly became unbearable. Releasing his grip, he watched the gun fall to the street. When it hit the paved road with a loud metal clank, his lips began to tremble with his efforts to hold back a sob. He glanced again at the man lying in the street and felt the weight of his crime land heavily on his shoulders.

He'd done a lot of things wrong in his short life, but this was by far the worst. He had committed an unforgivable sin. He was a killer, and knowing that he'd taken the life of another human being would haunt him for a very long time, possibly forever.

His friends called out to him again and Dexter looked up at the car parked by the side of the road a few feet away. A young boy stood by the open door, his dark eyes widened in terror. Dexter swallowed, his throat aching with unshed tears. The boy was an exact replica of the man lying in the street. He had to be the man's son.

"I'm sorry," Dexter murmured too softly for the boy to hear. "I didn't mean to do it."

This time when Carlos grabbed him, Dexter didn't struggle. Emotionally drained, he was too weak to fight. The last thing he saw as his friend dragged him away to their car was the eyes of the boy. Eyes that had narrowed and, despite the tears running down his brown face, blazed with hate. Eyes that he would remember for the rest of his life.

CHAPTER 1

"That's it!"

The explosive yell rent the early morning air a split second before a large, brown hand wrapped around Tyreese Johnson's throat. Lifted bodily from the ground, Tyreese found his feet dangling, his back pinned to the brick wall behind him, and his attention wholly focused on the enraged, black glare of Detective Christopher Mills.

Tyreese tried to nod his head. When that didn't work, he darted pleading dark eyes to Christopher's partner, Donny London. Donny turned his back and crossed burly arms over his chest as he ostensibly surveyed the empty street in front of him. Tyreese Johnson was on his own.

Christopher used his other hand to grab Tyreese's chin and switch his attention back to him. He was cold, tired, and was not going to put up with any more of Tyreese Johnson's nonsense. "I've been up all night and I've had enough of your shit. Now, are you gonna play ball, or am I gonna kick your ass from here to the corner of Colfax?"

Christopher tightened his grip, his expression growing fiercer by the second. Tyreese struggled against the force of the hand holding him firmly against the wall, but only succeeded in almost choking himself. His slightly glazed eyes widened in disbelief. The man staring up at him was someone he'd never seen before, and his expression emphatically stated that Tyreese might possibly end up a dead man if he didn't give up what he knew, and quick.

The problem was that Tyreese didn't know anything. He was hurting and had been looking for a quick fix. He'd sought out the man because Mills was usually good for a bill or two. That is, if the information proved useful. If not…well, Tyreese didn't even want to walk that road. With the grip on his throat making him dizzy, Tyreese scanned his brain, searching for at least one tidbit of information that would pacify the man who could, with a flip of his wrist, snap Tyreese's scrawny neck.

He tried to swallow and found that he couldn't. "Okay, Mills," he finally rasped. Christopher loosened his hold. "I got something I think you can use."

Christopher relented by letting Tyreese slide down the wall as Donny faced the men again.

"A shipment arrived this week with Santangelo's name on it."

Christopher's gaze narrowed to black slits. "How do you know?"

Tyreese made a show of rubbing the front of his throat and taking in deep gulps of air. Christopher pushed him into the wall. "Spill it, Reese!"

Tyreese mashed himself flat against the hard surface, putting as much space as possible between himself and Christopher Mills. "I was there, man. I saw the whole thing. Five crates—marked household goods. They came by truck and went direc'ly into Santangelo's warehouse."

Christopher reached into his back pocket for his wallet. With slow deliberation, he pulled out a twenty and watched a smile dent Tyreese's hollowed cheeks. "What else?"

Tyreese swabbed a dry tongue along swollen lips as he eyed the money. "Nothin' else, Mills. I swear. They unloaded the crates, stashed them behind some boxes, and I waited until they split before gettin' my black ass outta there. Santangelo's people don't 'preciate folks droppin' in on their private parties and I seen what they do to uninvited guests." Tyreese swiped the back of his hand over his mouth, then looked down at the sidewalk. "I don't know nothin' else, Mills," he mumbled.

Christopher took in the addict's bedraggled appearance and a shiver of disquiet ran down his spine. Drug addiction was a powerful master and it had taken down too many educated, successful men like Tyreese. Just a few short years ago, Tyreese Johnson had been on the fast track to the top in the DA's office. His life had come crashing down the night his wife found him in bed with another woman and, with revenge on her mind, leaked news of his twice a day *minor* habit with crack cocaine to the press.

By the time the media finished crucifying him and his divorce became final, Tyreese had lost his job, his friends, and all of the material possessions he'd accumulated. His addiction to crack had taken everything else, including his self-respect, pride, and dignity. Instead of the two-story, palatial palace in Douglas County Tyreese had once called home, he now spread his blanket in abandoned warehouses or sought warmth on the steam-heated manhole covers alongside the light-rail station at 14th and Stout.

Christopher had tried many times to help Tyreese overcome his addiction, but the man never stayed clean for more than a couple of months. With a shake of his head, Christopher lifted one of the man's skinny, dried up hands, and placed the money inside his palm. He smiled. "Thanks, Reese. What you've told me will be a big help."

Tyreese returned the smile, showing drug-stained teeth. He crushed the money in his hand. "Glad I could be of assistance, Mills. Only next time, keep yo' hands to yo'self." Tyreese pulled at the edges of a faded army jacket, patted down matted black hair that hadn't seen a comb in months, and stood a little straighter. He moved with caution around Christopher Mills, though. Ambling away, he began conversing with someone only he could see. "What I tell you, man? See what happens when you try and help a brother out? They try and jack you up. So, you take it from, T. Don't never let nooobody—"

The rest of his words were lost as Tyreese rounded the corner. Christopher and Donny looked at each other, shrugged, and headed for the black Jeep parked by the curb. Donny settled his broad frame into the passenger seat and buckled the seatbelt. "Why'd you give him the money, Mills? He didn't tell us anything we didn't already know."

Christopher started the engine and checked the side and rearview mirrors before steering the Jeep into the street. He'd seen Tyreese leaving the warehouse the night Santangelo's latest shipment had arrived. It was a good thing Reese had left when he did, because Christopher also knew what happened to someone found in the wrong place at the wrong time. "I'm aware of that," he said to Donny, keeping his eyes focused on

5

the road and the happenings in a neighborhood awakening to begin another day.

Soon the business owners and their employees would lift the bars on the windows and doors and start preparing to greet their customers. Those like Tyreese—the drug addicts, the pimps, the prostitutes, and the homeless—who roamed the streets under the auspices of darkness would disappear for a few hours.

Donny's brows furrowed as he surveyed the long city block. "Then I don't understand. Why did you give him money when he had nothing new to tell us?"

Christopher knew why he'd given up the dough. Guilt. Guilt for taking his anger out on Tyreese when he was actually mad at someone else. It wasn't Tyreese's fault that Manette Walker hadn't bothered to return even one of the many telephone calls he'd made to her house or to the boutique. He didn't look at his partner as he responded, "Just wanted to make sure Reese was still being up front with me. It pays to check up on your informants every once in a while."

Donny nodded, comprehension clearing the wrinkles from his forehead. He mulled over Christopher's words, then tucked the lesson away for use another night. "By the way," he said. "I traded off for a day shift tomorrow."

"Oh," Christopher said without any real interest in the young man's plans.

"I invited Chief Diggs to dinner to thank him for his help in getting me on with the department. He and my father grew up together, you know."

"So you've said."

"Yeah, even though Dad's no longer with us, I think he'd be happy to know that one of his best friends still thinks enough of him to help his kid out."

"Hmmm," Christopher responded.

"Carl Simmons will be there, too, I think. Hey, maybe you could join us, Chris."

Christopher restrained himself from commenting on Donny's tendency to name drop. Carl Simmons was the head of the local MET operation. MET, an acronym for Mobile Enforcement Team, was a federally-sponsored program that aided local police departments with the identification and arrest of criminals known to be involved in illegal drug-related activities.

Donny had transferred to the Denver Police Department after having some strings pulled by higher-ups. The man was flashy, too flashy for Christopher's taste. He could also do without Donny's daily update of his financial profile, which he'd increased considerably from a small inheritance received from his father. His bragging and boasting, expensive threads, and flamboyant black Camero had alienated the other officers. Their refusal to work with the cocky kid was the reason Christopher had gotten stuck with Donny four nights out of the week.

For Christopher, a man who liked to work alone, having the kid hang on his tail was tedious. It also didn't help that Donny was foolishly unaware that while who he knew could be important to his career, his on-the-job-performance would be the determining factor as to whether or not he remained on the force. A lesson he might learn sooner rather than later if he didn't stop flaunting his wealth in the faces of the other officers.

"No thanks. I have a couple of things to wrap up tomorrow."

"Well, maybe next time," Donny said.

Christopher sucked his teeth. "Yeah, maybe."

Shelby Reeves looked up when the bell over the door tinkled. Setting her cup of tea on the table, she crossed the room and walked up the three steps leading to the ready-to-wear store of Exterior Motives. A frown settled on her face as she watched her friend and business partner enter the shop.

Normally, the air around Manette Walker crackled with energy and her cheerful, bubbly personality drew smiles from everyone she encountered. Today, Manny didn't return the greetings from the sales associates already stationed on the floor, and she moved through the shop without her usual clamor. When Manny stopped to straighten a rack of silk blouses, Shelby saw the downward tilt of her mouth and the glum expression on her face. Concerned, Shelby watched Manny resume her trek to her office in the back.

Shelby sighed, went back for her tea, then made her way to her private office. Sitting behind her desk, she sipped from her cup and considered her options. She could try to talk to Manny, but now was probably not the best time. Though it didn't happen often, when Manny was in a bad mood, Shelby knew it was not wise to approach her unless she wanted to find herself on the wrong side of Manny's lightning quick temper.

That knowledge, though, didn't deter Shelby's need to know, and she was leaning toward taking the chance. However, the telephone on her desk rang before she could move from her chair. Shelby set her cup down and picked up the receiver.

"Exterior Motives, this is Shelby Reeves, how may I help you?"

"Shelby, its Chris."

She leaned back in her chair. "Christopher, how are you this morning?"

"Tired, Shel. Has Manny made it in yet?"

Her lips twisted as she contemplated her response. Since Shelby was sure that Christopher was the reason behind Manny's despondency, perhaps she didn't have to wait to satisfy her curiosity after all. "She's here, Chris, only she doesn't appear to be doing too well."

"Why, what's wrong with her?"

"Physically she's fine," Shelby said, in an attempt to ease the worry she'd heard in his voice. "It's just that Manny seems...well, down in the dumps."

"Oh." Christopher chuckled softly. "You had me worried there for a sec, Shel. Manny's probably upset because I had to cancel our date on Friday, and I pulled a lot of overtime this weekend so I didn't get a chance to see her."

Shelby had known Manny since college. Her friend was not the type of person who would let something as trivial as a broken date upset her. Manny was the type of person who had no problem chewing up and spitting out anyone who crossed her, unless that person was someone Manny cared for. Then, Manny would absorb the hurt and hold it inside until the wound healed itself. As much as Shelby wanted to believe Christopher, something else had happened to upset Manny.

Then too, Christopher was also a reserved person. Shelby knew she'd gotten as much information as she was going to get out of him. "Oh, okay, Chris," she said. "Then hearing from you should definitely cheer her up. Hold on and I'll put you through."

The ringing telephone didn't interrupt Manny's concentration on the sheet of numbers on the desk in front of her. The fingers on her right hand continued to fly over the calculator's keyboard, while her left index finger punched a button on the telephone.

"Call for you on two."

"Put them through to voice mail."

"But, Manny…"

"Shelby, I'm busy. These figures from last week's sales are not jiving. I can't take the call right now."

"But, Manny…"

"It's probably just a salesman and I don't have time to listen to his pitch. Just send the call to voice mail."

"Manny, it's Christopher."

Continuing to manipulate the calculator, Manny frowned when the number on the display still didn't match the number circled in red on the report. She began entering the numbers again.

"Christopher Mills," Shelby added when Manny didn't respond.

Manny automatically reached for the phone, and then, as if she'd touched a hot flame, just as quickly snatched her hand back. Christopher Mills was not a person she wished to speak with, especially not after what she'd witnessed last Friday after he'd cancelled their date with the excuse that something had suddenly come up.

Manny gripped her hands together, a physical sign of her internal struggle. It had taken a long time for her to accept Christopher Mills into her life. Just when she'd decided that he was the only man for her, she found out that he'd lied.

"Manny, are you still there?"

She took a deep breath exhaling loudly. It did not stop the wobbly beat in her chest, halt the trembling of her lips, or ease her desire to pick up the phone just to hear the sound of Christopher's voice. "I'm busy, Shelby. Send the call to voice mail."

Manny punched the button ending the connection and went back to what she was doing before Shelby interrupted her. When the numbers still didn't add up, Manny shoved the papers across the desk and leaned back in her chair, staring blankly into space, which was how Shelby found her when she entered the office a few minutes later.

"You should have talked to him."

Startled by the unexpected voice, Manny's body pitched forward and she nearly fell out of the chair. She braced her hands against the edge of the desk, righted herself, and fixed her stare on Shelby as she walked into the room. "Talked to whom?"

Shelby sat in the yellow wingback chair and smiled, despite the gloom in the air. "Christopher."

Manny blinked several times, which was the only indication of how much hearing his name affected her. "Oh him," she said flippantly, accompanying her tone with a shrug meant to convey that the name meant nothing to her. Inside her chest, her crying heart told a different story and its beat rattled out of control like a drum gone wild.

"Oh him," Shelby mimicked with sarcastic undertones. "Yes, him. Why don't you want to talk to Chris, Manny?"

"No reason, other than I don't have the time to waste right now."

"Waste!" Shelby blew out an impatient breath. "Christopher took time out of his day to call you, Manny Walker. The least you could have done was pick up the phone and say hello." Shelby set the cup of tea she'd brought with her on the desk and settled back in the chair.

"What's the matter, Manny?"

"Nothing." Swinging her chair around, Manny turned her back to Shelby and reached for a tissue from the box sitting on the oak credenza behind her. She blew her nose, deposited the tissue in the trashcan, and turned back to her friend. She tried to smile, but when she felt her lips quiver, Manny gave up the effort. She looked down as her gaze turned watery.

Shelby, more than concerned now, leaned forward. "Manny, what is it?"

Manny's shoulders lifted on a sigh. Seeming to put whatever was on her mind away, she looked at Shelby again. This time, she did manage a smile. "Nothing's wrong, Shel. I'm just a little tired, that's all."

Unconvinced, Shelby continued to study Manny and decided to try another approach. "Didn't you have a date with Chris on Friday?"

Manny's gaze hardened and froze. "I was *supposed* to have a date with Christopher, but he cancelled it."

"Why would that upset you? This is not the first date Christopher has cancelled. He was probably calling to explain."

Manny shrugged. "He can call, but it won't make any difference. I'm through with Christopher Coltrane Mills!"

"But why? You've been seeing Christopher for a long time, longer than anyone you've been with since I've known you. I thought the two of you were happy together."

"That's what I thought, too, but apparently Christopher Mills doesn't want to be with me anymore. He's made that very clear, and that's fine with me because I don't want to be with him either!"

Shelby rose from the chair and moved around the desk. She pulled Manny up by the arm and smothered her friend in a hug. She'd been so sure that things would work out this time and that Manny would find the love she'd been seeking for far too many years. "Oh, Manny. I'm so sorry."

Manny pushed away and resumed her seat. Picking up the telephone messages on her desk, she casually flipped through the pink pile. "I'm not. At least this time I found out before I committed my heart.

Men are dogs and I hate every last one of them."

"I guess," Shelby replied half-heartedly, as she sat on the edge of the desk and folded her arms under her breasts. If not for her husband, she might feel inclined to agree with Manny. Life with Nelson Reeves wasn't always a calm sea, but she had no reason to complain. Nelson was the find of her life and she'd hoped that in Christopher Mills, Manny had finally found her lifetime mate. However, despite Manny's drastic transformation—to Shelby's knowledge, the first she'd undergone for any man—it seemed that Christopher was not the one either. Only this time, Shelby wasn't so sure she agreed with the conclusion she'd drawn. Something in Manny's voice gave her pause to consider the matter a little further. "Did Christopher tell you why he wanted to break off your relationship?"

"He didn't have to tell me, I know why."

Shelby frowned. "I don't understand, Manny."

"What's to understand, Shel? Instead of keeping his date with me on Friday, Christopher decided to spend his free time with another woman."

"If you didn't see Chris on Friday, what makes you think that he was with someone else?"

Agitation marred Manny's face as her eyes shifted around the room in a struggle to keep her composure. How did she know? She knew because she'd seen him with her own two eyes. After he'd called to cancel their date, she'd decided to keep their reservation and go to dinner alone. Entering the restaurant, she'd immediately spotted Christopher sitting in a cozy corner with his arm around the shoulders of another woman. Frozen by shock, she'd watched the two of them exchange whispered comments before the woman had kissed him on the cheek.

While she and Christopher hadn't yet declared undying feelings of love for one another, Manny had felt strongly that their relationship had been moving in the direction of something permanent. Now she knew that he was a low-down, two-timing cheat, and Manny wanted nothing more to do with Christopher. The tears welled again and when one overflowed the brim and rolled down her cheek, Manny lost her battle to restrain her emotions. "Because I saw him with her!"

Manny dropped her head and hid her face in her hands. Shelby watched her, momentarily at a loss for what to do. In all the years she'd known her, she'd never seen Manny Walker cry, and her quiet sobs pulled at Shelby's heartstrings. Shelby leaned over and wrapped her arms around her friend. This was all her fault. She was the one who'd encouraged Manny's interest in Christopher Mills and she was responsible for the agony her friend now suffered. In trying to quell her tendencies at matchmaking, Nelson had told her to stay out of it, but Shelby hadn't listened. She'd thought Christopher to be a solid, strong, and dependable man—the kind of man Manny needed to help her settle down. Apparently, she didn't know Christopher Mills as well as she'd thought.

When Manny's tears subsided to soft hiccups, Shelby reached for the tissues. She plucked several from the box and handed them to Manny. "I know it hurts, Manny, but we'll get through this. If Chris has been two-timing you, then he's not worth another second of your thoughts. You just forget about him."

Manny sniffed. "That's a lot easier said than done, Shel. I really thought Christopher cared for me. He was so kind and patient with me and all the things he did—like calling just to say hi and rubbing my feet after a long day at the shop. He even brought me flowers and cooked dinner for me. Have you ever had a man do that for you, Shelby?" Manny looked down at the desk, dejection evident in the slump of her shoulders. "Of course you have; you have Nelson."

"You'll find another man, Manny, and he'll do all those things for you again. But the next time, it will be real and he'll treasure you the way you deserve to be treasured."

"But I love Christopher!"

The shock of Manny's words quickly registered on Shelby's face. Since her wedding, she had noticed a marked improvement not just in Manny's attitude, but also her appearance. Manny had traded her eye-popping, original outfits in favor of more traditional and sedate attire. Solid-colored pantsuits and longer skirts matched with silk blouses had replaced fur, spandex, and the other odd and glittery apparel that had once dominated Manny's wardrobe. She had swapped her snakeskin boots and her spiked heel collection for low-heeled pumps, sling backs, and flat, leather sandals. She no longer covered her face in heavy, almost clownish makeup, but now used only a light face powder, a little mascara, and colored lip-gloss. Manny had even removed the wildly colored braids from her hair in favor of styles more suitable for her age.

After years of trying, to no avail, to help Manny improve her outer appearance, Shelby had silently approved of her friend's new look. Now she knew the real reason behind the changes. Manette Walker was in love.

This morning though, Manette looked more like the Manny of old. A thick layer of foundation hid the smooth, tan brown color of a beautiful, heart-shaped face. Garish purple eye shadow and the long, black false lashes sank rather than enhanced her chocolate brown eyes. Manny had used a heavy hand with the blush that stained her cheeks and with the orange lipstick rimming her mouth. The eye shadow and lip color matched the deep purple sweater and bright orange miniskirt that covered Manny's slender frame. She'd painted her fingernails orange and styled her black hair into spikes that poked out all over her head.

Everything about Manny's appearance said she was screaming for attention. Examining her, Shelby finally saw the answer she'd been seeking since she'd met Manette Walker. As much as Manny professed to want a man, she used clothes and makeup as a shield to keep men from getting too close to her.

If not for the metamorphosis she'd personally witnessed, Shelby never would have figured it out, because Manny was so adept at guarding her feelings. She'd dropped that shield and exposed her true self for Christopher Mills, something he apparently hadn't wanted, and now Manny Walker had gone back into hiding.

Regretting the role she'd played in getting the two of them together and feeling her fury rise toward Christopher Mills, Shelby helped

Manny up from the chair. She reached into the bottom drawer of the desk and took out the purple purse. "Manny, I want you to take the day off—in fact, take the week. Go somewhere special and pamper yourself."

"I can't, Shel," Manny protested. "I have a meeting with the buyers this morning and I need to close out the accounts for month's end."

Shelby's tawny brown eyes glittered as she assessed her friend. "What you need is time away from here. You're way overdue for a vacation and you need some time to heal."

Though Manny took the purse Shelby held out, she hesitated. "Are you sure, Shelby? I mean, this thing with Chris is not that big a deal. I'm just feeling a little low right now, but I'll get over him, and I would never let my personal life interfere with my performance in the store."

"I know, honey. But today, I'm the boss and I'm ordering you out of our shop." Shelby watched as Manny gathered the rest of her things, then walked with her to the door. "I'll call you later and see how you're doing, okay?"

"You're a good friend, Shel, but don't worry about me. I'll be fine. In fact, I think I'll head to Boulder and visit the family for a few days."

Shelby nodded. Manny shared a close and loving relationship with her family and right now, her friend needed all the extra love she could get. "That's a good idea. Call me when you get back in town."

Shelby returned to the boutique and went into her office. Lowering herself in the chair, she set her cup on the desk and turned her mind to planning the payback she would deliver to Christopher Mills for hurting the best friend she had in the whole world.

CHAPTER 2

Manny unlocked the door and entered her house, just as the answering machine beeped and Christopher's voice filled the room.

"Manette Alicia Walker, pick up the phone!"

Manny dropped the items in her hands into a chair and crossed to the table holding the small black machine. Christopher Mills was nothing short of an idiot. If she wanted to speak to him, she wouldn't leave the security chains on the door, or she would have returned any of the numerous calls he'd made to her at home and at work.

"Come on, Honey-V. This has been going on all weekend. What's wrong with you? Why haven't you called me back?"

Manny turned away and sat on the couch. Besides, despite what she'd told Shelby, she really didn't care all that much for Christopher Mills anyway, and she certainly wasn't going to sit around while he ran back and forth between her and another woman. Leaning forward, she picked up the television remote from the table and clicked on the power. Turning up the volume, she tuned Christopher out and focused her attention on the infomercial advertising a plastic belt worn around the waist that promised to melt away the pounds. A sound of derision left her mouth. That belt had about as much chance of working as her relationship with the man on the phone.

She heard a female voice announcing a crime in progress and then her machine beeped, ending the call. Manny turned off the television. Shelby had told her to forget about Christopher. How was she supposed to do that if the man continued to hound her? Her mouth turned downward as her thoughts remained centered on Christopher Mills. Four years ago, Shelby had nearly died in a car crash, and Christopher had rescued Shelby. A few days later, Manny had called to invite Christopher to a celebration party. He had declined, citing work, but they had talked for hours and connected over the phone lines. He'd seemed like a nice man when they'd spoken and an intriguing enigma when they'd actually met in person at Shelby and Nelson's remarriage…

"So you're Christopher Mills."

"And you're the lady with the honey voice."

Manny held back a sigh by swallowing the gulp of air that accompanied it. His voice was so deep, so melodic, and so enchanting that it flowed over her like hot syrup on a tall stack of pancakes, and she was the pat of butter on top about to slide off into oblivion.

He had a presence, one Manny could not ignore. With his intense stare focused on her, she instinctively knew that he would be different from any other man she had ever known. Just looking at him made her thoughts scatter. The image she'd seen of him on television had not done him any justice at all. She diverted her gaze from his face and into the room, and willed her heart to start beating. "Honey voice, huh? That's a good one, Mr. Mills."

"The truth's sometimes hard to take."

Manny couldn't help tilting back her head as she sought a connection with his eyes. He was so tall; around six-three or six-four she figured. His eyes were beautiful, large and black as the night, framed by thick lashes that he used to conceal whatever thoughts he had on his mind. He was of medium build, which Manny preferred over burly and wide. His deep brown skin had a healthy glow and the barbered style of his short, cropped, brown hair suited his round face.

She'd also noted his walk, for it had been an instant enticement for her. Almost elegant in the way he moved, every step Christopher took seemed to flow into the next and he covered distance with each stride. Men might be bigger, heavier, and stronger, but Manny saw no reason for them to lumber along or pound their feet into the floor when they moved. "So are honey voices a turn-on for you?"

"Only yours."

So far, Christopher Mills was proving to be a man of few words and the couple he'd just tossed at Manny had her head swooning. He hadn't been that way on the phone. On the phone, he'd had long, talkative stretches when Manny couldn't get a word in edgewise. *Must have been the full moon.*

"When this shindig is over, would you like to go to dinner?"

Manny firmly believed in the old maxim: What you're doing when New Year's arrives is a good indication of what the coming year will bring. She had been staring at Christopher, and while it was already five minutes past midnight, she wanted to see if she could strengthen the bond of their visual connection.

Rather than respond to his question, Manny took Christopher by the hand and led him away from the crowd gathered to celebrate the remarriage of the Reeves. He willingly followed her into a secluded corner, raising a brow when Manny continued to stare up at him. His eyes widened in surprise when she reached up and placed her hands on either side of his face. Then she further stunned him when she rose on her toes and pressed her lips on his. Manny sighed when she released him. "I hope that was a turn-on for you, too."

Taking in the dazed expression on Christopher's face, she graced him with another smile. Then she all but ran across the room and out the front door…

She hadn't even meant to kiss him. To say the least, her behavior had been forward and inappropriate. To say the most, she'd made a spectacle of herself. The indifference Christopher had displayed toward her had irritated Manny and she'd wanted to show him…what? Manny shook her head in dismay—she knew. She'd wanted to show Christopher that despite his blasé attitude, he was as aware of her as she was of him.

Annoyed that she'd allowed herself to trip down memory lane, Manny turned off the television set and headed for the stairs. She hadn't seen her parents since Christmas and knew that her unexpected visit would both surprise and please them.

That night, Christopher stood at the counter in Manny's kitchen adding the last of the spices to the steaks. He'd arrived over an hour ago and she had yet to put in an appearance. He added marinating sauce to the pan and put the meat in the refrigerator. Then he turned to the table that held a large, wildflower arrangement and the bag holding the rest of the things he'd picked up on the way over to her house. Last Friday, he'd had to break his date with Manny, and while he hadn't been real specific, his reason had been a good one.

As he was preparing to leave, he'd received a call from Charlene Thomas, the wife of his superior, former partner, and friend, Samuel Thomas. Desperation had prompted the impulsive call. Charlene was worried about Sam. Since her hardheaded husband refused to listen to her, she'd hoped to recruit Christopher into the battle to get Samuel to take more notice of his health. Because of Christopher, Samuel was no longer in the field. He'd taken a bullet meant for Christopher. While Samuel claimed not to mind continuing his crusade for justice from behind a desk, Christopher knew how emotionally hard it was on a street cop confined to an office.

Though Manny had readily accepted his excuse of work, he'd heard the disappointment in her voice. Because of his job, they didn't spend nearly enough time together as it was. She worked during the day; he pulled the graveyard shift, which left a few weekends and the occasional days he sometimes took off. Tonight, Christopher had wanted to make up for his missed connection with Manny.

The thick steaks he planned to grill were already seasoned and in the refrigerator. The fresh broccoli was washed and the potatoes in the oven. Christopher grabbed the bag and removed his other purchases. He lifted out scented candles, then the scented oil he planned to warm prior to massaging it into Manny's skin. He set both items on the table next to the box of condoms he would need when he assuaged his desire for her in the heat of her body.

When he was done, Christopher looked at the clock on the stove and again wondered where Manny was and how much longer it would be before she came home. Before Manny, Christopher had made it a point to keep his heart and mind unattached to any one woman. He was a cop, and being a cop was a dangerous line of work.

His father had been a cop, and Christopher vividly remembered every detail of the day Donald Mills had been killed. After work, his father had picked Christopher up from the YMCA and they were on their way home when the car in front of them had run a stop sign. His father had pulled the car over, losing his life when one of the men in the car had pulled a gun and shot him in the head.

The senseless murder of his father had left a hole in Christopher's chest that had yet to heal, and at the age of ten, he'd made up his mind to follow in his father's footsteps. Nothing had deterred him from that goal and his proudest moment was the day they'd pinned that shining badge on his chest at the police academy.

Like his father, Christopher put his life on the line every day and though yet unscathed, there had been some close calls. For that reason alone, he'd built up his emotional defenses toward the opposite sex. Most of the women he knew considered him to be cold, emotionally detached, and unable to make a commitment, but Christopher knew differently. He was committed to bringing down the man who had killed his father, and he knew firsthand that to care was to open the possibility of a lifetime of pain.

The loss of his father and his mother's inability to cope had taught him that lesson well. Following his father's death, his mother, wallowing in anguish over the loss of her husband, had merely existed. She had lost interest in everything around her, including him. Two years later, she'd ended her life overdosing on pills. Christopher never wanted to see another woman suffer the way his mother had suffered when his father had died.

He walked over to the sink and through the window watched the twilight paint the Rocky Mountain skyline in deep indigo streaks and a dark grayish hue. How had Manny Walker broken through the defenses he'd so scrupulously built to keep women at bay?

He remembered that it had started with a telephone call and a voice that had run over his body like warm honey, leaving behind a trail of smooth velvet that had remained long after they'd said good-bye. That voice had held the promise of paradise and had caressed his ears as it delved into the deepest recesses of his mind.

He still wasn't sure how she'd done it, but somehow, Manny Walker had broken through his guard and learned the secrets Christopher held most dear; things that no one, not even the people closest to him knew. At her urging, he'd tried to describe the pain he'd felt over the loss of both of his parents, how deeply his father's death in particular had affected him, and about the anger he carried for his father's murderer. He'd expressed to her his feelings of abandonment when the child welfare authorities had forced him to live in the county orphanage, and his relief when Nelson's parents had rescued him after one year.

Manny had revealed almost nothing of herself, but had so expertly drawn him out that when it was over, Christopher had felt like a suspect who'd just undergone an intensive grilling by the cops. He'd asked himself a thousand times since then why he'd opened himself up to Manny Walker. He had finally concluded that it was the sound of her voice that had made him feel comfortable.

Their conversation that first night had lasted over three hours. After hanging up, Christopher, still reeling from his confessional, had used the sound of her silky voice to fill-in her looks. A tall and dark beauty with silky curls, a trim waist that fit in his hands, and long, long, legs that could wrap him in forever.

At the Reeves wedding, he'd watched the door, waiting for the long-legged beauty of his imaginings to come through. Nothing had prepared Christopher for the five foot, seven-inch dynamo that had blown into the house and skewered his heart with her chocolate brown stare. After the ceremony, Manny had taken him by the hand, sequestered them in a corner, and kissed him. That had been over four years ago and he still felt the sharp thrust of emotion that had hit him in the chest when he'd first seen her. It was a feeling that had yet to fade, and he knew that it would take more than a lifetime to satisfy.

Manette Alicia Walker was not his type of woman, but she was the woman Christopher wanted as his wife. As soon as he'd dealt with Dexter Santangelo, Christopher planned to retire from the work he loved so much. He would retire for Manny, only right now, he had no idea where the woman who held his heart was.

Manny fell back on the blue and white flowered couch, stuck her bare legs out in front of her, and rubbed her stomach. "Mama, I haven't eaten that much food since Christmas, but it was so good I couldn't put down my fork."

Loretta Walker swept a stray lock of hair liberally streaked with gray behind her ear and smiled at her daughter. Soon after her marriage, she'd given birth to three sons, and while nothing could replace the love she had for her boys, Loretta had secretly longed for a girl.

On her fortieth birthday, sure that it was too late, she'd put that longing aside. Imagine her shock when instead of confirming Loretta's suspicion that her body was undergoing the changes associated with the onset of menopause, the doctor had informed her that she was pregnant. In answer to her prayers, the Lord had blessed her with Manette, a surprising bundle of energy that had joined their family and turned the Walker household upside down.

Henry Walker's dark stare joined that of his wife's. At seventy-nine, his hair had turned snow white, his posture wasn't as straight as it had once been, and he tended to forget things every now and then. However, the one thing he never forgot was how much he loved his family and the special place that his baby girl would always hold in his heart.

Both of Manny's parents were still in good health, and both were worried about her. She'd taken a couple of rough hits early in life, but had been strong enough to overcome the terrible grief that had almost overwhelmed her. However, at thirty-six, it was long past time that Manny married and had children of her own. Watching her, Loretta was sure that something had prompted Manny's unexpected visit. She'd seen the desolate look in her daughter's eyes and the pain she was trying so desperately to hide.

Upon learning of Manny's arrival, the brothers had dropped by with their families and filled the house with the boisterous noise that always accompanied her sons. In the pandemonium of preparing to feed the large brood, Loretta hadn't had a chance speak with her daughter. Before Manny left for home, she would.

Manny ducked the white-fringed pillow that came flying her way and glared at the youngest of the Walker brothers. Younger versions of her still handsome father, if not for the one-year difference in their ages, her brothers could pass for triplets. She placed the pillow on the cushion beside her. "Will you ever grow up, Todd? I know your wife must be sick of your silly antics by now."

Todd stuck out a sculpted manly chin. "My baby loves me, Manny. She's not as sensitive as you."

"Yeah," Erik spoke up. He was the middle brother. "Maybe if you loosened up and learned to have a little fun you could find someone who would put up with you, too."

All except two sets of darkly colored eyes missed the stricken look that passed over Manny's face. It came and disappeared so quickly, had her oldest brother and mother not been watching, they would have missed it, too.

The owner of one of those pairs of eyes moved across the room and sat next to his sister. Maurice picked up one of Manny's hands and grazed his thumb across the back in a gesture of comfort and unity. He eyed his younger brothers. "You guys may as well back off. Every time Manny comes home, the two of you get started. Well, tonight I'm not having it, so find yourselves some other amusement. Todd, I believe that's your son I hear crying upstairs, and Erik, why don't you go and see if you can help your wife in the kitchen."

Duly chastened, the younger brothers rose to their feet and left the room. From the day their parents had brought Manny into the house, Maurice Walker had set himself up as her protector. Their bodies still held the faint remembrances of scars they'd received after tangling with their older brother over some small slight they'd rendered toward their sister.

Manny turned to her big brother and thought as she had so many times in the past how handsome he was. Maurice was one of the best men she knew and her sister-in-law was lucky to have him. "Thanks, Mawry."

Maurice smiled at the pet name. Manny was the only person on the planet who could get away with calling him that. "No problem, sister. That's what big brothers are for." Maurice rose and left the room, but not before leaving a brotherly kiss on Manny's makeup-free cheek.

As she readied herself for bed that evening, Manny felt a great deal better for having spent the day in the loving bosom of her family. Though the two younger brothers were merciless teasers, Manny knew that both held a deep love for her and that she just had to say the word and Christopher Mills would find himself twisted into a pretzel. However, Christopher was a problem that Manny had to work out for herself.

Climbing between the clean, scented sheets on the bed in her old room, Manny adjusted the pillows at her back, her thoughts still on her family. She had been born in Boulder, Colorado, one year before Mo Siegel had discovered a bountiful harvest growing in the fields around Boulder and began picking the herbs that would become the base for the teas sold by Celestial Seasonings, the largest herbal tea company in North America.

As a young city, Boulder had embraced the subculture brought by the hippies and beatniks of the era. Today, the population blended remnants of an unconventional culture long gone with the educational and technological advances of a modern city. Her father had moved to the city in the 1950s and had gone to school on the GI bill he'd earned during World War II. After obtaining his degree, he'd stayed on at the University, earning a Ph.D. and a professorship, where he sought to open young minds to the wonders of science. Her mother had taught math in the public school system. Both Todd and Erik had followed their parents' example and taken up teaching positions at the high school level. However, Manny and Maurice had struck out in new directions—he as the owner of a computer security firm—she as the business manager and part owner of Exterior Motives.

Only Manny had not found a lasting love; someone to share her life and her dreams. That's what Manny wanted most in the world, a life partner to rejoice with her in good times and console her when things were bad. A mate like her mother had found in her father and her brothers had found in their wives.

She had a long list of qualities that she wanted in a man, which she constantly revised as it suited her. Looks were not of major importance, but he had to be stable and she'd like him to be her friend. Most of all, he had to be capable of loving deeply, exclusively and with his whole heart. She wouldn't mind a couple of children or that house with the white picket fence, either. She wasn't naïve enough to think that the man of her dreams had to cater to her every whim, but he'd better do some darn good trying. In observing the loving couples around her, Manny had seen the devotion of true love, and she refused to settle for anything less. In return, she would treat her man like a king.

For a while, Christopher had shown all the signs of being that king. But instead of devoting himself to her, Christopher had chosen to spread his favors among the court. Men of color might be in short supply, but she wasn't about to share her king with anyone.

Pushing the disturbing thoughts aside, Manny snuggled down under the thick, pink comforter on her bed. After the death of her daughter, she'd gotten out of the habit of praying. However, tonight, just as she'd done hundreds of times as a little girl, she turned her head toward the window located on the east wall of the room. Looking up, she sought out the brightest twinkle she could find in the black velvet canopy. Manny made her wish, then closed her eyes, and sought atonement with the Lord. Feeling content, she drifted off to sleep, hoping upon hope that soon she'd meet the man who could fulfill her dreams.

In all of his thirty-eight years, Christopher Mills had never felt so frustrated. Two days had passed since he'd cooked and eaten a solitary dinner in her home and he had yet to see hide or hair of Manny Walker. He'd been to the house several times since, and his repeated calls to her home and Exterior Motives had gone unanswered.

He'd even called her parents' home in Boulder. If Manny was there, either she didn't get the message or she hadn't bothered to respond. Shelby Reeves had been unusually close-mouthed, too. He'd dropped by Exterior Motives on his way home this morning and all he'd been able to get out of Shelby was that Manny wasn't there; and if he wasn't mistaken, she'd seemed highly annoyed with him, as well.

Christopher pushed his long and lean body into the cushion of the brown leather chair and narrowed his eyes in concentrated thought. He simply didn't understand. Manny had been acting very weird for the past few days. Still, he couldn't understand why she would leave town without saying anything to him. He'd searched his mind and could think of nothing that he'd done to make her angry with him—if in fact she *was* angry with him.

Because Christopher had no clue about where Manny could have gone or whom she might have gone with, his thoughts were driving him crazy. His male pride was also at an all time low. Here he was, a decorated detective with over seventeen years on the force, and he couldn't even find his own woman.

A hand landing on his shoulder had Christopher leaping to his feet, his own hand already reaching for the weapon strapped to his chest. He eased off when Donny, who had a grin on his face and a white sheet of paper in his hand, came into focus.

"Where were you, man? I've been calling your name for the last five minutes."

With his heart attempting to slow its thudding beat, Christopher forced himself to relax, as he again became aware of the police station and the activities happening around him. Caught up in his problems with Manny, he'd shut out everything—not a good thing for a cop. That kind of inattention could get him killed fast.

With a shake of his head, Christopher stared at his partner. Donny wore his suit coat, a sign that he was ready to go. He pulled on the black leather jacket that was never far from his side, covering a black tee-shirt, matching black jeans and black leather boots on his feet—his standard uniform. Working the graveyard shift, Christopher liked to blend in with the night.

"Nowhere, man. Looks like you've got the info on that murder downtown, so let's roll."

Thursday morning dawned sunny and bright. Manny opened her eyes to find her mother seated on the bed beside her. She pushed herself up and accepted the glass of fresh squeezed orange juice Loretta held out.

"Morning, Daughter."

"Morning, Mama," Manny replied before placing the glass at her lips. She swallowed the juice thirstily, then set the glass on a white nightstand by the bed. Growing up, they had said good morning this way for as long as she could remember. It was an established tradition between mother and daughter; one Manny missed since she'd reached adulthood and moved out of her parents' home.

A few times on the weekends, she'd helped Christopher greet his morning with the offering. However, instead of the chaste kiss her mother had placed on her cheek, Christopher had shown his appreciation in a more physical and passionate manner.

A warm heat moved through Manny's body as thoughts of

Christopher's skills in the bedroom pushed into her mind, reminding her of the last time they had made love. Her eyes saddened with the memories. She missed Christopher Mills—his handsome dark face, smooth hard chest, wide smile, and the security and comfort of being held in his strong and muscular arms.

Manny pushed back, willing the memories away. Christopher Mills was not the man for her. She knew what she wanted. She wanted what Shelby shared with Nelson, what Starris had with Jordon and what Jacqueline had found with Henrico. She wanted a man to cherish her, and wanted to know and experience a love so deep that nothing in this world could destroy it.

"Did you have a good night, Daughter?"

"Yes, Mama."

The dark circles under Manny's eyes told a different story, and it was a tale Loretta's sharp eyes didn't miss. Her voice vibrated with warmth and a mother's love when she asked, "Where is he?"

Manny ducked her head, hoping to hide the dispirited look on her face. "Where is who?"

Loretta reached for one of Manny's hands. "The man who made you hightail it from the city to seek the love and comfort of your family."

Manny gave up the ruse, deciding that she might as well come clean. It was a waste of time trying to hide anything from her mother, who was very in tune with the minds and moods of her children. "Christopher is in Denver and I am not running from him. I came home because I wanted to spend some time with you and Daddy. I don't get up here often enough to suit any of us, at least that's what you always say when I arrive and leave."

The babbling did not distract Loretta from her mission. "Tell me what happened."

"There's nothing to tell, because it's over." Manny pushed out her lips in a sulking pout.

"Manette Alicia Walker, don't make me ask you twice."

Feeling herself about to break down, Manny turned her head away.

She quickly pulled herself together and looked up at her mother. "Christopher is a cheat, Mama, and Shelby already made me tell her. I'm not up to repeating the story."

Loretta smiled fondly. Shelby had been Manny's best friend since college. She was a woman with a good head on her shoulders and Loretta was sure that Shelby would not have let Manny get involved with a man whose character was questionable. Besides, Manny had brought Christopher up to share Christmas with the family. While she had claimed they were nothing more than friends, Loretta had observed Christopher's total devotion to her daughter. Henry and the brothers had liked him, too, and had treated Christopher as if he was already a member of the family. This said a lot for the young man, considering that the brothers, who still hadn't worked through angers and hurts of the past, took an instant dislike to any man who showed an interest in their sister. "What did Christopher do?"

Reaching into her memory bank, Manny talked about everything under the sun, except her recent discovery regarding Christopher Mills. When she did happen to speak of the man who so obviously held her heart, Loretta watched the subtle changes that transformed her features.

Manny's expression softened and her eyes glowed with the love she felt for Christopher Mills. Manny didn't often show her feelings. Growing up in a house with three boys had quickly taught Manny that leaving herself open to their ridicule was to have those feelings hurt. And Manny was easily hurt.

When Manny wound down, her mother said, "So are you finally ready to admit that you're in love with Christopher?"

"No!"

The denial came too quickly to suit Loretta. "Are you sure, Daughter? And this time, think about it before you answer."

Manny returned her mother's blatant stare and knew she could not deny her feelings. She sighed heavily, but did not sever their visual connection. "Okay, Mama. I do love Chris, but it doesn't matter because he doesn't love me."

"Manny, all things make themselves known in time—especially matters of the heart—and especially when it involves men. I believe that Christopher cares for you a great deal, but he may need more time to realize it himself."

"He's had plenty of time and he's decided that he wants someone else. I saw them together, Mama. They were sitting real close and he had his arms around her. If he cared about me, then he wouldn't have been with her!"

Loretta was well acquainted with her daughter's impulsive nature. Manny had always been the one who jumped first and thought about the consequences later. She was also short on forgiveness. Loretta's memory took her back to a time when her two younger sons had decided to play a joke on Manny and had taken and hidden her favorite doll. Though they'd given it back within the hour, her baby girl, who was only six years old at the time, hadn't spoken to the brothers for three months—not one single word.

Seeking absolution, Todd and Erik had saved all of their allowances, and had even gone through the neighborhood to earn extra money to buy three new dolls for their sister. However, it wasn't until her seventh birthday that Manny had finally decided to forgive them.

As she'd matured, Manny had learned not to be as hard on people who had wronged her. But her feelings were still fragile, and after a failed first relationship that had also resulted in the loss of her baby, she was very insecure.

However, Loretta had a strong feeling that Christopher Mills was the man Manny had been searching for and it would be a shame if she lost out on a chance at real happiness because of a simple misunderstanding. "Okay, Daughter. You saw Christopher out with someone else. What did you do?"

"What was I supposed to do, Mama? I got out of there as fast as I could."

"But you asked him about it later?" When Manny bowed her head and didn't answer, Loretta continued. "Manny, maybe the woman was his sister or an old friend. But instead of finding out for sure, you tried, judged, and convicted the man without even hearing his side of the story."

"He was kissing her, Mama. I didn't need to hear his side of the story when I could see the truth with my own eyes."

"But did it occur to you to ask him about it?" Loretta placed her hands on the sides of Manny's face. "Daughter, jumping to conclusions almost always leads to making the wrong assumptions. Talk to Christopher and don't let your temper stop you from hearing what he has to say. You could be wrong, you know."

Manny fell back on her pillows and swallowed the sob in her throat. She wasn't ready to talk to Christopher. Seeing him with another woman still hurt too much and she'd been down grief's highway too many times already. She couldn't talk to Christopher and hear him admit what she already knew to be true: He didn't want her. Somehow, she would have to find a way to go on without him.

Christopher paced impatiently outside the abandoned warehouse. He glanced at the black leather watch on his wrist. It was almost three in the morning and his contact was late. He cursed under his breath, cautious of keeping the noise down to a minimum. At this time of night, the streets of LoDo were long deserted, but anyone could be lurking in the shadows of the night. Leaning back against the wall, he decided that he would give the man ten more minutes.

While he waited, Christopher surveyed what he could see of the area and remembered his own arrival in the Mile High City. He'd wanted to experience something outside of the black township in North Carolina where he'd grown up and had chosen Denver primarily because of the availability of jobs in law enforcement. Having access to more sophisticated law enforcement tools to aid his search for the man who killed his father had been another draw. As an avid outdoorsman, however, what had clinched Christopher's decision were the newsy letters Nelson had sent home to his parents while in college. Nelson had whet his appetite for the city when he'd heralded his adventures in the majestic Rocky Mountains, the gentle climate, and low cost of living.

Christopher had spent his first week in Colorado camping and backpacking through the mountains and fishing for rainbow trout in the state's vast number of streams and lakes. Now he owned a home, which he'd purchased for a song during the city's economic depression, in Capitol Hill, one of Denver's most historic and diverse neighborhoods. Because of Jordon Banks' adroitness at predicting rising stocks, he also owned several other pieces of prime real estate.

His house was a vintage, red brick Tudor with red sandstone trim and flagstone sidewalks out front. The Molly Brown House was in the area and the Colorado State Capitol building was only a few blocks from his home. He loved the rich diversity of his neighborhood and its adjacency to Five Points, home to a very strong and vibrant, mostly African-American community, the Black American West Museum, and the Cleo Parker Robinson Dance Ensemble studios.

LoDo, the trendy name for lower downtown Denver, was a bustling business district where Union Station, once the rail queen of the West, but now a mostly nostalgic stop for railroad enthusiasts, still stood. During the economic crisis, LoDo had suffered just like the rest of the Metro area, leaving behind empty buildings and warehouses as shelter for the city's homeless, bums, and derelicts. It was an area once designated as skid row, but the toppling of old buildings to enhance the skyline and the development of the Sixteenth Street Mall had changed much of that. Evacuees from the West Coast had arrived with pockets lined with cash and had turned the old buildings into million dollar lofts and condos. Businesses had again taken up residence, along with fancy coffeehouses, restaurants, bars, nightclubs, chic art galleries, and museums.

Young and old alike meandered through the streets of lower downtown Denver, but especially the young and the yuppie. They had money to burn and a new place to spend it. Lower downtown Denver was a popular hotspot once again.

The homeless had fled farther down the banks of the Platte River to take up residence in the still abandoned buildings and warehouses that hadn't yet been touched by the effects of the renaissance. It was where Santangelo and others like him stashed their goods until it was safe to move them along established routes to their ultimate destinations.

It was in this area that Christopher waited for his contact. In the far, far distance, he could see the light of several small fires used to warm a group of people lost and forgotten in a city that had burgeoned from a laid back 'cow town' into a major metropolis. And, one that was too concerned with building its image to worry or care about them.

"Blackmon."

The whispered name echoed off the walls of the old buildings, startling Christopher out of his reverie. He peered into the darkness, seeking the owner of the voice.

"Jerome, man. Over here."

Christopher walked in the direction of the voice, his booted feet making no noise as he cautiously made his way toward the back of the warehouse. At the same time, he tried to slow his heartbeat. His contact knew him as Jerome Blackmon, an ex-con who'd served ten years in a federal prison for running drugs. He was close to Santangelo, and he had no intention of blowing it now.

Approaching the end of the warehouse, Christopher paused momentarily to check out the surrounding area before he strolled unhurriedly around the building. He used the rising and falling red tip of a cigarette to locate the other man.

Reaching him, he immediately faced outward, casually leaned back, and propped one of his feet flat against the side of the building. "You're late."

Benito Chavez dropped the cigarette on the ground and crushed the butt beneath the sole of one of his soft Italian loafers. "Actually I've been here for over an hour." A wary smile lifted Benito's lips. Christopher's focus remained on the man's hands, specifically the one in Benito's pocket. "Had to make sure that you weren't followed or 5-0 coming to take me out permanently."

Christopher wrapped the fingers of his left hand around the black belt at his waist. "Bullshit, Chavez. You've had me under the scope for three months. Anything they wanted to know about me, they found out within the first twenty-four hours. Now, am I in or out?"

"Ant'ny was impressed with you the other night, but I know my brother and he don't snuggle up too well to strangers, especially them that suddenly turn up out of nowhere. Know what I mean? But, since Juan and Luis got boxed last week, he's in a jam."

Christopher forcefully squashed a smile. Juan and Luis Chavez were on lockdown and he was responsible for the bust. If his luck held, Benito would soon be joining his brothers behind bars.

Chavez turned and stared into the night. "That makes ten of our boys in lockdown, and we need mules to move the merchandise out of the city. Since the crackdown, the rest of the boys have gotten real scared and some have taken off for parts unknown. Even the jugglers have made themselves scarce."

Christopher knew the term *jugglers* to mean the teenaged, mostly homeless street dealers who roamed the Sixteenth Street Mall and other areas of the city. The City called them mall rats and did their best to discourage their presence downtown. His interest perked up when Chavez added, "So, Ant'ny's gonna give you a tryout, Jerome. If you don't screw up this opportunity, he may take you on permanently. 'Course, that's only if the big man marks you first."

Christopher's heartbeat accelerated. The big man was Dexter Santangelo, the man Christopher had been hunting his entire adult life. He released a quiet, deep breath to ease the pent-up tension in his chest.

Upon the dismantling of the once powerful Cali Cartel of Columbia, Santangelo had secured his hold on the cocaine market by seizing control of their intricate and complex network of people. He ruled a vast empire that stretched across Latin and South America, and coast to coast in North America. The arrest of Santangelo would be a major boon to the agents that eventually took him down. Christopher wasn't interested in the publicity. He wanted to look Dexter Santangelo in the eye as he snapped on the cuffs and said the words, "For my father."

Questions he wanted answered burned in his mind, but Christopher held his tongue. It had taken too long to get this close to his quarry. There was no need to raise Benito's suspicious nature. "When do we leave?"

"Later in the week. I'll call with the when and the where. Until then, stay close to the ground. We can't afford to lose another mule." With a wave of his hand, Benito turned and walked away, blending in with the shadows in a matter of seconds.

Christopher moved off in the opposite direction, his face a study of seriousness. He hopped the free Mall shuttle and rode until he reached a light-rail station. Changing his mode of transportation, he climbed aboard the empty car and rode to the Park-N-Ride at I-25 and Broadway, where he'd left his Jeep parked to cover his tracks. Sliding into the seat, Christopher felt an immense sense of satisfaction in the night's work and the fact that he was one step closer to Dexter Santangelo.

CHAPTER 3

Friday morning found Manny back at her desk and in better spirits. That is, until she hit the power button to boot up her computer and nothing happened. Biting back a curse, she tried hitting the button several more times. Confirming that the computer's plug was in the wall before she reached for the telephone, she dialed the number of Mark Greene, the computer guru Exterior Motives contracted on an 'on call' basis.

"Manny Walker," Mark said as soon as he answered the call. His caller ID had identified her when his phone rang.

"The system's down again, Mark, or rather it might just be my PC."

"What's wrong?"

"If I knew that, I wouldn't have to call you, now would I?"

He laughed. "Sho' you right, Ms Walker, but I still need to know what going on with your machine."

"Absolutely nothing. I hit the power button and the computer just sits there."

"Hmmm," Mark toned. "And the machine's plugged in?"

"Of course," Manny said with a hint of irritation. "Do you think I would have called if I had not already checked that?" She had called him once, only to learn, to her complete embarrassment, that the problem was a plug halfway pushed into the socket. "Can you please just come out and take a look? I need my computer pretty badly today."

"Not a problem, Ms. Walker. I'll have you back up and running in no time. Hold on a sec and let me check my schedule."

While she waited for Mark's return, Manny first hummed, then began to softly sing the words to "Here and Now," a popular wedding song recorded by Luther Vandross. When she realized what she was doing, Manny stopped immediately. Naturally, it would have to be the last song she'd heard before turning off her car engine that morning and therefore the one stuck in her head.

"That was lovely, Manny."

"What was lovely?"

"Your voice. Have you thought about singing professionally?"

Manny turned all kinds of shades of crimson beneath her dark skin...glad not only for her coloring if someone happened to come into her office at that moment, but also that Mark Greene couldn't see her through the phone. "Ah, no," she said.

"You should think about it; you have a wonderful voice."

"Thank you, Mark." Manny cleared her throat. "Now, about my computer."

"Ah, yeah...I can be there around one o'clock. Will that work for you, Ms. Walker?"

"One o'clock will be fine, and Mark, thanks."

"Not a prob. See ya later, Manny."

She hung up the phone, then looked at her 'to do' list. A run to the bank was the next item; she might as well get that out of the way. Grabbing her purse and the bank deposits from the safe, Manny headed for the door. She stopped in the boutique to seek out Shelby, who was sitting at her drafting table hard at work on a new design. "Shel, my system's down again. I've already called Mark and he'll be over this afternoon to get it back up. I'm running to the bank to make the deposits, so you might want to keep your eye on the store until I get back."

Shelby laid down her drawing pencil, the name of their computer specialist catching her interest. Mark Greene had recommended and installed the store's computer system. He'd also been contracted to keep it running and had thus far provided excellent service. Lately, Mark had to make several trips to Exterior Motives and, if Shelby wasn't mistaken, the visits had less to do with her computer system than Mark's 'for all the world to see' crush on Manny.

Shelby knew nothing about Mark except that he had his own business and was a genius computer programmer. When he was at the shop, he spent most of his time with Manny. Though they talked, laughed, and sometimes shared long lunches, Manny, in her quest to find a husband, had overlooked Mark completely. Shelby's natural impulses kicked in. Could Mark Greene be the man Manny needed to help shake her depression over Christopher Mills?

Nelson had already given her the busybody lecture about Manny and Christopher, and knowing she'd hear about it later, Shelby tried in vain to stave off the urge to play matchmaker. This, however, was a golden opportunity she could not ignore. She could plan a dinner and invite a few friends over. Nothing elaborate—just a little barbecue at the house next Saturday. After that, she'd step out of the matter and let nature do what it did best. That way her husband wouldn't be able to accuse her of meddling. "Okay," she replied to Manny who still awaited her response. "See you when you get back."

The following Saturday, Shelby pulled the pink cotton blanket up over her sleeping daughter's body and quickly descended the stairs when chimes rang throughout the house. She opened the front door and froze on the spot when she saw the tall, good-looking man who stood on her porch. She'd meant to talk to Nelson and let him know discreetly that Christopher Mills was not invited to the barbecue, but had forgotten in her excitement over the prospect of Manny and Mark becoming a couple.

Though mad at him, Shelby could not ignore the fact that the man on her porch was very handsome. Christopher wore form-molding blue jeans and an open neck, blue-checked, cotton shirt with the sleeves rolled up to his elbows. A pair of shiny but much-worn black leather boots graced his feet, and he'd slung his black jacket over his shoulder. The goatee and mustache were recent additions on a face that wasn't as thin since he'd bulked up his physique, and the black Stetson, tipped at a rakish angle, hid a head he'd shaved bald shortly after her accident.

Christopher stood with his weight braced against the doorjamb, his stance one of raw, tamed power. Power Shelby knew many had challenged, but few had won out against. That powerful stance, however, belied the genteel charm of a man who went out of his way to help a friend and the gentle spirit reflected in the jet-colored eyes gracing her face with a look of admiration.

Shelby's eyes narrowed in a defiant glare. "What are you doing here?"

If the glacial greeting surprised him, Christopher's expression gave no hint. He smiled, casting two dimples in dark brown cheeks, and presented the bottle of chardonnay he'd picked up for the party. Though her recent manner with him still puzzled Christopher, he'd decided to ignore it. He and Nelson Reeves had grown up together, and anyone who knew Nelson also knew that his devotion to Shelby was unquestionable and complete.

Christopher didn't want to do or say anything that would cause the loss of one of his best friends. He just hoped that Shelby would work through whatever was bothering her so that they could get back to the easygoing friendship they'd shared over the years.

"Hey, Shel, hope I'm not too early." When Shelby didn't take the bottle or move back from the entrance, he added, "Am I too early?"

Whatever Shelby would have said in response, Nelson quelled when he arrived at the door. He took the knob from her hand and opened the door wider. "Chris! Glad you could make it, man. Come on in. I've just put the ribs on the grill and you can help me finish setting up the backyard."

Christopher entered, slipping by Shelby, who still stood semi-blocking the doorway. He handed the bottle of wine to Nelson, who slapped him on his back and led the way to the backyard. Shelby stared at the two men as they moved off, realizing the truth of an old Scottish saying, for her best-laid scheme had just gone awry.

An hour later, the doorbell chimed and again, Shelby hurried to the door. Everyone had arrived except Manny and Mark, and she'd piddled around in the kitchen so that she could warn her friend of Christopher's presence.

"Look who I found on the sidewalk, Shel."

Shelby smiled at Mark as she surveyed the sharply creased blue jeans, lightweight red pullover, and brown leather loafers. Sunlight gleamed on a head of dark brown hair neatly barbered in a fade and almost matched the gleam in the dark brown eyes staring adoringly at Manny Walker.

The crocheted top made of hot pink yarn stopped just below the navel on Manny's stomach. The hooked circles around the middle were large enough to show the smooth darkness of her skin and the enticing curve of her waist. A mock sarong wrapped around sheer pants, which were the same color as her top, and she wore white, low-heeled sandals on her feet. Her hair was a tumbling wave of black curls and hot pink earrings adorned her ears. A light covering of powder and a subtle pink lip-gloss, along with the bright color of her outfit, brought a natural glow to her beautiful face. Standing next to Mark, Shelby had to admit that they made one good-looking couple.

"Manny, you look great," she said.

"Thanks, Shel. So do you," Manny replied, openly eyeing the black Gypsy dress and matching sandals worn by Shelby. The long, flowing garment had a gold band and empire waist decorated with bits of multi-colored fabric and tiny mirrors.

Manny crossed to Shelby and turned her head to wink at Mark. "I had a feeling something good would be waiting for me here, so it took a little longer than normal to get ready. What do you think, Mark?"

His eyes widened at the not so subtle innuendo and openly stared at the pretty picture Manny made. Shortly, he found his voice. "I'll have to second that opinion." Mark had to take a deep breath before continuing. "You do look lovely today, Ms. Walker." He gave Manny a dazzling smile. "Oh, and you, too, Shelby," he added as an afterthought.

"Why thank you, Mr. Greene," Manny said. "I'm just glad there's someone here to appreciate it."

Shelby's cough broke the mounting tension. "Manny, do me a favor please, and check on Lauren. I put her down for a nap a while ago and she should be stirring about now. If she's up, bring her down to join the party."

"No problem, Shel. Be back in a few, Mark, so don't you go any-where."

"Oh, I won't," Mark replied, as Shelby him led away. He craned his neck to look back at Manny as she climbed the stairs on her way to Lauren's bedroom. Shelby tugged on his arm, then hustled him through the kitchen and out the back door. At the same time, she was trying to think of a way to hold off the disaster that was about to strike in a very a few minutes.

Mark removed the empty plate from Manny's hand and piled it on top of his own. He rose to his feet. "Would you like another drink?"

She smiled. The man hadn't left her side all afternoon. "Yes, I would. Thank you, Mark."

As he crossed the yard headed for the patio and the cooler, she leaned back against the picnic table and let her gaze slip to Christopher. He'd tried to approach her when she'd come down with Lauren earlier, but she'd handed the baby over to Shelby and studiously presented him with her back. She'd sought out Mark and grabbed hold of one of his hands as if it were a lifeline. Christopher had gone back to his table and hadn't tried to come near her again.

Surreptitiously, she studied him through the screen of her lashes. The man looked too good! She watched him laugh at something Jordon Banks said before he tipped the bottle of Coors in his hand to his lips. Manny barely contained a groan. The exposed throat and bob-bing Adam's apple had her remembering the many times she'd thrown her arms around his broad shoulders and laid her lips against the soft skin of his neck. It was one of his erogenous zones, along with the back of his thighs. She could get Christopher Mills to do just about anything if she paid special attention to those two areas once foreplay began.

Christopher liked to give her massages and Manny loved to receive them. As she allowed her mind to immerse itself in thoughts of their last time together, her breathing became a bit rushed. She could actually feel the touch of Christopher's strong and gentle hands caressing her body the same way they were caressing the bottle of beer he held now. Consciously, she told herself that if Christopher Mills cared anything for her at all, he wouldn't have left her in the clutches of another man all day. So what if he had lost interest? She hadn't lost anything except some time.

Inside, her heart took a different read on the situation. Pain motivated her flirtatious behavior with Mark Greene, and the pain of knowing that she had again failed to hold the attention of the man she loved. Thank God, she'd never told Christopher how she felt about him. Otherwise, she'd never be able to pretend she was having a good time, or that she enjoyed the attention Mark was showering on her. Or, that she didn't care a flip about Christopher Coltrane Mills.

Christopher had just about had enough. Manny looked so gorgeous and all he could do was stand by and watch while another man fawned over his woman. From where he stood, he could see the white of the lining cupping her ample breasts, and he didn't appreciate that the man she was with couldn't seem to keep his eyes off Manny's chest.

That, along with the teasing glances laced with disdain and the contempt she directed at him had turned his stomach into a roil of sheer rage. Manny was shamelessly flirting with another man and throwing it right in his face!

He'd tried to get in touch with her about attending the barbecue with him, but Manny hadn't answered her door and she certainly hadn't returned any of his phone calls. Her manner toward him when she'd arrived had been just short of hostile and Christopher was so confounded, he didn't know what to do. Her behavior today reminded him of their first shaky year together. For while Manny had professed early on that she was looking for a long-term commitment, her actions had stated otherwise.

While Christopher became a one-woman man, Manny had continued to go out with other men and he had exhibited the patience of Job waiting for her to get the party bug out of her system. Like today, he'd stood by silently while gratefully accepting whatever time she deigned to throw his way.

Now though, things were supposed to be different between them. The party bug no longer called to Manny. She came home directly from work now and, if he were able, they shared their evening meal. He spent his weekends at her house, doing minor repairs or just spending time, talking, cuddling, or making love to Manny.

Long talks with Manny were one of his favorite pastimes and Christopher thought he knew Manny well. She had an impulsive nature, which he complemented with his thoughtful approach. They both had easygoing temperaments, but she angered easily when it suited her. Not much bothered Manny Walker, but when she was irritated, he'd learned to make himself scarce.

She was outgoing and straightforward, and she had no use for people who played games or displayed haughty attitudes, except when she was hurt—then Manny exhibited the attributes of an introvert who wouldn't or couldn't tell you how she felt. She let you know in other ways, like she was letting him know today.

Manny didn't need to tempt herself, or him, with another man. She had him and he, she'd said, was all she needed to make her happy. She'd never said that she loved him, but that didn't bother Christopher. They just needed to spend more time together, time he would be able to devote to her once he finished this last case.

Trepidation stilled the beat of his heart and a lump formed in his throat. Christopher tipped the beer bottle to his lips and tried to swallow his hurt with a long, deep draw of the bitter ale. Manny Walker was supposed to be his woman, which was why her total disregard for his feelings cut through his heart like a knife.

When Mark returned and handed Manny her drink, Christopher stared openly. When the man sat down, put his arm around Manny's shoulders, and placed an impulsive kiss on her cheek, the tenuous hold Christopher had maintained on his emotions snapped. Christopher slammed his beer bottle down on the table, drawing curious looks from the people nearby. Ignoring their stares and low murmuring, he quickly crossed the yard.

Jordon, having seen the enraged glint in Christopher's eyes, stepped forward to stop him. Nelson placed a hand on his arm. "Let him go, J.R. Manny's been taunting him all afternoon and it's time Chris put a stop to it."

Nothing in his manner gave away the magnitude of Christopher's anger when he stopped in front of Manny and Mark. "We need to talk," he said in a tone that indicated she had no choice in the matter.

Manny firmed her shoulders in preparation for the battle she hadn't been all that sure would come. Sure, she'd been flirting with Mark and she'd done it to show Christopher, who had an uncanny ability to close himself off, that he wasn't the only fish in the sea. One minute he could be participating animatedly in a conversation, the next, staring in your face and not hearing a word coming out of your mouth. It was his shield, his armor, his way of keeping people from getting too close.

Manny had encountered his sudden bouts of withdrawal on numerous occasions. Most of the time, she just left him alone with his thoughts. Occasionally, she tried to break through the armor, coax him back to the present, and connect with the man underneath. She'd been waiting all afternoon for Christopher's reaction to her openly flirtatious behavior. That he'd finally decided to approach her again meant that his emotions, rather than his head, were controlling his actions.

As mad as she was at him, deep down, Manny was pleased. Christopher had just taken a step toward progressing into the caring and emotional man she knew he could be.

She turned to Mark, who was sizing up the man in front of him with the thought that he could take him, a serious mistake considering that Christopher's temper had been simmering all afternoon. The slightest provocation from either of them, and he would ignite.

"Excuse us please, Mark. I'll be back in a few minutes."

Christopher's antagonistic stare landed on Mark, almost willing the man to make a move so that he could vent his anger. "Don't wait around, Mr. Greene. Ms. Walker is mistaken. She won't be back!"

Gripping Manny by the arm, Christopher stalked away, fairly pulling her along behind him. Manny stumbled and lost a shoe; he didn't stop. She began tugging her arm in an attempt to break free. When he didn't slow down, she called his name and tried to hit him on the back, managing to knock the Stetson from his head. Christopher stopped long enough to swing Manny into his arms and resumed his march toward the patio and house amid the shouts of approval and applause from their friends.

Shelby ran forward, intent on helping Manny, but Nelson was there to cut her off. "This is your fault, Shelby Reeves, and now you're about to find out what happens when you meddle in other people's lives."

Shelby whirled on her husband. "This is not my fault, Nelson Reeves! You're the one who invited Christopher!"

Nelson crossed his arms. "Who invited Mark?"

She looked down at the ground. "I did," she admitted quietly.

"Why did you invite him, Shelby?" She had the good grace or sense to remain silent, which kept her from implicating herself any further. "You invited him, because you were trying to get Manny and Mark together. But you had to know that Chris would be here, too."

"I didn't think about that, Nelson. I just wanted to help Manny. She's been so unhappy and I thought—"

"No, Shelby Reeves, you didn't think, and that's the problem. I know that you want to help Manny, but it is not your place to interfere. All you know is her side of the story, sweetness. You haven't talked to Christopher. I have, and I happen to know that Chris cares a great deal for Manny, and that he has no idea why she's mad at him. So the next time you decide to jump headlong into other people's business...don't."

Nelson walked away without giving Shelby a chance to respond. She looked at the house and the door through which the couple had disappeared. Slowly, she crossed the yard to the sandbox where her daughter and the other small children were playing. Shelby sat down on the wood lining the edge of the square. Nelson was right; she really needed to learn how to mind her own business.

Inside the house, a showdown was brewing. Manny sat seething in the chair where Christopher had unceremoniously dumped her when they'd entered Nelson's study. He went back to the door, telling himself to calm down, but was too late. His wrath had been building for several hours into something he could not control. With a strong push, he slammed the door closed. Then he dropped his shoulders and leaned forward, pushing his forehead into the hard wood while grappling to regain mastery over his emotions.

Only one other person had ever brought him to this state, to the point where he would willingly kill another human being out of anger. He had to get control of himself because knowing that Manny had that kind of power over him scared the hell out of him. It was then that he realized that the saying was accurate: There truly was a thin line between love and hate.

Blowing out a deep breath, Christopher slowly turned and faced her. "What did you think you were doing out there, Manny?"

She jumped when she heard the deep rumble of his voice. He'd stood there for so long, she thought he'd forgotten about her and had been entertaining thoughts of escape, all impossible since he blocked the only exit from the room.

Vestiges of his internal struggle showed in his face, but Manny suspected that had less to do with her than with the spectacle he'd made of himself out in the yard. After all, he'd already shown that his devotion didn't lie with her. "That is not your concern, Chris, because just like you, I've moved on."

"Moved on?" The words were whispered, but more to himself than Manny. He frowned. What did that mean? "I don't understand, Manny. What are you saying?"

Rancorous brown eyes raked Christopher from head to toe as Manny tried to keep her mother's counsel and hold her temper. She didn't want to talk to Christopher about this. She wanted to go home where she could wallow alone in her self-pity. However, since he still blocked the door, she decided to spell it out for him. "I'm saying that I saw you last week, Christopher, and I saw who you were with."

Confusion, along with something else Manny couldn't identify, marred his face. For several tense moments, he merely stared at her and she knew he hadn't yet connected with what she'd just told him.

Christopher paced the floor, her words rolling around in his mind. Then he stopped abruptly and swung around to face her again. A nerve ticked in his cheek, the only sign of his agitation. "You were at that restaurant?"

Manny nodded, then rose to her feet. "And now that it's out in the open, let's get one more thing straight. I won't play this game with you, Christopher. You want to be with someone else, fine. Go and be with her!"

Christopher's eyes held a sorrowful appeal. "Manny, you're wrong."

"No, I'm not. I know what I saw and I'm not stupid. I might love you, Chris, but while you're out sampling another course, don't expect me to sit around waiting to take her leftovers!"

Christopher was so stunned, he couldn't even respond. Manny loved him! When had that happened and why hadn't she said anything before now? Maybe she had. Manny often accused him of not listening. Christopher shook his head. Had she said it, he was sure he would remember. He snapped out of his stupor when Manny began limping for the door. Impatient with the one shoe remaining on her foot, she bent down to remove it.

When she stood again, Christopher caught her around the waist and brought her back against his hard body. Holding her tightly, all the tension that had hummed through him melted away. Manny's hands came up to enfold his arms. Resting against his chest, she leaned her head to one side, content in the pleasant diversion of being in held in Christopher's strong embrace again.

He took advantage of her offering and his lips left a moist promise of passion along her slender neck until a barely audible sigh left her lips. Then he trailed a path of tender tongue strokes to her ear. "Did you say that you love me, Manette Walker?"

There was a teasing tone to his voice, but Manny didn't even hear Christopher. Lulled by the gentle caresses playing against her skin, she was busy waging a weak fight to keep her head above water. Christopher kissed the side of her mouth, a teasing touch really, and just enough to induce the smoldering burn of desire.

Craving the flame, she twisted in his arms and reached up to take his face in her hands. Their eyes locked in an electric gaze that sizzled in its intensity—hers with yearning pleading—his, desire tinged with puzzlement over her recent behavior toward him. Pleading won out and his hands spanned her waist, bringing Manny flush against his body.

Christopher groaned in resignation. This woman had a natural ability to move him like no other. Exciting him further, Manny shifted her hips back and forth across the obvious bulge of his need, then brought him into her gentle embrace when she felt the slight tremors coursing through his body.

She snuggled against him and the delicate love strokes of her hand on the back of his head were calming, but Christopher needed more. During their time together, he'd gotten used to the soothing way she had of settling him, especially after a long night of fighting crime and witnessing the results of man's inhumanity to man.

At times, Manny tried to play it tough, but the veneer was thin. She was a gentle spirit with a heart of gold and had a profound faith in her fellow man. Christopher knew a different fellow man, and he hadn't wanted to taint Manny's outlook with the harsh reality of that side of his life. When he was with her, Christopher tried to leave the hard-bitten cop outside. Their time together was special, man and woman, coming together in a soul-searing peace that filled him and made him whole again.

Nudging her back with his knee, but not out of his arms, Christopher lowered his head and laid claim to her mouth. As soon as their lips met, the passion denied, exploded. Securing his hold, Christopher cradled her body in a tighter embrace as the play of his mouth urged her lips apart. Feeling triumphant when she complied, he delved his tongue into her mouth and began an exploration of the warm hollow that had become familiar territory.

Despite her earlier words of love, he was seeking an outward sign that the hostility had ended and that her attitude of the past few days with respect to him would change. When she gripped his shoulders and whimpered, Christopher knew that his silent command had been effective and that Manny had given up the fight.

Releasing her, Christopher intertwined his fingers with hers and stared down into her passion-drunk eyes, a tiny smile lifting his lips. He dipped his head and placed his nose on hers, rubbing gently as he looked into the depths of her chocolate brown stare. "Honey-V, I don't know what you've been thinking, but there are no other women. You are the main and only course in my life."

In the strength of his embrace, Manny had lost herself in the blissful, emotional tide only Christopher could create within her. For a few brief moments, she'd given in to the sweet sensations of his touch and the wayward longing of her heart. With his words, the emotional truce they'd forged disappeared quicker than condensation in a strong breeze.

Christopher was good, but then in his line of work he had to be. As an undercover detective, he was an expert at wearing disguises and assuming whatever role suited his purposes. When a telltale glistening brightened her eyes, Manny jerked herself out of his loose grasp. She took several backward steps. "Good-bye, Christopher. And even though I couldn't, I hope she makes you happy." Manny treated herself to one last look, then executed a very unsteady turn, and walked out of the study.

Christopher remained where he was, knowing that he had to go after her, but unable to move. It was all there in her face. He'd hurt her. Manny had responded to his kiss, but Christopher knew that he'd have to do much more to win back her trust. However, he did have one advantage. Manny Walker loved him! She actually loved him! Knowing that she cared for him so deeply filled Christopher's heart with joy.

Then he sobered and his eyes reflected an inner torment. He loved Manny, too, but he couldn't tell her—not yet. Dexter Santangelo was responsible for the death of too many men. His influence and power spread a wide blanket, and he wouldn't think twice about exacting revenge on Manny if something went wrong.

Christopher sighed as he left the study. He couldn't declare his love, but maybe he could calm her fears and somehow let Manny know that he did care without revealing the true depth of his feelings until both he and she were safely out of harm's way.

CHAPTER 4

The first vase of flowers arrived at the store on Monday morning. Manny accepted the dozen pink roses and checked for a card. Not finding one, she handed the vase to one of the sales associates standing at the counter. "Enjoy."

Manny went back to her office, missing the happy expression on the woman's face and the whispers that followed in her wake. All week long, colorful pink bouquets arrived at the shop and Manny gifted one of the sales associates with the fragrant blooms. By Saturday though, Manny had to use all of the self-control she possessed not to throw the expensive buds on the floor and stomp them into smithereens. How long was he going to keep this up? Christopher had to know by now that she meant what she'd said. She was through with him!

She smiled for the benefit of the employees and customers as she accepted and signed for the delivery. Having been privy to the routine all week, the female associates gathered at the counter, each hoping to be the recipient of Manny's generosity. They were all disappointed when Manny left the shop floor, taking the flowers with her.

In her office, she set the glass vase on her desk and sat in her chair. She propped her elbows on the desk, rested her chin on the palms of her hands, and stared at the flowers. "Nice try, Christopher," she murmured in a quiet whisper. "But it won't work."

The man was sadly mistaken if he thought a bunch of flowers would change her mind. Now that she knew the type of man he was, there wasn't anything Christopher could do or say to make her feel differently about him. At least, that was the attitude Manny displayed outwardly. Inwardly, the heartache she felt was almost crushing at times. She needed to learn the lesson life had been trying to teach her. Men could not be trusted or depended on for anything except trifling with her emotions. The problem was her heart. It had a will of its own and continued to believe that somewhere in the world she would find her soul mate, she just had to keep looking.

Derrick Lewis. When his face popped into her mind, Manny's features crumpled in pain. She closed her eyes and tried in vain to will the memories away. "Derrick." His name slipped out in a whisper and her body trembled with agitation. He had been her first major disappointment in the love department.

Having turned sixteen and discovering a new fascination in the opposite sex, Manny had taken a great interest in the man who moved into the house across the street from her Boulder home. Derrick was twenty-three, fresh out of college, and he'd just landed a managerial position with one of the technological firms new to the area. Theirs had been a forbidden affair, and though her older brothers had warned her and Derrick to stay away from each other, Manny had been headstrong and in love.

She'd been so sure of his feelings, he'd easily coaxed her into giving up the precious gift of her virginity. At eighteen, she'd found herself pregnant. Though Derrick had done the gentlemanly thing and proposed marriage, her predicament had severely disappointed her parents, especially her father, an assistant pastor at the Baptist church attended by the Walker family.

In total disregard of their feelings, Manny remembered the excitement she'd felt planning her wedding. She'd thrown herself into the meetings with the wedding coordinator. She'd enthusiastically picked out her favorite pink tea roses, matching them with tiny blue bells and white chrysanthemums. She and Derrick had chosen their wedding ring sets together, along with the baby furniture and décor for the nursery he'd remodeled in preparation for the arrival of their child.

On the day of her wedding, Manny, now almost three months along, had awakened to the sound of booming thunder and flashing lightning. Though some believed that bad weather on a wedding day was a bad omen, it had not lessened Manny's joyful mood. She had dressed and gone to the church, her smile bright enough to replace the sun that had decided not to make an appearance on the happiest day of her life.

Three hours later, tears had replaced that bright smile. Like the sun, Derrick Lewis hadn't shown up at the church. When her brothers left to find him, they'd returned empty handed and without an explanation. The following week, a moving van had pulled up and emptied the house across the street. She never heard from Derrick Lewis again, and carried her child to term. After twelve hours of labor, the doctor performed an emergency caesarean section and had removed her still-born baby, a little girl, from her body.

Even with the unconditional love and support of her family, it had taken more than a year for Manny to get over her grief enough to pull her life together and attend college. There, she'd shared a dorm room with another lonely girl. As their friendship blossomed, Manny had confided the setbacks she'd suffered thus far in her young life. Even today, no one outside of Shelby and her family knew the depth of her humiliation over being jilted at the altar. Of her friends, only Shelby could personally relate to the everlasting anguish of losing a child.

Christopher Mills was just another disappointment in a life already filled with too many. Through it all, the one thing Manny had learned was that no matter what obstacles blocked your path, life continued whether you survived or not. And she intended to be a survivor!

Looking at the flowers, Manny sighed. Determined to throw off her blue thoughts, she pushed the vase to the side of her desk and pulled a pile of inventory sheets toward her. She never noticed the green envelope stuffed down in the middle of the arrangement, nor would she find and read it until much, much later that day.

Christopher leaned against the railing at Arapahoe Park Racetrack, which sat solitary and alone on the eastern plains just beyond the boundaries enclosing the City of Aurora. He clutched a ticket stub in his hand and feigned excitement for an activity in which he had absolutely no interest. When the crowd was quiet, in the distance he could hear the squeaky song of crickets and the soft yelping of prairie dogs whose underground homes extended across the fields surrounding the racetrack. Though his eyes seemed intently focused on the group of horses madly galloping down the dirt track to the finish line, Christopher's thoughts were about five miles down Quincy Avenue.

He was thinking about Manny and wondering if she'd arrived safely at the house she'd purchased on Stamford Street six months ago. Tired of renting, Manny had wanted the freedom and independence of owning a home, and Christopher had encouraged her decision by helping her find the perfect place to suit her needs, and if he were honest, his own. He'd already invested a large portion of the money he'd earned as a member of the DownTown Stock Club in several homes and businesses in and around the Metro area. He also owned two large tracts of mountain property, one of which held a huge log cabin where Christopher went to relax when he needed to get away from the bump and grind of the city.

However, the last decade had seen the price of homes in Denver, Colorado, skyrocket and unbeknownst to Manny, he'd added several thousand to the down payment she'd managed to save, bringing her monthly mortgage payments down to a reasonable amount.

Christopher frowned. *Had she locked up behind herself or remembered to let the garage door down?* Things Christopher had taken over doing for her or insisted she do when he called every single night since they'd been together after witnessing Manny's lackadaisical habits in regard to her safety came to his mind.

He had nearly blown a gasket the night he'd patrolled her street on a whim. Influenza had hit the Metro area big time and with the department already shorthanded, Christopher had agreed to take the shift of an ill officer. For the first time in years, he'd donned police blues and gotten behind the wheel of a patrol car. As an officer officially assigned to the Denver police force for the night, he'd had no business being in the city of Aurora.

Luckily, the streets of Denver had been unusually quiet, and a bored Christopher had taken a chance and driven out to check on Manny. He did that every night now, and in his Jeep and black clothes, had no trouble blending in with regular folks. That night, he'd arrived at three in the morning and the sight of the open garage door and a window where blue lace curtains blew inwardly in the breeze had set his heart to thumping. The lights in the house were out, and after first checking the perimeters and backyard, he'd let himself in with the spare key she no longer kept under a rock by the porch. Inside, he'd found Manny fast asleep on the sofa.

Staring at her and watching the rise and fall of her chest as she breathed, Christopher had felt such relief. However, with that relief, his temper had risen to epic proportions. Manny had no respect for the danger that abounded in the Metro area. She'd grown up in Boulder where, until recent years, people hadn't bothered to lock their doors. A few years back, he'd heard stories of similar behavior in the town of Parker, located a few miles south of Denver Metro.

But this wasn't the '50s, '60s, '70s, or even the '80s. This was present day Denver, and with the influx of people, crime had risen proportionately. When he'd awakened her, the yelling had begun. It was the one major fight they'd had during their entire time together and he didn't know how much of what he'd said had gotten through. Since then, though, when he ran his nightly trip by her house, he'd found the garage door down and the windows securely locked.

Loud shouts from the people around him brought Christopher out of his reverie, but not before he made a mental note to detour to the house as soon as he'd completed his business with Chavez.

Benito slapped him on the back. "You sure are som' lucky son of a bitch, Jerome. Bet you've pocketed over a grand tonight."

Christopher turned from the rail and began making his way up the crowded stairs leading to the ticket window. Yeah, he sure was a lucky son of a bitch. Lucky at the horses, but unlucky in love. He'd been calling Manny for seven straight days and she still refused to take his calls. After his shift had ended this morning, he'd dropped by the house, timing his arrival for when he knew she'd be awakening. Manny usually forgot to latch the security chains and he'd hoped the spontaneous social call would lead to some good old fashioned loving. All the unexpected visit had gotten him was a quick good-bye and a door slammed in his face, a reaction he'd not foreseen, nor was he ready to accept.

Manny Walker was stepping all over his heart in her crusade to remove him from her life. For now, he had to put up with the cold shoulder, messages she didn't return, and her refusal to take his phone calls. That, however, would soon change. When this case was over, Manny Walker was going to tell him again that she loved him and apologize profusely for every single thing she'd done to him, even if it meant locking her away until she regained her senses.

He glanced down at Benito, who stood at his side chatting eagerly while Christopher collected his winnings. The man was short, so short Christopher could see the balding spot on the top of his head. Anthony, Luis, and Juan Chavez hadn't grown any taller than their brother had. All of them had wiry builds, which they probably thought of as lean and mean. Christopher knew he could take any one of them out with a single punch. Unlike Benito, Anthony had risen to a position of power in the Santangelo organization. He reported directly to the man himself and was solely in charge of all activities in and around the Denver Metro area.

Benito talked incessantly, an annoyance which had Christopher wondering how he would withstand hours of being inside the cab of a truck with the man. He'd spent the last two nights with him, waiting for instructions that Benito assured him were coming. Christopher had already wearied of hanging out in bars and at the track, and he was most assuredly weary of Benito Chavez.

The man in the window shoved money forward. Christopher picked up the stack of bills, grinned his thanks, and turned away. He was reaching for his wallet when he noticed the tip of a white envelope in the middle of the pile. Someone had made him!

His head jerked up, but his quick and thorough scan of the area revealed nothing unusual. Still, now probably wasn't a good time to be standing out in the open. He'd be an easy target. "Let's go, Chavez."

Benito looked up from the racing form he'd been studying. His black, beady eyes glowed with excitement. "Why? I'm about to lay some dough on number seven." Benito slapped the form with the back of a stubby hand. "Just look at these stats. I'm A Lady is a sure winner in the tenth."

Christopher rubbed his tired eyes. "It's been a long night and I'm calling it a day."

Benito's face fell. "Damn, Jerome. You would wanna leave right when I'm about to score some cash."

"Look, Chavez, you can stay if you want, but I'm outta here."

"Okay, okay," Benito replied. "Just let me hit the can and we'll get goin'."

Christopher waited until Benito disappeared through the door leading into the bathroom, then made his way over to the wall by the ticket booth. The people making last minute bets would provide some cover, just in case someone had him in their sights. He quickly took out his wallet and retrieved the envelope. He ripped it open and took out the single, note size piece of paper it contained.

The note, written in a bold black scrawl said, "Lose the midget. Meet us down at the rails. You have one hour."

Manny entered her house, turned for the stairs, and suddenly stopped. She returned to the door. Christopher had a hang up about locking doors, and after judging hers inadequate, he'd spent one whole Saturday installing replacements and re-keying or adding bolts at every entrance of her home. At the time, his show of loving concern had touched her heart. Now she knew it was simply a matter of safety and that he would have done the same thing for anyone he thought in danger.

Still, she adjusted the vase of flowers to one arm, secured all the locks, and resumed her trek up the stairs. Moving into her bedroom, Manny paused in the rose carpeted doorway and surveyed the space for the perfect place to put the flowers.

Manny's bedroom was a testament to all things romantic and a haven for her after stressful days at the shop. It was filled with lots of silk and lace, potpourri, and large scented candles. Rose-colored panels covered the windows and Tiffany shaded floor lamps sat on either side of a canopy-draped four poster bed. Pictures of Christopher lined her walls and the top of a bureau on the left wall. She loved nothing better than snuggling under the mound of covers and pillows on her bed, seeing Christopher's face everywhere she looked. She entered the room and set the vase of flowers on the end of the dresser. Every one of those pictures of Christopher would come down tomorrow.

Hanging up her clothes in a spacious, walk-in closet, she wrapped her body in an old and fuzzy white robe, headed for the bathroom. Inside, she pushed aside the white bath sheet hanging from a pink rod to expose a large and very pink sunken bathtub with gleaming gold fixtures. Turning on the faucets, side jets automatically began spurting water. Reaching for the lavender-scented bath oil from the expanded back shelf, she poured several capfuls under the faucet, crossed to the sink and began removing her makeup.

Toweling her face, Manny surveyed herself in the mirror. The dark circles were still prominent. While the bubble bath would help ease her exhaustion, Manny knew she would get no sleep that night either. Her eyes moved of their own accord to the face smiling at her from the shelf. She needed and wanted Christopher Mills. Having gotten used to having him around and in her bed, her body craved his touch and the petting strokes he always used to calm her into a peaceful slumber. When she closed her eyes at night, it was Christopher's face she saw, and when she opened her fatigued lids in the morning, his image was still there.

Since the barbecue, she'd been trying to accept that the two of them were through, but the reality was that she hadn't accepted anything of the sort, and his constant reminders were not helping. When she'd opened her eyes this morning, Christopher had been hovering over her, and the exhilarating thrill that made her thump was as natural to her as breathing. Her first thought was that she'd died and gone to heaven…

"Morning, gorgeous," he said, right before his mouth had descended to cover hers.

By the time Christopher let her up for a breath of air, Manny's eyes had filled with happiness. His kiss tasted of ambrosia; his body felt harder and more solid than she remembered, and the resonant tone of his voice lingered in her ears, luring her into a hypnotic world that included only him.

Manny buried her face in his chest. "Christopher," she murmured. "I missed you so much."

Lowering his head, he placed a tender kiss on the side of her mouth. "I missed you too, Honey-V." Christopher checked the clock on the bedside table and lowered her back to her pillows. Then he stood, shrugged out of his jacket, and winked at Manny. "It's still early, which means that we have some time."

That's when Manny woke up fully. She rose to a sitting position and threw the covers back. "Time! Time for what?"

She saw the look of wariness enter his eyes before the shield rose and he hid the emotional reaction behind a wall of indifference. When he didn't respond, Manny left the bed. "I'll tell you what time it is, Christopher. It's time that you returned the key to my house."

A plea entered in his dark eyes when he reached for her. "Manny, don't. I know you're hurt, but don't do something that neither of us really wants."

She held out her hand. Christopher shook his head and reluctantly reached into the pocket of his jeans for his key ring. "Manny—"

"My key, Christopher, and then you can leave the same way you got in."

He removed the silver key and placed it in her outstretched hand. She followed him down the stairs and to the front door, her heart crying out for him to stay with each step. *Just tell me that you love me*, she thought. *If you can say that, everything will be all right.*

At the door, Christopher turned, "Manny, I…"

"Yes," she replied, unable to stop the lilt of hope that laced her voice.

She saw his shoulders drop in apparent defeat. "Goodbye, Manny." Then, he opened the door and Christopher Mills walked out of her life…

Manny lifted a hand and touched her mouth where the impression of Christopher's kisses still remained. This morning, she'd wanted nothing more than to throw herself into his arms and assuage the flames of desire flowing between them, quickly doused when she'd asked for her key and shown him the door. He'd looked so hurt, but she had to stay strong. She would not accept being just one of who knew how many women Christopher had in his life. For Manny, it was all or nothing.

Slipping into the tub, Manny relaxed in the luxurious, lavender bubbles and settled her head on the stack of soft towels at the base of her neck. With a sigh of contentment, she attempted to blank her mind to the strain and stress of her day. She'd managed to make it through another one, even though Carlotta Eldridge—a woman Manny could barely stand, and she pretty much liked everybody—had topped off her day with a visit, right before closing.

If the woman had just come into the shop and not said a word to her, everything would have been fine. But no, Carlotta Eldridge couldn't do that. The woman just had to snap that last piece of emotional rope holding Manny together by making one of her snide comments regarding her attire. Manny's first angry blast had left the woman speechless, and by the time the rubble settled, Carlotta couldn't remove herself from Exterior Motives fast enough.

Served her right, Manny thought, closing her eyes. Carlotta's superior attitude had always rubbed her the wrong way. In Carlotta's eyes, Manny was nothing more than a shop girl. It didn't matter that she was part owner of the ready-to-wear store or that her parents were both distinguished and honored educators. Having money didn't make a person better than anyone else. Manny knew that well from being with Christopher. He had money and didn't have to work. Yet every day, he risked his life on the streets of Denver, willing to pay the ultimate sacrifice to make the world a safer place. This morning she'd treated him horribly. Christopher would never admit how much it had hurt him to comply with her request and return her key. He didn't have to, because Manny had seen the sadness in his face.

With that thought echoing in her mind, a very troubled Manny had another equally troublesome realization. Christopher was a man of honor. He valued truth and justice above all else. He fought for those principles every single day of his life. She had, as her mother had said, tried, judged, and convicted him without giving Christopher the opportunity to defend himself. How unfair her actions must seem to the man that she was supposed to love.

Filled with remorse, Manny hung her head in shame and the tears she'd been holding in for days finally spilled from her eyes, the droplets hitting and disappearing into the hidden depths of the bath water.

Christopher parked his Jeep at the Park-N-Ride, grabbed his black jacket, and stepped from the car. Slipping on the coat, he thought about the clandestine meeting and the information to which he was about to become privy, his excitement growing over the possibility that it might be something he could use to finally bring Santangelo to justice.

He'd known all along that Benito was a mouthpiece with no real authority. The man was too short to use as muscle and had too much of a mouth to be trusted with anything of major import. However, Christopher didn't have time to ruminate on Benito's role in

Santangelo's organization. He had thirty minutes to get down to the rail yard. He turned to lock the door on the Jeep and tried to calm nerves that were taut with the anticipation of knowing that he was one step closer to his quarry and he was stepping into the unknown.

Christopher remembered giving a lecture at the police academy, "Tools Utilized by the Undercover Detective." He'd mentioned fear as one of those key tools, and some of the young yet-to-be officers had laughed before he could expound on the statement. He'd let them have their fun at his expense because he knew that they hadn't learned that a man who strode forth into dangerous situations without fear was a fool; and Christopher Mills was no one's fool.

Fear heightened the senses and the adrenaline raised awareness. Mindful of the natural stimulant energizing his body, Christopher began making his way toward the Sixteenth Street mall. In the Jeep, he'd been contacted again via the cell phone number he'd given to Benito. He'd received further instructions on where to go once he got to Union Station. Christopher knew that the designated location was one of the warehouses Santangelo used because it was one he'd been watching for some time.

At the entrance to the building, he paused. He had joined the force for one purpose—to find the man who had killed his father. As the years passed, he'd also found that he loved being a cop; loved the sense of justice he felt each time a criminal went to jail. Tonight, though, the single-minded purpose that had led him to this warehouse warred with regret. Because of the note, he hadn't been able to perform his nightly ritual of checking on Manny. That fact weighed heavily on his mind, especially since it was very possible that he might not walk away from this meeting alive.

Doing his best to shrug off the sentiment, Christopher opened the door and entered the building. He stood for a moment, letting his eyes adjust to the darkness and his ears to any sound that would alert him to the presence of others.

Hearing nothing, he was just about to call out when a hard blow to his stomach doubled him over. Someone grabbed the back of his jacket and jerked him up. Before he could react, a putrid smelling cloth sack came down over his head and tightened around his throat. Wresting himself out of the unseen hands, Christopher swung out blindly. His fist connected with bone and flesh. He was grabbed from behind and his arms were twisted behind his back. The next punch landed on the side of his face. Two more hit him center gut again and Christopher dropped to his knees.

Manny picked up a bottle of pear-scented lotion and crossed to her bed. She felt less stressed now and her posture was not as stiff. Tears had a way of doing that for you. They cleansed the soul and sometimes enabled you to see things in a different light. No new enlightenment had awaited Manny when she dried her face. She was as much in love with Christopher Mills as she'd been before and she was still alone.

She spread the lotion on her body, then crossed to the dresser and took out a nightgown. She slipped on the lacy pink garment and looked at Christopher's flowers again. He must have called her at least ten times that day and he'd left many more messages over the past week, but as much as she wanted to be with him, Manny wasn't ready to pick up the phone. Deciding that the nightstand by her bed would be a good spot for the colorful blooms, she lifted the roses. It was then that she noticed the small green envelope.

Manny plucked it from the bouquet, taking it with her as she moved the vase, and after arranging the flowers to her liking, she sat on the bed and opened the envelope. She took out the card, and then gasped out loud, realizing that she'd again jumped to the wrong conclusion.

"Hope you liked all the roses delivered this week. I remembered that pink was always your favorite. I would like to see you Manny, and meet my child. Please call me."

A phone number was written on the card and it was signed, "My everlasting love, Derrick."

CHAPTER 5

The next morning, Christopher rolled to his side and a painful groan slipped from his lips. Every single inch of his body hurt like hell. When and if he got up, he should probably head straight to the doctor, because he was fairly certain that at least two of his ribs were cracked. He didn't even want to think about the damage the rest of his body had sustained in the early morning skirmish, and he had no idea how he'd gotten himself home.

He raised his head and through a cloudy haze, fought the dizziness until the room came clearly into focus. It was a sparsely furnished space with his bed, a dresser, and a nightstand holding a lamp, phone, and a gold-framed photograph of Manny. Yellow curtains he'd purchased from a local discount store hung at the large window across from the bed. They were bright spots of color in a room dulled by gray carpeting and even grayer walls.

On a wall to the left, poster images of Martin Luther King and Malcolm X stood guard on opposite sides of the closet door. Inside, the left rack held a row of neatly pressed black jeans and the same color tee shirts. The right rack, the rest of his wardrobe and clothing that belonged to Manny, who would soon want to come over and collect her possessions, unless he could somehow mend their relationship.

Alone on the dresser, on a three-inch high wooden pedestal, a police cap sat protected in plastic. The hat had belonged to his father, and it was a daily reminder of why Christopher did what he did.

He should have hired a decorator years ago, because the rest of the house wasn't any better. Solely focused on his goal, Christopher hadn't paid much attention to his surroundings. That is, Until he'd watched Manny transform her new home into a showplace.

His head dropped back to the pillow and Christopher sighed

through another groan. He felt so bad that if someone came in with a gun, he'd gladly help pull the trigger to put him out of his misery. He needed some aspirin. What he wanted more was the sympathy and the tender touch of a woman's loving care, and he wanted those things from the person who'd been the indirect cause of his injuries.

With effort, Christopher managed to rise to a sitting position. He reached for the telephone and dialed Manny's home number. When the machine answered, he slammed down the receiver. Sharp jabs stabbed at every body part and he flopped backwards on his bed. That had been really stupid. He lay there with his eyes closed and as soon as the pain subsided to numbing aches instead of fiery spasms, Christopher made a decision.

A lesser man, battle scarred and sore, might have stayed in bed to lick his wounds. Christopher Mills was not that man and it was time to put down the combative stance Manny Walker had taken up against him. His thoughts helped further diminish the pain of his battered body and uplifted his spirit. The little war Manny had initiated was about to be over. He had several stops to make before launching a surprise attack of his own, and this time, Christopher intended to walk away from the conflict victorious.

He rose again, this time to his feet, and moving with all the speed of an elderly man with a cane, managed to make it to the bathroom. In the mirror, Christopher examined his wounds. His face had swelled with bumps; his bottom lip had split and his left eye felt tender and was an interesting shade of purple. Dried blood still clung to the whiskers on his chin and the knuckles on his right hand were scraped and bruised.

All in all, not bad, considering he'd had a burlap sack over his head and hadn't been able to see his opponents. The fight had been intense and by his estimate had lasted a good ten minutes. He knew he'd landed some blows. He could only hope that he had given as good as he'd gotten.

Christopher left the bathroom and sat on his bed again. His eyes narrowed as he relived last night's entertainment. For that's what he'd been. For all its intensity, it had been a staged fistfight. Had it been real, Christopher knew that he would not be sitting on his bed and able to analyze the events of the evening. His cold and stiff body would be lying in the fields somewhere down by the Platte River. His deliberation took a sharp turn as Christopher suddenly remembered something important.

After flattening him into a prone position, one of his attackers had removed the sack from his head. Lying on the ground, Christopher recalled seeing a heinous smile on the man's face. He had been rubbing his jaw as he'd leaned over him.

"You're a good man, Jerome," he'd said. Then he'd laughed and stuffed something inside Christopher's jacket.

Looking around the room, Christopher didn't see the black coat. One agonizing minute later, he was on his feet and headed for the living room. He saw his jacket thrown haphazardly on the back of an old leather chair. Christopher retrieved the garment and after a brief search of the pockets, pulled out a white envelope.

Inside, he found another note and a generous wad of cash. With his one good eye, Christopher scanned the paper in his hand, "Same time, same place. Two weeks from Friday. The run is on."

The bell above the door of Exterior Motives chimed and Manny's heart leaped as her gaze flew upward and focused on the two people who entered the shop. The woman, after a brief survey, smiled at Manny and moved to the shelves of marked-down accessories. The young girl never looked up as she crossed to the evening gowns on display.

Manny turned away, her frustration evident in the hands clenched into fists at her sides. She'd been watching that door all morning, waiting and wondering when Derrick Lewis would make his appearance, and she felt just this side of stupid. Even if the man did show up, she had nothing to say to him. Surely she could find something else to do besides standing there waiting on a man who'd made a fool out of her.

She tried to think, but couldn't make her brain cooperate. After reading the note, she'd gone outside and dumped Derrick's roses in one of the metal cans by the back fence in her yard. She'd spent the remainder of the night trying to divert her memories of him to that forgetful place inside her mind where she'd banished all past hurts.

This morning, she was tired, physically and mentally, and she'd also realized that she'd made a big mistake yesterday when she'd thrown Christopher out of her house. She needed him more than ever now, but when she'd called the numbers he'd insisted that she memorize so that she could reach him day or night, Christopher had not responded.

Derrick Lewis was somewhere in Denver. Christopher Mills was, too. Derrick wanted to see her. She wanted and needed to see Christopher. Derrick Lewis had plunged her into the depths of hell and hadn't cared if she survived the fiery fall. Christopher Mills made her heart soar whenever she thought about him.

What was the matter with her? Had she been looking so hard for love and for so long that she couldn't recognize it when it hit her smack in the face? So what if Christopher hadn't actually said that he loved her. Did she really need to hear the words when he had shown how much he cared in more ways than she could count? No matter what she thought he'd done, she loved Christopher Mills. Was she really ready to let him go so easily?

Manny signaled to one of salespeople that she was going to her office, and quickly left the sales floor. Christopher was the best thing that had ever happened to her and she owed it to him, and to herself, to sit down with him for that long overdue talk. If she hadn't already pushed him too far, he'd forgive her and she'd have another chance to show Christopher that she was the only woman for him.

In her office, Manny picked up the telephone, hoping as she said a silent prayer, that it was not too late. She tried all his numbers and when Christopher didn't answer, she hung up feeling frustrated. She'd just have to find another way to get herself back into Christopher's good graces.

Determination set her features as Manny worked diligently for the remainder of the morning, skipping lunch so that she could complete her tasks. At two o'clock, she rose from her chair, locked the file cabinet behind her, and retrieved her purse. Christopher might have decided to give up on her, but she was not going to give up on them. Her behavior had gotten her into this mess and direct action was what she would employ to reverse the damage she'd done to their relationship.

Five minutes later, Manny entered the boutique and found Shelby frowning over a sheet of white paper. "What are you doing?"

Shelby threw down her pencil and pushed away from the drafting table. "I was trying to get in touch with my creative muse, but I don't think that she's talking to me today."

Manny peeked over her shoulder. The outline on the paper appeared to be an image of a jumpsuit. The garment had a cummerbund waist with little circles lined up along its length. The bodice was short-sleeved with a zipper front and a cross pattern of more circles. The pants, roomy in the butt and hip area, tapered down to a tight band at the ankle.

"What are those?" Manny asked, pointing at the circles.

"When I'm done, those are going to be gold studs." Shelby considered the outfit again and retrieved her pencil. "I'm thinking of using leather. Or maybe it would flow better if I used a jersey knit. What do you think?"

Manny scrunched up her nose. "I think you should stick to what you do best." Manny took the pencil from Shelby and indicated that she should get up. Shelby stood to the side and watched in fascination as Manny took an eraser and rubbed out all of her work. Then, as if she'd been designing for years, Manny flipped the pencil and bent over the sheet for fifteen minutes of concentrated effort. When she finished, she sat up and held up the paper. "What do you think about this?"

The new jumpsuit had wider pant legs that flowed all the way to the top of the foot. Manny had lengthened the torso of the design and connected it to the bodice with a thin piece of elastic that gathered at the waist, and attached two large buttons to the front for a decorative touch. She'd drawn the bodice with wider shoulders and a rounded neckline. To the side, Manny had written the word 'crochet.' The garment had the effect of elongating the body, and the poly-rayon material Manny had noted for use offered versatility, and enhanced the sensual and natural movement of the body.

Shelby was more than impressed. Her friend was one talented woman! "Ooh, sister-girl. I think that you should be doing this instead of me." Shelby picked up the sketch and held it out in front of her as she mentally began visualizing the colors she could use to enliven the outfit.

Manny laid down the drawing pencil and rose from the stool. "I'm not the designer, Shel. You are. My thing is numbers and I have a pretty good eye for detail when it comes to selecting clothes for the shop."

An excited gleam washed Shelby's face. "Well, today you can just add designer to that résumé, because you've just sold your first outfit to Exterior Motives. I'll have samples made. I think we should use black and white for the first two pieces and showcase them in the store." Shelby walked away in the direction of her office, still babbling about manufacturing deadlines, commission fees, and price points.

Manny could only stare after her friend, hardly able to believe that Shelby, whose clientele included some of the wealthiest and most famous people in the nation, could be so in awe of something she'd whipped up on a whim. When Shelby disappeared into her office, Manny remembered why she'd come into the boutique. She'd wanted to let Shelby know that she was leaving and taking the rest of the week off. Winning back Christopher would take time and she had to get started as soon as possible.

Nothing felt right when Christopher parked his Jeep in front of his residence the following morning. He took his time leaving the car, bending over more than necessary to pull up the parking gear while his eyes scanned the street.

The tall, light skinned man standing by the tree across the street, he noted and dismissed. His rumpled appearance and hopeless gaze posed no threat. *Probably just one of the homeless who'd gotten lost in his wanderings.* Most of his neighbors had left for work, which pretty much left the street empty and he saw nothing else that captured his interest. However, as Christopher stepped from the Jeep and turned to lock the car door, a glance at his house did arouse suspicions.

The light on the porch was not on. A timer automatically shut off the floodlights in his front yard with the lightening of the day, but not the porch light. The only way to turn off that light was from inside the house. When a car's engine backfired, the sound jolted through Christopher like a gunshot. Breathing heavily, he quickly scanned the area again. The homeless man had disappeared. Christopher jogged across the street, looked behind the tree, found nothing, and using the tree for cover, he drew his gun.

Cocking the shiny black pistol, Christopher considered his options. Ten cement steps banked by a black iron rail led to his porch. Then there was the porch itself. Enclosed in brick and out of view of the street, anyone could easily lie in wait for him. Trying to cross the street would make him an open target. His other alternative was to track through his neighbor's yards and gain entrance onto his property from the back.

Christopher moved out. Ten minutes later, after trekking through the yards to the end of the block and back again, he jumped the chain fence along his border, smothered a groan, and crept up to his kitchen window. He waited there until the pain in his chest subsided, then moved around the house to the front porch. Taking a chance, he peeked over the wall and saw nothing. Thinking that his assailant might have moved, Christopher hauled himself over the top of the porch. He landed silently on his feet, but the jolt to his ribs caused him to bite back a curse. He checked his gun again and moved to the door.

Trying the knob and finding the door unlocked raised his pulse. Stepping inside and hearing the distinctive sound of a female voice singing in the back of the house set his black eyes ablaze.

Because Manny Walker hadn't told him that she would be at his house, he'd just made a fool of himself in his own neighborhood. Christopher replaced the gun in the holster under his jacket. Then he counted to ten, hoping it would calm him. It didn't, and Christopher stormed into the kitchen.

"Manette Alicia Walker! How many times do I have to tell you to lock the door when I'm not here!"

Manny whirled from the stove, her eyes wide as the knife in her hand fell to the floor. She was about to scream, but recognizing him, she stuttered, "Chris-to-pher!"

Then her body dissolved into visible trembles and he was beside her in seconds, holding her in a crushing embrace and muffling her murmured words in the hardness of his chest.

"I'm sorry, Manny. I didn't mean to scare you like that."

She buried her face in his shirt and when the initial fright wore off, she leaned her head back, her eyes closed, in expectation of more than his arms to comfort her.

Christopher stared down at the gorgeous brown face and the sound of his pounding heart filled his ears. He'd known that he missed her, but until now, he hadn't realized just how much. Nor had he wanted to acknowledge how much it had hurt him when she'd asked for her key. None of that mattered because Manny was here, in his kitchen, holding on to him as if she was afraid that if she let him go, he would disappear.

Christopher secured his hold on her body and lowered his head to satisfy her need—his need. Glad that she'd set aside the hostility, his lips roamed hers in a searching play for total forgiveness. He felt himself harden with the love-lust of wanting Manny for too many days and pulled her closer, deepening the kiss. He moaned when she opened her mouth in acceptance of his intimate tongue play.

Manny returned the kiss, massaging her lips against his in a blatant play of seduction. Even though he'd scared her, the terror had fled quickly when the long arms of the law—Christopher's arms—had her wrapped in paradise. She loved this man, and beginning today, she planned to show Christopher that he hadn't chosen wrong when he'd chosen her. She would do everything in her power to erase any thoughts he had of finding a replacement for her.

Her arms circled his waist, squeezing tightly as she pressed herself into his body. Christopher groaned again. This time it was a sound of pleasure mixed with pain. He'd gone to the doctor and while his ribs weren't broken, the flesh around them had taken a severe beating. With gentle hands, he pried Manny's arms from around his body and set her away. Unable to stop himself, Christopher leaned forward and grabbed the back of a chair, grimacing as he placed one of his hands on his chest, as if that would help stop the throbbing agony.

Manny stood where he'd moved her and for the first time since he'd entered the kitchen, really looked at Christopher. Holding his chest, he breathed short, hushed pants. His left eye was discolored and partially closed. His face was a map of bumps and bruises and his bottom lip looked angry and sore.

She watched him fight through the pain, her own fist at her chest as if she could somehow will his suffering to her. This was why she hadn't wanted to get involved with a police officer. Loving someone was tough enough. Manny hadn't wanted the additional burden of worrying about her man's safety or of spending her days waiting for him to come through the door, her nights worrying whether he'd live to see another day. Now it was too late. She'd given her heart to Christopher and one of her secret fears had just come to life.

Though Christopher stood before her wounded, but alive, her mind filled with thoughts of what could have happened to him. The image of his lifeless body sprawled in the street brought a horrified expression to her face. A cry of anguish tore through her lips too quickly for Manny to stop the sound. She slapped a hand over her mouth, then fled the room.

Christopher watched Manny run from him and wanted to kick himself for scaring her again. The look on her face had almost matched the one he'd seen on his mother's when she'd looked through the window all those years ago and had seen him standing on the porch with two uniformed officers. He now knew that his mother had known what had happened before she'd opened the door. She'd stood in the doorway and looked at him, her face a ghastly, pasty gray and eyes widened in a fright so horrifying Christopher immediately ran to her side.

He'd held up and held on to his mother, trying to impart some of his youthful strength to her when she wilted upon hearing that her husband had been killed in the line of duty. He would never forget that day. The memory had seared into his soul in the same way his love for Manny had seared into his heart, and he wouldn't let the terrified expression on her face be the last one he saw.

Gritting his teeth, Christopher pushed himself up from the chair. He released the air in his lungs, took another short drag, and began moving forward. He had to get to Manny because he knew that as quickly as she'd come back into his life, she was leaving again, and he couldn't let her do that.

He needed Manny. She was the sun that chased away the gloom and darkness in his life. She'd taught him how to laugh again. She'd filled him, completed him, and made him feel as if there was nothing he couldn't do as long as she was by his side. Manny was the most precious thing he had in his life, and Christopher was not going to lose her. Not like this, and not before he had a chance to tell her how he felt about her.

At the door to the bedroom, Christopher stopped and solemnly watched Manny. She was rushing around the room, pulling items from the drawers on the dresser and the open closet. Two black cases decorated with a profusion of pink roses were on the bed and one was already half filled with her things.

Christopher's heart dropped. Their relationship had matured to a level where each of them now kept some of their things in each other's home. Manny had two drawers in the dresser and part of the rack in his closet. One of her robes hung on a hook behind the bathroom door. Her toothbrush stood beside his in the medicine cabinet. Her perfumes, lotions, hair care products, and other items littered the counter in the bathroom and he'd gotten used to moving her things to her side of the sink when he was in the bathroom.

Doing his best to project a casualness he didn't feel, Christopher entered the room. "Honey-V, what are you doing?"

Manny looked up at him, her hands filled with the lingerie she'd just removed from the dresser drawer. Seeing him standing there injured from his beating only heightened her dread and a shiver of anxiety sliced her heart. When her legs began to tremble, she moved to the bed and dropped down. "I can't do this, Christopher."

He closed the distance between them, stopped in front of Manny, and despite his injuries, lowered himself to his knees in front of her. He placed his hand on one of her thighs and stroked the soft brown skin. "Manny, I'm all right."

Her head snapped up and through clouded vision, Manny surveyed every inch of his face again. She turned her head away. "You're not all right, Christopher, and I can't stand the thought that someone did this to you or that it might happen again."

"Look at me, Manny." When she didn't do as he requested, Christopher moved his hand to her face and held her chin, forcing her stare to lock with his. "Look at me and tell me what you see."

Manny first bit down on her bottom lip, the expression on her face a mixture of compassion and sadness. She stared at him for several long minutes before slowly reaching out her right hand. With the tip of her index finger, she began touching each of his injuries.

Christopher let her examine him, his manner quiescent and meek while he waited for her review to be complete, and for her answer. He couldn't force Manny to stay with him and he couldn't make her love him enough to accept the risks he had to take in the performance of his duties.

Suddenly the unfairness of it all struck Christopher with a force much like the punches his body had endured in the fight. Dexter Santangelo, and men like him, lounged in multi-million dollar homes portraying themselves as role models and pillars of the community. While he—an upstanding citizen and crusader against all that was unjust—had to fight to keep the love of his woman.

He also couldn't tell what was going through Manny's mind, but knew that her examination was something he had to withstand. Once she completed her analysis, he prayed that Manny would see beyond the outside bruises on his face and decide that she cared enough about the man on the inside to stay and work it out with him.

When she was done, Manny placed a light kiss upon his brow. She took his face in her hands and said, "Christopher, what happened to you?"

So far so good, and with that thought, a smile dimpled his bumpy cheeks. "You." Taking Manny into his arms, he leaned her comfortably against his body. "Honey-V, these bruises look bad now, but they will eventually heal." He took her hand and laid it against his chest. "But this heart would be destroyed if you left me."

It wasn't "I love you", but it sounded just as good. Lulled by the fervor behind his words, Manny gripped the back of his shirt in her hands. "I'm not going to leave you, Christopher. I've acted stupidly at times and made some foolish decisions, but you are the best thing that's ever happened in my life. It hurts me to my heart to know that some-body did this to you." She shook her head sadly. "And I don't think I'll ever be able to accept that anyone dislikes you enough to want to hurt you like this, but I would be a fool to walk out on you now."

Christopher rubbed his nose against hers. "And Manny Walker is nobody's fool, right?"

She smiled adoringly. "Right."

He rose from his knees with effort and pulled her up when he was on his feet. He placed an arm around her and looked at the bed. "Then why don't the two of us unpack these cases and put them and your things back where they belong. Then we'll be able to use this bed for another purpose."

CHAPTER 6

The sun bowed in a fiery ball accompanied by the resplendent purples, pinks, yellows, and blues of the waning day. The last of its light washed the dark mountainside and rolling green hills banking the valley below. Manny stood on the top of a cliff recording the gorgeous sight.

She whirled in a circle, her arms outspread. "This is so beautiful. I'm glad we decided to come up here, Chris."

On a whim one day, Christopher had rolled four of the large boulders scattered about the area together to fashion a chair of sorts. He'd added plenty of padding to the back and seat, which had made his chair quite comfortable. From it, Christopher watched Manny, his joy coming from her excitement. "I'm glad we did, too, Honey-V."

Manny ran over to him and lowered herself to the ground between his knees. "Chris, we've already spent the weekend up here. Are you sure we can stay through the whole week? Shelby didn't care when I called to tell her, but you've never taken this much time off work. Is your boss okay with this?"

His boss was okay with it because Christopher had already arranged for the time off. When he'd told his division chief that he was 'coming in', Samuel had taken one look at him and readily agreed that Christopher should take as much time as could be spared from the case to get his body healed. His plan had been to storm Exterior Motives, kidnap Manny, and bring her to his mountain hideaway. That hadn't been necessary after he'd come home on Friday and found her in his house. "Sam's okay with it."

They planned to spend a week at the cabin, which sat on top of a rising cliff in the heart of a clearing about five miles inside the city of Buena Vista, Colorado. Looking out into the distance, he could see the rugged slopes and snow-tipped peaks of three of the Fourteeners, a tag given to the sixty-eight mountains whose peaks broke the 14,000-foot high range in the North American Cordillera. Fifty-four of the Fourteeners were scattered throughout Colorado's mountain ranges, and Christopher had set a goal to reach the top of every one of them. So far, he'd found time to climb only twenty-three.

Manny had accompanied him on his last climb three months ago. They had hiked Mt. Bierstadt, which stood a commanding 14,060 feet high. It had taken them over four hours to reach the summit. Without Manny, he could have probably accomplished it in under two, but having his woman share one of his outdoor passions had made the climb all the more enjoyable. Once he retired from the force, he'd have all the time he needed to complete his goal with Manny at his side.

A gleam entered his eye and he gave Manny a speculative glance. "So, tell me, Ms. Walker, what would you like to do tomorrow?"

"Well, I was thinking—" she started, looking out on the beauty surrounding them and not paying attention to Christopher, whose mind had taken off in another direction. "What would you say about making an appointment at that health spa over in the next valley?"

Christopher was lost in his thoughts. In his mind's eye he saw the sparkling blue water of the nearby mountain lake. His net was in his hand and he could feel the flopping of the large trout as it fought for freedom. He added it to the bucket of fish in the bottom of the boat and the scene moved forward. Christopher saw himself sitting at the table, enjoying the fresh-cooked trout. The image was so vivid he could almost taste them.

"We could spend the day relaxing and getting our bodies pampered. What do you think?"

In an instant, Christopher's plate of golden brown trout, as well as his fork, knife, napkin, and the mound of fries he'd just added to his plate next to the savory collard greens disappeared. He frowned down at the top of Manny's shining, black head. "Huh," he uttered, not completely sure what she'd said, but certain that she hadn't said that she wanted to go fishing.

Manny twisted around to look up at him. "Christopher Mills, you are not even listening to me! I said I wanted to go to that health spa over in the next valley tomorrow. We could have our nails and feet done, get full body massages, and come back here relaxed and happy. Can we?"

Health spa? Have his nails done? Christopher looked down at his hand. There was nothing wrong with his nails. They were clean and neatly trimmed and he certainly wasn't gonna let anyone put any polish on them. He released a soft grunt. Health spa? He didn't think so. Not in this lifetime anyway. He gazed down into her expectant eyes. "No, thanks. Health spas are for women. I want to go fishing."

Manny opened her mouth, then abruptly closed it. What would her mother do in this situation? Or Shelby? They probably would not start an argument, which was what she'd been about to do. No, her mother and Shelby would simply comment on the matter and employ another method to get her father or Nelson to do what they wanted. She'd have to think on this. "We can discuss our plans for tomorrow later, Christopher. Right now, let's just enjoy this magnificent sunset."

By the time later arrived, another day which they had spent on the lake—she bored, Christopher happy with his fishing rod—had passed. However, Manny had already set her plan in motion. While Christopher napped on the coach, she'd called the health spa and made an appointment for nine o'clock the next morning. Her scheme also included a romantic candlelight dinner, followed by seduction, and ending with Christopher changing his mind about the spa.

In the kitchen, she placed a cutting board on the gold Italian-tiled counter, then began slicing carrots and onions which she threw into the pot on the island stove. The last time they had stayed at the cabin had been on a ski trip with their friends and, unlike his home on Curtis Street, with her help, the cabin's décor had been thoughtfully put together. Big, comfortable furniture made of the softest leather graced each of the rooms. Rich colors of evergreen, rust, maroon, gold, and brown blended in patterns that brought peace to a troubled mind and restored the soul. A large colorful rug resting at its hearth drew out the natural colors of the stone fireplace in the living room. His paneled, book-lined study was filled with the latest technological gadgets, and the three guest rooms were fully furnished. The master bedroom held a king size, shiny brass bed, and another stone fireplace.

Manny finished preparing dinner then went out on the deck to turn on the hot tub. After that, she went upstairs, headed for the black-marbled bathroom where she lounged for an hour in a scented bubble bath. Leaving the tub, she dried and smoothed lotion into her skin before going to the dresser and selecting the sheerest gown she owned. Though the lacy number had inch size discs of satin pale pink flowers interspersed into the white netting, the gown left little to the imagination.

However, since Manny didn't plan to entice Christopher with the sexy gown until later, she covered her body in one of the old, fuzzy white robes she normally wore around the house in the mornings. She piled her hair onto the top of her head with tendrils falling in lazy curls around her face and used plenty of the fragrance Christopher liked to scent her body. Manny turned to the mirror to assess her appearance. Pleased with her reflection, she turned for the doorway.

It was time to wake him up.

She tiptoed to his side and stood looking down at his sleeping form. Christopher lay on his back with his feet propped on the end of the couch. Manny lightly tapped his nose with the tip of her finger. His shoulders jerked and his hand batted at the unseen annoyance. She tapped his nose again, then watched long black lashes lift to reveal smoky, sleep-filled eyes.

A lazy smile touched his mouth. "Hi, gorgeous."

"Good evening, Mr. Mills. It's time for dinner."

Christopher threw his arm over the back of the couch. His intent was to lift himself up, but he fell back when his body stiffened in protest. Totally frustrated, he lay where he was, staring up at the high log-beamed ceiling in his living room. He'd soaked in the hot tub last night and that had helped, but some actions still hurt more than others did.

Manny bent down and picked up one of his hands. "Baby, let me help you." She saw in his face that Christopher wanted to refuse her offer. His eyes had that stubborn tint and his turned down mouth spoke volumes. Christopher Mills didn't want her help. "Boy, don't you dare pull that male chauvinistic crap on me. You need help and I'm the only one here to give it to you."

Whatever he'd meant to say, she'd swept away with her words and Christopher let Manny help him up from the couch. On his feet, he leaned heavily on her, even though he could stand perfectly fine by himself. "Ooh, you're so strong, babe. I sure am glad that you're here to help me. I don't know what I would have done without you."

A knowledgeable gleam brightened Manny's eyes. *Is that right?* she fumed, doing her best to hold him up, but knowing that any second both of them would hit the floor. "I'm glad I was here, too, darling, because if I weren't, I'd never be able to do this."

Manny released her hold on his body, then spun around, placed her palms against his chest, and shoved. Christopher lost his balance and his arms swung wildly until his butt hit the leather couch. He grimaced through a shot of fire in his chest.

His eyes were incredulous when he looked up at her. "Damn, Manny. That hurt!"

"Did it? Well, I have something that will make everything all better, only you'll have to get yourself up off the couch to get it." Manny left the room, smiling to herself.

Thinking about the well-shaped body hidden beneath the ghastly bathrobe, he watched her disappear through an arched doorway. Christopher tolerated the garment because it was one of Manny's favorites. For some reason, she seemed to prefer big and bulky to sheer and slinky. She said it was because she always felt cold and she continued to wear her robe although he'd shown her on numerous occasions that he could warm her up without the wrap.

Christopher raised his head and sniffed the air. Something smelled good in paradise and his stomach told him that he needed to go and see what it was. A few minutes later, he stood in the doorway to the dining room, his gaze on the table Manny had laid for him. She'd used the good china and candlelight washed the room in a romantic glow. A white vase, filled with fully bloomed purple lilac branches she'd pulled from the bushes in the backyard sat in the center of the black-clothed table, adding more fragrance to his already over stimulated senses.

Manny stood in the kitchen doorway with a covered serving bowl in her hands. Christopher wondered if it was the beef stew he'd hoped she'd prepare for dinner when he'd seen her rummaging through the freezer that morning. He saw the plate stacked high with yellow squares of cornbread, confirming the thought, and he smiled. If he couldn't have fried trout, then beef stew was his next favorite meal.

She moved to the table. "Come in," she said as she set the dish down, standing by her chair.

He crossed the floor and left a wet kiss on her cheek as he seated her before hurrying around the table to his own chair. Christopher said the blessing and was well into his second bowl of stew before he looked up at Manny. She hadn't really eaten anything, concentrating on the next phase of her plan.

"Baby, this dinner is great, but I have to say this—"

"I'm sorry," Manny interrupted, and she even managed to look somewhat contrite.

Christopher chuckled. "Oh, so now you know what I'm going to say before I say it, but I'm going to say it anyway. And don't take this the wrong way, but I've been meaning to talk to you about this for two days."

She raised a brow at his authoritative tone, but did not respond. To make sure she kept her mouth shut, Manny even picked up her glass of wine and placed it at her lips.

"Manette Walker, the next time I come home and find the door to our house unlocked, I'm going to put you over my knee."

Manny swallowed and the wine in her mouth went down hard. She had no idea what he was talking about and she certainly didn't know anything about any kind of door. Manny had apologized for pushing him when she knew he was hurt. "Huh," she toned, staring at him.

"The door, Manny. The front door at the house," he added when she continued to look at him in confusion. "It was unlocked when I got home the other day and a man who didn't live in the area was staring at our house. Do you have any idea what could have happened if he'd turned out to be some kind of maniac—"

Manny rose from her chair. She sauntered down to his end of the table and when she had his full attention, she took his face between her two hands and covered Christopher's lips with her own, which closed his open mouth. Then she turned her back to him, slipped off the robe, and let it trail behind her to the patio door. Manny pushed the sliding glass aside and faced him again. The expression on her face turned sultry as she slid the spaghetti straps off her shoulders and shimmied out of the gown. After that, she picked up the garment, tossed it in his direction, and disappeared into the night.

By the time Christopher gathered his wits, his thoroughly kissed mouth had dropped open again and Manny was up to her neck in the frothing waves churning in the custom-built hot tub, sipping a glass of champagne.

When Manny rose from the water and grabbed one of the fluffy towels from the stack piled on the deck, Christopher's heart swelled at the sight of her. She was so curvaceous, so dark, and so lovely. Though he'd first thought otherwise, physically, she was everything he had hoped to find in a woman. When Manny finished toweling herself dry, she headed for the house.

He scrunched down further in the hot tub, letting the water lap up over his shoulders. He took a sip of champagne from the flute in his hand as his thoughts took him back in time to their second encounter. It had been just as memorable as the first and had also led to their first date…

Christopher sat in his Jeep watching the protesters march in two separate circles of unity, each group brandishing placards with opposing views of the city's decision to locate a new jailhouse in a neighborhood of mostly minority inhabitants. Filled to overflowing, current detention facilities were dangerous not only for the inmates, but also for the employees. Too many people were behind bars for minor crimes, while others that needed to be in lockdown still walked about free because of the lack of space.

The city was also reviewing a proposed plan calling for the release of some inmates whose misdeeds could be reclassified as petty compared to the more heinous crimes perpetrated by others. While Christopher understood the protesters' outrage and didn't necessarily agree with the city's chosen site, he was a cop. When he arrested criminals, he needed a place to put them, and they had to build the new jail somewhere.

With his eyes looking for any sign of trouble, his mind turned as it invariably did to Manny Walker. For months after she'd kissed him, he'd pretty much walked around in a daze. The slightest stimuli, a ringing phone, a woman's smile, almost anything, and he could remember the tiniest of details about his first encounter with her. It was almost as if she'd cursed him, the way he was unable to forget her or the feel of her mouth on his.

His lips still tingled when he thought about the power of that one kiss, which, if he were honest about the situation, occupied his thoughts more often than he liked.

Even when he put forth the greatest of effort, Christopher could remember nothing of that night, except that Shelby and Nelson Reeves had married for the second time. However, everything about Manny Walker seemed burned into his brain—from the smoothness of her deep brown skin to the mint-green dress that had flared out from her shapely hips.

She was five-foot seven. Of this, Christopher was sure because she'd stood no taller than the middle of his chest, and he'd had a lot of practice estimating heights. Her lips were lush and full, and he knew how they tasted, for they had been the only part of her body he'd touched that night. He still remembered how they'd felt against his—soft—

satiny soft. Her black hair was thick, reaching her shoulders, and he wondered if it was as soft as her lips or even softer, like silk.

And those eyes...those wondrously dark, chocolate-colored eyes that had reached out and found a home in his soul. Those he'd seen up close, thick-lashed, curved, and set perfectly in a heart-shaped face. Manny's eyes held a depth of emotion so potent, Christopher felt pulled in her direction against his will. They could telegraph messages his body responded to as if bewitched by a spell.

He looked down. Even now, his body was reacting to his thoughts of her, having only her remembered image with which to work. Overpowering all of those traits, however, was the sound of her voice—low, distinctive, and sexy as hell. Remembering how euphonic it had sounded made his hand tremble and a rush of exhilaration shoot through him.

Christopher shook his head, bringing himself back into the present. True, Manette Walker *had* kissed him. However, what he couldn't understand was why it had left such an impression on him. Hell, he'd kissed hundreds...dozens...okay a lot of women, and none had ever affected him the way Manny had. Then again, Manette Walker was a woman unlike any he'd ever known. Yes, they had talked for several hours the night before the wedding, but they were still virtual strangers.

And why had she kissed him? Christopher wasn't sure whether to be flattered or insulted. He was from the South, North Carolina, and no woman, at least the women he'd known, would ever take such liberties with a man she hardly knew. Maybe there was something wrong with Manette Walker. Maybe she made a habit of kissing strange men. Maybe...

Christopher's thoughts paused when a little voice inside his head spoke up. "Maybe she just likes you. Did you stop to think about that?"

Well, no, he hadn't really considered that possibility. Smiling broadly, Christopher nodded his head as the thought took hold and stayed. Yeah, maybe she just liked him. Then he frowned. If that was true why hadn't she tried to approach him since? He'd seen her at several functions since the wedding, but after a hasty hello, she always retreated to another part of the room.

"Have you tried approaching her?"

There was that voice again. And he realized it was right. Manny Walker was either nuts or an over-amorous woman. As an officer of the law, Christopher decided that it was his duty to find out which scenario applied. If his investigation proved fruitful, and if he was lucky, maybe he'd get another one of those soul-stirring kisses in the bargain.

Just as he had that thought, the woman occupying his thoughts appeared on the steps of the Denver City and County Building. Unable to move, he watched Manny stop to respond to the questions shouted at her by a band of reporters. Whatever she said apparently angered some in the crowd, and like a slow-moving, badly written script, the formerly peaceful demonstration turned ugly.

A large man suddenly rushed the steps. Christopher was out of his Jeep and on his way into the disturbance in seconds. Minor flare-ups broke out all around him, but Christopher ignored them in his quest to get to Manny. He reached her side just in time to see her grab the man's sign and lift it above her head. Christopher reached out and grabbed her arm.

"Let me go!" Manny swung around still brandishing the cardboard sign and without thought to what she was doing, bashed it down on top of the head of her assailant. Her eyes widened in shock when she recognized Christopher. The sign, attached to the wooden stick with a nail, fell from her hands when she saw the trickle of blood that had spurted from his temple and begun a slow trek down the side of his face.

Though a little dazed from the blow, Christopher still had enough sense of mind to whip a set of handcuffs from a back loop on his jeans. He snapped one of the silver rings around the wrist of the arm he still held. "You, Ms. Walker," he said through gritted teeth, "are under arrest."

Tugging her away from the rowdy crowd, he escorted her to a white police cruiser, left her sitting in the backseat, and posted a guard to prevent her escape. Then he went to help put down the remains of a peaceful rally gone mad. The chaos that had descended in the space of a few minutes was almost unbelievable. Per protocol, the DPD had been aware of the potential for trouble when opposing sides clashed in representation of their views and had stepped up their presence at the protest. For Christopher and his fellow officers, it was just another day on the job.

Thirty minutes and five cans of mace later, the rally was over. Christopher rubbed the knot on his head, looked at the blood on his hand, and then headed for the ambulance to get some much-needed attention. A short while later, he rapped his knuckles against the window of the police car and observed Manny's struggle to sit up. He jerked open the car door and bent down.

Manny, shaking with fear, stared into eyes so black they resembled pooled tar. Given what had happened to him and her role in causing the disturbance, she was very surprised when Christopher reached into the car and gently helped her from the backseat. Wary of his calm demeanor, she tensed, expecting him to take her to task since she was the reason he now sported a head wrapped in white gauze.

Manny went for humor. "That's a good look for you. The white brings out the subtle reddish tone of your skin."

For a few moments, Christopher simply stared down at her. He was watching her lips and remembering how pleasing it had felt when she'd massaged them against his. He shook his head, dispelling the image. Right now, it didn't matter how great Manny Walker's kiss had felt, or how perfectly her lips had fit against his. Right now, what mattered was that she was the instigator of a ruckus that, if not for police intervention, could have escalated into a full-scale riot. He was the senior officer on the scene and it was time for him to take charge. "Are you all right?"

Manny shrugged a shoulder. "Sure. I'm used to this. I've been the cause of major riots all over the country." Christopher's countenance remained stoic and Manny quickly decided that being serious might be a better choice if she didn't want to be locked up for the rest of her life. "I'm fine, Christopher."

"Good," he said, taking her by the arm and turning her around. Manny thought that he was about to release her from the handcuffs. She could find no words to express her outrage when Christopher only checked to make sure her shackles were securely fastened before reading her the Miranda Rights.

The man was actually going to haul her butt to jail! Sputtering in anger, Manny began to struggle, twisting her body in an effort to get away.

"Resisting arrest will only make it harder on you, Manette."

She responded by swinging her right leg backward and landing the heel of her boot against his shin. Christopher howled in pain, then jerked her around. "You're going to pay for that shot, lady!"

Manny lifted her chin in a silent challenge for him to retaliate. Christopher thought about it—boy did he think about it—for one full minute. Then good sense prevailed and he shoved Manny back into the car. This woman was going to drive him nuts. He rubbed his shin with his left hand and signaled for one of the other officers with his right. When the man approached, Christopher stood straight and said, "Take her downtown and book her!" Then he looked Manny in the eye, daring her to say something else…

Christopher smiled as he finished the wine in his glass. Manny's stay behind bars had lasted no more than an hour, but she'd been furious with him for having the audacity to arrest her in the first place. He'd unlocked the holding cell and escorted her to the door of the station, where she'd stood in his face and threatened to sue not only the police department and the city, but also him personally for everything he owned.

She had been a raging ball of fire that needed dousing, and Christopher had done the only thing he could think of to shut her up. He'd yanked Manny into his arms and ravished her mouth until she'd moaned and leaned into his body. Then he'd taken her to dinner.

When Manny returned to the tub, Christopher held his glass above the swirling water and moved in her direction. He sat beside her on the light blue bench and held out his glass. "Lady, you sure have some way of ending a conversation you don't want to have."

Manny inclined her head and took the empty glass from his hand. She refilled it, handed it back, and leaned her head against the neck rest. "Just look at these stars, baby. I love being able to see them up close this way. They're so big. And the moon is so round and full, it makes me want to reach out, grab it, and see if I can bounce it like a ball."

He didn't respond and Manny glanced at the hard set of his jaw and firm line of his mouth. Because he had a point to make, Christopher hadn't yet switched gears to the romance she was trying so hard to interject into their evening. Christopher wouldn't click with the program until he'd had his say, and knowing that, Manny shook her head and sat up. "All right, Christopher, I get it. It wasn't that big a deal. I went out for the paper and didn't think about it when I came back inside."

Christopher blew out a breath and threw out one of his hands. He pounded it on top of water. "And that's just my point, Manny! You're always forgetting and I always have to remind you. I wish you'd think more about your safety, because I don't want to have to worry about the woman I love when I leave the house at night."

Manny gasped softly. For a moment, she heard nothing except the crickets in the woods and the soft lapping of water as it flowed over the rocks in the stream just outside of his property line. As a flutter started in her stomach and worked its way to her chest, her entire body became deathly still. "What did you say?"

Christopher's black eyes turned tempestuous. "Manny, this is important! So please pay attention."

As her body came back to life, Manny twisted to face him, her own eyes a virtual storm, but not a storm of anger. Hers was a squall of emotion…emotion dying for release. "I am paying attention, baby. So say what you have to say because I have something to say when you're done."

He released a deep breath and settled back against the bench. "Okay. Most perpetrators gain entry into the home because someone forgot to close and securely lock a door or window. I've seen it too many times, Manny, and I've talked to too many victims. The glaring truth of the matter is that most of them did not have to become victims. Being unaware or forgetting is not a valid excuse. *Make* yourself aware and *make* yourself remember. Because I don't, I truly don't, want to see the woman I love more than life itself become a victim because she forgot a simple thing like locking a door." Christopher grabbed her hand beneath the water and squeezed it tight. "So, I want you to promise me, right now, and I mean really promise me, that you'll be more careful in the future."

Twice. He'd said it twice, which meant that she wasn't mistaken and that she'd heard him correctly. Great day in the morning! Christopher Mills loved her! The stars should have been exploding in amazement and heralding the stunning news far and wide. Manny wanted to scream and dance. She wanted to walk that invisible staircase up to the moon above them and float in the gravity-free air. Most of all, she wanted to throw herself into Christopher's arms, lay a blaze of kisses on his face, and shout to the world that she loved him, too.

Rather than do that, Manny composed herself, hard as it was, and faced him. She laid her hand aside his face. "I promise."

"Do you really mean it this time?"

Manny leaned into his body, laid her head against his chest, and heard a beat that was strong and fast. Christopher had spoken from his heart, a truth he believed in, and Manny knew that she could believe it, too. "Yes, Mr. Mills, I mean it. And from now on, I will do everything in my power to keep the woman that you love safe."

The beat she heard in his chest abruptly skipped and Christopher's face contorted in a paradigm of shock. "What?"

Manny popped up. 'I said that I promise to lock all the doors and windows from now on."

"No, I don't mean that. I meant that last part—about me loving you."

Manny turned to grab the bottle of champagne. "Well, you do, don't you?"

Christopher had to think about that. "Well, yeah," he finally answered. "But how did you know?"

"Christopher," she said, as if talking to a small child, "you said it yourself, twice."

A lightning quick review of what he'd said, without the safety message, flashed through his mind and his stomach dropped. His hands started shaking and his brows quirked upward. "I did?"

Manny smiled to herself. "Yes, you did."

An embarrassed look stained his dark and handsome face and without another word, Christopher Mills pushed himself off the bench and slid into the water.

Stretching his body across the hot tub, he rested the heels of his feet on the bench across from him as he submerged his head and let his body float while he gathered his thoughts. Everything he'd promised himself that he would not do, he'd done over the last few days. The capper was telling Manny that he loved her when he knew in his heart that it was not safe to do so.

Although she seemed to be okay now, her initial reaction to seeing his injuries had been enough to let him know that if anything else went wrong, Manny would be devastated. The same way his mother had been devastated when his father died. Damn, Christopher thought. He needed air. His head broke the surface of the water and he glanced up at Manny's smiling face. She waved her fingers at him. He gulped and submerged his head again.

He'd known that Samuel was going to put him on Dexter Santangelo's tail before he'd taken up with Manny. He'd known because he'd purposely set himself up as the one person for the job. For that reason, he'd tried to leave Manny alone—she wouldn't let him. While she'd dallied with other men, she'd also spent just enough time with him to keep him interested. When he was fully hooked, she'd reeled him in, just like he'd reeled in the fish he'd caught yesterday. Now that she had him, she was going to force his hand. Christopher just knew it. Now that he'd told her that he loved her, Manny would want a wedding.

Once more, Christopher surfaced to refill his lungs. This time he didn't see Manny's face because she'd turned away and was staring into the night. He went back under the water. Okay, so he was lying. He'd known exactly what he was doing when he'd allowed Manny Walker into his life. As soon as their eyes met, a force that he could not control had taken over and though he'd tried to hold off, he'd had no choice but to go after her. The alternative was to let her get away and deep in his heart, Christopher had known that if he did, it would have been the worst mistake of his life.

Now that Manny knew that he loved her, maybe it was time to go the rest of the way. His brows crinkled into a frown as another thought occurred to him. His head popped out of the water again. "Hey…I told you that I loved you, right?"

Manny, who'd stretched out her legs on the bench and was calmly sipping from her wineglass and not paying one iota of attention to Christopher and his strangeness, turned her head to look at him. "Right."

"When I said that, why didn't you tell me that you loved me, too?"

"I did."

"No you didn't."

Manny, who had a mind like a steel trap, clearly recalled the moment when the words had slipped from her mouth. She, like him, hadn't meant to say them and because at the time they were at odds, she'd hoped that he hadn't heard them. As usual, he hadn't because he obviously didn't remember. "Of course I did, Chris. I said it first."

"When?"

"The day of the barbecue—during our little spat at Shelby's."

He grinned and grabbed both of her legs, the water in his dimples shining in the moonlight. With his firm tug, Manny slipped off the bench and into the hot tub, wineglass, and all, her head dipping beneath the water because she had not expected the move. She came up sputtering, her hair a ruined mess. She had no chance to speak, however, for Christopher's head lowered and he claimed her mouth in a blistering kiss that rocked Manny to her toes.

When he released her lips, Christopher looked deep into her desire-brightened stare. "Good," he said. "I was hoping you'd remember. Stay here, I'll be right back."

Manny pushed the hair dripping water out of her eyes, her frowning gaze glued to his bare bottom as he left the tub. By the time she thought to ask him where he was going, Christopher had disappeared into the house.

CHAPTER 7

Christopher paid no heed to the wet prints or water droplets he left across the wooden dining room floor or carpet as he ran up the stairs to his bedroom. He retrieved a suitcase from the closet, and after unzipping a pouch on the side, took out a small, blue-velvet box. He hastily descended the stairs again.

At the door to the patio, he stopped to observe Manny. She wore one of the black, silk wraps he kept stored in the cabana sitting off to the side on the patio, and his was lying on the deck beside her. She sat on the top edge of the hot tub, her butt on the deck, her feet still in the water, bent forward with her head in between her knees as she towel-dried her hair.

This was not how he'd planned it. They were supposed to be sitting in an elegant restaurant, surrounded by low, romantic lighting, flowers, and soft music, sipping champagne from fluted glasses. Manny, sated after an expensive meal, was supposed to be staring adoringly into his eyes and he was supposed to slip his hand into his pocket and present her with the ring. She was supposed to say yes, and then seal their engagement with a kiss.

Christopher had even gone so far as to let his imagination bring their wedding day to life. It had given him something to occupy his mind when he was passing the night on a stakeout in the warehouse district. Observing Manny, those images filled his mind again. Him, dressed in a black tuxedo standing at the altar flanked by Nelson, Jordon, Phillip, and her brothers, with her friends standing across from them in floor length gowns of pink, Manny's favorite color. The church decorated with bunches of white baby's breath intermixed with pink tea roses. The pews full of guests lost in the music played by a live organist. Manny, making her appearance in a beautiful gown that was lacy and white, with a short ceremony, followed by an elegant and fun-filled reception their friends would enjoy. And their honeymoon…

Christopher's recollection ended there. Some things needed to be a surprise. He looked at Manny again. Finished with her hair, she'd opened the robe and leaned back on her hands to let the warm breeze dry her body. Her hair, no longer dripping, hung in thick, wet tendrils. Her slender body with its full, pointed breasts, indented waist, leading to well toned thighs and a soft, rounded butt, was arched as if she were offering herself to the man in the moon. Christopher's body swelled with desire and he looked down to see himself straight, stiff. He wanted Manny and so very badly.

Well, at least they had the champagne. The moon and the stars would provide the romantic lighting and the song of nature's woodland creatures would provide the music.

He stepped onto the patio and a squeaky board alerted Manny to his presence. Her gaze first observed the hunger of desire in his face then dropped to the lower half of his torso. A tiny smile played at her lips when he grinned sheepishly and tried to cover himself with one hand. "There's no need to hide it from me, baby. I've seen it, done it, enjoyed it, and wouldn't mind having it again."

Christopher dropped his chin to his chest. Leave it to Manny to tell it like it was. Moving forward, he joined her on the deck. "Manny Walker, you are incorrigible."

She tipped her head to look at him, her face half-hidden by the arm she'd placed on her bent knee. "And you like it, Christopher Mills. I believe you said that I'm the woman you love."

His gaze turned serious. Damn the consequences, he wanted Manny; and he wanted her in his life permanently. It was time to get down to business. "You *are* the woman I love, Manette Walker, and I want you in my life for the rest of our time together on earth and beyond." Christopher lowered his body until he was on one knee in front of her and opened his hand. The small box sat in the middle of his palm. "Manette Alicia Walker, will you please marry me?"

Manny's hand touched her hair. Her eyes, wide as saucers,

screamed her answer before her mouth formed the word and Christopher braced himself for the blow. "No, Christopher."

Manny had said it, but he knew it was not because she didn't love him. He felt her love in his heart every time she looked at him or took him in her arms. Something else had motivated her negative response.

Christopher looked around the deck. It hadn't exactly been the best place for a marriage proposal. Neither of them was dressed, except for the open robe falling off Manny's shoulder. They had no candlelight or romantic music, but he dismissed their setting as the reason for her answer. Manny wanted to get married and she wanted to have children; they'd talked about it many times.

His eyes closed in despair as a gloomy and crucial piece of the puzzle fell into place. Manny wanted to get married and she wanted to have children; she just didn't want those things with him. She loved him, but she had no intention of marrying him. Marrying him would link them together, emotionally and spiritually. If anything happened to him…

Christopher observed Manny. Her eyes remained downcast and focused on her red toenails. Watching her avoid his gaze, he knew intuitively that he was right and he was just about to call her on it when Manny suddenly looked up.

"I have a reason, Christopher."

That intensified the ache in his gut, an ache so fierce that he felt its physical pain. Manny didn't want him. At least not for anything beyond the present and that was the end of it. He'd survive, just like he'd survived the death of his father and just like he'd survived the death of his mother two years later. Since the age of twelve, he'd been an orphan and orphans were traditionally alone, and—Christopher realized in that moment—very lonely people.

When he didn't respond, Manny stared at him with hurt eyes. "Do you want to hear it?"

Christopher rose to his feet. He shot her a fiery glare. "You said no. I got that. So what else could I possibly want to hear?" Bending down, he swiped up the black robe and walked away, leaving her sitting on the deck.

Manny watched him shrug into the garment, and then she got up and followed him to the half-wall made of logs that enclosed the wooden deck. She placed a hand on his back. "The reason I said no, Christopher."

He ran an agitated hand over the back of his head, then as if resigned to the fact that he wasn't going to get out of this, he slowly turned and faced her.

Manny offered a tense smile. What she had to say was hard enough without his grim countenance. A war was raging inside Christopher. The moon and lights illuminated the deck allowed her to see the clashing emotions and the raging tempest building in his dark and troubled gaze. Though extremely nervous, she tried to remain calm in the face of the growing storm.

Christopher was a pretty even-tempered man and he didn't often get angry, unless she'd been lax in some way that involved her safety. He was angry now, however, and he had every right to be. More than that, he was hurt, but that was because he didn't understand. They'd been together exclusively for more than two years and, while one could never be absolutely sure, it was long enough to know everything they needed to know about each other.

Manny felt that she did know Christopher. He was honest to a fault, and he'd hidden nothing about himself from her. She, however, hadn't been quite so honest. There were things that Christopher didn't know. After tonight, he would.

She touched his arm. It felt firm and strong beneath her hand. "Can we sit down?"

Christopher moved away from her again. This time, his strides, long and stiff, took him to a soft, black leather lounge chair. He flopped down in the seat with his legs spread on either side, leaned back his head, and closed his eyes.

He felt Manny when she approached him again. "May I sit with you?"

Dumbfounded, Christopher could only stare at her. Manny had a lot of nerve. She'd just stomped on his heart, set it on fire, and now she wanted to sit in the ashes. He wanted to tell her that he didn't want to sit with her. That he didn't want to touch her or hear anything she had to say. Things he couldn't say, because Christopher did want to sit, touch, and hear her voice. He wanted everything that was Manny Walker. But she didn't want him. He puckered his lips to keep from saying the things on his mind, then raised his head and his hand. He pointed his finger at a chair across from him. "Why don't you sit over there?"

Manny glanced at the chair and back at him. "Because I need to be with you."

Her eyes were big and wide, her bottom lip pouted out in a silent despair. She looked so forlorn, Christopher knew that he couldn't—wouldn't—deny her request. Despite the bad turn his evening had taken, Manny was still his woman, whether she wanted him or not, and he could never deny her anything. He opened his arms and she came to him.

Christopher first enfolded Manny in a strong embrace and after kissing her lightly on the mouth, settled her so that she faced away from him and leaned back against his body. He heard her deep sigh, as if his small concession had given her great relief.

"First, I want you to know that I do love you, Christopher, and that my saying no to you does not change my feelings in any way. You will forever and always have my heart."

Those two sentences were powerful enough to gain his full attention. Deeply moved, Christopher found his animosity melting away. He totally relaxed his posture and allowed himself to feel a semblance of joy from her words.

"I'm going to tell you a story, and when it's over, I hope that it will help you understand why, even though I love you, I can't marry you." Manny waited. When he did not respond, she leaned her head back on his chest. For a few minutes, she stared into the darkness searching for the courage to let Christopher in on her deepest, darkest secrets. She gulped in air, hoping it would stop the churning in her stomach as she silently worked through the pain of remembrance and faced the ghosts of a past that had haunted her for far too long.

No matter what she'd tried, she couldn't find a way to forget. She cradled her stomach with her hands, tuned out the night sounds around them, and tuned in the sound of Christopher's breathing. A sound that was hushed, and even, calming, an outward sign indicative of the patience he'd always shown with regard to her.

In that sound, Manny found the protection she needed to revisit that dark place inside herself, the place where she'd banished the humiliation, the pain, and the torment that had bruised her soul. It was from that place that she took a deep breath and once again began to speak.

"Once upon a time, there was a princess. Her family loved her and told her all her life that she was beautiful. They filled her head with dreams and spoke of a handsome prince who would one day come to claim her and take her to his palace where they would live happily ever after.

"But the princess didn't believe them, because she also had three brothers, all older and all very good looking. For a long time, the princess wondered why her family would lie to her. For when she looked into the mirror, she saw a scrawny body, a face with bumps, a mouth with buckteeth, and kinky, black hair that her mother couldn't seem to tame. In short, the princess thought that she was ugly.

"Shortly after her sixteenth birthday, the princess looked into the mirror and she didn't see the ugliness she'd seen before. She saw a small face with smooth brown skin; teeth that braces had taken two years to straighten, and hair that had been relaxed and styled into bouncy, shiny curls. The princess also saw that she had breasts and a body with curves and she'd noticed that boys, who'd never wanted anything to do with her before, now wanted to talk to her and take her out on dates.

"Then one day, when the princess was standing on her porch, tending her pink rose bushes, a long white van pulled up in front of the house across the street. A black car followed the van and when the man inside stepped out to survey his newly-found kingdom, the princess took one look and knew that she had found her prince. What the princess didn't know at the time was that her prince was in actuality…a frog."

Manny's voice wavered and she bent her head forward. Christopher squeezed her trembling shoulders, the expression on his face somewhat perplexed. Manny was talking about herself, and she was trying to tell him something—something of major importance, and something she'd obviously held closely vested for a long time. What had him intrigued and roused the detective in him was the manner in which she'd chosen to tell her story.

In his line of work, Christopher was skilled at questioning suspects and was very astute when it came to weeding out what was truthful and what was not. To supplement his natural perceptions, he also often employed the technique of 'statement analysis', a tool he and the other investigators commonly used to detect deception.

Although much more complex, statement analysis basically took the parts of speech—pronouns, nouns and verbs—along with extraneous information, lack of conviction, and the balance of the statement, and broke them down into individual components. He knew for example, that truthful people normally gave statements using the pronoun, *I*, rather than the pronoun, *We*, which was an indication that they were not afraid to take responsibility for their actions. Untruthful people mixed the two pronouns, using *I* to take ownership of actions that were irrelevant to the crime and *We* to distance themselves from any action that might incriminate them.

Manny hadn't used either pronoun, which was why Christopher was so mystified. Manny spoke in third person as if what she related had happened to someone else. He couldn't help wondering if she'd told this story to anyone other than him, and, if so, whether she'd related it in the same way.

Whatever had happened to her had hurt Manny so deeply that she couldn't even talk about the experience in first person. For her to have distanced herself in this manner had to have taken years of concentrated effort, effort that had not been wholly successful because she was speaking to him from her heart, a place where she was deeply and personally involved.

That put a frown of worry on Christopher's face. That could only mean that Manny hadn't gotten over the experience and that she was still in pain. The last thing Christopher wanted was for Manny to endure any type of hurt, whether she stayed with him or not. He had to help her. If he didn't, Christopher knew he wouldn't be able to live with himself.

He definitely wanted to hear the rest of her story, but he didn't want hear a fairytale. The only way for Manny to begin to purge the pain was for her to tell the story using the proper names and pronouns. That meant that mentally, she'd have to relive the experience. When she finished, and with his help, he hoped that she would be able to let it go.

"Um, would you mind if I asked a couple of questions here?"

She shook her head. "No."

"Manny, who is the princess in your story?"

He waited through a lengthy silence and thought he'd have to ask again when she finally said, "I'm the princess."

That was a good sign. "And the prince?"

"Derrick Lewis," she responded right away, but the answer was so soft he barely heard her.

Christopher ran the name through his memory bank. Nope, he didn't know anyone who went by that name. "And Derrick Lewis is?"

Manny twisted her body to look at him. "The prince-frog."

Christopher hugged her to him and placed his chin on top of her head. "I know Derrick is the prince-frog, Manny, and before you admitted it, I also knew that you were the princess. What I want to know is what Derrick did to you that was so bad you can hardly talk about it."

Manny stared at him. The moment for frank and open truth had arrived. She didn't know why she'd thought she would be able to communicate what she had to say by telling Christopher a story. The man was a cop, and one expertly skilled at getting to the facts. Facts she'd be able to give him if Christopher allowed her to do it in a way that was comfortable for her.

In order to get them out, she had to stay unemotional—detached. However, if she wanted Christopher to understand the enormity of what had happened to her, she was going to have to find a way to state the cold hard facts and let him deal with them on his own terms.

Manny examined his face, searching for any sign of pity or under-standing. She found neither. Christopher didn't interrupt her again. He listened to her talk about Derrick, the aborted wedding, and the loss of her baby, and through it all he remained as emotionally detached as Manny until she finished.

For a few minutes, Christopher sat still as the night. Then he pushed Manny away from him and rose from the chair. She rose, too, and observed his back. She saw the muscles bunched in tension beneath the thin silk of his robe and watched him work through the tautness by rolling his shoulders several times. His hand came down over the back of his head, and then…nothing.

Christopher stood stark still in a deafening silence, broken only by the hoot of an owl and the other sounds of nature. He was gone—lost in his thoughts. It was the way he was; the way he coped. Christopher Mills absorbed things and dealt with them in his own way and in his own time.

Manny wrapped her arms around her body, feeling lost and very much alone. She had wanted to tell Christopher about the flowers she'd received from Derrick and his request to see her. What she'd already told him was probably too much and after everything she had revealed of herself, she didn't have the energy left to go after him. This was one time Christopher would have to deal with things on his own. She turned for the house and was about to cross the threshold when she heard him sigh.

"Manny, I want you to do something for me."

She turned back, her eyes wary and her heart thumping inside her chest. "What?" she asked cautiously.

Christopher faced her, then walked slowly in her direction. "I want you to say, 'Derrick Lewis didn't want me.' "

Manny gasped. The sound was like a tire losing air. "What!"

"I want you to say, 'Derrick Lewis didn't want me.' "

"Noooo."

"Manny, please. Just do this for me, okay?"

He sounded so earnest; she knew she would do it. She just wondered why he wanted her to when he knew how badly she'd been hurt and what the loss of her baby had cost her. Christopher was supposed to love her, so why would he insist that she do something he knew would add to her grief? His hands reached out to grip and squeeze her arms and the look in his eyes encouraged her to be strong.

She firmed her shoulders and took a deep breath. "Derrick Lewis didn't want me."

He smiled. "But it doesn't matter."

But it did matter, and it mattered a lot. "But it does matter, Christopher."

"That's not what I said. Now, repeat what I said, word for word."

Manny pushed him away and glared at him, a fire lighting her eyes in challenge as she grated out each word. "But—it—doesn't—matter."

He stretched his arms open. "Because Christopher Mills does."

Her face dipped down even as her brows rose in question. Then she strung the whole statement together and let its melody play in her head. Before she opened up to him, Manny hadn't realized how much of herself she had locked away. With Christopher's words, that dark place, the place filled with painful bitter and bittersweet memories opened and freed her from captivity. When the lock sprang, the memories of her baby she allowed to flourish. Those of Derrick Lewis, she cast aside as if they were a recurring nightmare that once faced lost all power.

For the first time in a very long time, Manny felt free. Free to feel at peace, free to find joy, and most of all, free to love. These three things she would begin seeking, and she would start by accepting Christopher and the complete happiness he brought into her life.

When she didn't respond right away, he gave her a stern look. "Say it, Manette."

"Oh, Christopher," she exclaimed, right before she jumped into his arms. "Because you do!"

"That's right," he affirmed. "And here's something else I want you to think about. What happened to you was awful and losing a child is probably the most horrible experience a woman can endure. However, you have endured, Manny, and you've become a stronger person and the person you are because of it. Your baby, you will never forget and you shouldn't. Derrick doesn't rate a place in your memories and you should forget about him. He didn't deserve you and while I am sorry that you were badly hurt, I am not sorry that he walked out on you."

"All it means is that you were not meant for him. It simply means you are, and always were meant for me. Honey-V, I know that you are afraid to marry me, and I can't give you any guarantees." Christopher held her closer and tighter, until Manny's feet dangled in the air. "What I can guarantee is this: If you do marry me, I will do my best to make you the happiest woman alive for as long as breath flows in my body. And if I should pass before you, I will watch over you and try to help you remember the good times that we shared, and will wait for you to join me when it is your time, because what you and I share is eternal."

Manny secured her hold around his neck. This man, this wonderful, wonderful man, normally so sparing of words, had just strung together a sonnet that was so beautiful and more passionate than any poem of love ever written. How could she not marry this man? He was the prince she'd waited for all her life. "Christopher, put me down. I want to change my answer to you."

He chuckled and the deep vibration joined the throbbing beat of her heart. "You do?" She tipped back her head and nodded. "Well, I guess that means that I'll have to ask the question again."

He set Manny on her feet, then reached into the pocket of his robe and pulled out the ring box. This time, Christopher opened the box and Manny's eyes about popped out of her head. She reached for the four-carat diamond. He snapped the lid closed.

"You can't have this." He tensed his lips to hold back a smile.

She pouted. "Why not? It's mine."

"Not until I ask you to marry me."

"But you already did."

"Yeah," he replied. He turned away and hung his head as if saddened by the memory. "And you said no. Man, what an awful letdown. Oh, well, I guess I can get some of my money back. Better still, I'll give it to the next woman I fall in love with. She'll probably appreciate it more anyway."

Manny jumped on his back and wrapped one of her arms around his throat. "Christopher Mills, you give me my ring, right now!"

He was laughing and trying not to choke. "All right," he gasped when she began bumping and reaching for the end of his arm. He bent over and swung her off his back, and when she was on the ground, he flipped the box to her. "Here!"

Manny caught it, opened it, and had the ring on her finger in the space of about a second. She held her hand up to the light and watched the glinting sparkles, grinning like a cat that had just gotten the best of the cream.

"I'm supposed to put that ring on your finger, you know, *after* I ask you to marry me and you say yes."

She looked up. "Yes."

"You have to wait until I ask."

"All right, all right." Manny lowered her hand, but she did not remove the ring. "Ask me."

Christopher bent to his knee again and took her hand. He kissed the ring and looked up into eyes that were so full of happiness, his lungs stopped functioning. "Manette Alicia Walker, will you do me the honor of becoming my wife?"

"Yes!" And the scream that followed pierced his eardrums and woke up every living thing for miles.

CHAPTER 8

Christopher was busy finding new places to put his lips on Manny's body and delighting in the heartfelt moaning coming from her lips when she suddenly popped from her prone position on the bed. "Chris, I forgot to tell you something."

"What," he mumbled without slowing his efforts. Manny was long, flexible limbs, silky brown skin, sizzling heat, and untamed passion all put together in an enticing package for him to savor. And savor Christopher did, making it his mission to ignite every single one of Manny's erogenous zones. He lifted his head, but only so that he could switch his attention to the pointed nipple tipping her right breast, which was still taut from the attention he'd given to it earlier.

"I, um, I…" A flash sparked in her head and robbed Manny of her thoughts. She sighed and floated down to the bed just as the spark burst into a roaring blaze. Her arms circled his body and her hands spanned his back, massaging the taut muscles.

Christopher redoubled his efforts, knowing that any second Manny would lose control. He waited for that moment, and used his lips to push her over the edge. He wanted to hear her call his name. Just as she had on the deck, where he'd taken her after she'd accepted his marriage proposal, and just as she had in the dining room, when he'd taken her again on their way to the bedroom. Actually, Manny had started that little interlude, when she'd all but tackled him from behind and laid her lips to the back of his thighs. He'd paid her back in spades and had taken her again on the rug in front of the fireplace where after falling apart in his arms, she'd lain in his warm embrace, a trembling mass of spent emotion.

Upstairs, they had showered and retired for the night. After ten minutes of feigning sleep, Christopher had started this latest round of lovemaking. Manny was a wild and passionate lover and Christopher knew he would never tire of hearing the sounds she made in the throes of passion.

Manny thumped him lightly on the head. It wasn't hard enough to hurt, but enough to get his attention. "Chris."

He looked up frowning, rubbing the spot where her knuckles had landed. "Why'd you do that?"

"Because I have something to tell you."

"Oh," he replied, and lowered his head.

He kissed Manny's flat stomach and used his tongue to flirt with her navel. Each touch of his hot, wet mouth on her skin produced a flicker of heat that her rapid puffs of breath could not cool. She reached down with both hands and tried to capture his head. Christopher slipped lower and cupped her womanhood in the palm of his hand.

His fingers began a teasing quest and Manny arched her back. "Christopher!"

Satisfied with her response, his tongue continued to pulse over her skin, moving lower with more intensity until she began thrashing wildly and erotically beneath him. A rasping sound was all Manny could manage as the pad of his thumb teased her flesh, then delved deeper inside her inner core. Not even that was possible when his mouth replaced his fingers and a blinding shower of stars rained over her.

Christopher's stamina, quite simply, amazed him after all the times they had made love. Loving Manny was always a novel experience, and the sleekness of her skin and her untamed responses launched his senses into heights unknown. He was so aroused, Christopher was sure his passion would erupt before he could get inside her body.

He was wrong.

From somewhere, Manny garnered a burst of strength and within seconds, Christopher lay on his back. She climbed astride his body and took all of him in a long, drawn out moan. She leaned forward and his mouth eagerly sought her breast, in swipes and licks that pulled a flurry of babbling sounds from Manny's mouth.

In the hazy fog that followed, an emotionally charged vortex consumed them both. Manny closed her eyes and braced her hands on his chest, intensifying the tempo of her hips as she concentrated on giving Christopher the same enjoyment and gratification he'd given her. Soon, Christopher was the one thrashing wildly on the bed as Manny brought him to the brink, pulled him back, then thrust them both into a swirling eddy of light. There, in that wondrous place, their spirits met, touched, and melded into one.

Fighting for air, all Christopher could do was grip Manny tightly against his chest as she drained him of his essence, trying to find the breath that she'd robbed from his lungs.

In the glinting lights that followed, he felt, rather than saw Manny raise herself and move up to lie beside him in the bed. She rested her head on his chest and listened to his pounding heartbeat, pleased to know that she'd given him such pleasure and content with the more than relaxed state of her own body.

They were two very different personalities, she and Christopher: his tranquility to her excitability. The night they had met at Shelby's wedding, she'd done most of the talking. He'd responded at the appropriate times, but had basically spent the night staring at her as if fascinated with the fact that he couldn't quite figure her out. He'd asked her for a date. She'd declined, and it wasn't until many months later, after he'd arrested her for no reason, that she'd finally accepted his invitation to dinner…

The layered, fuchsia silk dress trimmed in silver flowed around Manny's body as she carefully followed the hostess to their table. The silver sandals on her feet had five-inch spiked heels, which she'd worn in an attempt to appear taller than she was to Christopher, who towered above her by several inches. Had she known about the shiny, hardwood floor, she would have worn different shoes, preferably something flat. Then she wouldn't have to pray that she didn't slip and break her neck.

When they reached the table, Manny grabbed onto the back of her chair and breathed a sigh of relief. Then she readjusted her cloak of confidence and took a quick survey of her surroundings. Bold Latin accents, tiered flooring, rust colored booths, and comfortable, old-fashioned chairs surrounded tables clothed in white linen. Overhead fixtures provided soft lighting and the stirring scent of artfully prepared entrees filled the air, along with the subtle sounds of conversation and jazz playing in the background.

Christopher thanked the hostess and helped Manny into her seat. She tensed when his hands landed on her shoulders, and stopped breathing altogether when he placed his face next to her cheek and the woodsy scent of his cologne clogged her senses. "I know I probably should have asked, but I do hope that you have a taste for spicy food."

Manny didn't respond; she couldn't. She was too busy concentrating on getting her heartbeat back under control and stopping the traitorous response of her body to his nearness. Watching him move around the table to his chair, her mind wandered back to earlier in the day when the two of them had stood on the steps in front of the police department.

When she'd kissed him, hers had been a brief touch of the lips, a light caress of titillation. His had been one of all out seduction that had rocked Manny to the core of her being. His lips had at first cruised over hers, testing their softness and leaving a trail of moisture that had felt as delicate as morning dew. Then he'd lightly nipped at her bottom lip and licked at the bud of fire left in his wake until she'd opened her mouth to accept his passionate invasion. She'd thought that once he'd gained entry, Christopher would plunder her mouth, leaving her lips bruised and her even angrier. To her surprise, he had slowed, even softened the kiss until she'd felt every nuance of his tongue's play against hers and on the inside of her cheeks and deeper inside herself until something light had touched her heart. By the time Christopher lifted his head and stepped back from her, Manny couldn't even remember her own name. Even now, she was still reeling from its impact.

Something was obviously wrong with her. Otherwise, one kiss

wouldn't have this kind of effect on her. She'd kissed plenty of men. So, why did she feel that with only the strength of that one kiss, Christopher Mills had imprinted his scent, his taste, his wants, his needs, and his desires on her soul? Her eyes rose and focused on his mouth and the absolutely enticing smile he displayed. Blood surged through her veins, heating her body and scattering her thoughts.

Refusing to give in to the longing desire for Christopher to kiss her again, Manny tore her gaze away from his mouth and waged another unsuccessful battle to stop the zings of pleasure making her nerve endings tingle. This had to stop, she chided herself, in a bid to convince herself that the last thing she wanted was another kiss from the man who'd locked her up as if she were nothing more than a criminal.

Taking his seat, Christopher unfolded his napkin and spread the white cloth across his lap. Sitting back in his chair, he stared at Manny Walker, wondering again why he was so attracted to her. He'd thought his tastes ran toward lofty, unpretentious women—women who were conventional in their thoughts, modest in their dress, and who held a philosophy that mirrored his own. His lips twisted into a half-smile. None of those things applied to Manny Walker. Manny stood up for herself and for her causes. Nor was she all that tall, and if her manner of dress this evening was any indication of her true personality, she was about as far away from modest as a person could get. He liked the dress she'd worn—the color was a perfect complement to her dark complexion. The arm full of silver bracelets, the large silver hoops in her ears, the silver spiked heels, and the silver scarf around her neck he considered…interesting.

Christopher suddenly sat up and signaled for the waitress. Maybe that was it. Manny Walker was uniquely interesting and the total opposite of the women he'd dated in the past; perhaps that was what had attracted him to her.

Manny released the last of the air she'd been holding in her chest and bought some more time to compose herself by spreading her napkin in her lap. Looking up and finding Christopher's dark stare on her again left her feeling self-conscious.

Christopher wore a tailored black suit with a plain white shirt. The only sparkle in his manner of dress was the gold watch on his wrist. Manny looked down at her own attire and shook her head. If Christopher were a Christmas tree, she could be the shining lights, colored balls, and the glittering garland all rolled up into one glaringly bright display of adornment.

"Manny?"

She looked at him again, saw the small bandage on his temple, and forced herself to remember that she was supposed to be furious with him. "Yes."

"I asked if you would like something to drink."

Still unsettled by her wayward thoughts, she began to fiddle with the silverware on the table. "No, Christopher," she finally answered. "The only thing I would like from you is an apology."

He coughed and stared at her. "An apology...for what?"

She leaned back in her chair and crossed her arms. "You were the one who had me arrested and put in jail."

"And deservedly so," he muttered under his breath.

"What was that?"

"I said you deserved to be put in jail."

"Oh really," she responded, her voice deceptively soft as she lifted a glass of water to her mouth. "And why is that, since I didn't do anything?"

Christopher noted the blaze simmering in the depth of her beautiful brown eyes and a tiny smile lifted his lips. He propped his elbow on the arm of the chair and relaxed his posture. "First of all, you were the main instigator of an altercation in which a lot of people could have been hurt. Second, you resisted arrest, and third, you assaulted an officer of the law."

Manny sputtered over the water in her mouth. "None of that is true, Christopher Mills, and you damn well know it!" She forcefully set her glass down on the table. "I did not instigate anything. If that man hadn't come at me like he did, I never would have hit you with that sign."

"Lady," Christopher said, waving away her response as if it were irrelevant. "You should count yourself lucky that I am not one of those people who holds grudges. Otherwise, you'd still be behind bars. And just so we're clear, I will never apologize to you or anyone else for doing my job."

Manny's mouth dropped open. The man had to be kidding, but the look on his face let her know that Christopher Mills was dead serious. There would not be an apology forthcoming from him, now or ever. "Fine," she stated. "Then I guess we'll see each other in court."

"Whatever, sweetheart," Christopher replied. "Now, what would you like to drink?"

Manny rolled her eyes and proceeded to sit in stony silence as Christopher ignored her bad mood and ordered drinks, appetizers, and entrees for the two of them. As soon as their waitress left, he began a one-sided conversation in which Manny refused to participate.

But she listened. She couldn't help it. The deep and sonorous sound of his voice drew her to him as Christopher peeled off more of his layers and opened himself to her. She glanced down at the champagne-poached oysters and grimaced. Then she stirred the food around on her plate with her fork as Christopher told her more about his childhood and his hometown in North Carolina.

He talked of his job and about how much he loved the work. He said that one day he wanted a family, but that his present lifestyle didn't allow for that to happen yet. He told her about his involvement with ROBY (an acronym for Rescuing Our Black Youth)—which Manny already knew was an organization that worked with African-American teenagers to help them get a firm foothold on life. He also told her of his plans to expand his role in that organization when he retired from the police force.

Manny heard everything he said, but her focus was on Christopher, the man. The way he had of dipping his left brow when he was making a point, the length of the fingers on the hands he used to emphasize his words and the excitement in his voice when he'd spoken of working full-time at ROBY. The sexy way his lips moved, and the stream of heat that shot through her every time she remembered the feel of that sensual mouth on hers.

Christopher Mills was classically handsome, a complete gentleman, and obviously stubborn to the core, as she'd learned when he refused her simple request for an apology.

"So what do you want out of life, Manette?"

"A husband."

As soon as the words left her mouth, Manny wanted to curl into a tiny ball and die. Would she ever learn to curb her natural instincts and think something through instead of going with the flow of the moment? Her gaze flew to Christopher's face. His expression of utter astonishment had her leaping up from her chair and slip-sliding her way across the floor toward the ladies' room.

Inside the charmingly appointed room, Manny plopped down on the plush-flowered couch and dropped her face into her hands. She was an idiot. Every single time she met someone with potential, something always went astray. What in the world had she been thinking to say something so stupid to that man?

Of course, that was the problem; she hadn't been thinking, and she could count on twelve hands the number of times she'd leaped off the mountain, thinking about the consequences of her actions only after she'd crashed into the earth. It had been that way when she was growing up. It had been that way in high school. It had also been that way with Derrick, the biggest mistake in her life. Actually, the more she thought about it, the more Manny realized that she'd given in to her impulsiveness for most of her life.

God only knew what Christopher thought about her now, and a woman could only humiliate herself so many times in front of one man. This particular man jiggled her nerves too much for her to keep subjecting herself to the episodic bouts of neurosis that hit her anytime she was anywhere near his proximity. She'd just swung her third strike—and Manny Walker was done.

"Miss, the gentleman would like to know if you are planning to return to the dining room."

Manny peeked up through her fingers. When she saw their wait-ress standing nervously in front of her, she quickly composed herself and rose to her feet. From somewhere, her inner reserve managed to conjure up a semblance of a smile. "Uh, yes," she said to the woman. "Tell the gentleman that I will be out in a minute."

With a shake of her head, Manny walked to the counter where she stared at her image in the mirror. In comparison, to say, the world end-ing, this wasn't so bad. This wasn't the first time she'd thoroughly embarrassed herself and she'd always landed on her feet; she could get through this, too.

Christopher stood when she returned to the table. He pushed in her chair, and then leaned over her shoulder. "Know something, Ms. Walker," he whispered. "I think you'd make a perfect wife."

Manny's heart drummed loudly when their eyes linked. She tried to respond…no sound emerged. She bit down on her bottom lip and turned away, certain that she was wrong.

For in the depth of Christopher's dark gaze she'd seen a bold dec-laration that her desire for a husband was possible with him…

However, as weeks turned into months, Manny had found that Christopher Mills was too quiet, and his thoughtful silences had left her feeling uneasy. Christopher observed and pondered. She leaped and partook. While she had liked Christopher, a great deal more than she was willing to admit then, she couldn't relate to his sudden reflective bouts of silence.

On more than one occasion, he had told her that he cared for her and she'd had no reason not to believe him. Except that she'd heard the same thing from another man, one who had claimed to love her, but had left her standing at the altar on what should have been the happi-est day of her life. Already once-bitten, twice shy, Manny had been too afraid to believe.

In an effort to get rid of the feelings she had developed for

Christopher, she'd continued to date other men. However, no matter how many men she went out with, she couldn't run away from her attraction to Christopher Mills. Something about the way he moved fascinated her. Something about the sound of his voice made her heart pulsate, and something about the way he looked at her set her body aflame with desire.

A wild child, a party animal. Terms her friends had applied to her when she'd continued to hang out in the clubs. None of them had understood, and to be honest, Manny could admit that from the outside looking in, it would appear that their assessments were on target.

What they didn't know was that Manny had needed noise and she had needed people. In the clubs and surrounded by people, she could focus on them rather than herself. She had needed to keep busy because too much quiet, and too much time alone left her open to grievous attacks from the past. Noise and people helped keep the memories at bay.

At the time, Christopher had had no way of knowing what motivated Manny and he hadn't asked. Instead, he'd let her do her thing and he'd waited, quiet, steady, and available whenever she decided that she wanted to see him. Through the months, Manny had found herself wanting to see more and more of Christopher Mills.

In trying to flee him, Manny had learned that all the partying in the world had done nothing to lessen her initial attraction to Christopher. Deep in her heart, she'd known that it was already too late. Theirs was a spiritual connection and one that had deepened the more she saw of him.

And when she'd tired of the party scene and decided to try the quiet, she'd turned to find Christopher, still waiting, still quiet, still steady, and still available only for her.

The more time they spent together, the stronger her feelings grew, and in the process of getting to know him, Manny had learned that quiet did not mean indifference. Nor did it mean boring, for Christopher knew how to have fun. It just meant quiet and usually only when he needed to gather his thoughts.

Christopher had shown her that he cared a great deal, not just about her safety, but about Manny, the woman. She couldn't help thinking about the house he'd helped her buy, the dinners he'd prepared for her, the flowers, the little gifts of affection he constantly showered on her, and the uninhibited passion he displayed in the bedroom. Christopher never sought his own pleasure until she had been completely satisfied. In fact, everything he did was for the sole purpose of making her happy.

Manny turned her head and found his intense stare on her. She smiled, and met his protruded lips in a feathery touch that sent her senses reeling. "Thank you for coming into my life, Christopher, and for putting up with me."

His brows rose in a tease. "Putting up with you, huh? Now that I think about it, I'm not too sure I should be marrying you. I don't know if my heart can take fifty more years of your shenanigans."

Manny punched him in the arm. "You'll take it all right, you big, strong, handsome cop, you."

"So, you do think I'm handsome. I kind of wondered, since you've never said anything before. But I have to ask if that's the only reason you're willing to marry me—because you think I'll give you some good-looking kids."

Manny's expression turned serious. "No, baby. I'm marrying you for the one reason that matters. I love you, Christopher Coltrane Mills, and that's the real deal whether we have any children or not."

Manny yawned and rolled to her side. Christopher helped her settle into his arms and spooned his body around hers. The fingers of one of his hands began moving in a light stroke across her brow, down her cheek, beneath her chin and up the side of her neck. It slid tenderly down her arm and back again to start the process all over and in a very few minutes, Manny Walker had fallen asleep.

Christopher continued to cradle Manny in his arms until he heard her even breathing, indicating that she'd moved into the realm of dreams. Then he shifted away from her body, and after pulling a comforter over her sleeping form, he quietly left the bedroom.

Downstairs in his study, he picked up the telephone. He hadn't reported in for four days and there was a pressing matter he needed to check on. His eyes lifted to the ceiling and he smiled with the thought that soon Manny would always find rest in his bed.

"Thomas."

The rasping voice of Lieutenant Samuel Thomas brought Christopher back from his mind's wanderings. "Sam, it's Chris."

"How's that body of yours, Mills? Santangelo's boys really put your butt through the ringer, eh?"

A strangled cough abruptly cut off Sam's attempt at a chuckle and Christopher shook his head. Samuel Thomas was a two-pack-a-day smoker and had needed to give up the bad habit long ago. Sam refused, saying that without the smokes, the on-the-job stress would kill him.

"The body's fine. I'm checking in."

"What for? You're on vacation, boy, which means that I don't want to hear from you. If there's something you need to know, I'll make sure I tell it to ya."

"That, I'm not worried about. I'm so close, Sam. I can feel it. And when it does go down, things are going to get real hot, real quick."

"When the time comes, I'll have your butt covered. Don't worry about it."

Christopher wanted to argue—not for his sake, but for Manny's. Sam might cover his butt, but Christopher knew, as he'd told Manny, that life held no guarantees. One stray bullet and their life together would end before they'd even had a chance to begin.

Manny would be completely devastated if something happened to him so soon after she'd given her promise to be his wife. He also knew that even in his grave, he would be just as ravished, knowing he'd given her a false hope of happiness. He wouldn't let that happen. Manny would be his wife and she would have the children she wanted.

"Just make sure that you do."

"You trying to tell me how to do my job, Mills?"

"Not at all, I'm trying to ensure that I'll be around to do mine."

"Got ya," Samuel growled. "By the way, since you are on the

phone, you might want to tune in the news tomorrow night. It'll be an interesting watch. See ya."

The phone clinked off before Christopher could respond. He replaced the green receiver back into the cradle, his mind lost in thought. Somehow, some way, he had to make absolutely sure that he walked away unscathed from the explosion soon to erupt.

"Who was on the phone?"

Christopher's eyes shifted to the doorway where Manny stood rubbing the sleep from her eyes. She'd donned a gown and looked so adorable that he couldn't help staring. The gown was pale pink and hit Manny at mid-thigh. In and of itself, the gown was rather modest, with its inch wide shoulder bands and a flirty white lace around the arms and hem. After what they'd shared so short a time ago, his heated gaze had no trouble piercing the thin silk and seeing the trim and slim body underneath. She walked into the room and Christopher, absorbing the sight, felt his heart swell with love as his body swelled with something else. Without giving her an answer, he opened his arms when she reached him.

Manny sat on his thigh. "When I woke up and you weren't there, I missed you."

"I missed you, too, gorgeous," he replied. His eyes weren't looking at Manny, but rather the front of the gown and the fleshy fruit he wanted to taste again. He picked up her left hand and watched the diamond sparkle in the light. Although he'd bought the ring, he hadn't planned to give it to her or ask her to marry him, at least not yet, and his brow crinkled with unspoken worry.

Christopher brought the hand to his mouth. His ring looked good on Manny's hand, and it belonged there. This felt right, so right that Christopher decided that he would worry about the consequences of his actions later.

Manny draped an arm around his shoulders and he turned his head, his tongue searching for one of the dark nipples covered by the gown. "Stop it and listen to me," Manny directed, pushing his head away. The subject at hand was the health spa. She was trying to convince Christopher that he would have the time of his life, hoping he'd agree to keep the scheduled appointment.

"When was the last time I told you how gorgeous you are?"

"About three seconds ago," she groaned as he rolled a taut nipple between his fingers. Manny pulled away from his hand. "Christopher, I'd really like the two of us to do this."

His gaze lifted to the moving lips and Christopher flicked his tongue at the corners of her mouth. Manny crossed her arms over her breasts, cutting off his access.

"Christopher Mills, will you please pay attention to what I'm saying?"

He bumped her off his leg and to her feet. "No, and just to make sure you understand, let me spell it for you. N! O! There is no way that I'm letting you talk me into going to a health spa."

Manny's lips protruded in a pout. "Baby, didn't you tell me that you loved me?"

He lowered hooded eyes at her. "Don't even try it, Manny Walker."

"But Chris, we have to go! I've already made the appointment."

"Now, there's an argument that will loosen me up. You make the appointment and then ask me? Not gonna happen, babe."

The convenient temper ignited until her eyes took in the rock hard set of Christopher's jaw. Manny backed down. "I'm sorry, Christopher. I-I don't know what I was thinking."

Fire lit the jet-black eyes that returned her stare and thunder rolled in his voice when he spoke again. "The problem is that you weren't thinking, Manny. By now, you should know me well enough to know that you shouldn't try to manipulate me or use feminine wiles to get what you want. I deal with deceitful people every single night—people who finesse and use others for their own personal gain. I won't tolerate that kind of behavior from my wife!"

Manny reached out her hand. "Christopher, I said I'm sorry, and I won't do it again."

He pushed her hand aside and at the same time, rolled his eyes with such flair, a response was not necessary.

Manny slapped the hand on her waist. "Are you going to accept my apology or not?"

"Or not."

"Fine!" Manny threw up her hands. "Then don't. I don't care and I'm not going to apologize again. I'm going back to bed."

"Have a good night," he shot back, watching her leave.

Manny waited outside the door to the study, sure that any minute Christopher would come to her. They would make up and everything would be right again. Ten minutes later, he hadn't made an appearance and astounded, Manny turned for the stairs.

She had really done it this time. She'd never seen Christopher so angry. She was going to have to discuss this with the girls and find out how her plan had gone so terribly wrong. Unsure of just how far she'd pushed him, Manny decided that it might be best if she slept elsewhere tonight.

She decided on a bedroom down the hall from the main suite and had just muttered her way to sleep when a pair of strong arms lifted her into the air. Christopher strode down the hallway, into the master suite, and dumped Manny on the bed.

"Don't even think about getting up," he warned, striding around to his side. He climbed in, pulled her toward him, and pressed their bodies together. He kissed her lightly on the cheek before settling the covers over their bodies.

At her ear, he whispered, "I was taught to never close my eyes at night angry with the ones I love. I love you, Honey-V, and I know that you love me. We'll be okay, Manny."

Manny didn't respond and she lay in his arms stiff as a board. It was a long, long time before her troubled mind allowed her to sleep.

Christopher sat on the couch, completely at ease with Manny's head resting cozily on his thigh. She hadn't said much all day and watching the way she moped around the house had left him feeling sorry that he'd yelled at her.

He was a man of honor and valued truth above all else. He'd been forceful because Manny had to understand that they could not have a marriage built on lies and that she could not take advantage of him by trying to manage him. He'd explained his position to her again that morning, this time using tender words and gentle touches, after which Manny had come back to life and they had spent a pleasurable day together.

Leaning over Manny, Christopher reached for the remote on the table and switched on the news. The lead story was about a late night raid on a home in central Denver. The bust had garnered two thousand pounds of cocaine, two crates of weapons, and an undisclosed amount of cash. The biggest coup of the night had been the arrest of seven men thought to be principal players in a local drug trafficking operation.

The chief of police, Herman Diggs, his chest puffed out like an overblown peacock, stood in front of the television cameras taking credit for the bust. Several DEA agents, who'd actually carried out the raid, stood at his side clenching their fists in frustration. The Feds had already forcefully suggested that the DPD 'step down' and let them handle the illegal drug activity in the Metro area, angering the police chief and the mayor who had just as forcefully refused the request.

Christopher watched the segment, his face devoid of emotion. The bust that the police chief was so intent on taking credit for should have been his. The drugs taken off the streets were supposed to have been part of the run he was to have made with Benito in another week. Wanting immediate retribution for the beating he'd undergone, he'd purposely revealed the location of the house, and encouraged Samuel to inform the Feds, knowing that they, in their eagerness to justify their existence, would rush in to claim another victory in the war against drugs.

Christopher didn't care who got the glory. He and Samuel had bigger fish to fry and the small bust amounted to nothing in comparison to what they knew to be the true magnitude of Santangelo's influence. Dexter Santangelo was who Christopher was after. When he found him, the man was going down. It was what he had dreamed about and worked toward since the day Santangelo had gunned his father down in the street.

He looked down at Manny asleep in his lap, and his heart filled with contentment. His woman was back where she belonged and she was going to marry him. It was only at that moment that Christopher realized that nothing was more important in his life than Manny or would ever make him feel any better than he felt right now.

High on a balcony of a luxury hotel in Bogota, Columbia, Dexter Santangelo sat outside his penthouse suite, sipping an apple martini and watching his two children romp in the heated Olympic-sized pool. He smiled and returned the gesture when his daughter waved at him and the smile held warmth for the flesh of his being. However, the eyes, inherited from his English mother, were icy in their blueness and stoked with an evil so vile, anyone entering his presence cringed under his stare.

Dexter kept a watchful eye on his babies, but his mind was on the call he'd just received from Anthony Chavez informing him of the loss of yet another shipment. He'd been losing a lot of money in the Denver cell lately and with this latest bust, doubts concerning Anthony's loyalty had resurfaced. Dexter Santangelo was not a happy man.

Though his life had been one filled with violence, looking back, Dexter felt proud of all he'd accomplished. It had started with the killing of a cop when he was a seventeen-year-old high school dropout with no plans and no future. He'd already had a rap sheet a mile long, and with no other options, he'd joined a local gang.

The day of the killing, he'd been on his way to fulfill the obligations of his initiation. Dexter had no real recollection of the cop, nor could he recall pulling the trigger. What he did remember was being hidden by his family until they could scrape together enough money to send him to live with his uncle in Columbia. Since then, he'd killed or ordered the killing of so many others that taking the life of one cop hardly mattered.

That uncle had been an associate of the once powerful Cali Cartel. Eighty percent of the world's supply of cocaine flowed out of Columbia, and at one time, the Cartel, which had represented the last of the old-style drug Mafia, had controlled more than seventy percent of that trade. The drug lords had lived extravagant lifestyles complete with lavish parties, beauty queen girlfriends and fancy cars, and they had murdered all who'd stood in their way.

Dexter's climb to the top had started as a runner and he'd learned the intimate secrets of his trade as he worked his way up the ranks. From the sidelines, Dexter had watched the collapse of the Cartel, and upon the death or imprisonment of the drug lords, he had seized the opportunity to establish his own operation. Like the Cali Mafia, Dexter was obsessed with computers and technology, and he spent millions keeping his networks outfitted with the latest technological advances. Unlike the Cartel, Dexter was satisfied with his piece of the action and felt no need to initiate wars meant to take out his competitors.

He'd assembled his organization into a network of cells spread throughout the United States, Latin America, and his home base in Bogota. Each cell was responsible for one geographic area, primarily run by family members or those closely related to preclude penetration by outsiders. The cells also operated independently of the others to prevent compromising the entire network.

Anthony Chavez had earned his current position through years of loyal service. As a division chief reporting directly to Santangelo, Anthony held responsibility for the overall management of several cells in the United States. Though he entrusted his chiefs with the day-to-day operations of the cells in their divisions, Dexter Santangelo, and Dexter alone, was the ultimate authority.

He'd built an empire that had made him rich, powerful, and feared. It had rapidly become apparent to Dexter that Anthony Chavez was the bad apple that could rot the entire barrel, and Dexter had no intention of losing all he'd worked so hard to gain.

He looked at his babies again and a gladness of sorts filled him, knowing that he was able to provide them with anything their hearts desired. The fact that his money came from drug profits that destroyed other people and other families didn't concern Dexter at all. Like any other business, his product supplied a demand. He could not be held accountable for what others did with their lives. If Dexter had any regrets, it was that he'd once been that scrawny, wimpy-ass kid who'd cried in the street. Crying was a weakness, and Dexter despised any type of weakness.

Mentally shaking himself, Dexter turned his mind back to his problems in Denver, Colorado. The authorities were systematically hunting and jailing his men on charges so tight, not even his best lawyers could free them. His merchandise was mysteriously disappearing and long-used routes being blocked.

Dexter slammed a fist against his thigh. Either the Chavez boys had suddenly gone dense or they'd decided to cut him out of the lucrative market. A serious mistake, since Dexter was the one who had given the 'not too bright with no future ahead of them' Chavez brothers the one chance they would ever have of making something of themselves.

He rose to his feet and signaled to his children that it was time for them to leave the pool. When they reached his side, Dexter wrapped them in large, white towels and gave them each a hug before ushering them inside the suite and handing them over to their nanny. Dexter headed for his study in the back. He had a few calls to place and flight arrangements to make. He could have sent any one of his men to check out the situation in Denver, but Dexter wanted to make the trip and see for himself exactly what was going on. Besides that, he could call in his faithful chiefs in the States for a long over-due meeting to make sure they were still all of one mind.

However, if he found anything that implicated Anthony Chavez in the downward turn his dealings had taken in Colorado, nothing on this earth would save the Chavez brothers.

CHAPTER 9

When Manny entered her office on Monday morning, she found Shelby already seated in the wingback chair. An air of eagerness surrounded Shelby, and Manny suspected that her friend already knew that something important had taken place at Christopher's mountain get-away.

"Morning, Shel," she said, shrugging out of the striped lavender and white linen jacket. Manny studiously avoided Shelby's knowing gaze by turning to hang the coat on the rack in the corner of her office. She patted the back of an upswept hairstyle, then smoothed her hands down the sides of the matching lavender skirt. Still without looking at Shelby, she moved to her desk and sat in the chair.

"Let's see it."

Manny studied the nails on her right hand. The left was in her lap. "See what?"

A smile tilted Shelby's lips. "The ring Christopher bought last month. And I also know that you said yes, because you're in love with Christopher, so don't try and play me, sister-girl."

Manny produced the hand, along with a dazzling smile. "Isn't it gorgeous, Shel? Can you believe it! I mean, who would have thought that Christopher loved me enough to give me something like this?"

Shelby glanced down at her own hand, where a half carat diamond twinkled in the light from the lamp on Manny's desk. She had a jewelry box full of diamonds now, as well as many other gem-encrusted pieces Nelson had presented to her. Over the years, he'd asked many times to replace the engagement ring he'd given to her as a broke college student, but Shelby always refused. She loved her ring. It was a symbol of the deep love he had for her.

Right now, Manny was still in the first stage of love where nothing mattered except that she had found someone who loved her enough to marry her. She still had to wade through the trials and tribulations of having her love for Christopher tested. As her love for him matured, Manny would learn that the size of the ring said nothing about the size of the man's heart. Shelby lifted her eyes and observed the glow in Manny's face. Then again, she was not Manny, and her friend had already experienced a lot in life, so perhaps she already knew. "Yes, sister-girl, it's absolutely gorgeous."

Manny stared at her ring. Yes, it was beautiful, but not as beautiful as Christopher was when he looked at her with love in his eyes. She looked up from her hand with a curious gleam in her eyes. No matter how innocent Shelby claimed to be, everyone knew that she was a natural born matchmaker and busybody.

Once she'd gotten her relationship with Nelson back on track, she'd purposely set Starris up with Jordon, and had been responsible for initiating Manny's interest in Christopher. "How did you know, Shel?"

"How did I know what?"

"That Christopher had purchased a ring and that he was going to propose to me? And how did you know that it would happen while we were in the mountains?"

Shelby laughed. "Nelson was with Chris when he purchased the ring, and you know my husband can't keep a secret. Though I must admit, Nelson did better this time. He didn't tell me until yesterday and even then it just kind of slipped out."

"What do you mean by 'slipped out'?"

"I mean that he was helped a little."

"Helped a little? By who?"

Shelby chuckled again. "By me, of course."

Manny grimaced, thinking about her own botched attempt to get Christopher to the health spa. Although they'd talked about it again the next day, Manny shivered, still fearing that she might have damaged their relationship, even if it was just a tiny bit, permanently. Rising, she walked to the window in her office door and quickly scanned the floor of the shop. Everything looked to be in order. Several customers were browsing through merchandise and sales associates were helping others with questions or ringing up their purchases.

Walking away from the window, Manny began pacing the floor. "I don't know how you do it, Shel."

"Do what?"

Manny sighed and resumed her seat. "I don't understand how you can get Nelson to do anything you want and never feel a backlash."

Shelby jerked back, somewhat surprised. "I beg your pardon?"

Manny removed the finger from her mouth and crossed her arms. "I've watched you, Shel, and I've watched Starris and listened to the others. All of you seem to be able to handle your men. By that, I mean that you can get them to do anything you want. I tried it with Christopher and he lit into me like an exploding firecracker. He told me that I didn't need to try to manage him or use feminine wiles to get him to do what I wanted. In fact, he stated emphatically that he didn't want to see that type of behavior in me." Her mouth took a downward turn and she shook her head again. "He was so angry, Shelby, I didn't know what to do."

"What happened, exactly?"

Good question, Manny thought. She wasn't exactly sure herself what had happened except that it hadn't worked on Christopher. She stood up and walked over to the coffeepot sitting on a small table in the corner. She picked up her mug and turned back to Shelby. "Okay, on Sunday we were lazing around and watching this gorgeous sunset when Christopher asked me what I wanted to do the next day. There is this health spa in Buena Vista that caters to tourists and when I told Chris that I wanted the two of us to go, he said no. But I decided that I wanted to go anyway and I tried to get him to agree to going with me."

"Oh, Manny, what did you do?"

Manny turned back to the coffeepot and filled her cup before returning to her chair. "At first, I was going to argue with him about it. Then I thought about what you might do, and I made the appointment. The next night, I cooked his favorite meal, candlelight and everything," Manny said, setting the cup on the desk. "I warmed up the hot tub and even had champagne that we sipped while lulling about in the water."

Shelby raised a brow. "And it didn't work, did it?"

Manny shot her a look of exasperation. "You want to wait for the ending, Shelby? Anyway, by that time I had actually forgotten all about the health spa, because it was about then that Christopher told me that he loved me." Manny smiled, recalling Christopher's admission of love and his slide into the water. However, she kept those memories to herself. "And asked me to marry him."

"How did he ask you?" Shelby's eyes were burning with curiosity. "Was it over dinner? Did he get down on one knee, and what were the two of you wearing? Something fabulous, I'll bet. What did you cook? How did you feel? But wait, you didn't know Chris was going to propose." Shelby lurched forward in the chair and slapped the palms of her hands on the desk. "Sister-girl, I need details! So give them up."

"Shelby," Manny said sharply to bring her friend back to the conversation at hand. She wanted to know what she'd done wrong with Christopher and all Shelby was interested in was how the man had proposed.

Shelby dropped back and folded her arms. "I told you how Nelson proposed to me, and as your best friend in the whole world, the least you could do is tell me how Christopher proposed to you."

Manny's face held amusement. "What was there to tell, Shelby? The whole campus saw Nelson up in that tree outside our window and heard his proposal to you."

Shelby shrugged. "Details, details, and that's what I want to hear from you."

"All right. Christopher did get down on one knee, but we were naked as the day we were born when he did it."

"You were making love?"

"No, we were out on the deck." When Shelby's brows rose in question, Manny added, "The hot tub. Wait a minute, come to think of it, Chris was the only one who was naked. I had on a robe."

"What did he say, though?"

"Oh, something about me being the woman he loved and spending the rest of our lives together."

Shelby gave Manny a dubious look. "You mean to tell me that you don't remember every single word that Chris said to you? I remember what Nelson said to me word for word, and that was almost fourteen years ago. Christopher just proposed a few days ago. How could you not remember?"

Of course, she remembered. Manny doubted that any woman ever forgot even the minutest detail when the man she loved proposed to her and she wasn't deliberately trying to be secretive. She just wanted to move on and find out what she'd done wrong with Christopher. "I do remember, Shelby. It was beautiful and poetic and I said no."

"What!" Shelby jumped to her feet. "Are you crazy? Christopher is one of the best men around. Why on earth would you *not* want to marry him, Manny?"

"Hmm," Manny toned. "Wasn't it just a couple of weeks ago that you wanted to wring his neck?"

"That was before I heard the whole story—his side and yours."

"Right." Manny fluttered the fingers of her left hand in the air. "As you can see, I changed my mind."

"Okay," Shelby conceded. "So you, rather he, was naked and at first you said no, then you said yes. So what happened in between?"

"I told him about Derrick."

"Oh." Shelby was glad that Manny had finally gotten the matter off her chest. She'd counseled her friend to come clean about her past months ago. After all, she hadn't done anything wrong, but Manny had ignored the advice, afraid that Christopher would want nothing to do with her if he knew. "And?"

"And he was okay with it."

Shelby nodded her approval. "See, I told you that Christopher was not the kind of man who would hold something like that against you or see you any differently than he always has."

"Yes, you did. Anyway, when I brought up the health spa later, Chris got so angry, I thought he was going to ask for his ring back.

Now, if you had done that, Nelson probably would have gone to the spa."

"No," Shelby said, "he wouldn't have, and I wouldn't have tried to trick him into going either. I don't use underhanded methods to deal with my husband."

"Didn't you just tell me that you tricked Nelson into telling you about Chris and me?"

"No, what I said was that I helped him along. However, I didn't con him into telling me and I didn't try to make Nelson do something he wasn't going to do eventually anyway. He just did it sooner than he expected."

"But how did you help him?"

"By watching the signs. I knew he had something to tell when I told him that it would be nice if Christopher proposed to you while you were in the mountains. Nelson became flustered and wouldn't look me in the eye. So I asked him point blank."

"You did?"

"Yes, and because we have no secrets between us, Nelson spilled everything he knew. Manny, I know there are women out there who believe that deceiving their men is the only way to handle them, but a lot of those relationships are on shaky ground at best. You and Christopher are going to be husband and wife, which means that you have to consider his feelings in addition to your own. Be honest with him in all things and trust his love for you. If you do that, the two of you will be just fine. As far as the health spa, I would have tried to talk to Nelson again, and if he still refused to go, I probably would have gone by myself."

Manny came around the desk and embraced Shelby. "You *are* the best friend I have in the whole world and I won't ever try something like that again. The next time Christopher tells me no, that's going to be the end of it."

"Good." Shelby rose from her chair and moved to the door. She surveyed the customers in the store. "Well, it's another day and business is looking good. Time for the two of us to get to work, sister-girl."

"You got it, Shel. We'll have lunch later, okay?"

"Can't today," Shelby replied, opening the door. "Mrs. Hathaway is coming by for her fitting and I had to squeeze her in over the lunch hour."

Mrs. Hathaway was a former neighbor of the Reeves and Exterior Motives' very first customer. Manny knew how fond Shelby was of the older woman, who'd taught her to cook. "That's okay. I've got a lot to catch up on here anyway. I'll probably skip lunch myself."

"I know," Shelby said. "Nelson and I will take you and Christopher out to dinner tonight."

"Does Nelson know about this?"

Shelby smiled. "Not yet, but he will. By the way, I also have a surprise for you this evening. See you later."

Christopher tried to concentrate on perfecting his stance and not on the laughter and purposely-loud remarks he heard coming from behind him. This was his last drive, and at the moment, he was winning the golf tournament initiated by Jordon.

This swing had to be good, one of his best. They each had one hundred dollars on the line. In addition, the loser had to buy the beer. After the way his friends had reacted when he'd told them of Manny's attempt to get him to a health spa, Christopher intended to clean out both their wallets this afternoon. He glanced over his shoulder to see Nelson leaning toward Jordon and Jordon roaring in hearty laughter. "Do the two of you mind? I'm trying to drive here."

"Oh, oh. We need to quiet down, J.R. Chris is taking a shot, and we wouldn't want to be the cause of him chipping one of his pur-ty, po-lished nails, now would we?"

Turning back to his ball, Christopher clenched his jaw and tried to tune out Jordon's response.

"I wouldn't worry about it, Nels. If he gets tense, he can always go back for one of those mud baths and facial massages." Both men cracked up again.

"That's it," Christopher muttered, and threw his driver to the ground. He probably should have kept his mouth shut, but he'd taken about all the ribbing he was going to take from these two clowns today. He stalked to the golf cart and stopped in a fighter's stance in front of his friends. "Okay, which one of your asses am I gonna kick first!"

"Oh, look-it, J.R., the girly cop is pissed."

Jordon observed the anger in Christopher's eyes and the fists raised in challenge. Mills really was pissed and they needed to back off. "Cool, it, Nelson." He turned to Christopher. "We're just kidding around, man. No harm done. None intended."

Christopher dropped his arms. He released a deep breath. "I know, J.R. I guess I'm a little touchy about it. So just lay off, okay?"

"Done, man. Why don't we finish up and get to the clubhouse so that Nelson can buy the first round of that beer he owes us."

Nelson stopped smiling. "What are you jawing about, J.R.? I'm not buying any beer. The last time we checked, you were the one losing this game."

Jordon pulled out the score sheets. "That was the last time we checked. Since then, you've been in two sand traps and hit one ball into the lake. At least Chris has some skills. I've been trying to teach your butt to play for ten years and you still can't hit a straight ball."

Nelson, whose tolerance for losing ebbed at an all-time low, glared at Jordon. "I'm just having a bad day. My game is normally up there with yours. Now, I'll admit I'm no Tiger Woods, but I don't swing my club like a baseball bat anymore, either."

"Yeah, yeah," Jordon replied. "Chris, take your shot."

Christopher did, and after he won the game, the trio retired to the clubhouse for beers.

At the table, Nelson passed around the bottles and took his seat. "So, when's the big day?"

Christopher swallowed the beer in his mouth. "We haven't set a date. Manny..." He stopped and stared around the patio. Now that he thought about it, they hadn't even discussed a date. Manny hadn't mentioned it and as far as he knew, she hadn't called her family with the news either. That struck Christopher as odd, considering the closeness she shared with her family. He made a mental note to ask her about it when he saw her later that evening. Jordon and Nelson were staring at him when he looked up again. "Uh, Manny hasn't decided."

"Oh," Nelson said, although it struck him as odd, also. As badly as Manny claimed to want to get married, one would have thought that she would have dragged Christopher before the minister before they left the mountains. "Well, I'm sure she'll decide soon."

"Yeah," Christopher agreed. He focused his gaze far out into the distance. He had something he needed to discuss. Under normal circumstances, he wouldn't hesitate to use Nelson and J.R. as a sounding board, but after the ribbing he'd taken all day, he wasn't sure if bringing up his concerns with them was the right thing to do. Christopher decided to go for it anyway. "I want to ask you fellas something."

Jordon leaned back and crossed long legs. "Shoot."

"Well, you guys are married, right?"

Nelson and Jordon exchanged glances. "Right," they said in unison.

"And both of you went through a lot with Shelby and Starris before your wedding day, right?"

Nelson leaned forward. "What do you mean by 'a lot'?"

Christopher rubbed the neck of the bottle between his hands as he gathered his thoughts. "What I mean is, do Shelby and Starris try to manage you? I mean, do they try to get you to do the things that they want?"

"I'm not following, Chris," Jordon said. "Are you asking if Starris tricked me into getting married?"

Christopher shook his head. "No, I'm talking in general. More like, do they try to tempt you into doing things that you don't want to do?"

Nelson sat back and grinned. "Of course they do. But," he added when Christopher's brows wrinkled together in a frown, "I never do anything I wasn't going to do in the first place."

"Yeah, right, Nelson. Shelby's been leading your ignorant behind around by the nose since day one and you're so in love you don't even know it's happening."

"Man, you're one to talk! Wasn't that a diamond tennis bracelet Starris was sporting on her wrist last week?"

Jordon sputtered. "So what? Since when is it against the law to give my wife a present?"

"It's not against the law," Nelson replied with a smirk. "But don't you sit here and try to pretend that Starris doesn't have you wrapped around her little finger. And don't try to tell us that you came up with that little item on your own either, J.R. I'm sure Starris dropped more than enough hints until that bit lug head of yours got the message."

Jordon swallowed his embarrassment with a gulp of beer. He looked at Christopher who appeared raptly interested in the exchange. "Yep," he agreed. "They try to manage us."

"But doesn't that bother you? I mean, why can't they just be up front and say what they want?"

"It's part of the love game, Chris," Jordon said. "Women see a man they want and immediately think that without them in their life the brother can't survive. Never mind the fact that we were doing just fine before we met them."

"Yeah," Nelson added. "It's in their makeup, their way of thinking that they have control. It's usually harmless stuff, and I love Shelby enough to let her get away with it."

Christopher's brows furrowed again. "So what you're saying is that they can't help it."

"That's it exactly," Jordon said. "They can't help it."

"What did Manny do anyway?" Nelson asked.

"Well, it's that health spa thing I told you about. I told her that I didn't want to go, and she somehow got it into her head that if she seduced me, you know, with the romantic candlelight dinner and stuff, that I would change my mind."

Nelson nodded. "Typical, but usually harmless."

"Harmless, but not honest!"

"Look, Chris," Jordon said. "What Manny did had nothing to do with honesty. It was just her way of trying to make you see something in a different light. She wanted to go the spa, you didn't. She simply tried to change your mind. There's nothing wrong with that. Nelson and I have both been through it and the evening that follows is usually worth it. We've known Manny for years and she's one of the most up-front people I know. I'm sure that she was just doing what comes naturally to the female gender. Starris and Shelby are the same way." Jordon leaned back in his chair with a thoughtful expression on his face "However, this next piece of advice comes from experience. Watch your back, because some of them are not as innocent or honest as our women and they will try to ruin your life."

All three men grew silent as thoughts of Jordon's ex-wife and the things she'd done to him took a prominent place in their minds. Jordon didn't sound as bitter now, but they all knew that he still harbored a little of the fear deep in his mind that things might not be as they appeared.

Nelson's thoughts of Shelby helped push Gloria Banks from his mind. They had been through some rough times, including a divorce, and there had been a time when he didn't think he'd ever recover from the loss of his son. It had taken some doing, but he'd won his wife back and now they had a daughter. There wasn't a day that went by that Nelson didn't thank God for his blessings.

Christopher mulled over the words of the other two men. Before Manny entered his life, he'd had one singular purpose and that was to find his father's killer. Now he realized how much joy Manny had brought into his life and couldn't imagine not having her at his side. There wasn't a doubt in his mind that sharing his life with Manny Walker would definitely have its high points. They would have some rough patches ahead, but Christopher felt he had enough love in his heart to weather the storms. He only hoped that Manny would never regret her decision to take him as her husband.

Jordon's thoughts of Starris and the life they shared pushed everything else from his mind. At times, he remembered the treatment both had suffered at the hands of their respective first spouses. However, those times were few and things were drastically different now. He had both of his daughters and a new son and his family was the source of his joy. In each other, he and Starris had found that true love did exist and it was a love that he felt would last forever. He rose from his chair. "Gotta go, fellas. It's almost four and my baby is at home waiting on me."

CHAPTER 10

Manny inhaled deeply and wiped tiny beads of sweat from her forehead. She surveyed the cluttered kitchen table and tried to slow her pounding heart. Dozens of catalogs and magazines littered the table's surface and the cover on each pictured a woman whose face glowed with happiness. She'd probably glowed like that once. Wrinkling her nose in annoyance, Manny pushed the magazine closest to her back into the pile.

Her troubled gaze lifted to observe her friends, particularly her best friend. Shelby Reeves had conned her. The supposed dinner at a restaurant had turned out to be an impromptu, pre-official engagement party at the home of Starris and Jordon Banks.

The babies, Lauryn and Jonathan, were asleep in the nursery upstairs. The teens, Dani and Jolie, were holed up in their bedroom, doubtlessly on the phone with some boy. The men, Jordon, Nelson, Phillip, and Christopher were in the great room, loudly engaged in some type of game.

Manny's eyes took in the women seated around the table and her mind noted, in turn, how beautiful each of them were, inside and out.

Shelby, her friend since college, had a head full of shining black curls, ebony skin, and honey-brown eyes. Shelby was her rock and represented stability, sensibility, and a useful sounding board when Manny needed to check her thought process.

The red henna highlights in Pamela Shaw's cheek-length brown hair complemented her medium brown skin and brown eyes. Pam had relocated to Denver from Detroit after selling her bookstore to a large conglomerate. Except for having a man in her life, she seemed to have acclimated to the Mile High City just fine. Pam was an editor of juvenile books for African-American children at JuneHart Publishing. A truly independent woman, Manny had come to admire the zest Pamela had for life.

Maxine Peterson, a paralegal, wore her black hair in a layered cap that emphasized the smoothness of her dark complexion and the shapely curve of her sharp black eyes. Maxie was persistent and loyal to a fault. She, like Manny, was a believer in love and her onward and upward approach to life was an inspiration to all of them.

Starris Banks, whose hair sat on her shoulders in a billowy auburn cloud, had hazel eyes and golden brown skin. A graphics designer and artist, Starris brought level headedness to the group and was a natural born peacemaker.

The only one missing was Jacqueline Tyler, or rather Jacqueline Augostini. Jacci and her husband, Henrico, lived in New York and Manny missed her friend terribly. She smiled when she thought about the auburn-haired, hazel-eyed beauty whose gifts to the group were a non-judgmental nature and a genuine caring for other people.

Most people could count themselves lucky if they found one true friend in life and though they had all begun their friendships in pairs, Manny now counted each of the women as a friend and a blessing in her life. At the moment, her friends were animatedly involved in planning a wedding.

Hers!

Only it was not a wedding Manny wanted. Had they asked, she would have told them not to bother, because Manny had no intention of planning another wedding. Normally outspoken, she should have told them how she felt. Seeing their excitement, though, she hesitated to say anything. Watching them, all she could think about was another wedding, one into which she'd thrown her heart and soul. One with all the traditional components: satin, lace, flowers, tuxedos and cake, and one which despite her perfectly planned day, had turned into one of the most disastrous times of her life.

Manny could still hear the hushed whispers and see the looks of sympathy of those in attendance, and the horrified expressions on the faces of her parents. Her brothers had been so angry, there had been talk of hunting down Derrick Lewis and shooting him on the spot. Manny had been so hurt that all she could do was cry.

All of it came back in a rush and, deep down, Manny knew she could no more plan another wedding than she could fly to the moon. She wanted to marry Christopher more than anything in the world, but she wanted to do it without the hoopla of a large affair. Manny wanted a ceremony that was quick and quiet, and preferably performed by the justice of the peace down at city hall.

To give herself something else to do, Manny rose from her chair and crossed to the sink. She reached for a glass from the cabinet and turned on the tap. Filling the glass, she turned slowly and raised it to her lips, silently observing her friends and listening to their discussion.

Maxie slapped an open magazine down on the table. "Look at this. Now, I think that this is the perfect dress for Manny, and I know that Shelby wouldn't have any trouble making it."

The other women frowned when they looked at the picture. The dress was a grotesque creation of satin with cut-away hearts above the breasts and in the belle of the skirt.

"No, that's not Manny at all," Starris said, presenting her find. Her dress was a simple design made of eggshell satin with a shoulder length veil. "Now this gown would be perfect. It's traditional and would look lovely on Manny."

"That dress would be perfect for you," Maxie stated. "But we are looking for a dress for Manny and her tastes run more to the exotic."

"Exotic is just a word, sister-girl," Shelby said laughing. "I'll never forget the alterations she made to the dress at my first wedding." Shelby shook her head ruefully. "Black spandex, fur and pink chiffon. Lord, what a sight she made."

"Well, at least she had it together by the time you got married for the second time," Pamela said. She twisted in her chair to face Manny. "Hey! Didn't you meet Christopher at Shelby's wedding?"

Manny nodded, but said nothing. Shelby, however, picked up the slack. "And I'll have you all know that I'm the one responsible for getting the two of them together. I knew that Manny and Christopher would hit it off, which is why I encouraged her to go out with him."

The well-meaning meddler in Shelby rose to the surface as she took in the women at the table. Starris was married off to Jordon, and Maxie had lived with Phillip Johnson for the last four years. Shelby felt their relationship had moved into the serious realm. Now, all she had to do was get Phillip headed in the direction of the altar. Although Jacqueline had found Henrico on her own, Shelby took credit for the union anyway. The night Henrico had showed up to claim Jacci, she was the one who'd gotten everyone out of the house so that the two of them could iron out their differences.

Her gaze moved on, landing and staying on Pamela Shaw. With a smile, Shelby pointed her finger. "And you're next."

"Oh, no you don't, Shelby Reeves. My life is just fine, so don't be getting any ideas of trying to fix me up. You got that, sister-girl? You just take those busybody skills of yours and apply them elsewhere."

"I'm not going to take offense at that," Shelby replied, sniffing the air with disdain. "Anyone looking at Starris, Jacci, and Manny can see that I am nobody's busybody. I simply match my friends with their soul mates. I just need to find yours."

"Stay out of my life, Shel! When and if I do meet someone, I'll make sure that you're the first to know. After me, of course."

Maxie looked up from her magazine. "Better back off, Shel, Pam sounds serious."

"And what about you, Maxine? I think that it's about time I had a little chat with Phillip to find out where his head is at on this marriage thing."

Maxie's expression changed to one of irritation. "Stay out of my life, Shelby, and Phillip's. We are doing just fine, and I don't want you sticking your nose in my business and messing up all the progress I've made with him."

Highly affronted, Shelby drew back in her chair. "Sticking my nose in your business! Weren't you the one who called my house just last week threatening to leave Phillip if he didn't put a ring on your finger?"

Maxie looked away, somewhat embarrassed. "So what? I threaten to leave Phillip every other week, and I'm still with the man, aren't I?"

Starris looked up. "Let's not start with that again. Regardless of whether or not he proposes, Maxie loves Phillip and that should be enough for us." The women exchanged glances, but didn't comment further. "Besides," Starris continued, "if Manny decides to get married before the summer is over, I have just found the perfect dress."

She placed the magazine on the table and the women studied the photograph. The wedding gown was ivory and the model wore a lacy veil with a circle band of intertwined baby's breath on her head. Made of satin, the gown had a beaded bodice and stopped at the knee. Manny would look beautiful in the off-the-shoulder design.

Still looking at the picture, Starris inquired, "When exactly are you getting married anyway, Manny?"

They all looked up when Manny did not respond and found to their surprise, that Manny Walker was no longer in the kitchen.

"What in the hell are you doing, Christopher?" Nelson shouted, throwing in the remaining cards in his hands. "I knew your Mama, so I know she didn't raise a no-account, spades playing fool!"

"That is not a place you want to go this evening, Nelson, because if you had been paying attention, you would have noticed that J.R. took the only trump I had two plays ago."

"Forget that boy, Chris," Jordon said, raking in the pot. "Nelson's still upset because we wiped his butt all over that golf course this afternoon."

"I am not upset," Nelson muttered darkly. "And I don't think it's too much to ask that Chris get his mind off Manny and on this game!"

Phillip rose from his chair and headed for the bar. "You take this stuff way too seriously. At some point in this life, you're gonna have to learn to lose and like it, boy."

Nelson banged his fist on the table and glowered at the three other men. "Forget all y'all, and get the hell out of my house!"

Jordon laughed. "While we'd like to accommodate your request, this is *my* house. Now deal the cards, so that we can take the rest of that chump change sitting in front of you."

Manny had wandered the house in a state of flux, seeking a quiet place to stem the emotional tide threatening to erupt within her. Without thought, she'd followed the sound of deep voices until she found herself standing in the doorway of the great room listening to the banter being tossed back and forth between the four men in the room.

Someone unaware of the circumstances might think that a serious argument was afoot, but Manny knew that the loud talk was no more than idle conversation. There was a depth of feelings in that room and a shared camaraderie built from years of friendship. It was much like the feelings she held for the women in the kitchen, and it felt good to know that people could love each other so much.

She stepped further into the male-dominated sanctum and slipped unseen into a chair at the back of the room. She hadn't come to interrupt their play; she'd come to be near Christopher and let the warmth of his presence settle her jangled nerves.

Manny sat silently, listening and watching the men for at least ten minutes before Christopher looked up from his cards and directly into her eyes. He immediately threw in his hand and rose from his chair. All was not right with his woman.

In seconds, he was standing in front of Manny and when she reached for him, he drew her into his arms, hugging her tightly as he lifted her from the floor. "What's wrong, Honey-V," he whispered in her ear.

Manny took his face in her hands and pressed her mouth against his. Their lips met and parted several times in light caresses that were more comforting than they were erotic. Manny sighed inwardly and secured her hold around his neck. Each peck of his lips on hers felt like a droplet of soothing rain: refreshing, fortifying, and calming. She relaxed in his arms, relishing the melting sensation that seemed to float her away. She didn't need words, a dress, or a wedding. All she needed was Christopher to hold her close like this and bring a sense of balance back into her world.

The sensations flooding Christopher's body produced the opposite effect. Something was wrong, but with Manny in his arms, everything and everyone else faded into the background. Her touch felt as if a heating coil had stroked his heart and spiraled through his body to stir his rising passion. With supreme effort, he managed to control his urges and return the soft and gentle smooches of Manny's sensual play. He knew they would have to stop when her lip play became a demand for something more passionate.

He lifted his head and let her slide down his body to her feet. "Are you okay?"

She nodded. She was okay, but now she wanted something more than a few tender kisses. "Can we go home?"

"Anything you want, gorgeous."

Nelson stood up. "Homeboy, you playing or what?"

Christopher didn't break his gaze away from Manny. "Would it be all right if I finish this hand?"

"Yeah," Manny replied. Her brown eyes, round and soft, told him to hurry, though.

"Good." Taking her hand, Christopher returned to his chair and after settling her comfortably on his thigh, he picked up his cards. He tried to concentrate on the game, but Manny's delicate touches and kisses on his face made that all but impossible; kisses he returned with enthusiasm.

Nelson rolled his eyes in disgust. "Manny, do you mind? We're trying to play here."

"Cool it, Nelson," J.R. interjected. "They're in love."

Nelson tossed out the ace of spades. "They can be in love at home. I'm trying to win back my money."

"There you are," Shelby said, as she and the other women entered the room.

Starris stopped behind Jordon and placed her hands on his shoulders, but she was looking at Manny and Christopher. When they broke apart for air she asked, "What happened, Manny?"

"Yeah," Maxie said, after dropping a kiss on top of Phillip's head. "We finally found the perfect dress."

"But when we turned to show it to you—" Shelby interrupted.

"You were gone," Pamela finished.

Shelby stood behind Nelson. "Are you all right, Manny?"

Manny smiled shyly. "Yeah, I just needed my man."

"That would be me," Christopher said, giving her waist a squeeze.

Nelson scowled. "We are never going to finish this game," he muttered under his breath.

Shelby bent down over his shoulder. "Hush, Nelson. There's nothing in your hand that's going to win anyway."

"Well, why don't you just tell the whole world, Shelby Reeves!"

She rubbed her hand over his back. "Hush, baby, something else is going on here besides your card game."

Christopher stood up. "Manny and I need to go."

"You can't leave," Nelson yelled. "We're in the middle of a hand here!"

"Ignore him," Shelby said. "It's time we were on our way, also."

"Phil and I need to get going, too," Maxie said.

Starris clapped her hands for attention. "I want to remind you guys about the People's Fair next month. I think we should meet at the fountain and plan the day from there."

"Sounds good to me," Shelby said.

"I'll need to check my schedule," Phillip said. "I'm pretty sure Max and I can make it, though."

"We'll make it," Maxie said definitively. "What time?"

"I think we should get there as early as possible," Starris said. "Every year, that fair gets more and more crowded."

"How about eleven?" Shelby suggested. "Will that suit everyone's schedule?"

"Chris and I will be there," Manny said with a smile.

When everyone else concurred, Shelby looked at Pamela, who had a glum expression on her face. "What about you, Pam? You are planning on coming with us, right?"

"I don't know," Pamela replied quietly. "I might have to work that day." What she didn't say was that she didn't want to come because she probably couldn't find a date and she didn't want to attend the function by herself.

The look on Maxie's face said, *Yeah right.* "Look, Pam. I have a friend and I can—"

Pamela cut her off. "No thanks. I can find a date on my own, thank you very much."

"If you find out that you don't have to work, then you can ride with us," Starris said. "You know how much the girls enjoy your company."

Pamela smiled. "That sounds fine, Starris, and I'll let you know."

Shelby raised a brow. It might sound fine to them, but it didn't to her. She would just make sure that Pamela had a date for the festival. "I'm going up to get Lauryn, so drive safely everyone."

It was too quiet inside the Jeep and Christopher glanced at Manny before turning his eyes back to the road. Usually, she held a running conversation in the car, but tonight, she seemed to have withdrawn into herself. They were halfway home and she hadn't spoken a word. Obviously, something was on her mind and while he believed in giving people their space, he wanted Manny to know that she could come to him with anything.

He picked up her hand. "Want to talk about it?"

She continued to stare through the side window. She had thought that telling Christopher about Derrick would free her completely from her past. It had helped, but sitting in that kitchen surrounded by reminders of a wedding day gone wrong had pointed out the error of her thoughts. The burden had lightened with the sharing, but after so much time, the past was still within her, haunting her.

She looked down at her left hand and unable to see her ring, she felt for it with her other hand and set her resolve. Shelby had told her to be honest with Christopher in all things and trust his love. She decided to give it a shot. "Chris, how would you feel about not having a wedding?"

He started, then gripped the wheel of the Jeep a little tighter in his hand. His eyes still surveyed the street and the happenings going on around them, but his mind went into a tailspin. However, before it went off completely in the wrong direction, he switched gears. "Are you saying that you've changed your mind about marrying me?"

"No, I want to marry you. What in the world made you think that?"

"You asked if I wanted to get married."

"No, I did not. I asked if you wanted a wedding." Manny jerked her hand out of his. "I swear, Christopher. Sometimes I wonder how you became a detective with your listening skills. It must make it impossible for you to obtain the facts."

"I listen just fine, Manny. All I'm trying to find out is why you don't want to get married."

Exasperated, Manny propped her elbow on the door and plopped her chin into her hand. "Christopher, what are we arguing about? I never said I didn't want to get married. I said I didn't want a wedding."

Christopher opened his mouth, then closed it. He stared hard through the windshield. "Oh."

"Oh, what?"

"Oh, you don't want a wedding, but you want to get married."

"And?"

"And I'm wondering why."

"You know why. I've already planned one of those things and this time I would like to have a quiet ceremony."

Christopher pulled into the driveway of Manny's house. She surveyed her two-story home and felt the pride of ownership. The exterior was painted eggshell white with dark blue shutters. There was a large bay window in the front and one on the side. Two spindly oak trees sat on either side of the front yard. In a few years, their leaves would provide shade for the porch. Colorful gardens flanked the side of the house and the fountain in the backyard.

Her eyes shifted to Christopher. He didn't think that she knew about the money he'd added to her down payment, but she did. Manny had carefully calculated what she needed to purchase her home, and based on what she'd saved, her monthly payment was several hundred dollars lower than it should have been had the bank taken only her funds into account. Since Christopher hadn't said anything, she hadn't either, but in her heart, she thanked him every time she entered her home.

Christopher pulled up the parking brake and turned to face her. He took a deep breath. "Manny, I have never been married and neither have you. This will be the one and only time I will get married and I want a wedding. A large one, with our family and all of our friends there to celebrate when I take you as my wife."

"A large wedding will be expensive. Think of the money we'll save by going down to city hall, and we won't have to wait so long."

He twisted his lips to stop a smile. Manny was reaching for straws. She knew the status of his finances. He reached for her hand again and tugged her toward him until she was up against his side. "Whatever the cost, you know that we can afford it, and I'll live with any date you set as long as you pick one soon and it's not too far in the future. I'm also ready to start having my children. Nelson has Lauryn. J.R. already has Dani, Jolie, and Jonathan and he says he's working on another son. I need to get started; I'm way behind."

Manny chuckled when she saw the frown on his face. He looked so serious. "And just how many kids, exactly, are you expecting to have, Christopher Mills?"

"Four or five would do to start. I'll need at least nine if I'm going to have my own baseball team, though." He added the last part to make her smile and she rewarded him with a tiny grin.

"Nine kids! You want nine children! How in the world would we feed them all? And we'd have to clothe and house them, too. By the time we finished raising them, the two of us would be very old, old people. I'm telling you right now that it's not going to happen, Christopher Mills."

"Then I guess I'll have to settle for one or two."

"That's better. I can live with that."

"But there's a problem."

"And that is?"

"We need to get married so that we can get started and that means you have to pick a date."

Leaving Manny to ponder that statement, Christopher opened his door and left the car. His eyes scanned the house, its perimeter, and the yard before he came around to help Manny out of the Jeep. He took her hand as he led her up the sidewalk and after unlocking the front door, entered the house first.

Manny followed him inside, then waited by the door until he'd made a cursory pass through the house. So much for being honest, she thought. Christopher Mills meant to have a wedding and he expected her to plan it. Manny watched him make his safety check and felt her insides shift. She just didn't know if she could.

Satisfied that everything was okay, Christopher returned to lock the front door, and then crossed to the closet to hang up his jacket. He watched Manny slip out of her shoes and his brooding gaze followed her as she went into the living room and set her purse in a cream-colored chair patterned in tiny navy blue dots. She moved to a solid cream-colored couch and sat down.

Pale blue walls complemented the décor that included many large and leafy plants in blue and beige patterned pots and dark walnut furniture. On the large table in front of the couch, Manny had placed a large scalloped vase and filled it with the rust-colored cattails she'd gathered in the mountains.

On the wall by the door, cream colored curtains hung from an ornate beige rod. They were held back by navy blue sashes that revealed the pale blue sheers underneath. For comfort, she'd placed navy-colored, cushioned pillows in the seats of the bay window.

Feeling weary, Manny stretched out her legs and laid her head on the arm of the couch. Christopher watched her for a minute, knowing that he had to tell her that he would be gone for a few days, and also knowing that they had not finished their conversation in the car. The thought of marrying Manny excited him and he wanted to share his happiness with the whole world. He'd also hoped that Manny would agree to get started planning their wedding so that she'd be so busy, she wouldn't have time to dwell on him while he was away.

Leaning over the couch, he brushed his lips across hers. "I'm going to the kitchen. You want anything?"

She shook her head no and reached up to wrap her hands around his neck. Pulling him back down, Manny took his lips again in a hot and passionate kiss. "I love you," she said. "But I still don't want a wedding and I need to tell you something else."

Though they had yet to settle the wedding issue, Manny had to try the honesty thing again. The strength of their love and their relationship depended on it. She sat up, making room for him to sit down. Christopher sat, but when she didn't relax her body against his or lie back and place her head on his thigh, his mind immediately became alert. Something was up.

Manny looked down at the beige carpet. When her eyes swept up to meet his again, distress marred her face. "Last week, I received some flowers at the shop." She hesitated and released a deep breath. "Actually, I received a lot of flowers; a vase of pink roses every day for the entire week. I thought they were from you—they weren't." She paused, giving him an opportunity to comment.

He raised a brow, but said nothing. Whatever Manny had to say, he planned to let her do it without interruption, but she seemed to be waiting for a response, so he asked, "Who were the flowers from, Manny?"

"Derrick." She looked away, unable to maintain the intense eye contact. "He wants to see me."

"Why?"

"He claims he still loves me and he wants to meet his child."

A muscle jerked in Christopher's cheek and he lowered hooded eyes at her. "Are you going to see him?"

"I've been thinking about it."

"Why?" Christopher asked with deadly calm.

Manny shrugged. "Well," she said on a sigh. "I thought that it might be a good idea to, you know, see what he has to say."

She glanced up at Christopher. The set of his jaw was rock hard and he was shaking his head back and forth.

"No, Manny. You have no reason to see that man after what he did to you."

"What he did to me *then* is affecting our relationship *now,* Christopher. I know you said to forget about Derrick, but how can I do that when I don't really know what happened. Besides, he doesn't even know that our baby died."

Christopher heard the genuine concern in her voice. Thunderstruck, he rose to his feet, unable to believe that Manny could still harbor feelings for a man who had walked out on her. "You mean the baby that he cared nothing about? Or its mother?" When she didn't respond, he continued, "I don't want you to see him, Manny."

"I think I have to," she whispered.

His voice wavered slightly with the next question. "D-do you still have feelings for him, Manny?"

"No," she answered without hesitation and with absolute conviction. "I love you. But sometimes I feel as if I'm not being fair to you, because there is a small piece of me that is afraid to love you completely, afraid that one day you'll walk away, too. I don't want to live like that anymore. I want you to have my whole heart, everything that I am, and I want everything that we can be together. But there were too many things left unfinished with Derrick, including my knowing why he left without an explanation. If seeing him will help free me of this doubt and also help me completely shed the past, then I think I should do it."

"You don't need Derrick Lewis to be free. All you need to do is set a date and start making plans for our wedding and our marriage." Christopher walked to the closet and retrieved his jacket.

"Where are you going? We're not finished talking about this."

"Yes, we are," he said, his tone cold. "I've made my position clear. Unless you still have feelings for Derrick Lewis, you don't need him for anything. You have my love and I'm never going to leave you."

Apprehension dulled Manny's eyes and her voice resonated with the disillusionment that had settled inside her chest. "But, baby, you're leaving me now."

Realization dawned quickly and Christopher froze in the middle of putting on his jacket. His head dropped as his mind worked to assimilate his actions with Manny's statement. He was leaving, but he wasn't leaving her.

As an only child, he'd shared a close relationship with both of his parents. They had spoiled him, and given him more love and attention than any child could possibly want. With the death of his father, all of that had changed for Christopher. He'd no longer had anyone to help him work through his problems, or hug him when he was upset or listen to him when he just needed to talk.

Sure, he'd had his mother for a short time after his father's death, but only her physical form. Her spirit and her disposition and all of the other human qualities that had made her a living and breathing person had died along with his father. The year he'd spent living in an orphanage had only made Christopher draw further into himself, and not even his rescue by Nelson's parents had brought back the happy, fun-loving child he had once been.

He glanced at Manny. Without meaning to, she had inflicted a great deal of distress on him and Christopher had resorted to the only method he knew to deal with his dilemma. In doing that, he was hurting the woman he was supposed to love. He removed his jacket, hung it back inside the closet, and returned to the couch. If they were truly going to be man and wife in every sense of the union, he had to change how he reacted whenever something upset him.

"I'm sorry, Manny. I wasn't thinking. I just needed to...never mind. It doesn't matter." He picked up one of her hands. "I don't want you to see Derrick, Manny. What he did to you was wrong and I don't want you exposing yourself to any more unnecessary pain. But, if you

feel that seeing Derrick is something you really need to do, then okay."
He sighed and leaned back on the couch, taking Manny with him, feeling his tension melt away when she squeezed him tight around the waist.

"Do you mean it, baby?"

"Yes," he growled. "But it better not be a long meeting. You listen to what he has to say and then you come home to me."

She tipped her head to stare deeply into his dark eyes. "I will. Thank you for understanding, Christopher."

He smiled. Manny had to do this, but he knew in his heart—felt it as if it were already a reality—that they were going to be okay. "You're welcome." He rose to his feet with his arms still around her. "I don't know about you, but I'm beat and I have to go to work in a few hours."

He turned off the lamp and together they ascended the stairs. Christopher showered and performed his nightly toiletries, then stood in the doorway watching Manny turn down the bed. "When are you planning to tell your family that you're an engaged woman?"

She dropped the decorator pillow in her hands on a chair. "Is this weekend soon enough? I thought we could drive to Boulder and tell them in person."

He wouldn't be here this weekend. He had a job to do and the time had come for him to let her know. He braced himself for her reaction. "Um, Manny, maybe we could just call your parents and let them know."

"I don't want to do that, Christopher. I want to tell them in person."

He heaved a breath. "Uh, okay, but we'll have to arrange another time. I won't be here this weekend."

"Why? Where are you going?"

"That I can't tell you, but it's the job."

Manny heard what he'd said and focused on all he had not. "Oh," she replied, struggling to quell her rising alarm. She desperately wanted to know where Christopher was going and what he'd be doing, but she knew better than to ask. "When will you be back?"

He studied her lowered head. "I'm leaving on Friday. I should be back in a couple of days."

I *should* be back, not I *will* be back, which to Manny meant that Christopher was about to place himself in a dangerous situation. Her heart jumped, then pummeled her chest and her lashes swept up revealing eyes full of torment. "But you're not well enough to go anywhere, Christopher. Besides, we're supposed to go to the People's Fair."

"I'm almost a hundred percent, and I'm ready to get back on the job. The festival is not until next month and I'll be back way before then."

His declaration of health had not helped. Manny's body visibly shook. He reached for her and hugged her tightly.

"Honey-V, please don't start worrying," he whispered. "I'm okay, Manny, and I plan to come home the same way I leave; whole in mind and body and still in love with you."

Christopher pressed lips tightened by a grimace against her temple and attempted to rationalize in his mind what might very well turn out to be a lie. He didn't know where he was going, or if he'd come back; and there was nothing he could say that would stop Manny from worrying. He just wanted the case over with so that he would never have to put her through this again. He led her toward the bed and climbed under the covers beside her.

Manny took his face in her hands and stared deeply into his black eyes. What she saw there brought her little in the way of comfort. His eyes were clear and confident, sure that no matter what happened he'd come back to her unharmed. She also saw his love for her and a plea for her to understand.

She tried, but it was useless. He hadn't even left and she was already scared. "Chris, what am I supposed to do if something happens to you?"

Her eyes were luminous and shadowed with alarm, and he didn't know what else to say to ease her worry, except to keep assuring her that everything would be okay.

Charlene Thomas. Christopher blinked when the name flashed

into his mind again. Why hadn't he thought of her before? Charlene had been married to Sam for more than twenty years, and if anyone could ease Manny's mind, it was Charlene. His eyes softened and he stroked the back of his hand across Manny's cheek. "Nothing's going to happen, Ms. Walker, except that when I get back, you and I are going to have a wonderful wedding and a happy marriage, and that's all I want you to think about."

He gathered her against him; the time for talking was done. Holding her close, Christopher feathered his fingers through her thick mane of black hair, massaging her scalp while laying a trail of tiny kisses over her face. The scent of honeysuckle and lavender wafted upward from the silky strands, alerting his mind, and elevating his body's response to her nearness. With considerable effort, Christopher tempered his need and continued his nighttime ministrations.

Manny soon relaxed, but then she began snuggling movements in an attempt to mold the softness of her body into his long and rock hard form. His pulse rate sped up and Christopher fought to take control of his rising ardor. He was supposed to be comforting Manny. He'd meant to handle her gently, caress her tenderly until only his touch filled her mind and she drifted into peaceful slumber. But if she didn't knock it off, something else was going to be occurring in their bed before too much longer. "Manny," he growled softly at her ear. "Be still and go to sleep."

She lifted her head and when she saw his eyes alight with the fire of desire he hadn't successfully banked, she shifted lower until her thigh brushed against the rigid source of his passion. "I love you, Christopher." Then she settled her head on his chest and closed her eyes.

He sent up a silent 'thank you' and closed his eyes, too. Despite what he'd told Manny, he needed his rest, knowing that his body had to be in top form to handle whatever was to come later in the week.

Enticed by his natural scent mingling with that of the soap he'd used in the shower, Manny managed to lie still as a rug for almost two full minutes before she pressed her nose into the side of Christopher's neck. Her tongue flicked out to dampen the smooth skin and her warm breath coupled with firm pressure of her lips only heightened the velvety sensations that immediately ignited a fire in his body.

Christopher's eyes flew open and he groaned in agonized pleasure. Of their own accord, it seemed, his hands trailed down the silken brown skin of her back and gripped her bottom in a tight squeeze. Still working her lips on his neck, Manny reached down to find him hard and ready. Taking him into her hand, she massaged his manhood until Christopher gritted his teeth and rolled her onto her back.

He kissed her thoroughly while his hands fondled breasts that were fully erect and begging for his attention. Manny moaned when his tongue skimmed the surface of each several times before his lips clamped around the hardened bud of his choice. He suckled and she arched her back, her hands wildly caressing the hard muscles in his arms. Mounting her, Christopher stared deep into her eyes. "I love you, too, Manny Walker, and I will come back to you unharmed."

He slanted a kiss on her mouth and thrust his hips forward in a stroke that penetrated deeply and filled her entire inner core. Manny gasped, then strained to keep up with the lightning tempo of the pace he quickly set and maintained until both careened into a rapturous fulfillment that left them barely able to breathe when they descended to earth. Once more, they kissed before both drifted into a soundless and restful sleep.

CHAPTER 11

Across the city, in a two million-dollar condo loft overlooking downtown Denver, Anthony Chavez shuffled the papers in his hands and kept his beady, black eyes trained on the tall man in the white linen suit. Dexter Santangelo had taken his sweet time getting to Denver, but Anthony had been expecting him.

Profits were down drastically. Merchandise continuously turned up missing along the route, and the police had hauled in too many of his men. Santangelo was rich and powerful; the kind of man Anthony had always aspired to be. He was also a man who kept his eyes firmly planted on the operation of his empire. Anthony only wondered why it had taken so long for Dexter to make an appearance. Without rising, he laid the papers to one side of the desk. "Mr. Santangelo, it's good to see you again."

Anthony's naïve display of disrespect was not lost on Dexter as he slowly approached the overly large, walnut desk that seemed to swallow up the small man seated behind it. The lack of respect served to confirm that despite nineteen years with the organization, Anthony Chavez still had no clue as to the type of man he was dealing with.

Everything about Anthony Chavez loudly proclaimed his lack of both class and sophistication. The gel-packed, slicked-back hairstyle had gone out with the fifties, along with the pale blue polyester suits, white belts, and shoes of the seventies. In one brief sweep, Dexter's eyes took in the red shag carpet on the floor, the heavy, black, imitation leather furniture, and the imitation walnut paneling on the walls. It was a room that personified bad taste.

With much ado, Dexter lowered himself into one of the chairs in front of the desk. He pulled at his white jacket and flicked non-existent lint from the legs of his trousers. Then he propped an elbow on the arm of the chair and crossed one leg over the other, his eyes lowered in an intimate study of the onyx and diamond pinky ring on the little finger of his right hand.

Like a flash of lightning, his lids suddenly swept up and an icy blue stare locked with the black eyes that now reflected an inward agitation. Dexter noted the tremble of Anthony's right hand when it came up to smooth back the hair on his head. "Anthony."

Anthony broke the stare and looked around his domain. He might have been looking for courage. When his eyes landed on the bar, he rose from his chair. "Can I get you something, Mr. Santangelo?"

"An apple martini."

Anthony put his hands on his waist, clearly at a loss. Apple martini? He crossed to the bar. "I got scotch, bourbon, gin, and rum." Anthony glanced over his shoulder at Dexter.

"Thank you, no. Please feel free to indulge yourself, though."

Anthony turned back to the bar and reached for the bottle of Jack Daniels. He was busy filling a glass to the brim when Dexter spoke again.

"I've been noticing that you're experiencing a few setbacks of late." The words, though quietly spoken, attested to the authority of the man who spoke them.

Anthony took a quick gulp from his glass. "Yeah, we've had a few problems, Mr. Santangelo," he replied, crossing back to the desk. "But with a little time, I know I can turn things around again."

Dexter's lips lifted in a mirthless smile. "I'm afraid that won't be possible, Anthony, because as of now, your time has run out."

Before Anthony could say another word, a small legion of men entered the room. Two of them took Anthony by the arms and escorted him out, while the rest scurried about, searching for and packing anything of importance into white boxes.

The following week was one of the busiest Manny would endure in the entire year. The ROBY fashion show/fundraiser loomed before them, and both she and Shelby were up to their armpits finalizing arrangements for the fashion part of the show. All week she'd been cataloging and tagging the haute couture designs sent for the show, confirming reservations, fielding questions from models, easing the worry of designers about their shipments, contacting vendors and technicians, and working with hotels and the managers of the entertainment booked for the evening, as well as performing her normal duties for the store.

ROBY's first fundraiser had garnered an audience of five hundred. This year's show had sold out in less than four hours and thirty-six hundred people had become the proud owners of what had become the hottest tickets in town. All available sponsorships had sold out months ago, but calls from local companies wanting to sponsor something, anything, donate auction items, or pay to have their banners flown, were pouring in daily to ROBY's office.

In addition, it was prom season and customers had been flocking into the store all week. Fortunately, Exterior Motives' sales associates were a well-trained team; otherwise, Manny would have seriously considered selling her ownership stake in the ready-to-wear store back to Shelby. However, with a large bottle of Advil as her personal assistant, Manny handled it all with her usual flair and efficiency.

She sighed as she bent down and lifted another exquisite creation from a shipment she'd received that morning. Well, at least she was keeping busy, which meant that she didn't have too much time left over to dwell on Christopher and the fact that by this time tomorrow he would have left on his mysterious mission.

"I swear I'm going to kill Tyrone Brooks!" Shelby brushed right by Manny and slapped the papers she carried in her hand down on the desk. "The fashion show is tomorrow night, and he just had the nerve to inform me that he has not yet selected or shipped his designs." Shelby threw up her arms. "I'm going kill that man when I see him."

Manny continued to unpack dresses. "The aspirin are on the desk. Feel free to take two, or three, or five."

Shelby leaned back on the desk and crossed her arms over her chest. "Aspirin? I don't need any aspirin. What I need is a hit man to take out my dear friend in New York. I spent all morning working on the designer lineup and because of Ty, I may have to start all over again."

"Whatever, Shel," Manny said wearily. "By the way, I ordered in sandwiches. They should be here any minute." As soon as the words left her mouth, one of the sales associates showed up at the door with the food. "Thanks," Manny said, taking the white bag. She moved to her desk and sat down. "I'm hungry, so let's eat."

Shelby drew in a deep, calming breath, then sat in the wingback chair, and took the sandwich and napkin Manny held out to her. For a few minutes, they took advantage of the quiet and consumed their food in silence. When the ringing telephone shattered their peace, Manny turned away to answer the call.

Shelby waited until she'd hung up before setting her sandwich on the napkin. "Have you given any more thought to the conversation we had this morning?"

"No," Manny said, replacing the earring in her lobe as she swiveled her chair around and met what she guessed was supposed to be an antagonistic glare. Manny bit back a laugh. The only person Shelby Reeves had ever intimidated was her husband and only because Nelson had been half out of his mind in love with Shelby since he'd met her. Manny maintained the hostile engagement until Shelby finally threw up her hands in surrender.

"Come on, Manny," she said in a tone meant to persuade. "You know I wouldn't ask if it wasn't really important."

"I said no."

This time Shelby balled her fists in frustration. "Why not?"

"Because Pamela has already told you that she doesn't want you meddling in her life. That's reason number one. Reason number two is that I'm not going to let you involve me in one of your little schemes. They always backfire and I don't want to find myself in the rubble of your mess."

"It's not a scheme," Shelby returned, a little put out. "It just so happens that Vance Caldwell is a well-known author of children's books, and has also penned several novels on western lore. He owns a ranch in Midvale, Colorado and will be in Denver for only a few weeks to conduct research on the state and look for a new publisher. The fact that he's good-looking and single has nothing to do with my inviting him to the festival. As a friend, I'm simply helping him by putting him together with another friend, who happens to be an editor."

If Manny didn't know Shelby Reeves as well as she did, she might have believed the sincerity she heard in her voice. But she did know Shelby, the quintessential matchmaker, who thought getting her friends paired up and married off to her idea of the perfect man was her second calling. "So, you're going to sit there and actually try to convince me that you're not hoping for a love connection between this Vance Caldwell and Pamela Shaw?"

Unable to meet the skepticism reflected in Manny's gaze, Shelby fiddled with a mother-of-pearl button on the front on her jacket. "I'm bringing them together for business reasons. If the two of them are attracted to each other in the process, who am I to stand in the way of blossoming love. And speaking of love," Shelby continued before Manny could reply. "Have you and Christopher set a wedding date?"

Manny felt her heart lurch. Leave it to Shelby to bring up the one subject she didn't want to discuss. The last thing she wanted to think about was a wedding, when she didn't even know if Christopher would be around to attend the nuptials. Playing for time, she shrugged her shoulders. "We're still working on that."

Shelby took in the somber look shading Manny's eyes. "What's wrong, Manny? For years, all you've talked about is finding a husband. If I didn't know better, I would think that you really don't want to marry Christopher."

Manny suddenly stood up and walked to the coffeepot. "Then I guess you know better, so let's just leave it at that, shall we?"

Hip to Manny's attempt to put her off, Shelby leaned forward, her ineffective hostile glare back in place. "Why haven't you set a date,

Manny?"

"Because Christopher and I haven't decided on one," Manny countered over her shoulder, which was technically true since he'd told *her* to choose one. She picked up her mug. "When we do set a date, I'll let you know."

"What about a July wedding? The weather will be nice and you can hold the ceremony outdoors."

Manny's heart began to thud so hard, she thought it would burst from her chest, as the palms of her hands turned clammy. Fearing that she would drop and break her favorite mug, she carefully set the cup back on the table. Then, she closed her eyes and prayed for strength. She loved the woman seated in her office like a sister, but Shelby had always had a knack for finding the right buttons to push. Coupled with Christopher's leaving and all the problems she'd dealt with over the past week, Manny had about all she could take.

She whirled around, her eyes ablaze with all the agitation jangling her insides. "I don't want to talk about a wedding date! In fact, I don't even want a wedding! So, will you please get off my back about it and, for once, just mind your own damn business!"

Shelby couldn't have been more shocked if Manny had walked up and slapped her across the face. This was not the woman that she'd known for over fifteen long years. The woman who'd stood faithfully in her corner during the loss of her child and the breakup of her marriage to Nelson. The woman who'd nagged and nagged at her until she'd finally admitted that she still loved her husband and reconciled with Nelson.

She sat up in her chair. "I just know that you are not telling me to mind my own business when you have used every opportunity you could find to interfere in my life, Manny Walker."

Shaking with the guilt of her outburst, Manny returned to her desk and plopped down in her chair. The air she created with the fall caused the magenta, multi-layered ruffled skirt she wore to float down layer by layer until it again settled into place. "That's exactly what I'm telling you, Shelby. Look, I know you mean well, but you also know why I don't want a wedding and I've already told Christopher. It was too hard the first time and I am not going to put myself through it again. And that's all I have to say about that."

Manny directed her eyes to her desk and began rearranging the items on its surface into a straight line. Shelby reached to still her hands. "Christopher loves you, Manny, and he's not going to run out on you. Not every man is Derrick Lewis."

Manny's head snapped up and a feral gleam lit up her eyes. "I don't want to talk about this, Shelby."

A wave of sympathy entered Shelby's voice. "I know, and I'm sorry. But Derrick is the reason why you won't let yourself accept that another man can love you and not hurt you."

"That's not true."

"Yes, it is, Manny. You have been saying for almost as long as I have known you that you want to find true love. Well, you've found it with Christopher. Don't let the memories of what another man did ruin the happiness the two of you share."

Manny's shoulders sagged in defeat. "I know you're right, Shel, and I'm sorry for snapping at you like that. I know I have to put Derrick and all the things he did behind me and I'm trying my best to do that. I know that Christopher wants a big wedding, but I don't think I can plan another one. If Christopher would just agree to get married at city hall, everything would be okay."

"I don't think he's going to agree to that."

"I know."

"So what are you going to do?"

"Plan another wedding, I guess."

Shelby smiled. "Now, that's the sister-girl I know. And Manny, I will be with you every step of the way, just like you are always there when I need you."

Manny hadn't thought that the bond of friendship she shared with Shelby Reeves could grow any stronger, but in that moment, it did. She was truly grateful for her friend. Planning another wedding would be hard, but knowing that Shelby was there to help her made the burden in her heart much lighter. "Thanks, Shel."

"You're welcome." Shelby picked up her sandwich. "Now, back to the festival and Pamela and Vance—"

"I'm not helping you, Shelby, and when Pam finds out what you're up to, I don't want to be anywhere in the vicinity."

"She's not going to find out."

"Of course, she is."

Shelby thought about that for a moment before saying, "But how?"

"Because I'm going to tell her." Manny took a bite of her sandwich.

Shelby's eyes widened in horror. "You wouldn't!"

Manny swallowed. "I would, but I might be persuaded to change my mind if you can admit that this business introduction you're planning has nothing to do with business and everything to do with your trying to match Pamela with a man."

"Okay, fine. I do want Pamela and Vance to meet before the surplus of women in this city get wind of the fact that he's new in town."

A flicker of victory crossed Manny's face. "Okay," she replied. "I'll help, but just so you know, if Pam does find out, I'm claiming ignorance."

"Great," Shelby said, clapping her hands together. "Now remember, don't say a word to Pamela. I want her to be surprised."

She'll be surprised all right, Manny thought, watching Shelby happily munch on her food, and Pam wouldn't be happy when she found out that she'd been set up. However, if Shelby could help her get through the ordeal of planning another possible wedding fiasco, the least she could do was try to have Shelby's back when Pamela Shaw laid into her for meddling.

Christopher was asleep on the couch when the telephone rang. He blinked his eyes open and reached for the receiver. "Mills."

"Chris, you need to get down to the station," Donny said. "Now."

Leaning up on his elbows, Christopher glanced over his shoulder at the wall behind him and the glass-encased clock. It read 9:00 A.M. *Damn*, he thought. His shift had ended at seven and he'd only been out for an hour. He sat up and scrubbed his face with one hand. "Why?"

"Calvin Saunders is in lockup and he's asking for you."

Christopher stifled a groan. Calvin was one of the boys enrolled in the ROBY program, and Calvin, who didn't seem to understand the purpose of the program, had been matched with Christopher.

"What did he do this time?"

"He was picked up on suspicion of armed robbery and assault with a deadly weapon."

"What!"

"You heard me, Mills. And this time, they wanna throw the book at him."

"I'm on my way."

Twenty minutes later, Christopher Mills burst through the doors of the station, a virtual storm raging in his black eyes. He strode to the front desk. "Where is he?"

"Cell number three," the desk sergeant replied.

"Move him to interrogation."

"But, Mills, the boy says he didn't do it. That's why he asked for you."

"And I said move him!"

Christopher left the desk to find Donny, who briefly filled him in on the case. Then he sat at his desk, made some calls, and completed paperwork he'd left unfinished the night before. Over an hour passed before Christopher felt calm enough to confront Calvin, whom he'd left to stew in the small, closet-size room.

He walked into the beige-colored space, bare of furniture, except for a brown rectangular table sitting in the middle of the floor, and three gray, metal chairs. No pictures adorned the walls and there were no windows. It was a room meant to make the suspect feel as uncomfortable as possible. It was a room meant to intimidate.

To Christopher's great surprise, he didn't find Calvin nervously awaiting his arrival. He found Calvin fast asleep with his arms folded on the table as a pillow for his head.

The little punk, he thought, moving forward with narrowed eyes. Upon reaching Calvin's side, Christopher lifted his foot and kicked the chair from beneath Calvin's butt. Then he stepped back, crossed his arms over his chest, and watched the startled expression on the boy's face as he picked himself up from the floor.

Highly indignant, Calvin scrambled to his feet. "Whatja do that for?"

"Because I am sick and tired of this crap with you, Calvin! How many times do you think I am going to come down to this station to rescue your stupid behind out of trouble? You like this place? You want to live here? Well, buddy, this time, I'll make sure you get what you want!"

Calvin's belligerence deflated like a lead balloon and terror shook his entire body. He'd never seen Christopher Mills so angry, and if he wasn't already so scared, he might have thought that the man was going to slam him into a wall. Calvin started talking. "I didn't do it, Mr. Mills."

"Tell it to a judge." Christopher reached for the handcuffs hanging from the back of his belt. He walked toward Calvin. "You have the right to remain silent. If you give up that right anything you say can and will be held against you in a court of law."

Calvin's legs turned to jelly and his mouth trembled in his effort to hold back the tears standing in his eyes. "Mr. Mills, I swear I didn't do it! I didn't rob no liquor store. I was at home that night. I swear I was. If you don't believe me, you can call and ask my mom!"

"You have the right to an attorney. If you cannot afford an attorney, one will be appointed for you." Christopher snapped on and secured the cuffs around Calvin's slender wrists. "Do you understand these rights as I have stated them to you?"

"Mr. Mills, please! I didn't do it!"

With a look of general dispassion, Christopher observed the tears streaming down Calvin's face. He reached down and righted the overturned chair. "Sit down, Calvin."

Calvin sat, sniffled, and then leaned his head to the side in an effort to wipe his wet cheek on his shoulder.

Christopher grabbed one of the other chairs, turned it backward, and straddled the seat. "Did you participate in robbing that store?"

"No, Mr. Mills. It's like I said. I was at home that night. I don't know who did it." The last sentence came out in a mumbled rush.

Christopher studied the young man through the screen of his lashes, his face a mask of stone. Calvin was lying and Christopher knew it. He might have been at home, but he was also holding out. "Then who did?"

Calvin glanced around the room, looking at nothing and everything except Christopher Mills. "I don't know," he finally repeated.

Disappointed, Christopher stood up. "I think you do, and perhaps a few days in jail will help clear your memory." He jerked Calvin up from the chair. "Donny," he called.

Donny entered the room, his expression solemn. "Yeah."

"Take this punk back to lockup."

Calvin's eyes widened in fright as he watched Donny move in his direction. He swung his head to Christopher. "Please, Mr. Mills. I don't want to go to jail. I'm cleaning up my act. I'm doing better in school. I've even been on time for work, every day."

"Who robbed the store, Calvin?"

Calvin shook his head back and forth, knowing he couldn't tell, yet at the same time, knowing that he had to. Overwhelmed with the weight of a decision he was not mature enough to make, Calvin dropped to the chair behind him and hung his head, crying like baby. "It was my cousin, Mr. Mills," he mumbled. "Jimmy robbed that store."

Christopher's stoic countenance relaxed as he watched Calvin again break down in tears. He knew well the unemployed cousin with five children by three different women. Jimmy Saunders put in regular appearances at the station, charged with one petty crime or another. Unfortunately, the man had just upped his profile to strike three, and when caught, it would be a long time before Jimmy Saunders smelled the air of freedom again. He nodded his head at Donny, who left the room to relay the information that would start the hunt for Jimmy Saunders.

When the door closed, Christopher crossed to Calvin and removed the handcuffs. "Where is Jimmy now?"

"I don't know, Mr. Mills, I don't. Jimmy only came into the house long enough to grab some of his stuff. Then he split."

"Sit down, Calvin." Christopher waited until the boy had taken his seat. "Son, I've been your mentor for three years and I don't understand why you continually place yourself in the path of danger." When Calvin would have spoken, Christopher held up his hand. "I know that this time you're innocent, but what about next time, Calvin? How many chances do you think you're going to get? You're seventeen and it's time you got your act together. It's time for you to start looking out for the self preservation of Calvin Saunders and to remove yourself from anyone or any situation which places you in harm's way or steers you off course from your goals."

"I'm trying, Mr. Mills."

"You have to do more than try, Calvin. You have to succeed."

Calvin looked up with sad, red-rimmed eyes. "Are you going to report me to Mr. Banks? If you do, I'll have to leave ROBY. Then where will I be?"

Christopher leaned back in his chair, tapping his fingers on the table. "I'm not going to report this, but this is your absolute last chance. You got me, Mr. Saunders? You mess up one more time and that's it."

"I got it, Mr. Mills, and I won't mess up again. You'll see. I'm gonna make you proud."

"Don't do it for me, Calvin," Christopher said. "Do it for yourself."

Later that afternoon, the bell above the shop door tinkled. When a young girl entered and offered a tentative smile, Manny returned the gesture and quickly finished ringing up the customer she'd been helping. Manny knew the girl only by sight, but she'd been coming into the shop every afternoon around this same time for the past few weeks.

Before today, the young woman had never made eye contact with anyone and she always declined assistance from the sales associates. Although she made her usual beeline for the prom gowns prominently displayed in the store, Manny sensed that something about the girl was different today. She thanked the customer as she handed over a white plastic bag boldly emblazoned with a large, red 'E' signifying the logo of Exterior Motives. Then she hurried over to the young potential customer.

"Hi," Manny said when she reached her. She glanced at the dress, which seemed to have caught and held the girl's attention. It was the same dress she gravitated toward every time she came into the shop. "Would you like to try that on?"

The girl swallowed and clutched something tighter in her hand. Manny waited with a friendly smile of patience on her lips. Finally, the girl thrust her hand forward. Manny took the paper and looked down at what was actually a colored, but faded photograph, which she immediately recognized. It was a copy of a photograph taken the night of her high school prom more years ago than she cared to remember. Staring at the picture, something else occurred to Manny. The dress she'd worn in the photo had an eerie resemblance to the gown the girl now held in her hands.

A haze filled Manny's gaze when she looked at the girl again. The child had large brown eyes, slanted slightly and shadowed by lengthy black lashes. Her neck was long and slender, her figure tall and slight. Well-defined cheekbones and a small turned down mouth highlighted golden bronzed skin that glowed with the bloom of youth. A cloud of black hair framed her small, oval face. Styled into thick and large curls, the hair had probably been hard to manage before a perm had relaxed it into its current tamed state. The girl looked to be in her mid to late teens and she was beautiful.

"Are you my mother?"

She heard the question, but thrust back in time, every single thought fled as the blood drained from Manny's face. Her heart began an erratic beat and she raised her hand and began patting her chest as if she could somehow ease the sudden pain. She continued to stare at the girl as her mind took her back into her past—to Boulder Community Hospital.

Manny lay in a bed groaning with the agony of labor and pleading with the doctor, her parents, or anyone who would listen to take the pain away. Next, she remembered sitting in the doctor's office listening to the doctor explain that her daughter had died in the birthing canal, choked to death by the umbilical cord that had, for months, sustained her life. Finally, she saw herself seated in a hard metal chair surrounded by a small crowd of people. In front of her, in an open grave, she saw a tiny white casket.

"Are you Manette Walker…my mother?"

The question shattered the ghostly images. Her mind, abruptly released from its hold on the past, dropped Manny back into the reality of the present. Still startled, it took great effort on her part to still the shakes rattling her body. From somewhere, she found her voice. "Honey, what is your name?"

The girl glanced nervously around the shop. "A-April. April Martin."

Manny reached for April's hand and after lifting it, she placed the photograph in the middle of her palm. "April," she began with a sad shake of her head. "My name is Manette, but I'm sorry, I am not your mother."

April's face immediately crumpled and large, fat tears filled her eyes and dripped down her face. "But I've been looking for her for such a long time and I was sure that this time I was right."

A loud sob erupted from her mouth and Manny's maternal instinct swiftly kicked in. She pulled the girl into her arms and hugged her tightly. Without speaking, she let April cry, rubbing the slender back trembling beneath her hands while trying to think of a way to ease a burden that had obviously been carried for a long time. When April quieted, Manny walked her to the counter. She pulled several tissues from a box and tenderly wiped away the tears on April's face. She kept her arm around the girl's waist as she led her toward a grouping of chairs set off to the side. Manny helped April sit, then lowered herself into the chair beside her.

Taking her hand, Manny took a deep breath. "April, where did you get that photograph?"

April looked positively glum as she stared unseeing straight in front of her. "My grandma gave it to me," she said, dully. "It was in a box with some pictures of me as a baby."

Manny nodded. "Did your grandmother tell you anything about the people in this picture?"

April lowered her chin to her chest. "No." Her saddened face finally turned to Manny. "I didn't even know her until a few months before she died. About two years ago, I was in my yard talking to one of my friends when this older lady got out of a car and crossed the street to my house. For a minute, she just stared me and my friend. Then she told me that she was my grandmother and that the people I lived with weren't my real parents. She handed me the box before she went back to her car."

"What did you do?"

"I ran into the house and told my mother." April's shoulders heaved as she sighed. "For a long time, my mom didn't say anything. Then she ran from the room and locked herself in her bedroom. When my father came home, I told him and he went to see my mother. I heard them arguing and about an hour later; they called me up to their room. When I got there, they told me that I was adopted."

April looked so unhappy, that for a moment, Manny wished that she could tell the child what she wanted to hear. Although she had no doubt that Derrick Lewis had fathered the girl—April looked just like him—she wasn't the mother and—

Manny's thoughts skidded to a halt. She wasn't the mother! Her gaze swung to April. "Honey, how old are you?"

"I'll be seventeen next month. On the tenth," she answered, rubbing a hand over her wet eyes

Manny gasped. Seventeen! April was only a few months older than her daughter, had she lived, would have been. Her eyes suddenly enlarged as another thought cleared her mind of the cobwebs that had fogged her thinking since meeting April.

April Martin was almost seventeen and she'd been born on June tenth—the same date of the same year Manny would have taken Derrick Lewis as her husband. Manny's eyes narrowed and a frown marred her brow. Christopher would probably say that the evidence she had, April's resemblance to Derrick and the date of her birth, was, at best, circumstantial. However, Manny couldn't help thinking that April's birth was the likely reason Derrick hadn't shown up for their wedding.

April pointed to Derrick's image in the photo. "Do you know where he is?"

"No, I don't." Manny abruptly rose to her feet. "April, I know you've been searching for your mother and father for a long time and I'm sorry that things didn't work out with me like you hoped. But I'm not your mother, and I think you should probably go on home now."

April stood, too. "I can't," she said, her voice a whisper almost too quiet to be heard.

"Why not?"

April hemmed and hawed before blurting out, "I told my mom that I was coming here to buy a dress for the prom and it's tomorrow night. I have to take a dress home with me."

Manny forced a smile to her lips. "Okay," she said. "Then let's find you a dress."

"I've already found the one I want; the yellow one." April reached into the pocket of her jeans. "I just don't know if I have enough money to buy it." She handed Manny the wad of bills.

Her heart still racing with newfound knowledge, Manny counted the money as she unfolded the bills. April was definitely short, by a lot, but the child had been through enough for one day and nothing in the world could have made Manny tell her that. Fairytale endings were elusive enough, but this was one time when she could make a dream come true.

She looked up with a genuine smile. "I believe that you have just enough," she said. "Why don't you take the dress and go to the dressing room to see if it fits. If not, we'll need to see a special friend of mine who can work magic with a needle and thread. By the time she's finished, this gown will fit as if it was specially made just for you and you'll be the prettiest girl at the dance."

April crossed to the counter and picked up a pen. When she returned, she handed Manny a piece of paper. "That's my phone number," she stated. "Just in case you remember anything about the man in the picture."

Manny could only stare at the paper in her hands. As April walked away, she said, "Thank you, Ms. Walker. And I'm sorry that you're not my mother."

Christopher had been sitting at his desk when the anonymous call came into the station. After dealing with Calvin, returning home and to his bed had been out of the question since he was now fully awake. He'd tried to call Manny earlier, and after learning that she'd stepped out to make a run to the bank, he immersed himself in the never ending pile of paperwork and reports he never seemed to have time to complete.

The call had led the police to an abandoned warehouse where, on the top floor, they'd found the beaten, bloodied, and dead body of Anthony Chavez hanging from a hook in the ceiling. Christopher had barely recognized Anthony's face. Apparently not satisfied with the abuse he'd undergone prior to his death, someone had put a bullet into the back of his head. With the other officers, Christopher had walked his way through the crime scene, feeling little remorse over the demise of Anthony Chavez.

Benito had called Christopher to inform him of Anthony's death and to request that they meet right away. They sat at the bar counter of a small club on the city's northwest side. Since it was still light outside, there weren't many people in the establishment and those in attendance probably filled their days and nights there trying to drink away the problems of life.

The quiet sobs from the little man seated at his side drew Christopher's glance. "Why'd they do Ant'ny like that, Jerome? What they did to my brother was wrong. Why, Jerome? Why'd they kill my brother like that?"

Christopher had no answers, except that Anthony Chavez had chosen a profession that had little to no chance of leading to a ripe old age. Most likely, he'd tried to rip off Santangelo, and had paid the ultimate price for his betrayal. As ludicrous as it sounded, even among robbers, thieves, and drug lords there was a code of honor. "I don't know, Benito. Maybe they were trying to make an example of him."

Benito looked up from the glass in his hand. "An example for what, Jerome? Ant'ny was the best division chief that organization had. He treated them right, and made sure they always got their cut. It wasn't his fault things started falling apart."

Christopher quirked his brow. Benito was probably correct there. Though Christopher had increased the pressure on the organization by having known associates arrested or paving the way for a bust every now and then, someone else was responsible for hijacking the truckloads of merchandise.

Briefly, he wondered if that was the reason Anthony no longer walked among the living. He also wondered why Benito had called him. They were not close, and he'd had only one meeting with Anthony. He didn't have to wait long for his answer.

Benito sniffled up his tears and signaled for another drink. When the bartender completed the task, he twisted on the stool to face Christopher. "I'm supposed to tell you that the run is postponed. No one knows when it will be rescheduled, but someone will get in touch with you when it's time."

Christopher thought about that, then asked the obvious question. "Will that someone be you?"

Benito shrugged. "Don't know. Depends on when it's supposed to happen, and I don't care, 'cause I gotta bury my brother."

Benito was so distraught that Christopher decided to take a chance. In his state of mind, maybe Benito would spill something useful. "Have the police arrested anyone for killing Anthony?"

Benito looked up, his crestfallen face full of sadness. "No, and they don't have any leads, but there's talk that it was a mob hit." Benito drained his glass and hopped down from the stool. "But I know, and the people who killed my brother will pay."

Christopher stood, too. "I wouldn't do anything foolish, Benito. If the police think the mob rubbed out Anthony, they are going to be looking at you, too, and it's a sure bet that they will find evidence of Anthony's connection to the organization. If that happens, all hell is going to break loose. If it was the organization that ordered the hit, it might be best if you laid low for a while. Maybe even go somewhere, leave the state and take a vacation, because they might come after you, too."

Benito shucked up his pants and stood a little taller. "Until the people who killed my brother are made to pay, I'm not gonna go nowhere."

Christopher shrugged, but didn't respond. They moved toward the door, Christopher grabbing Benito by the arm when the man stumbled. He'd done what he could to warn Benito Chavez. They weren't friends, so there would be no love lost if Benito decided to ignore his advice. At most, it would cost Benito his life. At the very least, the man was destined to pull a long haul in a federal prison.

Unlocking his front door, Christopher smiled when he entered the house. The air smelled of chicken, fried if he wasn't mistaken, and his ears picked up the lovely sound of Manny's voice as she sang along with the radio. Listening to her, he leaned back on the door and closed his eyes, letting a serene calm flood his being for the first time that day.

Dealing with Calvin and investigating the crime scene had been tiring. The meeting with Benito Chavez even more so, and he still had his shift to pull that evening. That, however, was several hours away. Right now, Christopher didn't want to think about anything except Manny and holding her in his arms.

He headed for the kitchen, stopping in the doorway when he saw Manny not only singing to the music, but also swinging her slender hips to the beat. She wore one of his old police shirts, it's bottom stopping just below hers as she moved around his kitchen as if she belonged there, which was something Christopher couldn't deny. Manny did belong, not just in his kitchen, but in his heart as well.

He fixed his gaze on the bare legs, long and brown, stretching beneath the material of his shirt and wondered if Manny wore anything underneath the garment. That thought raised his pulse. Unable to confine himself to observing the sensual motions of her body, he quickly crossed the floor. "Hi, gorgeous," he said, wrapping his arms around Manny from behind.

She leaned back against his body and accepted the kiss he readily placed on her lips.

He lifted his head. "Something sure smells good."

"I'm making chicken," Manny said, "with mashed potatoes and gravy on the side, corn and, oh—would you like peas or green beans with your meal this evening?"

"Either. I missed lunch and I'm hungry as a bear."

"Then perhaps I'll make both. We're also having biscuits and apple pie for desert."

Christopher's eyes lit up with anticipation. "You made a home-made apple pie? Where did you find the time?"

"Uh, it's not exactly homemade, but according to the write-up on the box, it's supposed to taste like it is."

Christopher chuckled. "What's the occasion?"

"No occasion," Manny replied. "I just felt like cooking, that's all."

"Hmmm," he toned. "You just felt like cooking and nothing happened today that helped put you in the mood. Interesting."

Manny stepped away and turned to the stove. She turned over the pieces of meat frying in the pan. "Okay, Chris. Something did happen today, but I thought we could discuss it over dinner."

Derrick Lewis immediately popped into Christopher's mind. Had Manny already met with the man? "We can discuss it now, especially if it has anything to do with Derrick Lewis."

She raised the cooking fork and pointed it at him. "We'll discuss it over dinner, which is almost ready. Why don't you wash up."

"But, Manny—"

"But Manny nothing. And when you're done, set the table."

Christopher grinned. At times, Manette Walker sounded just like his mother. "Yes, ma'am," he said as he headed out of the room.

Manny laid her fork on the side of her plate and leaned back in her chair. She observed Christopher's total involvement with his plate and smiled with satisfaction. The big occasions were nice, but it was the small, day-to-day activities, shared with the ones you loved that really mattered most. "Chris," she said, when he paused to reach for another biscuit.

He peeked up. "Yeah."

"I met someone today."

He reached for his knife and the butter. "Who?"

"A teenaged girl, who I believe is Derrick's daughter."

Surprise lifted his features before his brows came together in question. "Derrick's daughter?"

"Uh huh. She's been coming into the shop for several weeks now and I thought she'd come to look at prom dresses. She never asked for assistance, and she always left when any of the sales associates approached her. Today, I approached her and instead of leaving, she showed me a photograph. It was one Derrick and I had taken the night of my high school prom. She also asked if I was her mother."

Christopher's brows furrowed deeper. "But you said that your child died."

"She did, and I explained to April that I was not her mother. But I'm sure that Derrick is her father."

Christopher pushed his plate away, his appetite gone. "I don't understand why she would think you were her mother, Manny. Where did she get this picture? Why do you think that Derrick is her father?"

"She said her grandmother gave her the picture, and other than the fact that April looks like him, I don't have any actual proof that Derrick Lewis is her father. But there is more to this story," Manny said. "I think I also know why Derrick didn't show up for the wedding."

Giving him an opportunity to digest what she'd already told him, Manny picked up a chicken leg and took a bite. Chewing slowly, she watched a myriad of expressions flit across his face. When his features settled into skeptical acceptance, she continued. April Martin will be seventeen this year and she was born on June tenth." Manny raised a brow, then continued eating her meal.

June tenth. Something about that date was important and Christopher's mind spun into investigative action. He began by separating the facts Manny had just presented to him, dissecting each statement and rearranging them into a conclusion that could piece together neatly, if the evidence supported it. Interesting, he thought. However, he did have one other question. He looked up to see a gleam in Manny's eye. "You're testing me, aren't you?"

"Yes, Detective Mills. So, let's hear it."

"Well, I could draw this out and fit all the pieces together for you, but you've already done that, so I'll skip to the chase. You've decided that April Martin is the daughter of Derrick Lewis, who decided to skip his own wedding seventeen years ago to be present for his child's birth by another woman, right?"

"That *is* what I was thinking, but I'm still not sure about one thing."

"Why April doesn't have her father's last name?"

Manny rose from her chair and picked up her plate. "No, that's not it. April also told me that she was adopted."

"Then what?" he asked, rising, too.

"I'm not sure what to do about it. I haven't called Derrick, and since I believe I already know why he pulled his disappearing act, there's really no reason to see him at all, unless it's to tell him that his daughter is looking for him."

Christopher followed her to the kitchen. Both placed their plates on the counter and returned to the table to clean up the remnants of their meal. "That has nothing to do with you and you don't need to see him to tell him that. Call him and let him know that his child wants to see him. If he wants to see her, he can arrange it. Then again, if he put his daughter up for adoption, he probably didn't want her, and he may not want her to find him."

"But we don't know that for sure, Chris."

"You're right, we don't. But it really doesn't concern us. You have enough to deal with without taking on another problem, especially one that involves Derrick Lewis."

Manny let their conversation drop and together they cleaned kitchen. He related the incident with Calvin Saunders while she listened. Her mind, however, continued to review her options regarding Derrick and April, and by the time they retired to the bedroom that night, Manny had reached a decision. She was going to help April get in touch with her father.

Three hours later, Christopher opened his eyes. He glanced at the clock, dropped a light kiss on Manny's brow, and shifted his body away from her warmth. Leaving the bed, he showered quickly and pulled on his nightly uniform. Leaving the house, he secured the premises, climbed inside the car and started the Jeep. It wasn't until he'd entered the station and sat at his desk that Christopher remembered he hadn't told Manny that his weekend plans had changed.

CHAPTER 12

Manny Walker was not in a good mood. It was just a shame that the three people standing in front of her didn't know that. Her eyes narrowed dangerously as she glared at the three models. "I don't know who told you people that I was the information desk, but let me correct that impression for you right now. Wendy, I am not your dresser so I don't know what outfit you're supposed to wear next. Reggie, you're going to have to keep up with your own things as I believe you were warned in the information sent to you not to bring stuff like CD players in the first place. And I have no idea what you are even talking about, Jennifer. So all of you do me a huge favor and get the hell away from me!"

The models scrambled, and spotting the only unclaimed chair in the room, Manny dragged it into an out-of-the-way corner and dropped onto its hard plastic seat.

This was nothing short of complete and utter mayhem. At least, it would appear that way to anyone lucky enough not to have voluntarily agreed to become a part of the pandemonium that had exploded backstage at the Fillmore Auditorium.

Why? Why? Why had she agreed to do this again when she'd promised herself that she would never do another one of these fundraiser/fashion shows?

Every year, it was the same thing: Jordon Banks called Shelby, who then committed them both to doing the show for ROBY. One of these days, she was going to kill Shelby Reeves. Better yet, she should probably use that time getting her own head examined for letting her friend talk her into doing another one of these things.

The whole backstage area teemed with activity. Models, only partially transformed into the beautiful beings they would shortly become, waited by racks bearing their names and photos as dressers yanked down the clothing she'd spent hours labeling. Others wearing tee shirts and jeans, their hair twisted, curved, curled, and sprayed into spectacularly styled conglomerations, lounged on stools or whatever else was available for a few minutes of rest. Some chatted with other models, some meditated or read, and still others had their ears blocked by headphones in an attempt to remain focused and drown out the sounds of the chaos.

Manny couldn't help chuckling under her breath when she saw Manfred Stokes, the owner of a local jewelry store. His face had turned redder than the jacket on his back as he ran around in a total panic, frantically trying to account for the three hundred thousand dollars' worth of jewelry he'd loaned for the evening. On the back wall, a crew of twenty people and assistants worked on models' hair and makeup while callers shouted out names for the lineup and tried to organize those ready to make their entrance onto the runway.

Shelby's influence in the fashion world had garnered the appearance of some of the hottest designers in the world. Bonga Bhengu was there wearing braids, a jungle print jacket and sandals, overseeing his collection of colorful denim wear. Everett Hall had brought some of his classic suits for men. The Phat Farm had a few samples for the hip-hop crowd and a member of the local press was interviewing the male force behind Lady Enyce. Even B. Michael, world recognized as one of the leading couture accessories and millinery designers, had sent his good wishes for a fabulous show.

Of course, no show produced by Shelby would be complete without Tyrone Brooks, who'd brought his designs with him on the plane. At the moment, he was posing for photos with one hand tucked inside his traditional gray double-breasted suit. The interview he'd done for *Harper's* a few years ago had taken the name Tyrone Brooks and his label to the international level.

For the fifth time in as many years, Manny swore that she would never do another show. She'd said the same thing last year and the years before that. Yet, here she was again, with aching feet, a headache, and trying to cool her temper enough so that she wouldn't accidentally punch out one of those prancing models.

She laid the clipboard in her hand across her lap, slid her feet out of a pair of three-inch heeled clogs, and rubbed her tired eyes. The clipboard fell to the floor when she pulled her aching right foot into her lap and massaged the sole with both hands while taking in the colorful array of madness surrounding her.

"Manny-girl, you look like you got the low-down dirty blues. Why so sad, girlfriend?"

"Because I'd rather be anywhere but here, Tyrone. Every year it's the same thing, a bunch of ego-inflated models and designers who have nothing better to do than make my life miserable."

"You've been in this game long enough to know that you simply smile, pat them on the head, and move on."

"Well, just maybe I'd like someone to pat me on the head and give me a smile. Better yet, I'd skip the pat and take a hug."

Tyrone pulled her up from the chair and quickly accommodated her request. "Still manless and looking, Manny-girl?"

A pall of sadness entered Manny's eyes. No, she wasn't manless, but for all she knew, she very well could be. Christopher had left sometime during the night and she hadn't heard from him all day. Every time she'd thought to pick up the phone and call him, some problem had cropped up that she'd had to deal with right away.

Now it was too late. Christopher was gone and couldn't contact her, but it didn't stop her from hoping that he would. Thoughts of what he might be doing weighed heavily on her mind, and she was so afraid that something had already happened that it was all she could do not to break down in tears. She shared none of this with Tyrone, though. Rather, a characteristic twinkle lit her eyes as she resurrected her shield. "Still manless and looking, Ty-baby?"

"Touché, girlfriend. But you know God don't like ugly, and you should be happy about the good deed that you are doing. Once again, we're about to fill ROBY's coffers, which means that a lot of deserving boys and girls will be the beneficiaries of that wonderful program."

"I am well aware that this is for a good cause, Tyrone, but I'm tired of bitchy models, the rush of getting everything coordinated, and the screw-ups that come with the job. All the people out front see are handsome men and beautiful women draped in expensive, glitzy clothes and the excitement they generate when they slink down the runway to the joy of overzealous photographers. They never think about the people like me who keep this madhouse from crashing down around our ears. I don't know why I put myself through this craziness."

Tyrone crouched down and placed a tender kiss on her brow. "Ah, love. Don't you?"

"Yeah, I do. It's because I'm an idiot who can't say no to my best friend and business partner!"

"Shel is a love, isn't she? However, that's not why you're here, Manny. You're here because like the rest of us, you can't stay away from the glamour, the spotlights, or the action. This is fashion and fashion is fun."

"Not for me, it isn't. All I ever see is the chaos backstage and when I get home, all I have for my trouble is swollen feet and an aching back."

Tyrone sighed and rose to his full height. He pulled Manny up from her chair. "Manny-girl, I've heard enough, and tonight we're going to do something about that."

"Wait, Tyrone," Manny said, trying to snatch her hand back. "I can't go with you. I'm supposed to be checking up on the models and making sure the sound equipment is ready to go."

"Not tonight, Manny-girl. The sound crew knows what they are supposed to do and there are enough assistants running around back here to aid a truckload of models. You're coming with me because tonight you're going to see the other side."

One hour later, Manny stood at the back of the current line of models waiting to make their entrance onto the runway. She shooed away the hand of an assistant patting a powder puff over her face and tried to will down the fluttering that had caused every nerve in her body to dance in anticipation. She glanced at Tyrone, who stood just to her right, a huge triumphant grin splitting his face.

"Manny-girl, you look lovely."

She returned a trembling smile. "Thanks, Ty, but I don't know about this. Are you sure you want me to model this dress? What if I trip or—"

Tyrone lifted and patted her hand. "Manny, you're going to do fine. Now, get out there and strut your stuff as if you belong on that stage, and do my gown and me justice."

Manny would have responded, except the rocking beat of Stevie B's "Spring Love" suddenly filled the air, sending her already ozone-driven state even higher.

"Go," the caller announced.

Manny didn't move.

The caller shoved her from the back. "Go! You're next, so let's move!"

Manny stumbled forward a few steps and stopped. She closed her eyes and took a deep breath. She had no business on or anywhere near a runway, but Tyrone had faith in her. In her head, she told herself that fashion was a world of smoke and mirrors. The model was the instrument used to portray the garment in a positive and glamorous light.

She might not have the statuesque height required in this business or a slinky waltz to take her down the runway and back, but Manny had never been one to back away from a challenge. She could do this.

An intensity in the air and an energy born of the rush of adrenaline heightened both her senses and awareness. Manny walked from behind the curtain and a murmur ran through the crowd. When the warmth of a spotlight hit her, she steadied her nerves and pasted a smile on her lips.

Hiding her fear, Manny moved toward the catwalk and pretended that she was a princess at the ball, just like the ones in the fairytales her mother had read to her as a child.

Several hours later, Manny burst through her front door. When Christopher pulled into her driveway, she slammed the door shut, turned the locks, and hooked all the chains. She was halfway up the staircase when she heard his key in the lock and the door open.

"Manny, the chains are on."

She ran back down the stairs. "I know that, Christopher."

"Come on, Manny. Stop messing around. Take the chains off and let me in."

"No! You are not even supposed to be here!"

"Manny, they rescheduled the job until a later date. I tried to call you earlier to let you know, but I couldn't get through to you."

"You ever heard of leaving a message, Christopher Mills? Even if you couldn't reach me, you could have left a message. Besides, that is not what this is about."

She heard him exhale. "I know, Manny, and I'm sorry. For the tenth time, I am very sorry about what happened at the fashion show. It wasn't my intention to embarrass you. I thought that you were in trouble and I was trying to help."

"Some help you turned out to be," Manny muttered, as her mind dredged up the incident in living color for her to relive. There she was walking down the runway and concentrating on trying to look as if she belonged on the stage. She'd made it to the end of the walk and executed a near perfect turn when the audience suddenly went wild.

Manny had assumed their loud screams were in appreciation of the beautiful, lavender ball gown. The next thing she knew, Christopher had jumped up on stage, tackled her to the floor, and begun stomping on her dress. Dried-grass of the same lavender color fringed the hem of the ball grown. What Manny hadn't known at the time was that when she turned, the hem of the dress had accidentally brushed the top of the one of the small votive candles lining the runway.

Christopher had stomped out the tiny flame, partially ripping the bodice from the skirt. He'd also pulled Manny into his arms and yanked up her dress to ascertain if she'd been hurt. After satisfying himself that she was okay, he'd lifted her leg and kissed her calf right there on stage.

Some in the audience had gotten more than they paid to see and much more than she had ever shown outside of her bedroom.

Luckily, neither she nor anyone else had been hurt, except, perhaps, Tyrone, who'd almost cried when he saw the remains of his gown. And of course, her self-esteem had taken a sharp dive into the basement. While she could appreciate his need to serve and protect, she could have killed Christopher Coltrane Mills for making a complete fool out of her.

"What was that, Honey-V?"

"Nothing! Just go home, Christopher."

"Not until you let me in. What about that never-going-to-sleep-mad-at-each-other thing, Manny?"

"I'm not mad!" And she wasn't. Her pride was injured, her feelings bruised, and, because of him and his antics, her butt was awfully sore. But she wasn't mad.

The door closed, and Manny waited. She knew that Christopher wouldn't give up that easily and she tried to figure out what he was doing, but for the life of her, she couldn't imagine what was happening on the other side of that door.

She got her answer a couple of minutes later, when the door re-opened. Manny watched in shock as a large pair of black cutters slipped through the door and neatly snapped the security chains in half.

Christopher pushed the door open fully and stepped inside. "Don't ever try to lock out a cop," he said with a grin.

Manny growled deep in her throat. "You're going to pay to have those replaced," she said, shooting him a glare hot enough to singe his skin.

Christopher set the cutter against the wall by the door. "Not a problem, gorgeous. They'll be fixed tomorrow." He slowly moved in her direction, his eyes narrowed in amusement. "Now, back to our argument. Apologize to me."

Manny's mouth dropped opened. "Apologize to you. What for!"

"For locking me out of this house and for being mad at me for no reason."

"You'll get no apology from me tonight. If anyone should be apologizing, it is you, Christopher Mills." She raised a fist in warning. "And if you come any closer, I'm gonna blacken your eyes."

He stopped moving, noted the mutinous look on her face and the tiny balled up hand, and burst out laughing. It was a laugh that came from deep within and bounced off the walls of her living room. Did she really think that she could inflict any kind of damage with that thing?

Manny's glare turned murderous. "And stop laughing at me," she said. She could find nothing funny about the entire evening. Yet, watching him find humor at her expense, she had to work to keep her own lips from tilting upward. After all, it wasn't every day that a person could claim to be the cause of a blaze that could have burned the house down.

"I'm sorry," he said working to bring himself under control. "But Manny, you have to admit, this a pretty funny situation. I risk my life in order to save yours, and now you are standing here with a raised fist in an attempt to threaten me." He closed one eye in a saucy wink. "I've arrested you before and I'd have no problem hauling you downtown again." He moved in her direction once more. "Now kiss me and let's make up."

She backed away. "You come any closer and I'm going to let you have it, Christopher. I mean it."

He kept moving. "If you hit me, I *will* arrest you. How do you think it will look to have the papers report that a local officer arrested his fiancée for physical assault? I'd be the laughing stock of the department. You wouldn't want that, would you, gorgeous?"

"Why should I care? Because of you, I'm already the laughing stock of Denver."

"Manny, I was trying to help and I'm sorry for embarrassing you. Why don't you come over here and let me make it better."

Her legs hit the couch and she sat. When she shook her head and then lowered her face into her hands, Christopher hurried to her side.

"Don't cry, Manny. I wasn't laughing at you. I really wasn't."

Her head snapped up and she frowned at him. "Crying?" Manny rolled her eyes. "I'm not crying, Christopher. I'm trying to figure out how I'm ever going to show my face in public in this city ever again."

"It's not as bad as all that, Honey-V. In fact, quite a few people came up to me after the show to thank me for an entertaining evening."

She slanted a look at him. "They were being facetious, Christopher. For a little over twenty-five dollars, they got an auction, a showcase of fashion by internationally famous designers, and a peepshow. I'd say that they got their money's worth. Wouldn't you?"

He cupped her chin in the palm of his hand and with his thumb, softly stroked her cheek. "Manny, this isn't like you. Since when did you ever care about what other people think?"

She couldn't think when he was fondling her. She gazed into the dark liquid of his eyes and her insides shifted. She absolutely loved it when Christopher caressed her like this. His touch was so strong and yet so soft at the same time, and she was fairly certain that Christopher knew what he was doing to her. Manny closed her eyes, and right before her insides dissolved into a gooey mess, she put up a valiant fight to hang on to her resistance by leaping to her feet.

"I don't care. But you don't understand, Christopher. Tonight was…well…tonight was special. When Tyrone dressed me in that beautiful, beautiful gown, for the first time in my life I felt like the princess that my family always said that I was. I was Sleeping Beauty, and Cinderella, and Snow White all rolled up into one. I was Queen Nefertiti and Queen Cleopatra standing in front of the throne while everyone else bowed in deference to me." Manny plopped down on the couch and pushed out her lips in a pout. "And then you jumped up on the stage and ruined it."

To anyone else listening, the things Manny said might have sounded nonsensical. But Christopher knew how serious she was and everything she'd said he'd taken into his heart and tried to make sense of it. He reached for her hand and drew Manny into his lap. "Manny Walker, I'm not even going to pretend that I know how that mind of yours works half the time. All I know is that I love you, and regardless of what you think, you are a queen. My beautiful queen."

His lips closed over hers in a sensual seal that bonded them together for a lifetime. Manny melted against his chest, leaning into

Christopher and the kiss. She was a queen, his queen and for the rest of her life, she'd take care of Christopher, her king.

Laughter filled the air around the table where Shelby, Starris, Maxi, Pamela, and Manny sat having lunch on the day after the fashion show. Manny sat back so the waitress could place her plate, concentrating on her food and not on her friends, who'd been dissecting and finding total humor in her complete humiliation during last night's show.

"Oh, my God," Pamela cried, cracking up as the words spilled from her mouth. She tucked a strand of hair behind her ears and tried, unsuccessfully, to contain her loud chortles. "I've never seen a man move so fast in my life."

"I know," Maxie threw in, although she could hardly talk either since she was laughing just as hard as Pam. "Christopher Mills saw his woman in trouble and flew through the air as if he were Superman saving Lois. I haven't seen anything that funny in a long, long time."

Normally, Manny didn't mind being the butt of her friend's jokes, but the laughter ringing out from the other women at the table had even more of a flush warming her cheeks. She ducked her head in embarrassment. "Shut up, Maxie," she grumbled under her breath. "You wouldn't think it was so funny if it happened to you."

"Sister-girl, don't you pay Maxie or Pam a bit of attention," Starris put in as she tried to replace the smile on her face with a censorious look in their direction. "They're just being silly."

"That's right," Shelby said. "You and I know that accidents sometimes happen at these affairs." Even Shelby had trouble holding back a chuckle. "And after Christopher put out the fire, the rest of the show went off without a hitch."

Maxie picked up her copy of the *Denver Post*, which contained a large photo of Manny and Christopher hugged up on the floor. "I know I wouldn't have minded rolling around on the floor with that hunk of a man. Although I didn't really see the need for Christopher to hold

Manny in his arms for as long as he did. It was obvious within a couple of seconds that there wasn't a thing wrong with her, so why did he have to hike her dress up and kiss her leg like that?"

All the women looked at Manny, as if she had the answer.

"What did Christopher say when the two of you got home?"

"Nothing I want to tell any of you, Pam."

"She hasn't even told me," Shelby said, "and I asked first thing this morning."

"In that case," Starris said, "we'll leave it alone then."

"No, we won't," Pamela said. "Inquiring minds want to know. At least this one does."

Manny's lips opened with the air that blew through them. "I *said*, I don't want to talk about it."

"Fine, I don't really care anyway. I'm just messin' with ya."

"Don't I know it," Manny grumbled, obviously annoyed.

"Guess what, guys," Maxi reached into the side pocket of the red jacket she wore and retrieved the envelope she'd put there earlier. "I received a letter from Jacci today."

"Read it," Shelby said.

Maxi opened and removed two sheets of monogrammed stationery. "Okay, it says here that Jacci and Rico are doing well, and that they are planning to come to Denver in a couple of weeks."

"Hey, maybe they'll be here in time for the People's Fair," Starris said.

Maxie shrugged. "Yeah, maybe. Anyway, she also says that she has good news to tell us."

Pamela picked up her glass of coke. "What news?"

"Doesn't say."

"I'll bet she's pregnant," Shelby stated with confidence.

Maxi asked, "What makes you say that, Shel?"

"I've been dreaming about snakes lately and I don't think it's any of you."

"Not me," Starris said. "I have my hands full with Jonathan."

"Hardly," Pamela said. "I'd need to have some action for that to happen, and nothing's been in my bed except me and Jodi for the past year." Jodi was Pamela's stuffed dog.

"I'm on the pill," Maxi added. "So no, it's not me."

Manny was looking out the window of the restaurant, thinking about the call she'd decided to make to Derrick later that day. He hadn't tried to contact her since he'd sent the roses, but then that was just like Derrick. He had taken the first step in seeking her out, but he would never come to see her in person—that would mean a confrontation, something Derrick would avoid at all costs if he could help it. He was waiting for her to make the next move, and knowing that, Manny was reassessing her decision to contact him.

"Are you?"

Her friends were staring at her again and Manny didn't have a clue as to what was going on. "Are I what, Pam?"

"Are you pregnant?"

Manny frowned. "What kind of question is that to be asking somebody all out of the blue like that?"

Shelby sighed in exasperation. "If you'd been paying attention instead of thinking about Christopher, then you'd know what was going on. And if it's not you, then it has to be Jacqueline...like I said in the first place."

"For your information, I was not thinking about Christopher."

Manny could tell by the look in her eyes and the way she pressed her lips together that Shelby didn't believe her. Not that she'd expected that she would. "What are you guys talking about anyway?"

"Jacci's pregnant, or at least that's what Shel thinks," Starris answered. "She's been having snake dreams."

"I don't know whether Jacci's pregnant or not and until she confirms it, I'm not going to worry about it." Manny lifted her hamburger, took a huge bite, and consciously focused on counting her chews thirty-two times, which helped her tune out the talk of her friends and keep thoughts of Derrick Lewis at bay.

It wasn't until the next afternoon that Manny felt she'd worked up enough courage to carry out her decision to call Derrick Lewis. As much as it unnerved her to do this, she had to. Helping April was the right thing to do. She was also honest enough to admit that she was curious about Derrick and his whereabouts for the last seventeen years.

Manny entered her office and closed the door. Moving to the desk, she retrieved her purse and the green card listing his number. Her hand shook as she picked up the receiver and dialed. The telephone rang twice. Manny took a deep breath to steady the trembles that suddenly took root in her body when she heard the sleepy-sounding voice.

"Hello."

Stunned into a lapse of thought, Manny's lashes drifted downward, shielding an emotional squall that rocked her world. That voice, so deep in its resonance and sexy in its cadence, had once been the first thing she'd wanted to hear in the morning and the last she'd wanted to hear at night. She hadn't heard it in years, and Manny fought to equalize her senses, commanding her mind to conjure up Christopher's image and his voice to replace the timbre of the one echoing in her ear. Before she could think of something to say, he spoke first.

"Manny?"

She cleared her throat, finding her voice. "Yes."

"Manny, it's D."

"D?" She groaned when she realized what she'd said. Wasn't she the one who'd placed the call? It stood to reason that she should know whose number she'd dialed.

"Manette, it's Derrick Lewis."

"Oh," Manny responded, baffled by the inane direction of their conversation.

"I'm so glad you called, Manny. I didn't think you would, but I kept hoping that you'd give me a chance to say how sorry I am and to tell you how much I still love you."

Hearing those last four words chilled Manny to the bone and with a shiver, she pulled herself together. "You don't have to explain anything, Derrick. I met April." In the silence followed, Manny wasn't sure he was still on the line. "Derrick?"

Derrick's thoughts were on how badly he'd screwed up his life in the years since he'd walked away from Manny. He'd made some bad decisions and hadn't accomplished any of the goals he and Manny had talked about when they had planned their life together. Not only had he lost the woman he loved, he'd also lost his daughter. It wasn't his fault, but it was a failure his mother had never let him forget or forgiven him for.

He had been seeking redemption when he'd hired a private detective to find Manny. According to the report, she had never married; neither had he, and in Derrick's mind that had to mean something. Hoping she'd respond, he'd sent the flowers to pave the way for a meeting. He felt that if he could talk to Manny in person, he would have a better chance of convincing her to forgive him, and of possibly even taking him back. "I'm sorry, Manny, but at the time, I didn't know what to do. April's mother showed up at my house the night before our wedding. I didn't even know Cassandra was pregnant. When she said it was mine, we argued and she went into labor." Derrick sighed. "I don't want to discuss this over the phone. Can we meet some place and talk?"

"No, we cannot."

"But you have to give me a chance to explain. And what about my child? I don't even know if we had a boy or a girl. I want to see my child!"

"We have no child, Derrick. She died, and it's not something I'm going to discuss with you. The only reason I called was to let you know that your daughter is looking for you."

"April is looking for me?"

"Yes. She wants to know why her mother and father abandoned her."

Derrick exploded and Manny cringed. "I did not abandon my child! After her mother died, they took her from me!"

Manny cringed. She had forgotten about his temper. However, she had no reason to concern herself with Derrick Lewis any longer. "May I give April your number?"

"No. I want to see you, Manny," he whined.

"I don't want to see you, but your daughter does, so I'm going to do you a favor. I'm going to give your number to April. When she calls, I hope that you will see her and provide the answers she needs. And Derrick, don't ever try to contact me again."

"Manny, please. I've said I'm sorry. I loved you, and I wanted to marry you and I wanted to be a father to our—"

Manny hung up the phone. Christopher was right. Derrick Lewis had caused enough heartache in her life. Picking up her mug, Manny went to the coffeepot and filled her cup. She took it back to her desk and sat sipping at the hot brew. Though she'd taken control of the conversation, those few minutes on the phone with Derrick had shaken her more than she cared to admit. She needed some time not only to calm her nerves, but get her thoughts together before she placed the next call.

Feeling sufficiently calm a few minutes later, she set her cup down, picked up the phone, and called April Martin. After giving the grateful girl the number where she could reach her father, Manny Walker put both people out of her mind and went back to work.

CHAPTER 13

Christopher walked into the DEA building and directly to Samuel Thomas' office. Samuel, perusing through a folder on his desk, didn't bother looking up.

"Mills," he rasped.

"Sam."

"Got any news for me?"

Christopher took one of the chairs in front of the desk. "Santangelo's in town."

That got Sam's attention. "How do you know?"

"Anthony Chavez was found up near Wheat Ridge yesterday. He wasn't breathing."

"Interesting," Sam said. "But that doesn't prove Santangelo had anything to do with it. Chavez had his hands in everybody's pocket. We need solid evidence."

"True, but the only pocket that mattered was Santangelo's."

Sam spared little sympathy for the hood. "How are the brothers taking it?"

"Benito's broken up and it's a sure bet he's already informed Juan and Luis. Nothing they can do about it though, since they're still behind bars. I'm concerned about Benito. He's seeking payback, so he may try something stupid."

Samuel coughed, then had trouble catching his breath. Bending over, he waved Christopher forward, then pulled him down by the front of his black tee. "Keep your eye on Benito," he said in a raspy whisper. "I don't want that little bastard messing up all we've accomplished so far. If he tries anything, take him out, then go after the rest. I know you want Santangelo bad, and if he's in town, this time we'll get him. But, I smell rats from the MET office to DPD. Start at the top and do a thorough sweep to the bottom. Got that?"

"Sure, Sam. Sure," Christopher agreed. "Let me help you up." He helped Sam sit back in the chair.

"And another thing, Mills."

"What's that," Christopher asked, his eyes and voice full of concern over the ashen appearance of Sam's face.

"Call 911. I think I'm having a heart attack."

Christopher Mills did not like hospitals. The place was too quiet, the building too sterile. The medicinal odor was beginning to make him nauseous, and he was tired of waiting. He dropped his head to the back of the chair in which he sat. His friend was lying in one of those sterile rooms and no one had come to tell Christopher anything. He didn't know if Sam was dead or alive, and if Sam didn't make it, Christopher knew he would have to complete their assignment alone.

Though he'd worked as an undercover detective for the DPD, a year ago, Christopher had received a special appointment. Sam was his contact, and no one, with the exception of Sam, who'd also received a special appointment, had any inkling that Christopher was really working for the Feds.

The Attorney General had classified Denver as a High Intensity Drug Trafficking Area or HIDTA. His eyebrow had raised over the numerous times local law enforcement had requested MET assistance in stopping the flow of drugs through the area. While illegal drug activity always declined significantly after a deployment, any success in stemming the tide quickly eroded within a few months after the operation closed. His office had received another request for assistance, which had reinforced his suspicions that someone was aiding and abetting a known trafficking operation in the Rocky Mountain region.

Christopher's service record reflected outstanding on-the-job performance, and his work as an undercover detective revealed a knowledge of the local scene that could not be matched. As soon as he'd learned of

Dexter Santangelo's involvement, he had eagerly accepted the assignment. With Sam's assistance, Christopher was to clean the local house of MET and identify any and all agents or local police officers found to be in association with known criminals. If they apprehended Santangelo in the process, the Feds certainly wouldn't mind taking credit for bringing down another drug lord.

Christopher pounded his fist on the arm of the chair and surged to his feet. This waiting was almost unbearable. He headed for the hallway, intending to find somebody that could tell him something. He stopped when he saw Charlene Thomas burst through the doors with a cry of hysteria on her lips and a flood of tears pouring from her eyes.

He rushed to her side, nodding at the two officers with her, a signal that he would take over as he took Charlene into his arms.

Charlene gripped the front of his shirt and turned tear soaked eyes upward. "Where is he, Chris? Is Sam still alive?"

He walked her toward the waiting area. "They haven't said, but I think he's still alive. Otherwise, I'd have heard something by now. Wait here. I'll go see if I can find out anything more." He returned a few minutes later with the news that the doctor was in with Sam and that he would be out to talk to them as soon as his examination was complete.

Charlene opened her mouth to respond, but only managed a wail before she buried her face in his chest.

That was how Manny found them when she entered the waiting area looking for Christopher. He'd called her at the shop to tell her about Sam and though he hadn't asked her to come, she'd known from the sound of his voice that Christopher needed her to be there with him.

Now, and for the second time, she observed him with his arms around another woman, the same woman she'd seen him with before, if the slender build and brunette hair softly curved around her shoulders was an indication.

Manny swallowed, remembering how she'd jumped to conclusions the first time. They had since made up, and she had not asked about the woman nor had Christopher volunteered any information. This time, Manny wanted answers. She walked into the room, directly to their side and cleared her throat. "Christopher?"

He looked up and the shock of seeing Manny spread across his face. "Manny, I, uh, I didn't know you'd come down here."

"Obviously."

He released Charlene and tried to take Manny into his arms. She stepped away, furious. The look on his face and the stuttered words had told her all she needed to know. Whirling away, Manny left the room and began walking back down the hallway the way she'd come. Outside the exit, she moved to the side and attempted to clear her head and her anger.

Charlene laid a hand on Christopher's arm. "Was that Manny?"

He nodded and shook his head sadly. "This is not the first time she's seen us together and while she didn't ask that I explain, it tore us apart. I have to go after her, but I don't want to leave you alone, Charlene."

"Let me talk to her, Chris. I think I can get her to listen."

Charlene found Manny leaning against the brick wall outside the building. As soon as she saw Manny, her heart went out to the young woman, who looked so desolate. She hurried forward. "Manny."

Manny raised her head and upon recognition, she turned and would have fled had she not heard the plea in Charlene's voice when she called to her again.

"Manny, please wait!"

Manny stopped and inhaled deeply before facing Charlene. "What do you want?"

"My name is Charlene Thomas, and you can't leave because Christopher needs you."

"It sure didn't look as if he needed me a minute ago. The two of you seemed to be doing quite nicely by yourselves."

"Manny, I know what you're thinking, but you are wrong. Christopher is a friend, to me and to my Sam. He was only trying to comfort me."

Manny glanced out over the parking area, agonizing over whether to believe Charlene and go to Christopher or reject the explanation and go home to stew in anger over his deception. "I saw how he was comforting you."

"Manny, please. You have to know that Chris is loyal and trustworthy and that he would never do anything to hurt you."

"I know that," Manny ground out through teeth, highly annoyed that this woman knew Christopher so well.

Charlene looked around the immediate area and spotting a cement bench, she waved her hand toward the seat. "Why don't we go over there and sit for a minute. I want to talk to you about something." She walked away, taking slow, measured steps, hoping that Manny would follow.

When Charlene moved away, Manny saw her chance to escape. However, she wanted to know what Charlene had to tell her. She crossed to the bench and sat down.

"Thank you," Charlene said with a smile that stayed on her face as she looked off into the distance, seemingly more interested in what was going on around them than in Manny.

Manny wondered if Charlene really had anything to tell her, or if this was just a ploy to set her up to hear the bad news that Christopher really had been or was being unfaithful to her. She was just about ready to tell Charlene goodbye, when the older woman began to speak.

"Sam and I have been married for twenty years. I'm from a small town in Georgia and when I married Sam, I gave up everything, my job, my friends, and, frankly, my life to be with the man I loved. When I met Sam, he was a private in the army. We moved three times in four years, dealt with every imaginable problem, and produced two wonderful children. As hard as it was, I did my best to mold myself into the perfect military wife. It wasn't until Sam came up for re-enlistment that I learned of my husband's childhood dream to become a police officer."

Manny couldn't figure out what Charlene's story had to do with her or why the woman felt the need to reveal the details of her marriage. She wanted to leave, but something held her in place. Something told her that Charlene's story was leading somewhere and that when they got there, Manny would find the message meant for her. She tuned Charlene back in.

"All during Sam's military career, I knew that if a war should break out, there was a possibility that my husband might have to put his life on the line. Fortunately, I never had to deal with that situation. Now, however, that is the reality that I live with every day. Every time Sam leaves the house, I am aware that it might be the last time I see my husband alive."

"But how do you deal with that knowledge, Mrs. Thomas?"

"If we're going to be friends, Manny, I insist that you call me Charlene."

Manny's brow crinkled with her concern over how to put her fear into words. "I don't say anything to him, but every night, when Christopher goes to work, I worry so much it almost makes me sick to my stomach. I don't understand how you've gotten through this with Sam for all these years. I love Christopher, but I don't know how to deal with this. He says he's going to retire from the force when this last case is over, and I thought I could handle it until he does. But if this case goes on any longer, I just don't know if I can."

Charlene grabbed her hands. "Manny, listen to me. Choosing a career in law enforcement is challenging in and of itself. Falling in love with a police officer is even more difficult. I know that Chris works the late shift, which means there is little time for the two of you to spend together. I have eaten more dinners alone than with Sam, and I can't even begin to tell you of the countless times I've had to play the role of a single parent. Then, there is the shift work to deal with, the missed birthdays, holidays, and cancelled appointments. Add all of that to your own emotional stress and his, and you can understand why the divorce rate is so high among police officers."

"But you and Sam have been married for so long. How did you…? Why did you…? What did you…?" Manny tried to get her thoughts together. Questions she couldn't seem to voice jammed her mind.

"The simple answer is that Samuel Thomas loves being a cop and I love Samuel Thomas. The long answer is that I joined my life with his and pledged to do whatever it took to hold my marriage together. I won't try to lead you on by telling you that it was an easy road. It was not. It took a lot of effort, orchestrating, understanding, and compromise on my part and a little on Sam's to hold our marriage together. What helped the two of us is that early on we established some rules."

"What type of rules?"

I call them my rules of being married to Sam. Rule one: Before Sam leaves the house, we share a long and intimate hug. I tell Sam that I love him and he tells me the same. Rule two: When Sam comes home from work we kiss. After a shower and a change of clothes, he goes into his study for one hour of quiet time, no phone, no kids, and no wife. I do not know what Sam does in his study and I don't ask, because that is his time to relax and rid himself of the pressures of his day. If he needs a sounding board, he will invite me in. Otherwise, I do not go into his room. Rule three: Once Sam comes out of his room, we sit as a family and share dinner and the details of our day. Rule four: We end each day with the words 'I love you.'"

Manny frowned, thinking she must have missed something. "That's it?"

Charlene smiled. "That's it. It sounds simple, I know, but it has helped us stay together as a family and survive Sam's career in law enforcement. But that's the two of us. You and Christopher will have to decide what will work for you."

"Hopefully, I won't have to worry about it since Christopher is planning to retire."

Charlene patted her arm. "That's good, but I think that you should go to Christopher. He loves you, and right now he needs you very badly."

"Where is he?"

"Where you left him. Chris doesn't have a lot of friends, and Sam's been like a father to him. Go to him and let him know that he is not alone in this."

Manny managed a smile. "Thank you, Charlene. I'm terribly sorry about Sam and will pray that he pulls through this."

"Thank you," Charlene replied. "You're as lovely as Chris said that you were."

Reentering the hospital, Charlene went to the nurses' station, while

Manny returned to the waiting area where she found Christopher slumped over in one of the chairs.

"Christopher?"

He looked up, but the disillusionment in his eyes said that he hadn't expected her to return. "Y-you came back." He said it with hesitation, almost as if he couldn't believe that she was indeed standing in front of him.

"I came back, though I never should have left." Manny braced herself for his response, remembering the way he'd reacted the last time she'd acted impulsively without hearing his side of the story.

Christopher stood and looked down at her with kindly eyes. "You're right, Manny, you shouldn't have left, not without giving me a chance to explain. I love you, and I would never give you a reason to doubt my feelings for you."

"I know. It's just that sometimes, I get a little scared and even though I believe in my heart that you wouldn't hurt me, I can't help worrying that one day you might."

"Come here, gorgeous." She walked into his arms and he tilted her chin up so that she had no choice but to look him in the eye. "Manny, my name is Christopher Mills, not Derrick Lewis. I can't speak for him, but after all of these years, I consider myself an expert on you. You were sixteen when you met Derrick, and he was the first man who paid attention to you. We are both adults, and we came together first in friendship, then in love. Friends trust each other."

"You're right, Christopher. I know that, but—"

"So the next time you observe something that doesn't seem quite right to you, ask before you run away and give me the opportunity to tell my side of the story. It's what any friend would do."

"Hmmm, I've heard that piece of advice before."

He smiled as he lowered himself to the chair behind him and settled Manette on his lap. "From who?"

"My mother."

"Smart lady." He touched a finger to her nose. "And you should start listening to her."

"I will, but later."

"I think you should start right now."

"I can't, because if I do, then I won't be able to do this, Christopher Mills." Manny placed her hands on either side of his face and lowered her mouth to his. As soon as their lips met a fire exploded inside of Christopher. Manny was here, trying to offer him the comfort he so desperately needed while waiting for news of his friend's condition. When she touched him like this and kissed him so passionately all he could think about was finding a private place where he could ease his worry in the softness of her body. He deepened the kiss, plying his tongue in a playful duel with hers.

Neither noticed the man standing in the doorway of the waiting area or the black, beady eyes trained on them. Benito Chavez had just come from visiting his mother, who upon learning of the death of her son, had had a nervous breakdown. He was on his way out of the hospital when he walked past the waiting area in the lobby, stopped, then backtracked to the door and stared at the two people sitting in the chair holding on to each other.

He'd thought it was Jerome, but he could have sworn that he'd heard the woman call him by a different name—Christopher Mills.

Benito hurried out of view, then walked slowly toward the exit, his brows knitted together in confusion. Everyone thought that Anthony had been the brains of the outfit and that he, Benito, couldn't rub two nickels together to make a dime. How wrong they were.

He was adept at placing bugging devices in places people never dreamed of, mostly on orders from his brother. He knew a lot of things, things that Anthony hadn't even known that he knew. Like for instance, that Anthony had been skimming the profits for years, and, that Santangelo had scheduled a big meeting with all of his division chiefs in Aspen.

If Jerome Blackmon was really Christopher Mills, then who was Christopher Mills? In his car, Benito sat back in the white leather seat. Jerome had to be a plant. Thinking back on the last conversation he'd had with Jerome a.k.a. Christopher Mills, Benito realized that Jerome had been trying to tell him something when he'd suggested that Benito take a trip.

Something was going down. Probably soon, and it probably wouldn't bode well for Santangelo or the organization. He wondered if Jerome knew about the meeting. If so, he should probably try and make himself scarce.

Had he still held any loyalty for Santangelo or the organization, Benito might have thought about warning Dexter. However, as he started the car and backed out of the space, Benito only hoped that he could pull off his own surprise before the Feds arrived.

Charlene rushed into the waiting room and up to the happy couple with a wide smile on her face. "I'm going in to see Sam, but I wanted to let you know that he's going to be all right. It wasn't a heart attack. It was a stress attack. Sam has been under so much pressure lately that his blood pressure escalated. He'll be alright, but he won't be going home today. The doctors want to keep him here for a day or two to run some additional tests, just to make sure nothing else is wrong."

"I'm so happy for you," Manny said.

Christopher hugged Charlene. "I'm glad it was nothing serious."

Determination set her gaze. "Oh, it's serious, all right. From now on, Samuel Thomas is going to do exactly what the doctor and I tell him to do. No more cigarettes and no more bacon and egg breakfasts. That man is about to become more health conscious than he ever dreamed possible. I just feel sorry for you, Chris, because I'm setting you up as my watchdog. Sam will be in a perpetual bad mood, but if you see a doughnut or a cigarette in his hand, you're to slap it away. I'm counting on you."

"Sam's always in a bad mood, so I think I can handle it. Now, go and see your husband."

"Thanks for coming, and I mean that for both of you."

"You're welcome," Manny and Christopher called to Charlene's disappearing back.

CHAPTER 14

Three Saturdays later, Manny didn't feel right when she opened her eyes. The inside of her head felt fuzzy and airy as if stuffed with cotton. She touched a hand to her forehead, then held her stomach when a nauseous wave rumbled through her belly. When her stomach settled, she glanced down at Christopher.

He lay at her side and the even rise and fall of his bare, brown chest indicated that nothing had disturbed his night. Envy spread through Manny, followed quickly by irritation that he could sleep so soundly when she'd tossed and turned the entire night.

She kicked his leg. Christopher turned to his side, but he didn't open his eyes. She would have kicked him again, except that another wave in her stomach had her leaving the bed and making a mad dash for the bathroom. When the attack passed, Manny sat on the toilet and held her head in her hands.

It couldn't possibly be true. Not again, but all the signs were there. The sleeplessness, the nauseous feeling, and after doing a quick count, Manny realized that her monthly flow should have started last week. She shook her head, still not wanting to believe what her body told her was true. They had been so careful; she was on the pill and Christopher used condoms. How in the world had she gotten pregnant?

Then she remembered the night he'd told her he was leaving on his mysterious trip, and the way she'd coaxed him into making love to her. Conveniently dismissing that thought, her face screwed up in a tight frown and she looked toward the closed bathroom door.

This was his fault. He was the one always touching her and arousing her, making her so delirious that it was impossible for her to resist his advances. Irrational as her thought process was, Manny was angry. She stood shakily to her feet, left the bathroom, and got even madder when she saw that Christopher still hadn't awakened.

She marched to the bed and thumped him on his head. "Wake up, Christopher Mills!"

His eyes flashed open and Christopher's body lurched up to a sitting position. Rubbing his head, he stared at Manny as if she'd lost her mind. "What in the world is the matter with you, Manny Walker?"

As if blown by a stiff wind, Manny fell to the edge of the bed. She cast a dejected glance at Christopher, then stared at the carpet. "I'm pregnant," she mumbled.

Astonishment replaced the annoyance on his face, and for a second everything in Christopher's world stopped. Pregnant!

The word resounded in his head, rolling around and around like the echoing sound of a gong. His heart jumped and he felt just a little giddy. His mouth widened into a silly grin. For once, Christopher was sure he'd heard what Manny said. He just had to make sure that she'd said what he thought he'd heard, and he just wanted to hear her say it again. "What?"

Manny's eyes flashed fire when she looked up. That didn't stop the tear that rolled down her check. She wiped it away with a defiant swipe of her hand. "I said that I'm pregnant and it's all your fault."

He immediately reached out and tugged Manny's rigid body into a tight embrace. "Honey-V, don't cry. This is good news for us. I'm happy that you're pregnant."

Manny pushed him away. "Well, I'm not. Do you have any idea what this will mean for us?"

"Yes," he responded, still smiling. "It means that you and I are going to be parents."

"And that makes you happy?"

"Yes it does, and you should be happy, too. I've already told you that I wanted children and that I wanted to get started as soon as possible."

"Yeah, but children should be conceived after the wedding, not before. Sometimes I feel that's why my daughter didn't live, because she was conceived in sin."

"Manny Walker, sometimes you say the craziest things." He hugged her tighter, then stretched out on the bed, bringing Manny down with him. He was going to be a father and he couldn't wait to tell the guys. As happy as he was, though, he couldn't ignore the sadness he'd heard in Manny's voice. He wanted her to be as happy about their child as he was. "Manny, the death of your daughter was an accident, something that was beyond anyone's control. We conceived our child in love, not sin, and nothing is going to happen to take him or her away from us."

"Are you sure, Christopher? I couldn't take losing another child."

"I'm sure, Manny, and I'm going to be with you every single step of the way. We made this child together and we will bring our baby into the world and raise him or her together."

His kiss soothed her somewhat, but that whisper of fear within her stayed, and it would stay until she held her son or daughter in her arms and saw for herself that her child was alright. She felt Christopher's hand make rubbing motions on her stomach.

"Are you sure? About the baby, I mean."

"As sure as I can be without a doctor's confirmation."

He frowned. "Let's call your doctor now. Maybe they can see us today."

"Can't," Manny replied. "We're going to the People's Fair. Besides, it's Saturday, so the earliest we'd be able to see my doctor is on Monday."

Christopher folded his arms beneath his head and stared up at the ceiling, a happy grin on his face. "Manny Walker," he said after a few minutes of quiet, "we're going to be parents!"

She snuggled against his side, nudging until his arms came down to embrace her. "I certainly hope so, baby. I really do."

The day was sunny, warm, and ushered in by a breeze that kept the temperature from becoming too uncomfortable. It was perfect weather for the People's Fair, which was a neighborhood get-together of 300,000 plus people. Over three hundred booths featuring food, crafts, and information, as well as eighty-nine local musical acts on six stages throughout the park were on hand for the enjoyment of those in attendance.

The fair was sponsored by Capitol Hill United Neighborhoods, Inc. or CHUN, a neighborhood association devoted to preserving and improving the past, present, and future of the Greater Capitol Hill area. Held at Civic Center Park on Broadway and Colfax Avenues, the fair attracted visitors of all races from all over the state.

Manny, who'd been studying the enormous floral gardens through-out the park and 'borrowing' ideas for her own gardens, sent another longing glance toward the booth to her right. The aroma of smoked turkey legs filled the air and her mouth watered at the prospect of sink-ing her teeth into the juicy and tasty meat.

Her problem: She'd been eating all day and had just finished off a three-tiered ice cream cone. And that after polishing off a large ear of roasted corn, a funnel cake heavily dusted with powdered sugar, and licorice she kept swiping from the stash in Christopher's pocket. Unable to resist the alluring smell of grilling meat, she turned to Christopher. "Baby—"

"Say no more," he said, reaching for the wallet in the back pocket of a pair of beige shorts he'd worn with a sky blue polo shirt and black loafers. He handed over a twenty, then watched the sway of Manny's hips as she moved away to the booth. She looked adorable in the white one-piece, shorts outfit with a pink tee underneath. Her legs were bare and she had flat white sandals on her feet. Though she wouldn't be able to wear the curve-hugging outfit much longer, Christopher could hardly wait to see her stomach swollen with his child.

"Hope you brought along a lot cash, Mills," Phillip said with a laugh. "Because that lady's going to eat you into the poorhouse today."

"I don't believe it," Jacqueline said, watching Manny take her place in line. "Don't tell me she's going to eat one of those, too."

"Yeah," Maxie said. "Sister-girl's been eating all day. One would think she'd be full by now."

"If I didn't know better...," Pamela said, forcefully pulling her gaze away from the handsome man standing too close to her side for comfort. His name was Vance Caldwell, and he was a friend of Shelby and Nelson. According to Shelby, he was also an author who'd left his ranch in

Midvale to come to Denver for a few weeks to conduct research for his latest project. Pamela wasn't sure what it was about the man that attracted and held her attention, but nevertheless, attracted she was. He had to be at least seven feet tall, with nut-brown skin, gorgeous gray eyes, and a long straight nose that sat in the middle of a clean-shaven face.

His hair was thick, dark brown and curly, and the dimple in his chin, as well as the massive build of his body only served to heighten her awareness of him. He was definitely handsome, in a rugged sort of way; and if she was reading the signals correctly, Vance appeared to like her, too. "If I didn't know any better," she repeated. "I'd think Manny was pregnant."

Christopher chuckled. "She is."

"What!" Pamela exclaimed, whipping around to face him. "You're kidding."

"Nope," Christopher proclaimed with a gigantic grin. "Though we haven't confirmed it with a doctor, Manny is quite sure that we are pregnant."

After closing mouths dropped open in astonishment, the women rushed off to surround Manny.

Nelson slapped Christopher on the back. 'Way to go, brother! I'm glad to see that you're finally joining the ranks of parenthood."

"Thanks, Nels. I'm glad, too."

Phillip looked skeptical. "It's great news, Chris, but frankly, I'm glad it's you and not me."

"Congratulations, Christopher," Henrico said, placing a hand on his shoulder. "With any luck, I'll be joining you soon."

"Takes more than luck, Rico," Nelson interjected. "You're going to need to heat up the action in the bedroom if you want to produce children."

"I can assure you that I have no problems in the bedroom, Nelson, and when the time is right, Jacqueline and I will have children."

Jordon, who held his son in his arms, extended one of his hands. "Congratulations, Chris. Becoming a parent is one of the best things that's ever happened to me. But," he said, keeping a watchful eye on his daughters, "they grow up too fast, so enjoy them while they're young."

When Dani and Jolie stopped to converse with a group of teenaged boys and one of them pulled Jolie into a tight hug, Jordon handed his son to Christopher. "You might as well get in some practice, Mills. Excuse me while I go and fetch two 'think they're grown' teenagers and bring them back into the fold."

Manny looked around in bewilderment when the women rushed her, pulled her from the line, and hugged her each in turn. Her brows furrowed in disappointment when the line in front of the turkey leg booth lengthened considerable. "I just lost my place."

"Oh, forget that," Shelby said. "We want to hear about the baby. When exactly am I going to be a godmother?"

Manny raised a brow. "What baby?"

"The one Chris just told us that the two of you are having."

Manny glanced at Christopher. She had wanted to keep the news between the two of them for a while longer, until she was sure. She tried not to fault him, though. He was so happy about becoming a father. "I'm not sure, Starris, but probably sometime in February or March."

"Wonderful," Pamela exclaimed. "You guys keep this up and I'll have so many children, I won't have to have any of my own."

"By that time, Rico should be settled in his office, so I'll be here for the birth."

"That's right, Jacci," Shelby said. "And I'm so glad that you're coming home."

Maxie glanced down at the ground, then focused her stare on Phillip. She was happy for Manny, but she could hear her own biological clock ticking. How much longer was she going to have to wait? She had a smile on her face when she looked at Manny again. "Congratulations, Manny. I'm so happy for you."

"Do you want a boy or a girl?"

"I-I don't care, Pam. I just want a healthy child." Her tone sounded light, but Shelby hadn't missed the hitch in her voice.

"It will be, Manny. I just know it."

"Thanks, Shel."

"Is there anything we can do for you? You know all you have to do is say the word and we're there."

Manny glanced over her shoulder. "As a matter of fact, Starris, there is," she said with a grin. "Would one of you mind standing in that line and getting me a turkey leg?"

The sun took a final bow and slid behind the walls of rock making up the Colorado Rocky Mountain range. The sky changed into a mixture of lavender and baby blue shot through with streaks of golden orange and hot pink. Following the brilliant colors, the austere gray of twilight heralding the night brought with it a cooling drop in the temperature.

Although many patrons had left, the park was still crowded with those who'd stayed to hear the last of the local bands. Christopher, Manny, and the rest of their group had camped out on blankets near a bandstand and were listening to Jordon wring a soulful tune from his saxophone, accompanied by Fantasy, a band he'd played with in the past.

Manny, who'd spent the day eating her way through the park, had exclaimed her excitement over hearing Jordon play. Within two minutes of the first note, she'd curled herself into Christopher's lap and gone out like a light. He pulled the cotton blanket up over her shoulders, content to brace her slumbering weight against his body.

According to the guys, he could expect more of this, along with backaches, swollen feet, eating for several, and sudden mood swings that came out of nowhere. Christopher looked forward to every bit of it. Manny was carrying his child. When her back ached, he'd rub it. When her feet swelled, he'd carry her. When she was hungry, anything she desired he would provide and he'd hold her through the mood swings until she calmed.

Concern shadowed the love in his eyes. Christopher knew he'd make a great father, but the slight possibility that he might not have the opportunity to prove that increased his worry tenfold. He couldn't quit the case when they were so close, but with Manny pregnant and his knowledge of her last ordeal, the pressure on him to stay by her side was almost unbearable.

"Nelson," he called in a whispered voice.

"Yeah."

"Can I talk to you for a minute, man?"

Nelson handed a sleeping Lauryn to Shelby, then he stood and sat down again beside Christopher. "What's up?"

Christopher clenched his jaw in indecision as he wondered how much he could safely tell his friend. "I need a favor, Nelson. In a few days, I have to go out of town. It's the job," he said when Nelson raised a brow in question. Christopher breathed deeply before continuing. "I should be back in a couple of days, but I need you to keep an eye on Manny for me, just in case something happens."

Though Nelson knew that Christopher would never divulge the specifics of a case, he threw propriety to the wind. "Just in case something happens? How dangerous is this job? Where are you going?"

Christopher shook his head. He'd already said more than he should have. "Those are questions you know I can't answer, Nels. I just need you to look out for Manny and make sure she's okay. She'll need you guys until I can get back to her."

"You know you don't have to ask. Manny's like a sister to me; a meddlesome get-on-my-nerves kind of sister, but a sister nonetheless."

That pulled a hushed chuckle from Christopher. "Watch it, Reeves. You're talking about the woman I love and my soon-to-be wife."

"I love her, too, but she's still a meddlesome busybody. By the way, have the two of you set a date?"

"Not yet, but with the baby coming, it'll have to be soon. I'm planning to press Manny before I leave."

"Just don't press too hard. Manny loves you, but she doesn't react well to pressure. Chances are that if you push her, she'll choose a path in opposition to yours."

"I know she can be stubborn."

"As a mule," Nelson agreed.

"Well, this is too important to me. I want to know before I go exactly when Manny is going to marry me. It'll be one less thing on my mind when I'm on the road."

"Yeah," Nelson remarked, and a solemn quiet fell between them as both men turned their attention to the stage. Nelson's mind was filled with unasked questions. Christopher's, with answers he couldn't give.

Nelson rose to his feet as the last notes of Jordon's sax solo faded into the distance. "I'd better get back to Shel. Fantasy is about to launch into their final number and she'll need help packing up."

Christopher looked up at his friend with heartfelt gratitude. "Thanks, Nelson."

"Don't mention it. Manny won't be alone, we'll all keep an eye on her."

On the ride home, Manny did her best to keep their conversation on lighthearted topics. They discussed the wonderful day they'd shared with their friends, possible names for the baby and guesses as to her due date. Everything except what Manny had overheard in the park.

She awakened at the sound of the two deep voices and she'd heard their entire conversation. A shiver ran the length of her body and its chill settled at the base of her spine. Manny tried in vain to quell her rising fear. Christopher was about to do something dangerous and he was worried that he might not come back.

Like a sinister stalker, her past had come back to haunt her. She was pregnant, unmarried, and could quite possibly lose the man she loved. Her life seemed to be repeating itself, and if something happened to Christopher or to her baby, Manny was sure she wouldn't be able to handle it this time.

The call came the next night, and it was Benito who delivered the message. On Friday, Christopher was to be at the warehouse at 11:00 P.M. He was to come alone, bring nothing, and ask no questions.

On Monday morning, Christopher went to see Sam as soon as his shift ended. He stepped inside the office just in time to duck a flying coffee cup.

"Get the hell out!"

Samuel was standing behind his desk and the vein in his forehead looked ready to burst. Christopher looked from a ranting Sam to the woman cowering in the corner. He moved slowly toward the desk, patting the air with his hands in a conciliatory gesture. "Sam, man. Calm down or you *will* have that heart attack you've been courting."

Sam's heated gaze cut to Christopher. "Not until that buffoon posing as an assistant gets out of my office!"

Both heard the muted cry. Sam lit up the air with a descriptive expletive while Christopher crossed to the woman. "Maybe you could come back later."

Wringing her hands, she directed an agitated glance in Sam's direction. "But I was only trying to help. I didn't know it would upset him so much."

"If she thinks she was helping, she's loonier than she looks. Because of her, I can't find a damn thing I need in here. If I had wanted my desk cleaned, I would have done it myself. Get her outta here, Mills, before I do something she'll be sorry for!"

An apologetic smile lifted Christopher's lips. "He's not normally like this, but it might be best if you left now. In the meantime, I'll try and calm him down."

The assistant gave a grateful nod and hurried from the room. Christopher took a chair in front of the desk.

Samuel curled his lip. "Don't even say it, Mills. Goddamn government hotshots always poking their noses into things that ain't none of their damn business. If I had wanted an assistant, I would have asked for one."

"You're going to have to apologize to her, you know. If you don't, you might find yourself sitting in front of a review board."

"Why are you here? Char send you to check on me?"

"She did not. Look, Sam, just tell the woman you're sorry and give her some flowers or something to calm her down."

"Who are you? A spokesman for the civil rights commission?"

"Come on, Sam. You know you can't treat people like you just did. Besides, it's not her fault that you've had to change your lifestyle, and I need to know that you'll still be sitting behind this desk on Friday."

Sam raised his brows. "You've been contacted."

"Yep. Friday at 11:00 P.M."

Sam studied Christopher for a moment. "For someone who's spent years hunting his prey, you don't look like a man who is about to nab the big prize."

"I'm as happy as a flea on a dog."

"Is that right?" Sam remarked. "What's bothering you, Chris?"

Christopher leaned back in the chair and stretched his feet out in front of him. "I'm going to be a father."

"Hot damn," Sam yelled. "That's the best news I've heard since Char took away my smokes. Congratulations, son!"

"Thanks," Christopher replied, his tone sounding wooden.

"Oh, oh," Sam said. "I take it there's more."

"Yep. I also asked Manny to marry me; she said yes."

"Whew, Lord," Sam said, thumping his hand on his chest. "Somebody stop this heart of mine from jumping around. I can't believe that Christopher Mills is finally going down. When am I going to meet this lady of yours?"

"Hopefully, when I get back."

Sam stopped smiling. "Hopefully? What's the matter with you, boy? You're about to take down one of the most powerful drug lords in the world and become the darlin' of the AG's office. You're getting married and you're having a baby. Four homeruns in a row, and no one deserves it more than you, Chris."

"I just hope that I'm around to enjoy any of it."

Sam pushed himself up taller in his chair. "Okay, Mills. That's it. This sad sack crap is starting to get me. I'm under enough pressure and not up to wallowing in the mud with you. Danger comes with the job, but then I'm not telling you anything you don't already know. Get your head together, boy! You'll need all your wits about you when you tangle with Santangelo."

Sam believed in calling black, black, and was apt to say whatever was on his mind. In this case, however, he didn't need to say any more, and he purposely didn't mention any variation of the word death, a definite bad omen among fellow police officers, but Christopher knew exactly what he'd meant. He did need to focus on the goal. Only after reaching it could he turn his full attention to Manny, their marriage, and their child. "Thanks, Sam."

"Don't mention it. I'll make sure everything's in place by Friday. I'll want to see you around noon to go over the details. Hand me that pitcher of water over there and a glass." Christopher rose to comply. Sam poured his drink and after draining the glass, he sent a contemplative look in Christopher's direction. "When's the big day?"

"We haven't picked a date yet."

"Get one set before Friday. Char's going to need time to shop for a new dress and it'll give you a reason to get back here. In the meantime, you're going to take the rest of the week off. Spend that time with your lady and get your mind in the right place."

Christopher rose to his feet and replaced the chair against the wall. "I'll do that, Sam," he said, heading for the door. "You take care and I'll see you on Friday."

"Oh, there's one more thing, Mills."

"Yeah," Christopher said.

"You wouldn't happen to have a cigarette on you, would ya?"

Christopher left Sam's office with a lot on his mind and a long list of things to do. He stopped first at his lawyer's office, then paid a visit to his realtor. He made two more stops, at Manny's bank and a cigar store, before going to pick up Manny at the shop for their ten o'clock appointment with her doctor.

As soon as the doctor confirmed Manny's pregnancy, Christopher handed the physician one of the cigars, along with everyone else they passed on their way out of the building. After lunch, Manny went back to work and Christopher drove to Boulder.

Loretta opened the door and surprise widened her eyes when she saw Christopher standing on her porch. She looked around him for Manny and when she didn't see her daughter, anxiety lit her gaze. She brought her hand to her pounding chest and called for her husband.

Unsettled by her reaction, Christopher spoke quickly to arrest her fears. "Manny's okay, Mrs. Walker," he said just as Henry arrived at the door. "But I would like to speak with you and Mr. Walker, if that's okay."

"Come in, son," Henry said, stepping back from the door.

Loretta and Henry exchanged glances as they waited for the young man sitting on their couch to speak. Christopher was trying to find a way to express what he had to say without causing undue worry.

"Would you like something to drink, Christopher?"

Pulled from his reverie, he looked up at the older couple. "No, thank you, Mrs. Walker."

Henry tapped his pipe on the arm of the chair. Maybe he could help the boy get started. "Though you've told us that Manette is all right, this does have something to do with our daughter, or you wouldn't be here. Am I right, son?"

Christopher shifted his weight on the couch and looked Henry in the eye. "Yes, sir. It's that…well, you see. What I'm trying to say is—"

"Manette is pregnant?"

"What?" Both men spoke simultaneously as their gazes flew to Loretta Walker.

She looked at Christopher. "That's why I was so worried when you showed up here alone. I thought something had happened to my daughter."

"How did you know?"

"Yeah, honey. How did you know?"

"Manny called to tell me earlier today. She also told me that you asked her to marry you."

"And just when were you planning to tell me, Loretta Walker? Am I or am I not Manette's father? I have a right to know what going on with my child, too."

"You were napping, Henry, and I didn't want to disturb you. I would have told you later, but now I don't have to. She said yes, by the way."

Henry's nut-brown gaze turned to Christopher. "Did you propose to my daughter before or after you found out about the baby?"

"Before, sir, which is why I'm here now."

"It's a little late to ask for Manette's hand, son."

"I understand that, and I apologize, but time is of the essence. As you know, I have been an officer with the Denver Police Department for the last fifteen years. But what you don't know is that last year, I was appointed as a special agent for the DEA."

"Oh, my," Loretta sighed.

Henry glanced at his wife, then cut his eyes back to Christopher. "Does Manette know this?"

Christopher shook his head no. "And I don't want her to know. I'm currently working a case that's about to come to an end, and once it does, I'm planning to retire from the force."

"Oh, my, my." Loretta used her hand to fan the air in front of her face.

"The reason, I'm here," Christopher continued, "is that I'm scheduled to go out of town for a couple of days and I'd like to marry Manny before I leave."

Henry studied the young man he'd hoped to one day call his son-in-law. He'd liked Christopher Mills when he'd met him last Christmas. All during that weekend, Christopher had seen to it that his daughter had lacked for nothing, materially or otherwise. The entire family had seen how much he loved Manette, and while Christopher had left many things unsaid about his assignment, Henry was astute enough not to ask. Being a cop was a dangerous profession. Then again, the Lord promised no one a tomorrow. "What is it that you need us to do, son?"

CHAPTER 15

Feeling much better when he drove back to Denver, Christopher stopped at Tony Roma's for a slab of Manny's favorite ribs and all the fixings. He needed her in a good frame of mind when he revealed his new departure date. When she arrived home, she headed directly for him, laid a passionate smack on his lips, and handed him a small bag. He reached inside and pulled out the tiny brush/comb set fashioned from clear plastic decorated with blue, pink and yellow designs.

"That's our first present for the baby," she said. "I chose the clear set since we don't yet know whether we're having a girl or a boy."

Manny looked so happy that Christopher was reluctant to spoil her bright mood with his news. So, he held off until they had retired for the night. In bed, he pulled Manny into a tight embrace, told her that he had to leave on his assignment on Friday. Then he made passionate love to her for most of the night.

On Tuesday, Christopher went shopping. Seeing Manny's gift last night had intensified his need to personally do something for his child, just in case. Christopher hastily cut off that thought. Sam was right; he did need to get his head in the right place.

He entered the exclusive baby boutique and stood in the doorway surveying the store without a clue as to where to begin. All he knew was that he wanted his child to have the best of everything. Relief filled him when a salesperson approached and inquired whether he needed help.

He followed her, explaining Manny's preference for dark furniture. Together they chose dark walnut to furnish the nursery. She helped him make arrangements for a home designer to come in and help Manny decorate the room according to her liking. Christopher left the store loaded down with bags filled with baby goods.

Manny was ecstatic when she saw all of the bags that he hauled into the house that night. She was moving from bag to bag happily examining the contents when the reason that he'd purchased the items suddenly popped into her head.

"Christopher, what if you're not here—" Manny stopped, unable to finish voicing her question.

"I'll be here, Manny," he said.

"But what if something—" She stopped again and sighed. She wanted reassurance, which was something Christopher couldn't give her. "You know what? Playing the 'what if' game is stupid. No one can predict what will happen tomorrow, can they?"

He smiled with pride, knowing that Manny was doing this for him. Last night, when he told her he was leaving, he'd expected her to fall apart. At the very least, he'd expected an emotional debate. Manny had done neither. When their lovemaking ended, she'd kissed him on the lips, turned into his arms, and settled in for the night. "No, Honey-V, they can't."

She went back to her inspection of the items he'd purchased, exclaiming over the things she loved, and frowning over those that she was not too crazy about. Christopher crossed to her, tipped her chin, and locked his gaze with hers. "Manny, everything is going to be all right. Believe that, okay?"

"I know," she said, though she wasn't sure if belief alone would be enough.

"I have an idea," he said. "When you're done here, why don't we go to a movie, your choice."

The movie they saw was a sappy, chick flick. For the life of her, Manny couldn't remember much of what she'd seen, except that the male and female characters had walked off into the sunset looking forward to sharing a long life together. The thought of them living happily ever after had made Manny feel so low, she wished that she'd gone with the action flick Christopher had pointed out. She took his hand as they strolled around the lake in Washington Park. Looking up at him and seeing his profile in the moonlight, Manny couldn't help feeling saddened by the thought that her love story with him might end—

sooner than either had expected.

On Wednesday, Christopher drove up to his cabin and spent the day fishing and taking in the scenery. He came back down the mountain in time to fry up the trout he caught for Manny's dinner. That night, they shared a bubble bath and after drying her, he heated scented oil and massaged it into her skin until Manny groaned in the throes of pleasure.

As soon as he set the small black tray on the nightstand, Manny attacked, and by the time she let him up, Christopher's mind reeled with ecstasy, gratification, and regret. No one made love like Manny Walker. He always felt blissfully happy, thoroughly satisfied, and only regretted that this might be one of the last times he'd ever make love to the love of his life.

Manny nudged his side and moved into his arms. "I love you, Christopher."

He settled her against his still racing heart. "I love you, too, Manny, and that's something that will never change." Spooning their bodies, Christopher began his loving sleep-time strokes on her body until Manny relaxed into a deep slumber.

On Thursday, Christopher rechecked all the locks on Manny's house and while the firm he'd hired replaced her alarm system, he sat at the kitchen table with a pen and pad. For a long while, he simply stared into space while his thoughts, like a movie reel, took him back through every single minute he'd spent with Manny Walker. More than a few times, he smiled; a couple of times, he frowned, but mostly he savored their time together. When the review ended, Christopher sighed and picked up the pen. He pulled the pad forward and began to write.

His first letter was to Manny. In it, he included his recollection of the highlights of their relationship, detailed the arrangements he'd made for her future and that of their child's, and thanked her for her patience, her belief in him, and for her love. His second letter was to his unborn child.

Later that morning, Christopher began making phone calls. When

Manny arrived home from the shop, he handed her two dozen pink roses and sent her upstairs to dress for dinner out.

She entered the bedroom, laid the flowers on the dresser, and walked to the bed. She dropped on the spread in a daze. Her gaze moved slowly around the walls in her bedroom, stopping to stare at each of the smiling celluloid images of Christopher. She tried to take comfort in the thought that he was downstairs and hadn't gone anywhere yet. It didn't help as the tears she'd been holding at bay surfaced.

All week, sensing that Christopher needed to see her strength, she'd tried so hard to pretend that everything was normal. She reminded herself that she had a great career, wonderful friends, and a loving family. She had a handsome, caring man who wanted to be her husband and she sheltered the child created from their love in her womb. She had everything that she'd ever wanted in life, and no reason to complain. God had been good to her. Though Manny had mentally repeated this mantra all week, and did so again as she sat on the bed, the mental strain she'd placed on herself finally reached its peak.

Her lips trembled and she lowered her head. She wasn't going to be able to do this. Tomorrow, Christopher was leaving and she might not ever see him alive again.

Life was so damned unfair. She'd waited so long to find the man of her dreams and just when everything had finally come together in her life, she again faced the prospect of having it all taken away from her. As much as Manny wanted to weep over her situation, the scalding anger she felt at the unjustness of it all dried her tears. She jumped to her feet, and needing to lash out at something, crossed to the dresser. She picked up the picture of Christopher in his police uniform.

He looked so handsome and the wide smile on his face was an outward sign of his pride. The uniform represented all that he was: fair, honest to a fault, helpful, and willing to put his life on the line to help right the wrongs of the world. In that moment, all it represented for Manny was death and another sign that God was still punishing her.

Enraged to the point where she could no longer control the emotion, Manny raised her arm and let the photograph fly. In the next instant, remorse hit her like a ton of bricks, and she dropped to her knees, unsure of what had come over her.

Christopher heard the crash, rushed up the stairs, and crossed to Manny, who was trying to piece together the photograph she'd thrown against the wall. He took the broken frame from her and laid it aside, then picked her up and lowered himself to the floor.

She pushed away from him, her face set in a commanding scowl. "Don't go."

In the depth of her eyes, he could see her desperation, and the look on her face was so resolute, Christopher didn't know how to respond. He sought but couldn't find the words he needed to console her. "I have to go, Manny. I think you know that."

"But I need you." She placed one of his hands on her stomach. "We both need you."

"And I need both of you, but I have no choice. I have to see this through."

"There's always a choice, Christopher! I am carrying your child and I don't want to raise it alone. Nothing should be more important to you than that!"

Nothing was more important, he thought, directing his eyes away from her distressed expression. But he had to stop Santangelo and the poison he spread, and avenge his father's death. It had been his mission for too many years for him to just give up now and walk away. "It will be all right, Manny. I told you that I would always be with you. No matter what, you will never be alone."

"I don't want some spiritual being looking out for me. I want you! Here, in the flesh. Where I can look at you, and talk to you, and touch you. Tell them to put someone else on this case. Please!"

"I can't, Manny. I'm the one they chose for this job. I'm the one who brought it to this point, and I'm the one who is going to see it through. Now, I promise you that I am taking every available precaution, and because of what we're dealing with, Sam has arranged for additional protection. Nothing should go wrong, and in two days, I'm going to be right back here with you and the baby." He gripped her chin and kissed her hard on the mouth. Lifting his head, he stared deeply into her eyes. "I don't want you to think about this anymore. What I want you to do is start planning our wedding and to do that you need to pick a date. I've been thinking that we should do it soon, and…"

The doorbell rang before he could say anymore.

Leaving Manny with an admonishment to get dressed, Christopher straightened his clothes and hastily made his way down the stairs. He opened the door to a crowd of well-dressed people standing on the porch and sidewalk outside the house. All carried something in their hands and he raised a finger to his lips in a signal for them to keep quiet. No one spoke until he'd led them through the house and into the kitchen.

"Can we go up?" Shelby asked in a whisper.

"Not yet," Christopher said. "I haven't had time to warn her."

"That's not good," Maurice Walker said. "Perhaps I should go and tell her that we're here and why."

Christopher shook his head. "No, I'd better do it."

Loretta Walker stepped forward. "I think her father and I should go, too."

When the older Walkers and Christopher left the room, Jordon took charge, assigning tasks and generally overseeing the work as it progressed. Upstairs, Christopher and Manny's parents entered the bedroom, where they found her wearing one of her comfy old robes and a pair of fuzzy, pink house slippers. She was sitting on the bed with a bottle of lotion in her hands.

"Daughter?"

"Mama!" Manny jumped to her feet. She ran across the bedroom and into her mother's arms. They exchanged a giant hug before Manny stepped back. "Daddy, you're here, too." She frowned as she looked back and forth between their faces. "Why?"

"I can answer that," Christopher said, reaching for her hand. "Honey-V, I wanted to prepare you for this, but time kind of ran out on me. It's about our wedding and, well…it's going to happen tonight."

Manny's confusion deepened as she stared at Christopher for several long and uneasy seconds. Her heart began a rapid beat and breathing became a hit and miss operation. In the mounting tension, Henry and Loretta clasped hands as they waited for Manny's reaction. The seconds continued to tick away until finally Manny was able to grasp onto a coherent thought and her mind cleared. Yes, this crazy, sweet man had said that they were going to be married tonight.

She turned to her parents, smiled, and hitched a thumb over her shoulder. "He's kidding, right?"

"Daughter…before you go with that thought, take another look. Your father and I didn't dress up and come all this way for nothing."

Her father wore his good black suit, with a beige shirt, coordinating tie, and shiny black shoes. Her mother wore a pink silk dress with matching low-heeled pumps. Her hair had been professionally styled and she had a sprig of baby's breath tucked in the curls. Then she looked at Christopher again. He wore a white, banded collar, silk shirt beneath his designer black suit and there was a pink rose in his lapel. Manny waved her hands in the air as she crossed the room to the bathroom. "You all look very nice, but I'm not getting married tonight."

The door closed on the last of her words and Christopher turned to Loretta and Henry with a grin. "All in all, I think that went rather well."

Loretta cast a shrewd glance at the bathroom door. "Would the two of you mind leaving? I need a few minutes alone with my daughter."

The men left and Loretta sat on the bed. "Manette Alicia Walker, you have three seconds to come out of that bathroom."

It took five, but the door eased open and Manny popped her head around the door frame. "Is he gone?"

"Yes."

Manny breathed a sigh of relief and entered the room. "Good. I cannot believe that the man actually thought that I would marry him this evening, especially when I didn't know a thing about it. I think he's gone off the deep end. I mean, what could he have possibly been thinking?"

Loretta listened to Manny babble until she stopped to take a breath. "Manette, sit down."

Hearing the authoritative tone, Manny hastily obeyed her mother's command. She raised eyes somber with wariness to her mother, knowing what Loretta was going to say before she said it.

"Manny, for far too many years you've been trying to pretend that what happened with Derrick and that losing your baby didn't affect you deeply. And I've stood back and watched my beautiful girl hide herself away from the world. You've told everybody that you are looking for love, and yet you have purposely run off any man who showed more than a passing interest in you. That is, until you met Christopher, the one man who touched your heart."

Manny hung her head. For years, she *had* claimed that she was looking for love, and watching her friends find golden stalks of wheat in a field overrun by weeds, she'd told herself that she wanted the fairy-tale, too. In reality, Manny had really believed that love was not in the cards for her and she'd been too busy protecting her bruised heart from any more hurt to allow any man a chance to convince her otherwise. She'd tried to run off Christopher, too, but he'd remained firmly planted in her life until his love had taken root and attached itself to her heart.

"Manette, do you love Christopher?"

"Yes, Mama," Manny murmured. "I love him."

"Are you sure, because it doesn't sound like it."

"Yes, ma'am, I'm sure."

"Then do this for Christopher, Manette, and for your child. Marry that man, because there is no doubt in my mind that he is very much in love with you."

"I can't, Mama. Chris is working on a special case, and tomorrow he's leaving to do something that will put his life in danger."

"All the more reason for you to marry him tonight."

"But he might not come back! I can't marry Christopher tonight, knowing that tomorrow I might be a widow."

"Daughter, if you don't marry Christopher tonight and something does happen, you might very well be responsible."

"What do you mean?"

"I mean that Christopher needs a clear head for whatever he has to do. How do you think he is going to feel if he has to go off knowing that the woman he loves and the one carrying his child refused to take him as her husband?"

"I don't know how Christopher will feel. All I know is how I feel and that I'm tired of feeling like God is still punishing me for one mistake I made years ago. I'm not going to marry Christopher tonight, only to lose him tomorrow."

"Manette, I know that you don't honestly believe that God is punishing you. He is a God of love and your father and I raised you to believe that. You also know that bad things happen in life. Some come about because of our own actions, others happen for reasons that He will never reveal to us. Regardless, God never gives us more that we can bear and you are living proof of that. Now, you say that you love Christopher. Well, he feels strongly that he has to marry you tonight. When you love someone with your whole heart, Manette, it sometimes means sacrificing your feelings for the sake of theirs."

"I think I've sacrificed enough in this life, Mama."

Loretta rubbed Manny's back. "Yes, you have, Daughter, and while there are some things we will never understand, God understands it all. Life holds no guarantees, which is why you have to count your blessings as He bestows them. Christopher Mills is one of your blessings, Manette. The Lord has seen fit to let a good man come into your life. And since He is capable of all things, leave the future and whatever it holds for the both of you in His hands."

Manny thought about what her mother said and tried to find comfort in her words. For so long, she had believed that God was punishing her. Otherwise, why would He have taken her child from her?

Moreover, she'd been looking for a man to share her life for so long, and having no success she'd thought sure that something was wrong with her.

Thinking about it now, though, Manny knew that God had nothing to do with that aspect of her life. Until Christopher, she was the one who'd run off every man who tried to get close to her. God wasn't punishing her; she was punishing herself—something that she was going to stop doing right this minute. Manny reached for her mother and embraced her in a tight hug. "Thank you, Mama. I don't know what I would do if I didn't have you and Daddy in my corner."

Loretta chuckled. "Henry and I may have provided the genes, but you're a survivor. Now it's time for you to do more than survive. It's time for you to be happy, Daughter." Loretta kissed her cheek and stood. "I'm going downstairs to see how things are progressing. Shelby and the others will come up in a minute to help you get ready. So, wash your face and smile, because you found a man whose love for you outshines all the stars in heaven. And that's a rare find, indeed."

This wedding idea had apparently been a huge mistake. Christopher came to that conclusion as he moved to the end of a row of chairs assembled for the guests and sat down. Though he'd gone on impulse to see Manny's parents about marrying her, spilling his heart on those sheets of paper had reinforced to him that his decision was correct. Manny carried his baby, and although he'd left everything he owned to her and his unborn child, it was not enough of a permanent tie. Christopher felt strongly that she had to carry his name, too.

Tapped on the shoulder, he looked up. He rose nervously to his feet when he saw Loretta standing in front of him.

"It's okay," she said. "Manette will be down as soon as she is ready."

An hour later, Christopher stood in front of Manny's father, his gaze fixed on the landing. Nothing was as he'd envisioned. All of the people who meant the most to them were in attendance, but his groomsmen wore good suits in varying colors. Manny's friends had fleeced their wardrobes for something to wear, too, and none wore pink.

They were not in a church; there was no red carpet. Their honeymoon would have to wait as well, and yet, none of that mattered to Christopher as he watched Manny descend the stairs on the arm of Maurice Walker.

Shelby had spent her day searching for the perfect dress and Manny looked beautiful in the off-the-shoulder satin gown. Her hair had been styled into large curls that framed her face and her makeup was flawless. In her hand, she carried six of the pink roses he'd given to her tied together with a white satin ribbon. It was a sight he would never forget.

His gaze lowered to her feet and he laughed out loud, drawing curious stares from the people in the front row of chairs. Instead of shoes, Manny still wore the pink bedroom slippers that had seen their best days long ago.

The ceremony was short and quick, the reception a fun-filled affair. Afterwards, Christopher and Manny stood in the doorway waving goodbye to their family and friends. When the last one drove away, he turned to her, lifted her into his arms, and carried her across the threshold of what would be their home.

Manny's face dissolved in heat when she saw her feet. He set her down and she immediately hid her face in his chest. "Why didn't you say anything?"

"Because marrying you was the one thing I wanted most in this world and you did that for me."

Manny looked up and into his eyes. "Okay, I can understand that, but I don't understand why none of my friends said anything. They must have noticed that I had these house slippers on my feet."

"They did notice, and they didn't care." He placed a kiss on her nose. "This is not the first time you've made an original statement either. Your girlfriends have been regaling me with tales of other weddings all evening."

Manny tilted her head back and the horrified expression on her face was comical. "They didn't!"

"They did. Besides, this was your wedding, too, and if you felt comfortable wearing those slippers, it made no difference to me."

That night, Christopher took Manny in his arms and by the time he released her from his loving hold, the light of another day had broken on the horizon.

CHAPTER 16

The sun was high in the sky when Manny finally stirred the next morning. Keeping her eyes closed, she savored the ray of sunshine hitting her cheek before she stretched her more than contented body and reached for the man who had become her husband the night before. When her hands came up empty, Manny sat up.

Cocking her head, she listened for sounds of movement or the voices of the TV anchors relating the morning news. She heard nothing, and knew. Christopher had left and he hadn't awakened her to say good-bye.

Her stomach rumbled and Manny crossed her arms over her middle, knowing that at any second she would have to make a mad dash for the bathroom. At the moment, though, the hurt she felt ran deep and she continued to stare at his empty side of the bed as though she could somehow make Christopher appear. Then her stomach revolted.

In the bathroom afterward, she sat on the commode with her head in her hands. This morning's bout had been the worst she'd experienced so far. It was as if her child knew that something was wrong and had made its feelings known in the only way it knew how.

She had wanted to spend the day with Christopher and tell him that while she would still worry about him, she had accepted that he had to do his job. She hadn't wanted him to go off on his secret mission thinking that she would be a basket case. Talking to her mother had made her realize that while life had thrown her a couple of curve balls, she was still standing at the plate, and that she was strong enough to survive almost anything. She could let Christopher leave without making a scene, and she would wait, strong in her belief that he would return to her unharmed.

Manny waited a few more minutes before rising to her feet. She brushed her teeth and walked back into the bedroom, saying a prayer that Christopher would come back safely. Since Shelby had generously given her several days off, Manny crawled back in the bed and pulled up the covers. Still drained from her bout with morning sickness and the energetic activity of the night before, she closed her eyes and fell asleep before she could count to ten.

Thirty minutes later, a pair of smooth lips covered her mouth and kissed Manny awake. "Good morning, Mrs. Mills."

"Morning."

Christopher, who'd expected a more enthusiastic greeting after the night they'd shared, stepped back from the bed when Manny sat up. "What's wrong, Honey-V?"

"Nothing, except that you weren't here when I woke up earlier."

"Oh, is that all?"

"Is that all! Christopher, do you have any idea how I felt when I woke up and didn't see you? I wanted to talk to you and you weren't here!"

He sat on the bed. "I'm here now, so talk to me."

Manny climbed into his lap. "I wanted to say that I love you."

His lips twitched with the beginning of a smile. "Is that it?"

"No." Her fingers played with the buttons on his shirt. "I also wanted to tell you that I understand why you need to go. You have a job to do and it's important. I just wanted to say that you don't have to worry about me worrying about you while you're gone."

His heart surged with love. After last night, when she'd begged him not to go, he'd been so worried about how she'd react when he did finally leave. She would worry; Christopher knew that. However, for him, Manny was calling on the strength he knew resided within her to let him leave with a clear conscience.

He didn't think it was possible to love her any more than he did at that moment. His hand gripped her chin and his mouth covered hers. "Thank you," he said when he lifted his head. "You are one hell of a woman, Manny Mills, and I'm very happy that you are mine." He set her in the bed and rose to his feet. "The reason I wasn't here this morning was because I went out to get breakfast. I figured we'd both be too tired to cook after last night. It's downstairs." He observed the scowl on Manny's face. "Was it bad this morning?"

"The worst. It was probably all those spicy chicken wings I ate last night. In a couple of months, this phase will be over. Then we'll only have to deal with backaches, paralyzed nerves, and swollen feet."

Christopher didn't chuckle as expected. Since she'd told him about the baby, he'd made it a point to be with her every morning. He couldn't share the physical pangs of her pregnancy, but he could hold and comfort her when his child made her so ill. "I'm sorry I wasn't here, Honey-V."

"It's okay, but I think for a little while, we'll need to add saltines as a staple on the shopping list."

"Do you have any idea how much I love you?"

"Actually, I do." Manny popped a tiny piece of croissant bread into her mouth. She was trying to fool the baby into thinking that she wasn't really eating in the hope that the food would stay down this time.

"Oh, that's right. You know everything. Pardon me for forgetting."

"You're pardoned. To answer your question, though, you loved me enough to marry me. You're giving up your home and moving in here and you even love me enough to hold my head when I'm vomiting over the toilet. If that's not love, then I don't know what is."

Christopher pursed his lips and tried to hold on to his appetite. "That roll staying down?"

"For now."

"Manny, I'm not sure I want you here alone, especially while this morning sickness thing is going on. While I'm gone maybe it would be a good idea for you to stay with your parents. We could drive up later this afternoon."

"Now who's the worry wart? I'll be fine, baby. Besides, I know what to do. I've been through this before."

"True, but you had your parents with you then."

"And I have you with me now."

"I guess that means no."

"I have only two days to sort through that stuff in your house and make arrangements to have your things brought here. That doesn't give me a lot of time."

"You could wait until I get back."

"I could, but it will be better if I'm occupied. I'll need to keep busy."

So you don't worry so much about me. Christopher knew what she was thinking even though she hadn't voiced the actual words. "Well, don't try and lift anything and don't go into the attic. And make sure—"

"Christopher," she interrupted. "I know what to do."

"I just don't want anything to happen to you or the baby," he persisted.

He was always looking out for her. What was she going to do if he didn't come back? "I'll be careful, baby. I promise."

"You'd better or be prepared to be taken over my knee when I get back here."

Manny grinned. "You would spank the woman who is carrying your child?"

Christopher pointed his fork. "Damn straight. So, she'd better watch it and take care of herself and my child." He stood up. "Want some more milk?"

Manny pushed away from the table. "No thanks. I'm going to go and lie down for a while."

"Want some company?"

"Depends."

"On what."

"On whether you're the company." Manny turned for the stairs. "Last one to the bedroom has to clean up the mess from breakfast."

Christopher returned to the table and began clearing their plates. He'd happily clean up the mess and when he was done, he hoped that

Manny would still be awake to thank him properly.

The next day, Manny entered her office at five and lowered her tired body into the chair behind her desk. She slipped off her shoes, propped one leg on top of the other, and massaged her aching foot. Not knowing what to do with herself after Christopher left, Manny had called to check on things at the store. When Shelby inadvertently mentioned that two of the sales associates had called in sick, Manny had gladly stepped in to help. A special week-long sale had started that morning and shoppers had poured into the store as soon as the doors opened. Her day had been busy, for which Manny was truly grateful. Working in the store and focusing on the needs of the customers had kept her mind occupied. She'd had very little time to dwell on Christopher.

Yesterday, except for a brief meeting he'd had with Sam, they had spent the entire day together. This morning, she'd been proud of the way she handled herself. She hadn't cried or clung to him. She'd walked him to the door and watched Christopher drive away with a smile on her face. He'd be back, Manny assured herself while rubbing the sole of her other foot.

The phone rang and she reached for the receiver. "Exterior Motives, Manny Walker speaking. How can I help you?"

"You can help by going to dinner with me this evening."

"Jacqueline?"

"Yes, it's Jacci. So, are you busy tonight or can you spend some time with a friend?"

"Actually, I do have plans."

"To do what?"

"Sort through the stuff at Christopher's place. We've decided to make my house our home."

"Why don't you wait until he gets back? I'm sure he'll want to help."

"No, I'd rather do it now. With Chris gone, I will avoid a lot of dis-agreements over what goes and what stays. You know men and how they cling to old junk like it's treasure."

Jacqueline laughed. "I know what you mean. Why don't I meet you at his place and give you a hand? I can be there in thirty minutes."

"No, need. Mostly, I'll be weeding through the boxes in the attic."

"Didn't Chris tell you not to go into the attic?"

Manny's eyebrows rose in surprise. "How did you know that?"

Jacqueline coughed. "Um, I didn't. I guess I just assumed that with your condition, he wouldn't want you climbing stairs and prowling around in a dusty old room."

The excuse was not even close to sounding plausible, but Manny let it pass. "I need to get going, Jacci. Thanks for the offer, but I think I can get through this by myself."

"Well, call if you change your mind."

"I will. See ya."

Before Manny could gather her purse and briefcase, the telephone rang three more times. She declined another dinner invitation from Starris, put off going to the movies with Maxie and Philip and begged off attending a concert with Pamela. If Manny didn't know better, she'd think that her friends were in on some sort of conspiracy. Grabbing her things, she headed for the door.

"Where do you think you're going?"

Manny whirled at the sound of Shelby's voice. "Home. Actually, to Christopher's. I want to start going through the stuff in his house."

"Can't it wait until he gets back?"

"It could, but I'd rather do it now and get some of that junk in the attic sorted through before Chris gets back."

"Didn't Christopher tell you not to go into the attic?"

"But...wait a minute. I just had this same conversation with Jacci. What's going on, Shel?"

Shelby turned to a rack of blouses and began straightening the padded hangers. "Nothing that I know about, why?"

"Did Chris say something to you, like, 'Watch out for Manny and don't let her do anything stupid', for instance?"

Shelby concentrated on the blouses. "No, he didn't," she hedged. It was not a lie. Nelson had told her and she had taken it upon herself to spread the word to everyone else.

"Well, it's just so odd the way everyone is calling and inviting me places all of sudden."

"What's odd about that? We've always done things together, separately and as a group." Shelby walked to the counter. "I think being pregnant is making you more sensitive than usual. I wouldn't worry about it, though. This too shall pass."

"I guess you're right," Manny responded slowly. "But you can call off the dogs, Shel. Christopher will be back and I'm dealing with it just fine. See ya tomorrow."

"Nite," Shelby said, although her thoughts were elsewhere.

At Christopher's house, Manny had just managed to pull down the stairs to the attic and was climbing to the top when she heard honking outside the house and the peal of the doorbell. By the time she got to the door and opened it, all of her friends were crowded together on the porch and there was a large U-Haul truck sitting out front.

"The crew is here," Jordon said, stepping around her while rolling up the sleeves on his shirt. "Tell us what you want done, then take a seat."

"Yeah," Henrico added. "We'll have this place cleared out in no time."

"Move, Manny, you're in my way," Nelson said, dragging a dolly behind him.

"And you heard what J.R. said," Phillip admonished. "So, find a chair and tell us what needs to be done."

Shelby stepped into the house next. The apologetic look in her eyes was almost genuine. "You might as well do as they say, Manny. These guys aren't leaving until the house is cleared."

Manny stared at her friends and tried to rein in her frustration. She was lucky that she had people who cared enough about her to come to her aid when she needed them, even if Christopher had orchestrated the whole thing. He might not be there in body, but he was still looking out for her. Though still mildly exasperated, Manny stepped back from the door. "Please, won't you all come in."

Christopher covered a yawn with the back of his hand and stretched his long legs as much as he could in the narrow space of the car. They'd made the delivery in Fairplay, Colorado, a small community once a mining camp about eighty-four miles southwest of Denver.

Christopher and Benito had spent the last two nights at a small resort, where rather than sleeping, Christopher had used his time to scope out the operation. This morning, he'd stood back as Benito supervised the unloading of the goods. They had left the merchandise in the hands of several suspicious looking Nigerians, and exchanged the moving truck for a 1987 Ford Escort before hitting the road again at five that afternoon.

Nigeria hadn't gotten involved in the drug trafficking business until the mid-1980s when a group of Nigerian naval officers training in India had begun trafficking Southwest Asian heroin. Since then, many Nigerians, who labored for very little, had chosen to act as drug couriers, lured by the prospect of making a lot of money. This group had been posing as waiters and kitchen help at the resort. If everything had gone according to plan, Sam and his men were now at the resort, arresting the Nigerians and confiscating the merchandise, along with whatever else they found. Christopher also suspected that once they researched ownership of the resort, they'd find Santangelo's name on the deed.

They'd made the delivery and his identity was intact. Now all he had to do was find out the location of the meeting and he could go home. He glanced down at the jacket folded across his knees, and then at Benito.

For the talkative sort, the man hadn't said a whole lot on the trip up or during the drive back, and Christopher wondered what was going through his mind. He hesitated to ask, fearful Benito would start talking and never shut up. Instead of questioning Benito, his mind turned to Manny. Even this far away from her he could feel her worry, hear her sighs, smell the flowery fragrance of her hair, and still taste the goodbye kiss they had shared at the door.

Since they'd decided to live in her home, she was probably already at his house clearing out his stuff. As much as he wanted to be there with her, helping, he was glad that she had something to keep her mind occupied and friends to watch over her for him. Thinking about their baby, a warm buttery feeling slid over Christopher and settled in his heart. He had a family and the thought that he was no longer alone felt so good, he almost smiled.

He looked out the window and frowned. Something was not right. They were supposed to be heading northeast, not further west. He looked at Benito again. The man had a strange, almost serene looking smile on his face.

"Er, Jerome. There's something I need to tell you."

Christopher's senses went on alert. "What?"

"Delivering the load was only part of the job. Mr. Santangelo has scheduled a meeting with all of his division chiefs and called in all available hands. He needs flunkies to act as drivers and such. Don't worry. If all goes well, you should be back in Denver by Monday afternoon or evening tops."

Christopher dropped his head back on the seat and exhaled. He hoped that Samuel was listening to their conversation. They had known about the meeting, but all of the information he'd obtained previously had indicated that Santangelo had scheduled it for next week. The DEA planned to be there in force and with little fanfare, take not only Santangelo, but all of his men into custody.

"Where exactly is this meeting being held?"

Though they were traveling down the mountain, Benito turned his head and for a moment stared directly into Christopher's face. "In Aspen," he said, turning his attention back to the road.

Despite the change in plans, Christopher had to maintain his carefully built cover, and he had to reach deep to come up with the appropriate reaction. "Damnit, Benito. I have plans this evening! Why didn't you tell me about this before we left Denver?"

Benito shrugged, seemingly unconcerned about Christopher's display of temper. "Didn't know before we left. I was told when we made the drop."

Christopher's heart began pumping in correlation to the adrenaline flowing through his body. Aspen was not part of the plan. Benito was supposed to spill the location of the meeting during the ride home. Then DEA agents were supposed to pull them over, discover the packet of cocaine he'd hidden beneath the spare tire in the trunk, and arrest them both before whisking Christopher off to safety.

He closed his eyes and tried to control his soaring pulse rate. Could Sam make the necessary adjustments in time?

Bone weary and tired when they arrived in Aspen, Christopher stepped from the car and shook off the stiffness of his body. He had to be mentally alert and ready for anything that might happen. Surveying the area, he counted no less than twenty cars of various makes and models parked on the property.

One in particular caught his attention—a green Bronco that looked so familiar, Christopher walked over to the vehicle for a better look. He knew the car. It belonged to Chief Herman Diggs. Carl Simmons drove the red Explorer parked next to it.

However, seeing the black Camero parked on the other side of the Bronco was a major disappointment. It hadn't taken Donny long to get in with the wrong crowd. Christopher clenched his jaw. Sam had said he smelled rats, and Christopher had just stumbled into the nest. Regardless of who was involved, he meant to clean house.

As far as he was concerned, corrupt officers who threw their lot in with criminals after swearing an oath to serve and protect were worse than almost any other lawbreaker walking the streets. When the sting was over, he planned to make damn sure that the three officers got exactly what they deserved.

Christopher forced himself to focus on his mission as he returned to the Escort to retrieve his luggage. With all three men in attendance, the chances of his being discovered and uncovered had just jumped dramatically. Turning, he stared up at the house. If any one of them made him before Sam and his reinforcements showed up, Christopher knew that he'd never leave Aspen, Colorado, alive.

When the car carrying Christopher and Benito rolled into the circular driveway of his residence, Dexter was standing in the window of the master bedroom. He looked down at the two men who exited the car. The run had been a test. One he'd first thought to cancel all together. Changing his mind, he'd given his approval and personally requested Benito Chavez as the driver, figuring it would be a good way to find out where Benito's loyalties lay, in light of his brother's untimely demise.

That Benito had come through told Dexter a lot about the man and his thought process. Profit before family, something he didn't personally agree with or practice, but expected from the men under his command.

His gaze moved from Benito to the tall, black man who'd accompanied him on the run, the new man, the one Anthony Chavez had talked so much about. Anthony had felt that Jerome Blackmon would be an excellent and loyal addition to the organization. Then again, Anthony had always been one to accept people at face value. Dexter held no such illusions. He knew from experience that people were no more loyal than a dollar bill.

He watched Jerome Blackmon walk over to the cars parked in his driveway and couldn't help wondering what the man was up to, but he shrugged when Jerome returned to the Escort to retrieve his bag. Some of his division chiefs couldn't help showing off their wealth by driving expensive cars and Jerome was probably just taking a closer look at some of the vehicles.

When Jerome looked up at the house, the air left Dexter's throat, and he stood frozen in place as he stared down into the eyes he had never been able to forget. Eyes that had haunted his dreams for as long as he could remember and made him break out in cold sweats in the middle of the night. A shudder coursed through him as his mind took him back to that summer day so many years ago. The day he'd killed that police officer and left his son standing by the side of the road.

Dexter shuddered again and forced his mind back into the present. His gaze narrowed as he examined the man in his driveway again and tried to blend his features with those of the young boy tied to his past, which proved to be an impossible task. Releasing a sigh, Dexter turned from the window and walked back to his bed wondering why he'd imagined the ghostly image from his past.

At the massive walnut entrance, a man with somber eyes dressed entirely in black, offered no greeting when he opened the door. Christopher breathed a sigh of relief as they entered the house, glad that it hadn't been someone else. The man beckoned them with a hand signal, then turned and led them down the long hallway of a lavish and expensively furnished home.

Though he listened intently for any signs of activity, Christopher heard nothing as he followed the man and Benito up the steps of an intricately carved oak staircase to the top floor of the house. In his assigned room, Christopher dropped his bag and flopped down on the large feather bed. Its softness, combined with the strain of the last two days. penetrated the tiredness in his body and Christopher closed his eyes. He did not fall asleep, however, but rather used the down time to focus his mind on the reason he was there and on the arrest of Dexter Santangelo.

CHAPTER 17

On Sunday morning, Manny awoke with the rising sun. She sat up in the bed, glanced at the empty space where Christopher should have been, and rather than dwell on the fact that he wasn't there, forced herself to get up and get moving. On her feet, she waited a few moments for her child to begin its customary, bathroom-rushing attack on her system, but when nothing happened, Manny continued into the bathroom with a feeling of inner peace.

It was as if the baby sensed her stress and had decided not to add to her load this morning. To Manny, it was a good sign on a day that had held the promise of loneliness. However, she decided not to dwell on that, but rather on the fact that later that night Christopher would be home.

At breakfast, she even managed to eat two spoonfuls of the hot cereal she'd prepared before her stomach rumbled with a warning to stop or face dire consequences. Manny cleaned up the small mess she'd made in the kitchen, entered the living room, and stood with her hands on her waist.

The guys had sorted through, boxed up, and moved the contents of Christopher's former residence into her home. At her direction, they had dumped the entire load in the middle of her living room and part of the dining area, with the promise of returning to help her put everything away. Since she was technically still on her honeymoon, and not needed at the store today, Manny decided to get started.

It took her forty minutes to unpack the first box because every item she pulled out turned her lingering thoughts to Christopher. Seeing his things only increased her yearning to see him with her own eyes. Touching his things made her long to touch him and run her hands over his body to make sure he was okay. Smelling his scent in his clothes only heightened her desire to press her nose into the side of his neck and make wild, passionate love to him.

Giving up the fight, Manny sat on the couch and gave in to her apprehension. Where was Christopher? How much longer would it be before he came home?

The ringing doorbell brought Manny out of her reverie and she left the couch to answer the door. Unlike last night, she was so grateful to see her friends that she ushered them in with hugs and a welcoming smile. With everyone's help, the boxes were unpacked and Christopher's things stored in their appropriate places. Then, as if sensing that Manny needed the company, the guys fired up the grill while the women joined her in the kitchen to prepare side dishes.

As soon as they went home, Manny poured a glass of milk and picked up the spreadsheets Shelby had left. She sat at the kitchen table and began reviewing the figures detailing the sales for the week. Immersing her mind in that project killed another two hours, but when Manny looked at the clock and watched the long hand move to the eight, dread flooded her body and her hands began to shake.

She forced herself to calm down, but her eyes stayed on the clock. Five more minutes ticked by before she rose from her chair. This was nuts. She couldn't sit here driving herself crazy with thoughts of all the things that could be happening to Christopher. She needed some air to clear her head. Grabbing her car keys, Manny headed out the front door.

Twenty minutes later, Manny took a determined breath and rang the doorbell. Starris had pitched the idea to all of them some time ago and she had been thinking about it for quite a while. Christopher's absence, along with her propensity to worry, had been the impetus that had pushed her toward finally making a decision, and she'd decided to inform Jordon, who opened the door, of her decision right away.

"Manny! Didn't I just leave your house? Wait a minute, what's wrong? Has something happened? Are you okay?"

"I'm fine, J.R."

"Well, get on in here girl. Starris is changing Jonathan's diaper, but she'll be down in a minute."

Manny stepped into the foyer. "Actually, J.R., it's you I've come to see."

He stepped back, surprised. "Me?"

"I wanted talk to you about becoming a mentor for ROBY."

"Now that is good news. Although Carlotta pledged her support, she neglected to offer any warm bodies."

Manny scrunched her nose. "Well, I wouldn't have expected anything else from Ms. Eldridge."

Jordon laughed and wrapped his arm around her shoulders. "At least your heart is in the right place. Let's go back to my study. Everything we need is there and we won't be disturbed."

In the study, Manny settled herself in one of the large leather chairs in front of the desk, while Jordon rifled through the files in a drawer of his desk. When he'd pulled out all the necessary forms, he sat back in his chair. "So, what made you decide to volunteer your services to ROBY?"

Manny shrugged. "Starris is a good pitch woman."

"That she is," he agreed. "But as I understand it, Starris talked to you ladies about serving as mentors a while ago. At the time, you said that your schedule wouldn't allow enough time to serve adequately in the role. Why the change of heart?"

"That was several months ago. Now I have the time."

"What about when the baby arrives? Have you thought about how making a commitment to ROBY now will affect your time once your child is here?"

Manny leaned forward. "Look, J.R., do you need mentors or not?" If not, just say so and I'll be on my way."

"Whoa, girl. As badly as I need women to volunteer, I'm not trying to talk you out of this, so don't get your drawers in a bunch. People volunteer for different reasons. As the head of this organization, it is my responsibility to ascertain what those reasons are. I have to make certain that you've thoroughly considered what making a commitment of this magnitude will mean, and the effect it will have on your lifestyle."

He held up his hand when Manny would have interrupted. "Understand that my first concern is for the girls enrolled in this program, and that they receive the care and guidance from the mentors as outlined in the program materials. That means we take every precaution to prevent failure by matching the children with the right mentor from the start.

"My second concern is for the mentors themselves. Being a mentor requires a large time commitment, and one of the requirements is that you sign on for a minimum of one year. The child we match you with has to know that they can depend on you and on the relationship that will develop between the two of you. It is crucial that they are not made to feel as if they are a burden on the mentor in any way."

Manny waved her hand impatiently. "I already know all of that, J.R. Chris is a mentor and he's already told me what it's going to take on my part if I decide to do this. I want to be a mentor and I want to get started right away."

"You're sure?"

"Yes, J.R., I'm sure."

"Okay." He picked up the packet on his desk. This folder contains all of the information you will need to get started, the first being that you complete the application and get it back to me so that my staff can start the review process."

"The review process? What exactly does that entail?"

"Nothing quite as serious as you may be thinking." Jordon removed the application from the folder and handed it to Manny. "As you can see, other than basic information, name, address and so forth, the balance is where you tell us all about you. The kind of person you are and the type of activities you like to engage in. Why you want to become a mentor. What strengths you can offer to the program and other questions noted on the application form. We won't dig into your finances or your personal business. However, we will run a background check." When Manny raised her brows, Jordon continued, "It's necessary, Manny."

"Oh," she said. "I guess I can understand that."

"Good. Now, seeing as you're a personal friend of the director and that he has known you for years, I can almost guarantee your acceptance by the committee. How does that sound?"

"Great."

"However, first you need to review the materials in the folder. If you have any questions, just pick up the phone and give me a call. And Manny, if you change your mind after reading through everything, I'll understand."

"Oh, I don't plan to change my mind."

Jordon nodded. "Well, let's leave it open until you've reviewed the information and have had all of your questions answered. Okay?"

"Sure, J.R. Oh, I have another question."

"Shoot."

"What do I need to do if I know of someone who could benefit from being involved in ROBY?"

"Would this someone be an enrollee or a mentor?"

"An enrollee."

"To tell you the truth, Manny, I have a waiting list a mile long and not nearly enough volunteers of the female persuasion."

"But I think ROBY would be good for her."

Jordon smiled. He could feel the goodness in Manny's heart shining through like a light bulb. "Okay, Manny. I can't make any promises, but here's my card. Have her parents or guardian give me a call and I'll see what I can do about getting her on the waiting list."

Manny took the card and placed it inside the folder. "Thanks, J.R."

"Don't mention it." Jordon stood up. "Why don't we go and find Starris? She's probably done with the baby by now and I know she'll be happy to see you."

Arriving home, Manny pulled into her driveway and sat in the car staring at her house. She was trying to see what Christopher saw every time they came home from an outing. She was trying to view her home through a cop's eyes. Through the curtains, she could see the light she'd left on inside and a house illuminated by the floodlights Christopher had installed when she'd moved in. She saw her two spindly trees doing their best to stand up in a sudden brisk wind and the shadows they cast against the front window. Not seeing Christopher's Jeep parked in the driveway saddened her, but Manny shrugged off the emotion. She'd had enough of the melancholy blues.

She opened the door and was about to leave the car when she heard Christopher's voice admonishing her to pull into the garage and to lock up the house for the night. Manny shook her head and smiled. Christopher would be happy to know that his lectures on safety had finally penetrated her brain.

Before Manny could restart the engine, however, someone tapped on the window. She jumped, then turned to find a man standing outside the car. Manny's heart rate shot up and her eyes widened in fright. She fumbled for the button to lock her car doors, and at the same time tried to turn the key in the ignition.

The car's engine started, but the man grabbed the door handle and yanked the door open. Manny screamed when he bent down and looked inside the car.

"Manette! It's me, Derrick."

She murmured something unintelligible and shrank back from the hand he held out.

"Manette, it's Derrick Lewis."

She closed her eyes and opened her mouth to let air into her lungs. With her heart still thumping wildly inside her chest, Manny opened eyes that were blazing. "You idiot! Are you out of your mind! Do you have any idea how badly you just scared me?"

He stepped back, hoping to dodge the laser aim of her fury. "I'm sorry, Manny, but I had to see you."

She stepped from the car. "Well, I don't want to see you. In fact, I made that quite clear on the phone."

"My God, you're beautiful!" She stared at him and didn't respond to the compliment. "I-I mean, I always thought you were beautiful, but I never imagined how gorgeous you'd be when you became a woman."

"What do you want?"

A docile look appeared on his face. "I wanted to talk to you…to explain so that you'd know and understand what happened the night before our wedding."

She rolled her eyes. "I've already heard your explanation, Derrick."

He looked down and stubbed the toe of his shoe into the ground before his lashes swept up revealing eyes full of sadness and regret. "I'm sorry, Manny. I kept hoping it would all be over in time for me to make it to the church. I meant to call and tell you to wait for me, but Cassandra began experiencing complications. She needed me and I couldn't leave her at the hospital by herself. I wanted to call and tell you why I wasn't at the church, and to let you know that I still wanted us to get married."

"If that's true, then kindly explain to me why when my brothers went looking for you the next day, you were nowhere to be found, and why movers cleaned out your house the following week?"

"By the time April was born, I knew it was too late and that you'd already left the church. I panicked. I knew you'd be angry, and that your family would be angry and I just couldn't face you after what I'd done." He stared at the ground. "But I always loved you, Manny," he mumbled. "I still do."

"You don't know the meaning of the word. April is only a few months older than our child would have been, and that could only mean that you were sleeping with April's mother at the same time you were with me. If you truly loved me, then I don't understand how that situation could have occurred." She held up her hand when he would have responded. "Save it, Derrick."

He hung his head. "I loved you, Manny, and I know that what I did was wrong. Maybe one day you'll find it in your heart to forgive me.

"You're forgiven." She closed the car door and started for her house.

He followed. "Thank you for that at least." He caught her arm, halting her progress. A tiny smile lifted his lips. "But what about us, Manette? Is there a chance that we can try again?"

She pulled away, stepped up on the porch, and turned to face him. Derrick Lewis was still a handsome man, but the doe-brown eyes she'd once found so attractive were filled with desperation. Years ago, Derrick had been so confident, a man sure of what he wanted, and capable of doing anything his heart desired. He'd often told her how lucky she was to have someone like him in her life. Caught up in her lovesick fantasy, she'd admired his self-assurance and had felt proud that he'd found her worthy of his love.

Maturity and the love of a real man allowed her to see Derrick Lewis as he really was, and had probably always been. A weakling and a coward, and so self-absorbed that his ego had allowed him to believe that a flimsy explanation and a pathetic apology would sway her to take him back after all this time. Manny wanted to scream and slap his face to wake him up, but she stopped herself right before she erupted. Derrick Lewis wasn't worth it, and she'd had enough of this conversation.

She flashed her left hand in the porch light. "Derrick, there is no us. I have a husband."

Derrick grabbed her fingers as waves of shock rocked his body. "This can't be," he cried as he stared down at the twinkling diamond solitaire flanked by gold. "That detective I hired told me that you had never married!"

"Oh, but it can be, Derrick, and I've never been happier in my life." She turned and inserted her key in the front door.

"Manny, wait! Just let me explain what I've done for—"

"No more waiting, Derrick, and no more explanations," she said over her shoulder. "Goodbye, and good luck to you and to April."

Manny entered the house and closed the door. In a way, she felt sorry for Derrick and at the same time almost giddy with the thought that she was glad that he'd left her standing at the altar. Otherwise, she'd never have met Christopher, the one man she knew for certain that God had meant as the only man for her.

Very late in the afternoon on Monday, Christopher and Benito walked around a long rectangular table filling glasses with water and making sure that the bar was stocked with whatever else Santangelo's men would want to drink. He knew the men were in the house, but so far, he hadn't run into any them, because Christopher had spent most of his time in the garage polishing cars or in his assigned room. The last thing he needed was to run into Donny, Diggs, or Simmons and have his cover blown. Benito went to get more ice, and Christopher checked the jacket he'd strategically draped over the back of a chair in the corner, near the head of the table. They had just about finished setting up when Benito offered to complete the last of the tasks and Christopher, thankfully, headed for the kitchen.

Thirty minutes later, Benito walked into the room. "The meeting's started, but we gotta stick around, in case they need anything in there."

"No problem," Christopher said, taking a seat at the table. He felt safer here in the kitchen and out of sight.

"Want somethin' to eat?"

"Nope."

Benito seemed unusually happy and he had reverted to his old talkative self. He sat at the table with his sandwich, chattering away. Christopher blocked out the noise. His thoughts were on Samuel, and he hoped that his boss was on his way as he concentrated on the arrests that were about to go down.

Still greatly irritated by Donny's decline into the gutter, he briefly wondered just how far back Diggs and Simmons' association with Santangelo went. Then he shook off the thought, because it really didn't matter. All three were dirty cops, and they deserved whatever punishment the justice system meted out to them.

An hour later, the phone on the kitchen wall rang and Christopher rose to answer it. "Yes, sir," he responded. Then he hung up and turned to Benito. "The tequila's running low."

"I'll take care of it."

Ten minutes later, Benito reentered the kitchen. "We have to go, Jerome."

Christopher looked up with a frown. "I thought we were told to stick close in case they needed anything."

Benito smiled. "Christopher, we have to go and we have to go now."

Christopher was on his feet and around the table before Benito knew what had happened. "How do you know my name!" Benito just shook his head. Christopher jerked the little man forward by the front of his shirt. "Damn it, answer me!"

With lots of effort, Benito managed to dislodge himself from the tight grip. He stared at Christopher for a couple of seconds and said, "You tried to help me. Now, I'm trying to help you." Then he turned and ran for the back door.

Christopher quickly followed, and had just reached the door when a deafening explosion rent the air and the backside of the house exploded in a ball of fire.

Twenty minutes after the explosion, Christopher opened his eyes to find himself prone on the ground. His head reverberated with a loud ringing that hurt his ears. Trying to sit up, he grimaced from the searing pain coming from the back of his right leg, his left arm, and his head. Looking down, he saw that his shirt was nearly gone and the legs of his pants hung in ragged tatters.

Christopher lifted his hand to his temple, touching the place that seemed to be the source of the pain radiating through his head. He fought through the agony, then lightly touched the lump, while surveying the area around him.

All he could make out were the nearby bushes and large dark shapes reaching upward that he assumed to be trees. There was a bright glow in the distance, but because his sight was hazy and his depth perception off, Christopher had no idea what it was. It hurt too much to keep his head up and he fell back to the ground.

What in the world had happened to him? He clenched his jaw when another wave of pain worked its way through his head. Once it subsided, he took a deep breath and labored to get his mind to focus. Then it all came back in a rush. Him chasing Benito, him reaching the back door just as a loud blast propelled his body forward and across the yard. He sat up, then tried to rise to his feet. A shaft of pain shot up his left leg and dizziness threatened to overwhelm him. Both had him falling back on his butt.

Frustrated, Christopher rubbed at the aching spot near his temple. The lump felt large and he lightly pressed his fingers against the bruise, at the same time staring at the scraped flesh on the back of his arm. There was something else he was supposed to remember. Then it came to him—Santangelo and his division chiefs were having a meeting and he was there to take them all into custody.

A rustling sound in the bushes diverted his attention. Forgetting about his own ailments, Christopher scrambled to his knees and peered into the waning light. He saw a flash of white darting through the trees, coming in his direction. Christopher reached for his gun. It wasn't there and he could only presume that it had been lost in the blast.

Rising to his feet with difficulty, Christopher hobbled over to the nearest tree and threw his back against the hard trunk, biting back a curse when his left arm hit the rough bark. When the pain subsided a little, he took a chance and twisted his head in the direction of the noise. He saw the flash of white again. It was closer and even with the cover of darkness, recognition dawned. Only one man at that meeting would have been wearing a white suit. It was a rule enforced by the man himself, and that man was Dexter Santangelo!

He continued to watch Dexter scurry through the wooded area, moving closer, and closer to where Christopher stood rock still. Not wanting to give away his presence or his position, Christopher held his ground and his breath.

Too busy making his escape and pushing branches out of his way while checking over his shoulder to see if he was being followed, Dexter Santangelo never saw the dark form that stepped from behind the tree. He smacked the ground hard when Christopher stuck out the foot on his good leg. Jumping up, Santangelo began swinging his fists, blindly punching out and hitting nothing. Christopher landed a hard right on his jaw and Santangelo hit the ground again.

This time Dexter didn't get the chance to rise because Christopher jumped on him, smashed his face into the ground, and twisted his arms painfully behind his back. Reaching for the cuffs hooked on his belt, Christopher snapped the bracelets in place and after rising, hauled Santangelo to his feet.

He looked at the man who had murdered his father and a storm of emotion swirled up around Christopher, clogging his mind and making him want to heave. The urge to wrap his hands around Dexter Santangelo's neck, and squeeze until he choked the life from his body was so overpowering, Christopher could hardly breathe. With Dexter struggling to free himself from Christopher's restraining grip, Christopher willed his control into place. He'd finally captured the man who killed his father, fulfilling his life long goal. It was enough.

Breathing harshly, Christopher jerked Dexter around and looked in the dark depths of a cold-blooded killer's eyes. "For my father," he said. "Dexter Santangelo, you are under arrest."

Two days later…

The darkness was all consuming and he was sinking further into its depths. Christopher flailed his arms and legs in a desperate fight to stop his descent. It wasn't his time to go. He had to get back. Manny was there, waiting on him, and he'd promised her that he would return to her unharmed.

But he was tired and he didn't know how long he could hold out against the unseen forces working against his efforts to rise to the surface. Christopher had no idea how long he'd struggled in that murky obscurity when something covered his hand and squeezed it tight. He somehow knew that whatever it was that held him was trying to help and he squeezed back. Then he heard the sound of a sweet, honey-dipped voice.

"Christopher."

That voice belonged to Manny, and she was calling his name. That gave him hope and the will to fight harder and before he knew it, he was back in the light.

"Christopher."

He heard her voice again and slowly opened his eyes, blinking when the brightness surrounding him blurred his vision. When he was able to see clearly, Christopher examined the dark circles beneath Manny's eyes and the worry lining her face. He gripped her hand tighter. "Manette." His voice was a scant whisper.

"Yes, baby, I'm here."

Groggy and hardly able to keep his eyes open, Christopher squinted up at his wife. "Manny, are you all right?"

A raw chill ran the length of her spine, followed by a bolstering bath of blessed relief. According to Sam, as soon as he'd handed over Santangelo, Christopher had passed out cold. He'd spent three unconscious hours in a local hospital in Aspen before being transferred to Denver General, where he'd been doped up with enough pain medication to send him into another coma.

Manny closed her eyes and shook her head, wanting to laugh and cry at the same time. Here he was laid up in a hospital bed with his body battered and broken in places, and he was worried about her. "I'm fine, baby, and I'm the one who should be asking that question. Are you all right?"

Before he could answer, the door to his room opened. Manny backed out of the way when his doctor and two nurses entered.

"Welcome back, detective."

Christopher's jaw twitched, but he didn't respond.

"How are you feeling, young man?"

"Like I was in an explosion."

The doctor chuckled. "Good, at least you're cognizant of what happened to you."

Seeking out Manny, Christopher locked his gaze on hers as the nurses checked the IV drip, bandages, casts, and fluffed his pillows while the doctor poked and prodded his body, and asked him a bunch of questions testing his awareness. Christopher endured it all as calmly as he could, knowing that as soon as they had finished, he could hold his wife in his arms.

Manny stared at Christopher from across the room, her heart crying out in silent anguish. She'd been so worried and scared that he wouldn't make it. When she first heard the newscast, horrible sounds and images that she couldn't control had immediately taken over her mind: Christopher trapped inside a house while a bomb exploded around him. She'd heard his screams of pain, seen his body shattered and bloodied flying through the air; watched his eyes close and his chest stop moving as his life force slowly drained from his body. And then Nelson was there, with Shelby and the others, calming her and helping her fight through her agitation and fright.

For two days and nights, she'd held her vigil in the chair by his hospital bed, and except for short bathroom breaks, refused to leave his side even to eat. The nurses, upon learning from her friends that Manny was pregnant, had brought her meals and snacks, which Manny ate only because they wouldn't leave until she'd finished the food.

Then she went back to talking to Christopher about their life, their baby, and their future, all the while praying to God, well, begging, really, that he allow Christopher to come back to her.

As soon as the doctor and nurses left, Christopher lifted his head. Various parts of his body twitched with discomfort, but Manny had suffered, too. He could see her pain etched in her face and all he wanted was to take his wife in his arms and kiss her senseless. He needed to reassure her that despite his injuries, he was okay. "Honey-V, come here."

Manny shuddered, then drew in several calming and fortifying breaths. "Is it over, Christopher?"

He lifted his hand. "Honey-V, come to me."

Walking stiffly, Manny slowly crossed to the bed. Christopher took her hand in his. "Manny, I found the man I was after and he's behind bars. Once I testify at the trial, the case is over for me."

She tenderly stroked his cheek with her fingers. "Oh, Christopher, look at you." Her eyes had a glassy sheen, but she held back her tears and the temptation to throw herself on top of him.

"It's okay, Manny. I'm not hurt all that badly and in a couple of months, I'll be good as new and we'll have forgotten all about any of this." He tried to smile, but only succeeded in grimacing in pain.

She simply stared and tried to assimilate the gauze-covered man with the one she loved with all her heart. "I'll never forget, Christopher. I almost lost you."

"But you didn't lose me. I'm here, just like I said I would be." He tugged her forward, until Manny had to use her hand to brace her weight against the bed in order to stop herself from falling on top of him. "Kiss me, Mrs. Mills, and take away your husband's pain."

Manny offered a strained smile. "A kiss is not going to do anything for your pain. Do you want me to call the doctor?"

"Ah, Honey-V," he said solemnly. "You're only saying that because you don't know the power of your kisses and the effect they have on me. Now kiss me, Manny."

She leaned over, meaning only to touch her lips to his, but Christopher trapped her head in his hand, holding her still while he pressed his mouth long and hard against hers. He needed this kiss and he wasn't going to let Manny cheat him out of what was rightfully his.

Softening the kiss, he used the tip of his tongue to lick her upper and lower lips in a slow, tantalizing, teasing motion until Manny groaned and parted her lips. Christopher slipped his tongue inside, thoroughly exploring her mouth and the sides of her cheeks before engaging her tongue in a duel of passion in which Manny gave as good as she got.

They were both moaning, their ardor rising, until Manny, who needed to get closer to Christopher, slipped off her shoes and tried to climb into the bed with him. He sucked on her bottom lip and shifted over, then held her tightly, ignoring the pain when she wrapped her arms around his waist. Releasing her mouth, Christopher landed a series of butterfly kisses on her brow, her eyes, and her cheeks before taking her mouth again in a deep and heated kiss that seemed to melt away his pain.

He smiled when their mouths parted again. "See, I feel better already."

Even as he spoke the words, the medicated fog claimed his mind again and Christopher closed his eyes. "I love you, Manny Mills," he whispered.

"I love you, too, Christopher," she said on a sigh as she snuggled closer. "And I'm so glad that you're home, and safe, and that I won't have to worry about you any longer." Christopher, having already fallen asleep, never heard her and Manny smiled when she heard his quiet breathing.

Supporting herself on her elbow, she rose and made a visual inspection of his body. The doctor had talked to her as soon as she arrived at the hospital, so she knew that none of his injuries were life threatening, but his left ankle was broken and would require surgery. The numerous cuts and lacerations had been treated and bandaged, and his left arm was in a temporary cast.

However, all that mattered to Manny was that Christopher was alive, and for that, she sent up a prayer thanking God for bringing her man home to her.

EPILOGUE

"She looks just like you."

Leaning heavily on his cane, Christopher leaned over the bed and looked down at the infant cradled securely in her mother's arms. Dark colored eyes surrounded by a head full of shiny black curls and features that mirrored his own stared back at him. Christopher stroked a finger across her cheek, and Erika Rose Mills rewarded him by tilting her lips into what Christopher would swear to his dying day was her very first smile.

The indictments for Dexter Santangelo, his cohorts that had survived the blast, and the three former officers had been swift, largely due to the evidence presented by Christopher and Benito's willingness to expose everything he knew about Santangelo's organization. Christopher still had to testify at the various trials, but knew that Dexter Santangelo's next stop was a federal prison, where he would remain behind bars for life.

His ankle had required three surgeries, the last of which had been performed a month earlier, which was why he still needed the cane. The rest of his body had healed just fine and everything was in working order.

"She's beautiful, Honey-V. Only…"

Manny lifted a brow. "Only what?"

Christopher limped to one of the chairs in the room, pulled it forward, then sat heavily on the padded seat. "Only she's a girl, and I thought that I specifically requested a boy."

"You requested no such thing and I can't believe you even have the nerve to say something like that, Christopher Mills."

"Well, I told you months ago that I wanted a baseball team."

"And I told you that it wasn't going to happen."

"Yeah, you did," he replied, directing his eyes back to his daughter.

He watched her tiny mouth open and release a small yawn. "She's tired."

"Believe me, I'm just as tired."

"You did good, Honey-V."

"Thank you."

"Now, when can I have another?"

"Not for a long, long time."

Christopher frowned. "How long, is long, long?"

"I don't know, Chris."

"We need to start planning, because now that we have Erika, we have to start working on the rest of the team."

"*You* are a nut case."

"But you love me, and as long as I have that, I'm a fulfilled man."

Manny nodded in agreement. Her life could not have been more perfect. She had a wonderful husband, a beautiful daughter, and the love of family and friends. When the door to her room opened, Manny smiled as the first shift spilled into the room.

"Where's my beautiful granddaughter?"

"Right here, Daddy," Manny said, handing her baby over to her grandfather's arms.

Loretta kissed her grandchild's cheek, then sat on the bed. "How does it feel to be a mother, Daughter?"

"I'm not sure," Manny said. "I mean, Erika arrived only a few of hours ago and while I'm glad she's finally here, I guess time will tell what kind of mother I'll be. Hopefully, I'll be as good a mother to my daughter, as you are to me."

Christopher leaned forward in his chair. "You'll be a great mother!"

"I think so, too," Loretta said, rising. "Well, there are about ten other people out in that hallway who want to get in here, not including Erika's uncles who must have bought out every single toy store in Boulder before we came down last night." She planted a kiss on Manette's brow. "Your father and I will be back as soon as everyone else has had a chance to see the baby."

"I'm not going anywhere, Loretta. I came to see and hold my granddaughter and that's exactly what I'm going to do."

"Henry Walker, there will be plenty of time to hold Erika later. Besides, we agreed to let the others in."

He scrunched up his face at his granddaughter, then grinned from ear to ear when she batted her lashes at him. "They can come in, but I'm staying."

"Let him stay, Mama," Manny said.

"Oh, all right." Loretta headed for the door. "I love you, Daughter."

"Love you, too, Mama."

Christopher rose and sat on the bed. He wrapped his arm around her shoulders while reaching into his pocket. "Know something, Manny? I still owe you a honeymoon."

"It's a little late for that, Chris. We're parents, and from now on our time will not be our own."

"Yeah," he said with a grin. "But being a father will have its own rewards." He pulled a flat case from his pocket and dropped it into Manny's lap.

"What's this?"

"Something to thank you for giving me my daughter."

Excitement lit Manny's eyes when she opened the red velvet case. The ruby and pearl necklace was exquisite. "It's beautiful."

"Not as beautiful as you, Manny Mills."

He removed the necklace and hooked it around her neck. "The pearls symbolize a happy marriage, which you and I are going to have for the rest of our lives. The ruby represents the intense love, passion, and desire I will always feel for you, and the contentment I feel having you and Erika share my life.

Enchanted by his words, Manny sighed. "Oh, Christopher, that's so romantic."

Reaching up, she brought his head down and connected their lips in a sensual and arousing lock of passion that would have gone on longer if Nelson Reeves had not entered the room.

Nelson glanced at the bed and the two people doing their best to devour each other, took one look at Erika Rose, and loudly exclaimed, "Hey, Chris…this baby of yours isn't a boy!"

ABOUT THE AUTHOR

As a twenty-five year veteran or casualty of the cable television industry, **Wanda Y. Thomas** has worked in various Administrative and Affiliate Sales & Marketing Management positions. In 1994, God led Wanda to the dusty desert and Decadent City of Las Vegas. "Though God may have had a hand in it," says Wanda, "It was actually a home shopping network, which relocated about 100 people from across the country to Las Vegas, and then laid us all off within a month." That experience and the lessons learned prompted Wanda to review the goals on her Life List, and to pursue the one that said: Write a book and get it published.

To date, Wanda has authored four full-length romance titles and a novella.

- *Truly Inseparable* – African American Literary Award Show, 2004 Open Book Award Nominee
- *Forever Love* – Heartbeat Award
- *Subtle Secrets* – 2001 Romance In Color, Genesis Press Release Of The Year
- *Passion's Journey*
- *Treasured Dreams*, a novella in the Homeland Heroines and Heroes, Vol 2.

Excerpt from

I'M GONNA MAKE YOU LOVE ME

BY

GWYNETH BOLTON

Release Date: March 2006

CHAPTER 1

Palm   er Woods Historic District, Detroit

"It's just so archaic—a throwback to the dark ages or at least pre-enlightenment!"

Grimacing as he watched his wife brush her hair, Kyle thought about the best way to respond to her statement and decided humor was the way to go. "Well, I don't know, Karen. Seems like you could bump it up to at least the Victorian era. I don't think people were arranging marriages for their children in the dark ages."

Fixing the bow tie on his tuxedo, he gave her a smile as she paused brushing her hair and glare at him.

"It's not funny, Kyle. Really, Black folk just don't do this kind of thing. We don't pick spouses for our children."

Sighing because he thought they were through with this discussion, he tried to think of yet another way to get his wife to understand what she clearly did not wish to understand. Having long since made the deal with Jonathan Whitman that allowed him to regain control of Taylor Publishing; he was too far in to back out. Whitman made him an offer he couldn't refuse—a chance to save the Taylor legacy, business, and family name.

"You'd be surprised at what Black folk do, especially *our kind of people*. It's about control, breeding, and family. I've heard stories about mergers in my family that did not start out based on love, as we like to think about it." Untying his failed attempt at a bow, he tried again. "Believe it or not, those mergers were the very mergers that brought the family the most success. *Love* didn't get my parents anywhere."

Were it not for his father's gambling and bad habits, Kyle wouldn't have even considered the offer. In many ways, they were lucky the Taylor name still meant something. A scandal like the one his father had left would have annihilated a lesser family.

The overly indulgent lifestyle his own father had led almost ruined the family name and made Taylor Publishing vulnerable to a hostile takeover by Whitman Enterprises. Whitman offered a chance to earn it back, albeit at a high cost.

"Well my father is a Kansas City barbecue king, and although I grew up well-off and attended all the *right* schools, I was not among that elite group of *your kind of people*. So, forgive me if I don't understand this!" Karen put the brush down, crossed her arms over her chest, and narrowed her eyes on him. "Those two kids that you and Whitman hope will one day marry *cannot* even stand each other. They argue every time they are near one another!"

Kyle sighed. He knew the children didn't get along and hoped the childhood rivalry between his daughter and Whitman's son would eventually go away.

"You know." Karen's voice calmed to a whisper. "If your family arranged a marriage for you, or if you didn't have the guts to date and fall in love outside of your tight knit group of black elites, you and I would not be together now."

"Probably not. If my life had followed the path I started out on, if my father were half the man he should have been…" Stuttering slightly, he closed his eyes in search of the words that would make her understand.

"I have a chance to rebuild my family's legacy. To do all the things my father wouldn't or couldn't do."

"And it will only cost your daughter's future. Her right to choose who she wants to fall in love with? Don't you see it's crazy? And did I mention, Alicia *can't stand* Darren Whitman. The two of them are like oil and water!"

"What I see is that if I don't try this, my child won't have the lifestyle she deserves. I can't abide with that, Karen. I won't! She will have the world and will grow up in a world where the Taylor name still means something." Reaching out and touching her shoulder, he continued, "They are kids now. Most boys and girls don't like each other when they are young. She might grow to like him, even love him one day."

Karen lowered her gaze. By the way she clenched her teeth and clutched the brush in her hands, he could tell she was simmering. "I don't like it, Kyle."

"It will work... It has to work. When you think about it, what more could two parents wish for? Our daughter will marry one of the richest men in the world. Could it be so bad for our little girl to grow up and become Mrs. Darren Whitman?" Hearing his own voice, he realized that in addition to trying to convince his wife, he was trying to convince himself. Things had to work out.

Letting out a ragged breath, he continued, "Jonathan Whitman is letting me run my family's company. I'm making a lot more now than what I made when I was trying to work my way up the corporate ladder. Taylor Publishing is my legacy. The dinner party that we are hosting this evening is just the start of the big things to come. Think of the important people who will be here. I'll have a chance to build the company back to its original luster. I know I can do it. It's my birthright.

"I'll get to run it for now, and once they are married, part of the company will revert back to the Taylor family. Once there is an heir, another part of the company will revert to the Taylor family. Doing this will give Alicia and her future children the family's legacy."

Straightening his slouched shoulders, he shrugged and sighed. Things were truly out of his hands. "If Alicia grows up and decides she just cannot marry the young, rich man her daddy picked out for her, then we'll lose everything. Don't you see I had to try? I *have* to try."

When his wife finally turned her gaze back to him, he used his own expression to plead with her to understand. He hoped one last time that she did and that they would not have to rehash this discussion.

Alicia giggled as she eavesdropped on her cousin Kendrick and his friends, Darren and Troy. The three boys irritated her to no end, and she awoke each morning thinking of ways to ruin any idea of fun they might think up. The one thing an eight-year-old girl with braces and pigtails hated most was twelve-year-old boys who teased her and pushed her around at whim.

Each of the older boys annoyed her and Alicia could not decide which boy annoyed her most. Her cousin came to visit every summer because her father said Uncle Kelvin was a loser like the grandfather who died before she was born. Darren Whitman and Troy Singleton were just boys who came around whenever Kendrick was in town. Troy lived right across the street in a big red brick house, and Darren lived in a huge mansion in Bloomfield Hills.

The rich boy, Darren, was the one she decided she hated him most of all. Not only was he rich and a pain, he was also the meanest. He tugged her pigtails anytime she got within arms reach and called her names like metal-mouth, brat, and antenna head. The nerve of him calling anyone names when he was so bony and his voice went all low and then high, sounding like tires screeching all the time.

The boys were planning to come inside out of the heat and watch a stupid karate movie on the VCR. Racing into the family room of their six-bedroom classic Tudor home in Palmer Woods, Alicia turned on the TV.

"Get out, metal-mouth; we want to watch a movie on the big screen!" Darren barged into the room followed by Kendrick and Troy.

"I'm watching it, so you can't." Gripping the remote control in her small hands, she gave the boys her best attempt at a threatening glare.

"Come on, Licia, you have a TV in your room. Let us watch our movie in here." Kendrick's request was just a little nicer than Darren's.

Letting out the kind of exasperated sigh she saw glamorous women give in the movies whenever someone was getting on their nerves, she replied, "What part of no don't you understand? You have a TV in your room. I was here first. Get lost."

"I'm tired of this! Give me the remote and get out of here, brat!" Snatching the remote Darren yanked her left pigtail extra hard before walking away.

She let out a loud piercing scream, and her mother, Karen Taylor, came running from upstairs where she was supervising the help and getting ready for a big dinner party.

"What is it now? You children know I am busy getting things ready for Kyle's dinner party. I really don't have time for this." Karen placed her hands on her hips and gave each child a pointed stare.

No visible tears accompanied Alicia's sobbing. "I was here first watching something, and they came in bothering me. I was here first, and Darren hit me. He's mean and horrible! Mommy, they know the rules. But they don't care." Burying her face in her dainty hands, Alicia dramatically fell unto the sofa.

"Boys, was she here first?" Karen used her no-nonsense tone.

Almost tempted to peek up from her production to watch, Alicia didn't want to risk having the tone turned on herself.

"Yes," the boys murmured in unison.

"Well you know the rules. Go and watch TV in Kendrick's room until Alicia is finished."

The boys followed her mom out of the family room with Darren bringing up the rear. Lifting her head just in time to stick out her tongue at Darren, she relished the view of his face twisting up in anger.

The show that was playing, like every other show, was a re-run and didn't interest her. Her best friend Sonya was away at Jack and Jill camp for *two weeks*, and Alicia had no one to play with or talk to. Although Alicia was also a member of Jack and Jill, her father felt she was too young to go away for two weeks. So she amused herself day after day.

Deciding to go and spy on the boys again, she got there just in time to follow them out to a huge cluster of oak trees that extended just a few yards from the backyard of their home. The backyard was huge, and just behind it was what the kids felt was a mini forest. It didn't have nearly as many trees as a forest, but for kids living in the city, it was just as good. Forbidden to go back there alone, Alicia reasoned she wouldn't *really* be alone. She would be with the boys, only they wouldn't know it.

Darren kicked the rocks with all the force his twelve-year-old feet could muster. Unaccustomed to not getting his way, he focused his anger on that metal-mouthed brat Alicia. He was almost tempted to call his driver and go home, but there was nothing to do there and no one else to play with.

He really loved spending time with Kendrick and Troy. They were like brothers. In fact, they'd made a blood brothers' pack in their secret spot earlier that summer. They were now headed to their secret spot to come up with ways to make sure the brat didn't ruin the rest of the summer. They stopped under the dark shade where oaks met so closely they almost made a circle.

"Well she did it again. She messed up a perfect afternoon." Vocalizing what they all thought, Troy was the first to speak.

"Well, we could spend the rest of the summer at one of your houses." Bowing his head, Kendrick kicked a rock.

Irritated, Darren pointed out, "If we do that she wins. No way is that little brat going to win. It's us against her! We can't let that metal-mouth win."

"It's like she always knows what we're going to do next, and she beats us to it," Troy complained.

A slight noise in the bushes drew Darren's attention. Motioning for the boys to be silent, he caught a glimpse of the yellow ribbon at the end of Alicia's long-curly pigtail as she darted behind a tree.

"That's it, brat! When we catch you, you're toast!" he yelled.

Alicia let out a high-pitched scream and took off running. The boys followed, but she was fast. They each took different directions, hoping to corner her. Gaining ground, Darren had her right in his sight. Glancing back at him, Alicia did not see the big rock in her path.

He watched as her foot hit a big rock, and she tumbled to the ground. He stopped in front of her and saw that she was holding her leg and crying. It wasn't the loud fake sobs that she had let out earlier, just streams of tears down her cheek. He sat down beside her and put his arm around her.

"It's going to be okay, Licia. Can you move your leg? Can you walk?" He had heard people on TV ask people who were hurt if they could move the injured body part.

Alicia moved her leg and continued to cry. The others came running up from different directions.

Throwing up his hands, Kendrick groaned. "Oh, man, this is guaranteed punishment for at least a week."

"She's hurt her leg. You two go get your aunt and uncle, and I'll stay here with her." Guilt ridden, Darren wanted to make sure that Alicia was okay.

The other two boys ran back to the house, and he talked to Alicia while waiting. He could have sworn that he even made her smile—either that or she was grimacing from the pain.

Relief washed over him when he saw Mr. and Mrs. Taylor come running through the woods followed by Dr. Samuels. They were all dressed in fancy clothes, and he knew that he and the boys were going to be in big trouble for interrupting the dinner party.

He smiled down at Alicia. "See, I told you everything would be okay. Here's your mom and dad." He waited until the adults got there before removing his arm from her shoulder.

While examining her, Dr. Samuels asked if she could move her leg and Darren smiled.

Mr. Taylor picked Alicia up to carry her back to the house. The doctor had said she had a bad sprain, and she wouldn't be running around for a while. When Darren was on the verge of feeling sorry for her, Alicia lifted her head from Mr. Taylor's shoulder and stuck her tongue out at Darren. Furious he'd wasted his time being nice to the little metal-mouth brat, he kicked a rock.

ENCHANTED DESIRE

2006 Publication Schedule

January

A Lover's Legacy
Veronica Parker
1-58571-167-5
$9.95

Love Lasts Forever
Dominiqua Douglas
1-58571-187-X
$9.95

Under the Cherry
  Moon
Christal Jordan-Mims
1-58571-169-1
$12.95

February

Second Chances at Love
Cheris Hodges
1-58571-188-8
$9.95

Enchanted Desire
Wanda Y. Thomas
1-58571-176-4
$9.95

Caught Up
Deatri King Bey
1-58571-178-0
$12.95

March

I'm Gonna Make You
  Love Me
Gwyneth Bolton
1-58571-181-0
$9.95

Through the Fire
Seressia Glass
1-58571-173-X
$9.95

Notes When Summer
  Ends
Beverly Lauderdale
1-58571-180-2
$12.95

April

Sin and Surrender
J.M. Jeffries
1-58571-189-6
$9.95

Unearthing Passions
Elaine Sims
1-58571-184-5
$9.95

Between Tears
Pamela Ridley
1-58571-179-9
$12.95

May

Misty Blue
Dyanne Davis
1-58571-186-1
$9.95

Ironic
Pamela Leigh Starr
1-58571-168-3
$9.95

Cricket's Serenade
Carolita Blythe
1-58571-183-7
$12.95

June

Cupid
Barbara Keaton
1-58571-174-8
$9.95

Havana Sunrise
Kymberly Hunt
1-58571-182-9
$9.95

2006 Publication Schedule (continued)

July

Love Me Carefully	No Ordinary Love	Rehoboth Road
A.C. Arthur	Angela Weaver	Anita Ballard-Jones
1-58571-177-2	1-58571-198-5	1-58571-196-9
$9.95	$9.95	$12.95

August

Scent of Rain	Love in High Gear	Rise of the Phoenix
Annetta P. Lee	Charlotte Roy	Kenneth Whetstone
158571-199-3	158571-185-3	1-58571-197-7
$9.95	$9.95	$12.95

September

The Business of Love	Rock Star	A Dead Man Speaks
Cheris Hodges	Rosyln Hardy Holcomb	Lisa Jones Johnson
1-58571-193-4	1-58571-200-0	1-58571-203-5
$9.95	$9.95	$12.95

October

Rivers of the Soul-Part 1	A Dangerous Woman	Sinful Intentions
Leslie Esdaile	J.M. Jeffries	Crystal Rhodes
1-58571-223-X	1-58571-195-0	1-58571-201-9
$9.95	$9.95	$12.95

November

Only You	Ebony Eyes	By and By
Crystal Hubbard	Kei Swanson	Collette Haywood
1-58571-208-6	1-58571-194-2	1-58571-209-4
$9.95	$9.95	$12.95

December

Let's Get It On	Nights Over Egypt	A Pefect Place to Pray
Dyanne Davis	Barbara Keaton	I.L. Goodwin
1-58571-210-8	1-58571-192-6	1-58571-202-7
$9.95	$9.95	$12.95

Other Genesis Press, Inc. Titles

A Dangerous Deception	J.M. Jeffries	$8.95
A Dangerous Love	J.M. Jeffries	$8.95
A Dangerous Obsession	J.M. Jeffries	$8.95
A Drummer's Beat to Mend	Kei Swanson	$9.95
A Happy Life	Charlotte Harris	$9.95
A Heart's Awakening	Veronica Parker	$9.95
A Lark on the Wing	Phyliss Hamilton	$9.95
A Love of Her Own	Cheris F. Hodges	$9.95
A Love to Cherish	Beverly Clark	$8.95
A Risk of Rain	Dar Tomlinson	$8.95
A Twist of Fate	Beverly Clark	$8.95
A Will to Love	Angie Daniels	$9.95
Acquisitions	Kimberley White	$8.95
Across	Carol Payne	$12.95
After the Vows	Leslie Esdaile	$10.95
(Summer Anthology)	T.T. Henderson	
	Jacqueline Thomas	
Again My Love	Kayla Perrin	$10.95
Against the Wind	Gwynne Forster	$8.95
All I Ask	Barbara Keaton	$8.95
Ambrosia	T.T. Henderson	$8.95
An Unfinished Love Affair	Barbara Keaton	$8.95
And Then Came You	Dorothy Elizabeth Love	$8.95
Angel's Paradise	Janice Angelique	$9.95
At Last	Lisa G. Riley	$8.95
Best of Friends	Natalie Dunbar	$8.95
Beyond the Rapture	Beverly Clark	$9.95
Blaze	Barbara Keaton	$9.95
Blood Lust	J. M. Jeffries	$9.95
Bodyguard	Andrea Jackson	$9.95
Boss of Me	Diana Nyad	$8.95
Bound by Love	Beverly Clark	$8.95
Breeze	Robin Hampton Allen	$10.95

Other Genesis Press, Inc. Titles (continued)

Broken	Dar Tomlinson	$24.95
By Design	Barbara Keaton	$8.95
Cajun Heat	Charlene Berry	$8.95
Careless Whispers	Rochelle Alers	$8.95
Cats & Other Tales	Marilyn Wagner	$8.95
Caught in a Trap	Andre Michelle	$8.95
Caught Up In the Rapture	Lisa G. Riley	$9.95
Cautious Heart	Cheris F Hodges	$8.95
Chances	Pamela Leigh Starr	$8.95
Cherish the Flame	Beverly Clark	$8.95
Class Reunion	Irma Jenkins/John Brown	$12.95
Code Name: Diva	J.M. Jeffries	$9.95
Conquering Dr. Wexler's Heart	Kimberley White	$9.95
Crossing Paths, Tempting Memories	Dorothy Elizabeth Love	$9.95
Cypress Whisperings	Phyllis Hamilton	$8.95
Dark Embrace	Crystal Wilson Harris	$8.95
Dark Storm Rising	Chinelu Moore	$10.95
Daughter of the Wind	Joan Xian	$8.95
Deadly Sacrifice	Jack Kean	$22.95
Designer Passion	Dar Tomlinson	$8.95
Dreamtective	Liz Swados	$5.95
Ebony Butterfly II	Delilah Dawson	$14.95
Echoes of Yesterday	Beverly Clark	$9.95
Eden's Garden	Elizabeth Rose	$8.95
Everlastin' Love	Gay G. Gunn	$8.95
Everlasting Moments	Dorothy Elizabeth Love	$8.95
Everything and More	Sinclair Lebeau	$8.95
Everything but Love	Natalie Dunbar	$8.95
Eve's Prescription	Edwina Martin Arnold	$8.95
Falling	Natalie Dunbar	$9.95
Fate	Pamela Leigh Starr	$8.95
Finding Isabella	A.J. Garrotto	$8.95

Other Genesis Press, Inc. Titles (continued)

Forbidden Quest	Dar Tomlinson	$10.95
Forever Love	Wanda Y. Thomas	$8.95
From the Ashes	Kathleen Suzanne	$8.95
	Jeanne Sumerix	
Gentle Yearning	Rochelle Alers	$10.95
Glory of Love	Sinclair LeBeau	$10.95
Go Gentle into that Good Night	Malcom Boyd	$12.95
Goldengroove	Mary Beth Craft	$16.95
Groove, Bang, and Jive	Steve Cannon	$8.99
Hand in Glove	Andrea Jackson	$9.95
Hard to Love	Kimberley White	$9.95
Hart & Soul	Angie Daniels	$8.95
Heartbeat	Stephanie Bedwell-Grime	$8.95
Hearts Remember	M. Loui Quezada	$8.95
Hidden Memories	Robin Allen	$10.95
Higher Ground	Leah Latimer	$19.95
Hitler, the War, and the Pope	Ronald Rychiak	$26.95
How to Write a Romance	Kathryn Falk	$18.95
I Married a Reclining Chair	Lisa M. Fuhs	$8.95
Indigo After Dark Vol. I	Nia Dixon/Angelique	$10.95
Indigo After Dark Vol. II	Dolores Bundy/Cole Riley	$10.95
Indigo After Dark Vol. III	Montana Blue/Coco Morena	$10.95
Indigo After Dark Vol. IV	Cassandra Colt/	$14.95
	Diana Richeaux	
Indigo After Dark Vol. V	Delilah Dawson	$14.95
Icie	Pamela Leigh Starr	$8.95
I'll Be Your Shelter	Giselle Carmichael	$8.95
I'll Paint a Sun	A.J. Garrotto	$9.95
Illusions	Pamela Leigh Starr	$8.95
Indiscretions	Donna Hill	$8.95
Intentional Mistakes	Michele Sudler	$9.95
Interlude	Donna Hill	$8.95
Intimate Intentions	Angie Daniels	$8.95

Other Genesis Press, Inc. Titles (continued)

Jolie's Surrender	Edwina Martin-Arnold	$8.95
Kiss or Keep	Debra Phillips	$8.95
Lace	Giselle Carmichael	$9.95
Last Train to Memphis	Elsa Cook	$12.95
Lasting Valor	Ken Olsen	$24.95
Let Us Prey	Hunter Lundy	$25.95
Life Is Never As It Seems	J.J. Michael	$12.95
Lighter Shade of Brown	Vicki Andrews	$8.95
Love Always	Mildred E. Riley	$10.95
Love Doesn't Come Easy	Charlyne Dickerson	$8.95
Love Unveiled	Gloria Greene	$10.95
Love's Deception	Charlene Berry	$10.95
Love's Destiny	M. Loui Quezada	$8.95
Mae's Promise	Melody Walcott	$8.95
Magnolia Sunset	Giselle Carmichael	$8.95
Matters of Life and Death	Lesego Malepe, Ph.D.	$15.95
Meant to Be	Jeanne Sumerix	$8.95
Midnight Clear	Leslie Esdaile	$10.95
(Anthology)	Gwynne Forster	
	Carmen Green	
	Monica Jackson	
Midnight Magic	Gwynne Forster	$8.95
Midnight Peril	Vicki Andrews	$10.95
Misconceptions	Pamela Leigh Starr	$9.95
Montgomery's Children	Richard Perry	$14.95
My Buffalo Soldier	Barbara B. K. Reeves	$8.95
Naked Soul	Gwynne Forster	$8.95
Next to Last Chance	Louisa Dixon	$24.95
No Apologies	Seressia Glass	$8.95
No Commitment Required	Seressia Glass	$8.95
No Regrets	Mildred E. Riley	$8.95
Nowhere to Run	Gay G. Gunn	$10.95
O Bed! O Breakfast!	Rob Kuehnle	$14.95

Other Genesis Press, Inc. Titles (continued)

Object of His Desire	A. C. Arthur	$8.95
Office Policy	A. C. Arthur	$9.95
Once in a Blue Moon	Dorianne Cole	$9.95
One Day at a Time	Bella McFarland	$8.95
Outside Chance	Louisa Dixon	$24.95
Passion	T.T. Henderson	$10.95
Passion's Blood	Cherif Fortin	$22.95
Passion's Journey	Wanda Y. Thomas	$8.95
Past Promises	Jahmel West	$8.95
Path of Fire	T.T. Henderson	$8.95
Path of Thorns	Annetta P. Lee	$9.95
Peace Be Still	Colette Haywood	$12.95
Picture Perfect	Reon Carter	$8.95
Playing for Keeps	Stephanie Salinas	$8.95
Pride & Joi	Gay G. Gunn	$15.95
Pride & Joi	Gay G. Gunn	$8.95
Promises to Keep	Alicia Wiggins	$8.95
Quiet Storm	Donna Hill	$10.95
Reckless Surrender	Rochelle Alers	$6.95
Red Polka Dot in a World of Plaid	Varian Johnson	$12.95
Reluctant Captive	Joyce Jackson	$8.95
Rendezvous with Fate	Jeanne Sumerix	$8.95
Revelations	Cheris F. Hodges	$8.95
Rivers of the Soul	Leslie Esdaile	$8.95
Rocky Mountain Romance	Kathleen Suzanne	$8.95
Rooms of the Heart	Donna Hill	$8.95
Rough on Rats and Tough on Cats	Chris Parker	$12.95
Secret Library Vol. 1	Nina Sheridan	$18.95
Secret Library Vol. 2	Cassandra Colt	$8.95
Shades of Brown	Denise Becker	$8.95
Shades of Desire	Monica White	$8.95

Other Genesis Press, Inc. Titles (continued)

Shadows in the Moonlight	Jeanne Sumerix	$8.95
Sin	Crystal Rhodes	$8.95
So Amazing	Sinclair LeBeau	$8.95
Somebody's Someone	Sinclair LeBeau	$8.95
Someone to Love	Alicia Wiggins	$8.95
Song in the Park	Martin Brant	$15.95
Soul Eyes	Wayne L. Wilson	$12.95
Soul to Soul	Donna Hill	$8.95
Southern Comfort	J.M. Jeffries	$8.95
Still the Storm	Sharon Robinson	$8.95
Still Waters Run Deep	Leslie Esdaile	$8.95
Stories to Excite You	Anna Forrest/Divine	$14.95
Subtle Secrets	Wanda Y. Thomas	$8.95
Suddenly You	Crystal Hubbard	$9.95
Sweet Repercussions	Kimberley White	$9.95
Sweet Tomorrows	Kimberly White	$8.95
Taken by You	Dorothy Elizabeth Love	$9.95
Tattooed Tears	T. T. Henderson	$8.95
The Color Line	Lizzette Grayson Carter	$9.95
The Color of Trouble	Dyanne Davis	$8.95
The Disappearance of Allison Jones	Kayla Perrin	$5.95
The Honey Dipper's Legacy	Pannell-Allen	$14.95
The Joker's Love Tune	Sidney Rickman	$15.95
The Little Pretender	Barbara Cartland	$10.95
The Love We Had	Natalie Dunbar	$8.95
The Man Who Could Fly	Bob & Milana Beamon	$18.95
The Missing Link	Charlyne Dickerson	$8.95
The Price of Love	Sinclair LeBeau	$8.95
The Smoking Life	Ilene Barth	$29.95
The Words of the Pitcher	Kei Swanson	$8.95
Three Wishes	Seressia Glass	$8.95
Ties That Bind	Kathleen Suzanne	$8.95
Tiger Woods	Libby Hughes	$5.95

Other Genesis Press, Inc. Titles (continued)

Time is of the Essence	Angie Daniels	$9.95
Timeless Devotion	Bella McFarland	$9.95
Tomorrow's Promise	Leslie Esdaile	$8.95
Truly Inseparable	Wanda Y. Thomas	$8.95
Unbreak My Heart	Dar Tomlinson	$8.95
Uncommon Prayer	Kenneth Swanson	$9.95
Unconditional	A.C. Arthur	$9.95
Unconditional Love	Alicia Wiggins	$8.95
Until Death Do Us Part	Susan Paul	$8.95
Vows of Passion	Bella McFarland	$9.95
Wedding Gown	Dyanne Davis	$8.95
What's Under Benjamin's Bed	Sandra Schaffer	$8.95
When Dreams Float	Dorothy Elizabeth Love	$8.95
Whispers in the Night	Dorothy Elizabeth Love	$8.95
Whispers in the Sand	LaFlorya Gauthier	$10.95
Wild Ravens	Altonya Washington	$9.95
Yesterday Is Gone	Beverly Clark	$10.95
Yesterday's Dreams, Tomorrow's Promises	Reon Laudat	$8.95
Your Precious Love	Sinclair LeBeau	$8.95

ESCAPE WITH INDIGO !!!!

Join Indigo Book Club©
It's simple, easy and secure.

Sign up and receive the new releases
every month + Free shipping and
20% off the cover price.

Go online to www.genesis-press.com
and click on Bookclub or
call 1-888-INDIGO-1

Order Form

Mail to: Genesis Press, Inc.
P.O. Box 101
Columbus, MS 39703

Name _____

Address _____

City/State _____ Zip _____

Telephone _____

Ship to (if different from above)

Name _____

Address _____

City/State _____ Zip _____

Telephone _____

Credit Card Information

Credit Card # _____ ☐ Visa   ☐ Mastercard

Expiration Date (mm/yy) _____ ☐ AmEx ☐ Discover

Qty.	Author	Title	Price	Total

Use this order form, or call

1-888-INDIGO-1

Total for books	_____
Shipping and handling:	
$5 first two books,	
$1 each additional book	_____
Total S & H	_____
Total amount enclosed	_____

Mississippi residents add 7% sales tax